ABSORPTION

The debut novel by Kelly Farrington

Absorption – First Edition

First published in 2023 by Kelly Farrington, trading as **Snakepass Books.**

Kelly Farrington is the author and is acting in law as a sole trader.

Office Address:
140 Warton Street,
Lytham,
FY8 5EZ

A CIP catalogue of this book is available from the British Library.
ISBN 978-1-8380661-2-3 (Paperback)
ISBN 978-1-8380661-3-0 (MOBI)

Cover design by **George Contronis**
Interior Layout by **Dean Wanbon**
Edited by **Fiction Feedback**
Printed and bound by **Ingram Spark**

Snakepass Books

Invasive Species: What You Can Do

The Nature Conservancy lists six easy ways to combat invasive species:

1. Make sure the plants you are buying for your home or garden are not invasive. Contact your state's native plant society for a list of native plants.

2. When boating, make sure to clean your boat thoroughly before putting it into a different body of water.

3. Clean your boots before you hike in a new area.

4. Don't take home any animals, plants, shells, firewood, or food from different ecosystems.

5. Never release pets into the wild.

6. Volunteer at your local park, refuge, or other wildlife area to help remove invasive species. Most parks also have native species restoration programs.

Extract taken from the National Geographic website, April 2019.

Unfortunately, not all invasive species are from this planet.

PROLOGUE

The planet nestled fifth of twelve planets from its sun. The system, thirty-nine light years from Earth, was in the Aquarius constellation. The planet had been beautiful, with several continents, ice caps and large oceans. The two moons that orbited it had once cast their seductive light across mountains, forests, plains and seas.

Home to myriad biological species, the diversity of the planet had been ended by an invasive force. A cancer. A disease that had absorbed all life, merging it into a soup of fused DNA. It had taken several Earth centuries for the contagion to reach near saturation, spreading across the planet's surface and ending all indigenous life, metamorphosing it into something new.

The process was close to completion. Former manifestations of life lost their individual identities, interblending into strange shapes emerging from what resembled a primeval swamp. The planet's apex predators no longer preyed on the weak and vulnerable. They existed as a combined mass of seething, frothing, unified life. Nothing survived with a living advantage over another.

All life was close to being absorbed into one joint entity that covered the entire planet. A few remnants of former species occasionally surfaced from the mass, shifting patterns pulsating in an ugly biological Armageddon as their original identities were slowly destroyed.

But a short time before the process concluded, a planetary Armageddon of another variety occurred. A huge meteorite slammed into the alien world. With a force of several million nuclear detonations, the explosion tore the planet's surface to shreds, spraying debris into the outer atmosphere, much of it escaping into space.

Like a giant sneeze launching flu bacteria, such exhalations were a significant reason that the terror had, over aeons, been able to propagate and expand its life force across the galaxies, ultimately becoming the most successful single entity to have existed throughout space and time.

The menace had conquered innumerable worlds where sentient beings were ill-prepared to counteract the threat. The alien had proven indiscernible to all but advanced science. It could land on planets undetected and in multiple locations.

The advantage of stealth owed nothing to conscious planning. It was an unholy accident of nature The end of worlds often involved explosive forces, flinging any infected surfaces out into space.

Fragments thrown out by this particular planetary blast entered an orbital path around its sun. The trajectory acted to slingshot them out of their solar system and into the deep, frozen void of space.

The small meteoroids travelled on, cooling to the ambient deep space temperature of minus 270.45 Celsius. The living structure contained within the meteoroids froze. Dormant, but still a living entity. The shower headed on a path towards another universe and, nearly two million years later, into a different solar system, journeying inexorably past a frozen outer planet and then past a larger world with a huge red gaseous eye.

The meteoroid shower finally became attracted by the gravitational pull of the little blue planet orbiting third from the sun. Nearing the end of a journey that had started millennia earlier, they missed the planet's single moon on their collision course with Earth.

ONE

His best friend was to carry out the execution and report back that evening. As the time of the anticipated murder came and went, he felt his nerves starting to fray.

What was taking so long?

It would be the second killing sanctioned within a matter of weeks. He was not a reckless man and complicity in two deaths was not a decision taken lightly. Two executions would surely mean the death penalty, but he could see no other way out. The decision to kill again had spun around in his mind many times with the same conclusion – his hand had been forced, and the territorial rival needed eliminating.

Or maybe he was going to be a triple murderer?

The belief he had killed someone a decade earlier continued to be an irritating companion, one that regularly dogged him. He had pushed the blade in and felt little resistance as it entered the kid's gut. But he did not know for sure if the young gangster had died. The knife had gone in deep – he knew that much.

Now over a decade, a crossed ocean, and a new life later, he once again re-imagined the scene, like it happened yesterday. In dreams, the gangster's corpse rose like a zombie to chase him. The chase was always brutally vivid, running through the dingy London estate until he could hardly breathe. He always woke at the point of being caught, with leaden legs preventing escape, his body's own chemicals blocking the neurotransmitters to his muscles. The helplessness of paralysis scared him the most. It mirrored the helplessness of his youth and threatened the adult world he desperately wanted to control.

The zombie visage was significant, though. He saw it as a sign confirming the stabbed gangster had died. So, three deaths then. Three felt like a magic number, giving him more credibility. Three murders defined him as a serious player. Big league stuff, right? He was not to be messed with. And, as he paced around his kitchen, he repeated that mantra out loud: 'Don't fuck with me.'

With each inflection of tone, he hit the outside of his thigh with his clenched fist and then mentally admonished himself. Cursing was not a trait of an accomplished gangster. Nor was the frequency with which he checked his burner phone for news.

Impatience served to bring on anger and, though sufficiently self-aware to know his anger came from a damaged, dark place, he could feel the rage within surfacing again. He allowed himself to give way to the fury because he felt it was justified. Someone was trying to invade his turf and take what was his, threatening his precious status. Such an affront was a personal challenge and nullifying his competitor a necessary consequence.

Where was the confirmation text?
He looked at the cellular phone again. The screen was still blank. Not daring to put the phone down on the kitchen worktop, he held it tightly, willing it to buzz, waiting to feel the vibration and hear the sound alert. The job had been in progress for over four hours.

Why was it taking so long?
Time was not his friend tonight. Each occasion he looked at his Rolex it had only moved on a minute or two. He cursed its slow advancement. The guaranteed sweep of the second hand seemed suspended in an expensively cruel hesitation.

He took to playing mind games with himself, trying to forget the time, avoiding glancing at his watch or phone. But before the end of every diversionary task, he would cave in and look.

'Come on, Ben. What's taking so long?'

The sound of his own voice stopped him in his stride.

Doubts invaded every thought. Had Ben encountered problems? Resistance? Darker still, had Ben decided to not carry out the hit, or turned against him? Ben had been with him from day one of the operation. They shared a history that made their friendship unbreakable.

No, surely Ben was just delayed, that was all.

As the storm clouds in his mind gathered, another twenty minutes seemed to elongate into what felt like an hour. How could time move that slowly?

'This f-fucking watch!' he stuttered at his innocent Rolex.

Just as he was on the verge of breaking their security code and texting Ben, his burner phone pinged. Fumbling, he read the message. It said 'pets fed'. Two words that confirmed the problem was eliminated. He imagined the body weighted down in the swamp. Alligator food. The message swept away his nervousness and he felt a smile of satisfaction wash over his face. Worries about betrayal were dispelled as his mood lifted. It had been a bad idea to back him into a corner. He controlled his environment and those within it. Those who dared cross him paid the price.

Did he feel remorse?

No.

I'm no cold-blooded killer. Extreme actions were justified as simply the order of things – of life. Survival had to override the rights of others. Call it self-preservation in a dog-eat-dog world. The clichés abounded in his mind's dialogue.

Reaching for a cut-glass decanter, he poured a comforting measure of whisky into a matching tumbler. Holding the nectar up to the window, he watched the glass sparkle, and allowed the light to mesmerize him. As his mind drifted, he drank, feeling the nectar quell his anxiety, pushing the demons back into the shadows. The liquid flattened his self-doubt while enhancing a feeling of invincibility.

He pictured the sad child he once was – James Wardell – the boy who had grown up in North London. The child he had deliberately buried deep inside himself.

The boy had morphed into the man, Damian Gent. Long live the man, Damian, he thought, raising his glass to toast the latest victory in the battle of disassociation from his youth.

He liked his name and recalled how he had lifted Damian from a gravestone in a Miami cemetery over a decade earlier. His renaming had been part of a survival strategy – necessary to create a new identity in a faraway land.

As the whisky took hold and his tension abated, Damian leaned both hands on the kitchen counter, head bowed, thinking. It always came back to the same thing. The actions of another and how they'd affected him during his impressionable formative years. He considered the man who'd created his inner darkness. The man who'd killed the sweet-natured child he once was. He pictured his boyhood nemesis and vowed silently to return to London and kill the man responsible for his inner turmoil. *Yes, I will kill the imposter who called himself Dad.*

Damian poured himself another measure of the fiery liquid. If anger about the injustices towards his younger self was his sword, then alcohol provided a soothing shield.

The Scottish malt soothed him and helped block out memories of his later childhood. How he'd given up his home, abandoned his mother and fled his country of birth to forge a new life from nothing in the United States.

But his rage was always there, lurking below the surface, and he felt himself increasingly enjoying the violence. With far more to lose, both material wealth and responsibilities, he needed to preserve his status. Passivity would invite attack.

Any kind of opposition could and would not be tolerated.

Faint sounds of gunfire came from down the hall and he froze. The TV in the bedroom. It sounded like one of those cop shows his girlfriend liked. Damian topped up his glass and decided to join her in bed. Maybe sex would lift his mood.

TWO

An innocuous white Nissan NV approached the dilapidated warehouse, slowing to a crunchy halt on the dirt track. The huge figure of a man jumped out and pulled open the shutter, allowing the van to edge its sticky hot tyres inside onto a concrete floor strewn with loose bits of debris – a cumulative neglectful build-up. As soon as the van came to rest, its three other occupants jumped out.

The first gang member's herculean shape was silhouetted against the sun-drenched opening, tugging on a rusty iron chain to close the shutter. A slam reverberated, bouncing off the cool concrete. At once the searing Floridian sun was blocked out.

The gang had reached its base.

Damian paced across the concrete and flicked on switches next to the front entrance. Somewhere in the background, he heard the oil-fed generator whirring into action. No mains electricity reached this far out. The shed's old fluorescent tubing stuttered to life, revealing a stark but functional interior. He looked around, making sure everything was in order. Objects at the far end of the warehouse cast threatening shadows, and he subconsciously touched the reassuring steel of his holstered Glock 19. The weapon had not been required during the earlier heist.

He relaxed, allowing himself a smile of satisfaction. Acquiring the deeds of the Lake Winder shed a few years back had been a good move. He was unsure of the building's full history, only that it was built by Mormons who later sold the property. Its position in the Lake Winder Conservation Area made it difficult to find. There was only one single dirt track in and out from the trailhead at the end of the North Wickham Road. He'd only ever seen a couple of vehicles accidentally make it down as far as the building.

His eyes acclimatised to the gloom and the mostly empty space was revealed. Cheap partitioning to the left housed a small office, storeroom, kitchenette, and a single WC. An airboat sat at the back of the shed facing another shutter. The craft was his method of transportation around the surrounding shallow marshes, where a standard outboard engine with submerged propeller would be impractical.

Damian liked the name 'swamp boat', given to such craft by locals. He enjoyed pushing the boat to high speeds and feeling its shallow draught, driven by a caged aeroplane propeller mounted above the rear transom, carve arcs through the state's waterways. He looked at the boat wistfully. Perhaps he would travel home by boat rather than be driven. He decided to leave the decision over transportation till later – there was money to count. Lots of it, he hoped.

Damian watched Mason Reeves lift a holdall out of the van and haul it to an old table next to the partitioned rooms. Mason was a recent addition to Damian's inner circle, promoted from his small network of thieves. Mason had an encyclopaedic knowledge of types of safe, meaning he could place drill holes in precisely the right spot to pop any brand of high-security safe. He also knew how to use technology to bypass home alarms, a transferable skill Damian had needed to knock out the currency exchange's security system that morning.

The bag thudded on the tabletop, indicating a good haul. It was clear to Damian that the significance of the heavy sound was not lost on his driver, Noah Scott. Noah looked wide-eyed at the bulky bag. Mason appeared to have caught the expression too, because he winked at the youngster as if to say *not bad, heh?*

The huge frame of his business partner and best friend, Benjamin Johnson, joined them at the table. Damian was satisfied. The Clearwater raid had gone as well as the first over in Tampa. Hitting currency exchanges was proving to be a masterstroke. As he hoped, the exchange staff had handed over the money without any dramas.

The four gathered in silent tribute to the haul presenting itself and Damian felt the relief of completing another raid safely.

'OK, let's get it counted,' he said.

The holdall was moved from the table to a desk in the partitioned back office. Mason took out wads of notes and began the painstaking process of calculating the haul's value.

Damian knew from the first raid that the count took Mason some time, so joined Ben and Noah in playing cards and drinking beer, reliving the first two raids – building up their parts and exaggerating the experience. Occasionally Damian noticed Noah glancing at the closed office door. They were all keen to find out what the final total would be.

'I can't believe how easy it was,' Noah said, opening his second beer.

'You shouldn't tempt fate like that,' Ben said.

'I'm not tempting fate.' Noah looked peeved.

'Well, be thankful there were no have-a-go heroes,' Damian said.

'I prefer it this way,' Ben said. 'Our fate is in our own hands. We are not at the mercy of Florida Man.'

'Hmmm.' Damian contemplated. Ben was referring to the thief who had threatened to turn him in to the police three months earlier. That problem had been eliminated, but another gang had recently made a move for their territory by tapping into their network of burglars.

Ben was right. It was better not to place so much trust in outsiders. He had one lucrative job to complete before putting the robberies on ice. The danger of being caught fencing stolen goods was currently too high.

In the meantime, they would continue raiding currency exchanges. It was their new avenue of criminality – one he knew was potentially more dangerous than moving on stolen property. Damian glanced towards the back shutter, picturing the waterway beyond. He briefly imagined the body Ben had disposed of, weighted down no more than two hundred yards from where they were sitting drinking and laughing. Another body might have to follow it. He would worry about that later.

But, despite two early successes raiding currency exchanges, the reasons for the change of career path niggled him. Everything had been going smoothly until the night Randal Button had been caught on a house burglary twelve weeks earlier.

Nothing had quite felt the same since.

THREE

Twelve weeks earlier

Randal Button cursed his carelessness. Everything about the property indicated a routine job. A creaky old mansion house, miles out from the city, occupied by a lonely old widow. Rotting wooden window frames, easy to break into, and no tech on show anywhere.

And yet, there had been an electronic trip or pressure pad somewhere. How had he missed it? He'd taken his time inside the house, so the police were already waiting for him, cuffing him as he straddled the side window.

Busted while stealing to order for Damian Gent.

Button accepted that Damian had done his research on the pieces. He'd promised Button that the old biddy owned some real dazzlers, and he'd been right – the security box secreted at the bottom of her dressing room wardrobe was jammed full of expensive jewellery. Gold necklaces and bracelets adorned with diamonds, rubies and emeralds, probably his most valuable haul ever. Or it would have been.

He should have been warned about the security and cursed Damian for not having the house scoped out thoroughly. He regretted taking the job and wished he'd never been introduced to Damian.

After meekly giving himself up to the deputies waiting for him, Button found himself held alone in custody for several hours, being left to sweat it out, no doubt. When the hour of reckoning came, Button was a nervous wreck. He had not expected the police to come down so hard on someone with no criminal record. But they outlined a wave of similar robberies, only two of which were his, making it clear that he was to be indicted for them all. 'Every single last one of them,' the officer had said.

Yes, they suspected someone else was behind the wave of jewellery thefts, but that was just 'too bad'. Then, right at the end, they offered him leniency in mitigation for information to apprehend the mastermind. He wanted to tell them, but Damian's warning stopped him and made Button fight against the idea of selling out.

Back in his cell he grappled with the consequences of his decision, either way. *Fucking Damian.* How was it fair to be taking the rap for robberies committed by other slimeballs in Damian's network? He smashed his fist against the cell bars. *It's not my fault. You put me in this position.* Yet, Damian had made the contract clear. If anyone was caught stealing and ratted out, they would be dealt with, even behind bars. Damian would get to them and kill them.

Button believed the threat and his belief had been reinforced by the man who'd accompanied Damian at that meeting. A large man with menace in his eyes. Button had asked who he was. 'I'm a man you never want to see again,' had been the reply. Button spent a sleepless night in the cell before the second interrogation. Again, he denied the involvement of anyone else. The officers looked resigned and terminated the interview.

'It's your choice. Be prepared to live with it for a very long time,' one officer had said. In his cell, the hours and pressure took their toll, and Button came to a decision. He would accept the deal and give up Damian Gent to the police.

Then fate stepped in. There was activity at his cell door. He was led to the reception desk. The lead officer said Button was to forgo any pre-trial detention to allow him time to consider making a deal, pending his court hearing scheduled for the following month. On his return, if Button did not name the gang leader, he would be charged with the other burglaries.

Button was told not to leave the county and, signing the sheet for his stuff, said he understood, but it was all a blur.

Walking free bought him valuable thinking time. The next day Randal Button stood on Damian Gent's doorstep in the sweltering heat, knocking loudly.

'Are we expecting anyone?' Damian asked his girlfriend as he moved towards the hall.

'Don't think so,' Sarah replied.

Damian looked at the security monitor and recognised Button.

'What the fuck is he doing here?' Damian asked out loud. 'Sarah, make yourself scarce while I sort this.'

Sarah looked puzzled but did not question the instruction.

'Don't worry,' Damian said. 'This shouldn't take long.'

He opened the door and, checking the street in both directions, ushered Button into the hallway. Aside from Button's car parked next to Sarah's, the street was empty.

Closing the door, Damian indicated Button stretch out his arms and patted him down thoroughly. Damian hid his fury at Button turning up at his home unannounced. There was no telling if Button was being tailed by police or not.

Once he was satisfied Button was not carrying a piece or wired up, Damian moved them through to his large kitchen diner, all shiny white quartz and steel, opening on to the private pool area.

Damian walked to the opposite side of the central island and leaned back against the counter. 'So ... how the fuck do you know where I live?' he asked.

'Whitepages.'

'I'm not on that.'

'You are to those who pay a fee to find you.'

'Fucking no way!' Damian would check if that was true later. Was that smugness creeping across Button's ugly face? He would wipe away that look. 'I heard you'd been busted. Does Whitepages cover prison cells, mate?'

Button looked scared. 'I had to come here. It's the police. They know about you.'

Damian was alarmed. 'What? You gave them my name?'

'No, not your name. They just know I'm not the man.'

'The man? You mean me? So, you did give them my name.'

'No, I didn't give you up. I swear it.'

'What did you tell them then?'

'Nothing. I remembered what you and your friend said. I told them nothing. Promise.'

Button was breathing rather hard for someone standing still. He kept looking around and outside the back.

Damian allowed the silence to hang there a moment before gesturing Button to continue.

'It's like this. Now, I respect you and all, but I can't do the time. Not without compensation. I figured—'

Damian cut him short. 'You've come here for money?'

Button looked strangely relieved. 'Yes, I've come here for money. I think I earned that much.'

'Go on, how much?'

Button looked around the kitchen and towards the pool. Damian guessed he was calculating how much to ask for.

'I see you here with all your fancy stuff, and I figure if I talked this would all end, and I know you like your things. You have expensive taste and I—'

'How much?'

'I guess sixty thousand ain't a great deal for a man like you.'

'A man like me?' Damian smirked. He was expecting a much higher ask.

'Fifty then, but I ain't going no lower. I'm looking at five years. I need something when I come out. Look, you owe me, man.'

'But you'd be out in half that time, surely? I know about *gaintime.*'

Button looked unsure. 'Even with gaintime, I'd be doing well over half.'

Damian considered. His burglars all knew the risks and Button was not following the rules. He should be keeping his head down, ready to take his medicine quietly. Instead, here he was demanding a pay-off in exchange for silence.

Damian did not take kindly to threats, especially ones made in his own home. The fact Button had been scared of him enough to not give him up to the police, but not scared enough to ask for money, was puzzling. Maybe Button would have been better off trading his name to do less time, but it was too late now.

Looking Button up and down, Damian considered the thief inept and small-time, and the derisory sum demanded by Button confirmed that thinking. Button had done two previous jobs for him, stealing goods to order worth tens of thousands of dollars to Damian's collectors, and had been paid seven thousand and ten thousand in return. Button would make considerably more longer-term from their business arrangement. All he needed was to keep quiet and do the time, and then his loyalty would be rewarded, well beyond a paltry fifty grand. Damian felt himself struggling to contain his anger. He thought about pulling out his Glock and putting a bullet in the thief's head.

No, he was not going to do that. Not with Sarah along the hall.

The late afternoon sun streamed through the kitchen window, light dancing on the sparkling quartz. Reflected light shone into the face of the ungrateful thief shuffling uncomfortably opposite, avoiding eye contact with Damian. The silence in the room was palpable.

The sun's warmth bathed Damian too, burning his cheeks in a fuel of outrage. Button had no shame, trying to blackmail him in his own home.

The danger posed by Button's threat to make a trade with the police had come as a shock. The plea-bargaining scum could ruin everything. Damian came to a decision. He would use the ultimate sanction in defence of his interests.

'OK, let me think how we're going to do this,' he said as he moved across to a cupboard and casually poured himself a large glass of single malt. With mock civility, he offered a glass to his 'guest'. Button squinted against the sunlight towards Damian and declined the offer.

He wants to grab the money and run.

The pantomime of swirling his tumbler, taking in the

peaty aroma of the whisky, gave Damian time to think. It also allowed him the cruelty of baiting Button and watching him shift uncomfortably. Button wiped a bead of sweat trickling down his temple, and Damian contemplated a far more serious blood sport. One involving alligators.

By the time Damian had finished his drink, his next steps were crystal clear.

'I don't keep that kind of cash here,' he said. 'I'll need twenty-four hours to get the money.'

Button seemed to believe him, and the place for the handover was agreed. It was to be the following evening. Moments later he was watching Button's beat-up old brown Chevy drive around the corner and out of sight.

It was only in solitude that Damian's vitriol exploded with tenacious force.

He became lost in his private imaginations of retribution, imagining Button's head being punched to a pulp against the hood of the Chevy. The monster inside Damian resurfaced as deep exhalations through gritted teeth. The slight tic that had plagued him as a child returned as it tended to in moments of extreme emotion. 'No f-f-fucking w-way!'

Damian twitched as he repeated the cursing; to the point he raised the now empty whisky glass in readiness to throw against the wall.

Something made him stop as his control returned. Breathing deeply, he looked at the sparkling Waterford crystal in his hand. He set it down on the breakfast bar like it was a grenade about to explode. The small victory against temper eased any remaining fury. Damian heaved a sigh and looked up. Sarah was at the door watching him. He had no idea how long she had been there, but he did not like her seeing his episodes.

It was a scenario he had learned to live with. When under threat, he'd trained himself to remain focused and to quell the raging beast within. By the time he was on the phone to Ben, authority had returned, all anger banished from his countenance.

'Ben, we need to talk. Will you come around to mine? Now.'

A quarter of an hour later Ben arrived to be given his macabre instructions.

The following night, Randal Button was dead.

FOUR

Damian opened the warehouse's office door and looked in on Mason to see how the currency count was going. The Safescan machine was whirring through a bundle of notes quickly.

Satisfied, Damian returned to the table, leaving Mason to finish off. Noah was explaining to Ben how to drift cars around bends. Noah was a talented driver who had completed promising trials with NASCAR teams at Chicagoland Speedway. Despite Noah's huge promise, his rich father had turned him down for the money to buy a seat in a team.

Noah had gone against his father's will and borrowed money to buy that drive in NASCAR but gambled the entire loan away. He had borrowed from the type of people you should never owe money to and had fled his city of birth to start a new life in Florida. Damian had met Noah in a local bar, flat broke and asking for work, and decided to give him a chance.

Damian guessed Noah's father had likely wanted his son to earn the drive for a top team through hard work as a test driver, but there was something about Noah's plight that touched a nerve and made Damian want to help.

The count continued and Sarah arrived. She chatted with Noah and Ben – something about the Dolphins vs the Bears. Ben and Sarah were teasing Noah about the performances of the Chicago Bears that season. Wow, she certainly knew her American football and was comfortable bantering with the guys. It was a skill Damian had mixed feelings about.

Mason stepped out of the office, bringing the conversation to halt. 'We have ourselves a total,' he said, 'and it's a good one.'

He handed over a small scrap of paper torn off his notepad.

Damian read out the total before having a quiet word with Ben and then Noah to clarify the share they would receive once it had been laundered.

'So where to next, Mason?' Damian asked.

'I've already been thinking about that question,' he said. 'Avoid heading south, I'd say. We need to create a false pattern where our location isn't in the middle. I've mapped out a few options based on size, potential take, risk assessment vis-à-vis security, and—'

'Wow, I didn't expect a lecture,' Damian said. The others laughed.

Damian saw Mason's face flush and the indignant techie tried to defend himself. 'I'm just doing my job. You know about license plate readers? LPRs can log vehicles in the vicinity of every job. They can extract numbers to find suspect vehicles. I've been mapping the locations of static cameras too. We need to stay off the highways. Florida Highway Patrols have them in their cars too.'

'Well, that's dumb. We change the plates each time, so there's no issue,' Noah said.

'But even false plates raise red flags to FHPs and can get us pulled over,' Mason retorted.

The post-job euphoria was on the wane.

'OK. You're right, Mason. It's been a long day,' Damian said, 'and it'll be better if we discuss the next target tomorrow. Come on, guys, we just made seventy-two grand!' The total was more than Damian believed even the bigger bureaus kept on site. The heist was a windfall.

The large frame of Ben stood up, except he was wedged into the cheap garden chair he'd sat on. For a comical moment, the arms clamped either side of his midriff, rising with him like the chair was a fused extension of his backside. Ben grinned and everyone laughed. The tension was broken.

Damian felt in the mood for a post-job celebration and arranged for the team to meet up the next evening.

'Go get some rest,' he said. 'I'll sort the money tomorrow and then it's … party!'

FIVE

He was calling her.

'Just a minute,' Sarah replied.

She looked up from the sink to her reflection in the mirror. The woman looking back showed defiance – a purse-lipped resolve where soft features should have been. Not long to go now and she would escape. Weeks, not months, she hoped.

On the other side of the bathroom door lay the source of her anxiety. Steeling herself, she swallowed a couple of pills from a secret stash. *They should dull the senses.* Growing up in a trailer park under the care of her drunken mom, she had learned how to block out pain.

How had she let herself become trapped in this situation? Tears welled up and the image of the woman facing her became bleary. She splashed cold water on her face and reached for a towel.

She told herself she was still the same Sarah Mitchell who had battled through numerous disadvantages to gain a degree in tourism from Florida International University. She was the Sarah who had financed long hours of study with money from bar work. She really needed the strong Sarah now because, at that moment, she felt helpless.

Why had fate conspired against her? She had worked hard, graduating two years after the economic crash. Despite the optimism of her tutors, the tourist industry had not recovered to its pre-2008 heights. She'd had to lower her sights and work as a booking clerk for a boat charter and holiday rental company. But with no support and very large loans taken to fund her education, she had also done some topless waitressing, which was where she'd met the man waiting for her on the other side of the bathroom door – Damian Gent.

With a deep sigh and one final glance at the mirror, she slipped out of her underwear and entered the room, naked. Just how Damian preferred.

'You've been a while. What were you up to in there?' He seemed preoccupied on his cell phone, so she ignored the comment. Setting aside the phone, he turned his attention to her, patting the bed beside him.

'That was one hell of a day you've just had. You must be exhausted. I really don't mind,' she said.

Damian laughed. 'Nah, come here, sexy.'

She heard his British twang at its strongest in such moments, the colloquial traits of a man whose accent switched between the native and the alien.

She obeyed and he drew her towards him, cupping her breasts. She felt his hot whisky breath on her mouth and then her neck. Soon his mouth was on her nipples, and she felt him stiffen against her thigh. His head went lower and, despite herself, she moaned as his tongue played. He moved up the bed and kissed her, sharing her taste as he bit down on her bottom lip. As he did so he nudged her legs apart with his free hand and rode on top of her for a while.

Which Damian would she see tonight?

She sensed him escaping to another place, any connection between them broken.

His hand gripped her blonde locks and tightened. As hard as he thrust, he pulled down on her hair. Next, he gripped her under the chin, choking off her airway. She longed for the tenderness they had once enjoyed. The cruel Damian had returned.

Damian climbed off her and pushed her on to her front – a position he recently seemed to prefer. He entered her behind with an uncompromising push that made her wince. He thrust hard and bent over her, once again grabbing her hair.

He pulled her hair with a force that jerked back her neck. The tension referred down her shoulder blades and spine. He was pushing so hard into her that a sickly sensation rose from the pit of her stomach to her throat. The sensation was fear.

As his breathing deepened into a trance-like rhythm, hers became short and uneven. She knew he was somewhere else and wondered where. Was he with someone else? If so, who was she?

Damian was barely nine years old, safe and warm in the bosom of his mother.

'James ...' whispered his mum, stroking his hair. They were cuddled up watching television. It was how he liked to spend Sunday afternoons after coming home from playing football. Sometimes he'd watch the Sunday afternoon match in his Charlton football shirt. Charlton was the team his father had supported, and he'd wanted to play for them one day. It was a great season, their highest ever in the Premier League.

His father had died in a work accident and for five years he'd been the main man in his mother's life. Or so he thought. It was a chilly autumn afternoon when the van pulled up outside. A man got out and carried boxes and bin bags into the house. The man looked much older than his mother, and every time he returned to the van, he turned to wave. The man's jaunty gesture carried with it the promise of friendship. When the van was emptied, the man sat down on the sofa opposite, surveying him over a mug of steaming tea. His mother introduced the man as 'Michael, the one I've been telling you about'. His mum made it clear that Michael would be living with them. She said something about it making 'financial sense'.

The infiltration of his home occurred with casual ease. He barely remembered the wedding. He sat by an aunt and was swung around on the dance floor by Michael. 'I'm your dad now,' Michael said.

Sarah heard a man talking in the next room. The trailer had paper-thin walls. Her mom was drunk again and had brought yet another stranger to their home. She despised her mom's drunken laughing, the overly faked compliments. 'Oh my, aren't you the strong one.' She tried to block out the overly loud orgasms too, surely faked. It was so demeaning, and Sarah hated living with the shame.

The reality of the man the next morning never lived up to the sexual soundtrack played out the previous night. The men were invariably ugly, smelly druggies, petty thieves and worse. She twice had to fight men off to prevent herself being raped, yet her mom had blamed her for the incidents and showed no remorse for recklessly endangering her own daughter.

She felt the man's rotten breath on her.

'Your mommy didn't tell me about you, my pretty …' The man was clawing at her top. Hurting her.

Pain snapped her into the present.

'Damian, you're hurting me. I don't like it. Slow down, please.' He was totally detached, pounding her without feeling. She was hurting, both physically and emotionally. 'Stop, please stop …'

Damian was still in North London. It was raining. He was wet. He was looking at the bloodied knife in his hand and down at the motionless Albanian kid. Then he was running. Fleeing.

Sweat dripped from his face, making salty splashes on Sarah's back.

His climax took over and brought him into the present.

'F-f-f-u-ck …' He stopped moving, breaths becoming shallow pulses as he pulled away, collapsing on to his back. His heart was pounding. Swallowing hard, he reached out to his bedside table glass of whisky. Half turning, he gulped down the liquor, some of it dribbling down his chin and onto the sheet. He exhaled, and turned back towards Sarah, whose body was now facing away from him in a foetal position. He felt numb – physically and emotionally spent. The nightmare was vanquished from his earlier thoughts, leaving him with a strange mix of feelings. The success of the raid comforted him, but it was tinged with a note of sadness. He could tell Sarah was crying. Her breathing moved in time to the staccato rhythm of suppressed sobs.

He'd had a sense beforehand that he was losing control. It was a situation that had been repeating itself for the last few weeks and he felt powerless to stop it. It was always the same – he would try to fight the urges but fail. He hated himself for his weakness.

He spooned his naked body against hers, kissing her shoulder gently as he tried to justify his actions to himself. It had been a difficult few weeks, and today had been stressful. He had needed the release of rough sex tonight and would be more gentle next time.

Then doubt nagged away at him. He was getting increasingly lost during sex. Was he deluding himself? He had acquired a taste for something different, and dreams of violent sex were beginning to supplant his usual nightmares. Somehow the violence was helping him cope with the past and pushing those cold, dark London memories away. Maybe he needed more than Sarah to satisfy his expanding appetite.

He knew she needed a bigger challenge and he had plans to open a business for her. That boat hire company she liked to talk about. It was exactly what they had been working towards before Covid hit, wasn't it? The heists would provide the capital to fund the dream. He would do the right thing and look after her.

He drifted into sleep, back in Florida. Safe and warm away from the rain-soaked streets of North London.

Sleep was more difficult to come by for Sarah. Silent tears trickled down her chin, wetting the sheet in symmetry with the whisky stain. Her back ached. Damian's games were becoming more physical, but at least tonight she'd been spared his new sex toys. She had not been handcuffed or beaten with a riding crop. Tonight, she had escaped lightly.

The private humiliation was now matched by his public displays against her. He had recently goaded her in front of the gang for being his 'ungrateful rescue job'. She was a freeloader and lucky to have him. All this was laughed off publicly and taken as a joke, but resentment had swelled as she plotted an escape from her insufferable boyfriend. A boyfriend she had loved so much, but whose disrespect towards her was increasing weekly.

Moreover, her resentment meant that she was starting to enjoy pushing back. She knew it infuriated him. She liked wearing daring low-cut tops and it annoyed her that he now asked her to cover up and not show 'too much' to other men. She began deliberately inciting his flashes of jealousy, even though she risked paying the price later. She needed the satisfaction of controlling some of the space in which they coexisted. She enjoyed seeing his jealousy and hated herself for it.

She would only have to ride it out a little longer before taking what was fair – the reparations that had accrued with each attack – all of his banked money. She would start her own boat rental business and a new life far away in California. She knew how to access Damian's bank accounts because she knew where he hid his login details.

Sarah consoled herself with thoughts of revenge as sleep finally rose to meet her.

SIX

The old man sat on his porch swigging his favourite beer. About halfway through the bottle his attention was caught by a meteor shower arcing through the clear Floridian night sky, leaving a silvery tail behind it.

He was lucky to have looked up at that moment – the display was a thing of beauty – and he understood some of the science behind what he was witnessing. Light trails were the optical manifestation of tiny fragments of space material burning up as they entered the Earth's atmosphere.

Weren't meteors and comets once viewed as warnings from heaven, a sign from the gods? He was sure he'd read such a thing, or maybe seen it on TV. Something about the ancients making prayers, and sacrifices offered to avert impending doom.

He tilted his rocking chair back, so he'd not have to crane his arthritic neck looking up. It had nothing to do with religion. It was simply an interesting light show to accompany his bottle of beer.

The man looked from sky to beer and took in another gulp of the refreshing brew. His favourite beer from upstate went well with the celestial entertainment. The label on the Floridian beer made him smile. The brand was Hop Gun and came with advice from the fat little Buddha on the label to 'Suntan your soul'. What did that mean, exactly? And why use a religious symbol like a Buddha? The old man had no idea. He stared at the bottle, no longer seeing the pictures on it. His thoughts had blurred to images of pagan rites and altar stones. He was not a religious man, but something made him feel uneasy. The bushes whispered in the breeze and the crickets had fallen silent. It made him shudder.

Despite growing up in a religious state, the elder son born to a God-fearing family, he spurned religion. He had seen his baby brother taken from him in a car accident at a young age and, from that day, stopped believing. He thought about his brother every day, and his son too.

He looked up again; the lights were further north and fading out of sight, dying before his eyes.

His son was dead too. Or might as well be. With a university major in computer science at UF, his boy had used his top-of-the-class abilities to rob and defraud. He had brought shame on the Reeves family name by spending time in Manatee County Jail.

The last time his son had visited, the old man had said some words he knew could never be taken back. He had not believed his son's promise to end his association with crime. He knew his son had no job, and yet he seemed to have come into money. He had called his son a liar and told him that it was unfair he should live when so many good people in the world died young. He had told his boy to go, and never visit him again. They were words he regretted.

A tear ran down his cheek and he placed the empty bottle down. The light trail had disappeared on the horizon.

Giving a final backward glance towards the heavens, he shuddered again. Despite the humidity he felt chilly and headed indoors for his bed. He passed a photo of himself and his son, Mason, hanging on the landing. They were both grinning proudly, holding a marlin caught while fishing off the nearby Keys, back when they'd shared better times. Before Mason moved out and started keeping bad company.

The old man carried the gut-wrenching disappointment in his son around like a curse. It turned his ageing blood cold on balmy nights such as this.

He folded back fraying bedsheets and hoped a good night's sleep would vanquish his sad thoughts. The ticking of the clock seemed louder tonight. Sleep was not going to arrive easily. When it finally did, dreams of monsters punctuated his restless slumber. He wrestled with sweat-soaked sheets that clung to his torso like the horrible visions of his imagination.

Two hundred miles to the north, a cluster of meteorite particles, no wider than a dime in diameter, slammed down through the roof of a solitary warehouse. The warehouse was located to the north-west of the Melbourne conurbation, in a conservation area.

The final fragments of the obliterated meteor shower came to rest against the mildew-soaked wall of the concrete shed. They had completed a journey of gigantic proportions and now cooled off after their super-heated entry through Earth's atmosphere.

As they cooled, outer molecules of the innocuous shards sent out tiny impulses. Imperceptibly, life forms were waking up and reaching out, feeling for other life.

Bedded against the living fronds of lichen and moss, the fragments pulsed into action. Subtly and slowly, the extraterrestrial material transferred energy to microscopic bugs that lived as part of the green morass.

In an area no larger than a small saucer, tiny bugs scuttled and crawled. In the violent world that encapsulated such creatures, they hunted for prey and, in turn, were hunted themselves. Prolonging life and the ability to replicate their enzymes or procreate meant success. Darwinism and luck dictated which creatures lived and which died. Each species carried unique elements, placing them within an ordered hierarchy of living things. The successful ones gained dominance over their surroundings by killing the weak or forcing competitors to try to survive in neighbouring environs.

A process that had continued for millions of years was coming to an end. Small impulses penetrated millions of microorganisms, breaking down their genetic codes and fusing competing life forms into combined matter. The tiny creatures merged into the debris, losing their individuality and becoming part of a small and growing collective.

The damp moss extended to a third the height of the warehouse's back wall. The moss was hydrated by a tributary running behind the building, water seeping in through decaying masonry. The moss's fronds gripped the inanimate objects in contact with the floor at the base of the wall. Green-hued micro-vegetation established itself on the label of a bottle of beer. The little fat Buddha on the label became clad in a green suit as the slimy substance encroached up his thick chins and on to his mouth.

The moss wall provided a useful canvas for the alien life to take hold. Slowly but surely, more and more tiny elements of living matter were assimilated into the growing entity. The foreign matter expanded without conscious thought. Without fear or pity, it systematically absorbed everything it encountered.

The beauty of the earlier light show at the fringes of Earth's atmosphere was a stark contrast to the darkness that had just made landfall..

SEVEN

It was just past 9.00 p.m. and Melbourne's Indian River bars were busy. Confidence had returned as the Covid restrictions of previous years became a distant memory.

Damian shouldered the heavy wooden door of the Rebel Yell open and ushered Sarah in. He followed her into the musty dark interior. It was his favourite restaurant bar and it felt like he was stepping back in time. Damian liked the wood-panelled, candlelit atmosphere and knew the owner lovingly cultivated its Old South feel.

As usual, the owner was behind the bar and nodded in his direction. Damian raised a hand in acknowledgement and looked round for the others. He was pleased to see they had already arrived and were occupying the furthest corner seats. The booth was his favourite, the one he always reserved.

He was guiding Sarah through a small group of tourists towards the booth when a firm hand pulled on his shoulder. It was the owner, David Anderson.

'Got a moment?' Anderson said.

'What, now?' Damian looked over to the booth. There were already drinks on the table.

'If you don't mind, just a little business to clear up.'

'OK, what is it?

'Not here.' Anderson nodded towards the bar.

Damian sighed. An afternoon of laundering money had prevented him drinking, and he needed a dram of something to warm his throat. He followed Anderson through a raised hatch and into the back corridor. Anderson unhooked a large bunch of keys attached to his belt and, after rattling them around for what seemed an age, found the right one for his office door. Damian rolled his eyes and glared at the back of Anderson's head.

Anderson rounded his mahogany writing desk and sat down. He gestured to the seat opposite, but Damian preferred to stand. He knew Anderson liked to talk.

Please get on with it, Damian thought, although he did not want to appear too uncivil, not when money was at stake.

The bar owner had latched on to Damian's British accent several years earlier and they'd formed a loose friendship. Anderson had outlined a British ancestry he claimed extended all the way back to the state's 1830 settlers. He even bragged about distant relatives fighting at Gettysburg.

Damian remained dubious, but never argued the point. Anderson was a keen collector of Dixieland memorabilia and was always on the hunt for new items. Consequently, Damian had become something of an American Civil War expert. The bar was themed with symbols of the Confederate States of America. The Rebel Flag appeared in various locations around its oak-panelled walls. Images of Robert E. Lee and heroic portrayals of the Battle of Gettysburg took pride of place around the booths. The paraphernalia around the tables were all cheap replicas. They were not the items he acquired for Anderson.

All the genuine collectibles were safely tucked away in Anderson's private collection. Damian had fenced a variety of interesting Dixie treasures for Anderson, stolen to order. The man paid good money and large bonuses for special items. The bonuses came in the form of crates of beer, cases of wine, and various whiskies which were consumed in large quantities by Damian.

The other quid pro quo was access to booths at short notice, which was where Damian wanted to be at that moment. He waited for Anderson to talk.

'It's about the cross, Damian. I really need it quickly.'

'Yes, you said, but it's not something we can rush. The church museum has security in place and—'

'I know that's what you said, but it's been a fortnight now and I have an important event coming up. I've promised my associates we'd have it.'

'OK, David, I'll see what I can do. But no promises. I like to do things properly. It helps keep us both out of jail. What's so important this time around?'

'Ah, you see, that Anglo-Saxon artefact dates back centuries. It travelled over with the first settlers. For us, it would be a small victory to set against the Lost Cause. Its Anglo-Saxon symbolism is crucial for our first Klan event.'

'Klan? You don't mean the Ku Klux fucking Klan, do you? No way.'

'Why, is that a problem?' Anderson looked disappointed. 'You know the guys would welcome you. You are a true WASP. Your purity of blood cannot be questioned.'

Damian had listened to Anderson's romanticised version of the Old South many times. Although Anderson was deluded, Damian believed him to be harmless enough – a sad relic of a dying culture of white supremacists who once held sway across the state.

'I wish you'd told me what it was for,' he said.

'Get it to me on time and I'll pay twenty per cent more.'

'You'll pay double if that's what you're using it for.'

'OK, I'll make it double,' Anderson said without hesitation.

The offer was too tempting. Anderson was about to pay twelve thousand for a battered old silver cross.

'I'll make a call and get back to you soon. Will that be all?' Damian said as he turned towards the door.

'Well, there is one thing …'

Damian turned back. He guessed what was coming next.

'You know I wish you wouldn't,' Anderson said.

'Oh, don't start on that again.'

'You know we don't like Blacks in here, that's all.'

'And you know Ben is my friend and business partner.'

'How you conduct your private life is your own business, but just don't bring … his sort into my establishment.'

His sort. Damian laughed. 'Let me tell you, it was his sort who looked out for me when I had no one else. You may not like it, but there was a time when nearly all my friends were his sort.'

Anderson looked surprised. 'You never told me that before.'

'Why would I?'

'Because you know it matters to me.'

'And being loyal to a friend who helped me matters too. We agree on one thing, though. I should never have brought Ben in here. What must he think of me?' Damian gestured towards the framed memorabilia on Anderson's office wall. 'I used to think all this was quaint nostalgia, but the KKK? This is 2025. What the fuck are you thinking?'

'Damian, Damian, open your eyes. Look around you. See how much our great nation has declined. International communists and financiers are taking over our country. Immigrants have taken our jobs, Jewish bankers are working with the Chinese to destroy our economy. The Democrats are helping them from inside Capitol Hill. The Democrats bleed the working man dry. This time around we got our woman in. We need the South to rise again and join with the new president to stop the communists and make the United States great again.'

Damian was stunned. 'Jeez, you actually believe all that shit.'

'It's all there online. They may own mainstream media, but they can't hide it from us any more.'

'I don't know what to say,' Damian said. 'An intelligent man like you ...'

'Then maybe we need to reconsider our business arrangements.' Anderson slammed his fist down on the desk.

Damian shrugged. 'Yes, I think we should,' and he turned again to leave. He'd reached the end of the corridor when he heard Anderson's shout.

'Stop.' There was a hint of desperation in his voice.

Damian sighed and turned back. He needed that drink.

Anderson looked at him earnestly as he returned to the office door.

'Look, no offence meant. I don't blame you or anyone for not understanding. The media is controlled by them. CNN, NDC, *The New York Times*. Oh, and MSNBC and NPR. All of them. I don't even fully trust Fox. They turned against Trump, remember. No wonder you and many others don't see it. Let's talk about this when you're in here alone. I don't want us to fall out.'

Damian thought he could feel himself shaking, but it was his phone vibrating in his pocket. He needed to get to the bar.

'OK,' he said. 'We can talk about this another time.'

Anderson looked relieved. 'We're sticking with the new arrangement, aren't we? With the cross, I mean. You deliver on time, I pay double.'

Damian contemplated for a moment. The robbery of the cross was already commissioned, and the job now promised a heftier payout.

'OK, I'll get you your precious cross. One last job. Just don't fall short on your side of the deal.'

Anderson's voice softened. 'I won't. When have I ever let you down? I'll even throw in an extra half case of your favourite whisky.' Anderson scribbled something on a notepad. 'Maybe we should resume this conversation another day. When we've both had a chance to cool down. I'm sure we can accommodate each other's opinions.'

Damian was surprised by Anderson's conciliatory tone. *Wow, this cross must be very important.*

As uncomfortable as he was with the intended end use for the artefact, Damian was not going to turn down that sort of reward. He nodded and walked out.

He entered the bar and checked his phone as he waited to be served. It showed a missed call and a new text from his longest-serving and most trusted burglar, who went by the handle 'Gold'. Damian read the text twice. It was not good news. He really needed that drink now.

A sickly feeling rose inside him as Ben looked up and smiled from across the room. Anderson's revelation about the KKK had shocked Damian. It seemed the bar was a hotbed of fascism.

Ben was smart, and Damian wondered how much his friend understood about Anderson's operation. If Ben knew the truth, why had he never mentioned anything? He would talk to Ben about the subject and find another venue for his celebrations. This would be the final night – he'd never bring his associates to the Rebel Yell again.

At the bar he ordered a bottle of Timber Creek Florida Reserve bourbon and asked for one glass. He carried them to the booth, where he wedged himself between Sarah and Noah and poured himself a healthy measure. It tasted good. The infusion of Florida limestone spring water they used in the blend's production was just what he needed.

Everyone seemed relaxed, which meant the drinks were flowing. Waving his hand, Damian summoned a waitress and ordered a fresh round.

He looked over at Ben. His giant friend looked relaxed. Then he looked at the memorabilia on the booth's walls. It dawned on him that nostalgia for the Confederate past was accompanied by a collective amnesia of the horrors of slavery. He had bought into the bar's atmosphere without considering some of its historic meaning.

Ben was now looking at him. As if reading his mind, he mouthed, 'You OK?'

Damian succinctly shook his head and mouthed back the word 'Gold'. It was a problem they needed to sort quickly, and he wanted to tell his friend he was sorry.

Ben frowned. Had he understood?

The exchange, intended to be private, had attracted the attention of the others. Damian looked around at the group. He would talk to Ben a bit later. In the meantime, he was determined not to let thoughts of either Anderson or Gold spoil their evening.

Damian raised his glass. 'Here's to you, team. I mean it. Here's to you all.'

'No, no, no,' Ben said. 'Here's to *us.*'

Everyone raised their glasses and said, 'Cheers!'

'How's Lewis Hamilton tonight?' he said, looking across at

Noah.

'I'm good – can't wait for the next heist,' Noah shouted across the table.

Sarah was shaking her head. 'I think there's someone at the back of the bar who didn't quite hear you.'

'Oh, sorry.' Noah instinctively looked down and pulled up his shoulders.

Ben was also shaking his head, a look of resignation on his face.

'The next trip, Noah, is something I will be discussing soon,' Damian said, nodding in the direction of Mason. 'How's our new boy enjoying his night out with us? Keeping up, I hope?'

Mason immediately picked up his bottle of beer and smiled back awkwardly.

'Don't worry, you'll get used to all this,' Ben said, laughing.

'It's a condition of employment here,' Damian said, jiggling his bourbon and winking.

Mason laughed and directed a question to Ben, so that they could all hear.

'How fast can you run the hundred metres? Without drugs, that is?'

Ben and Damian had heard variations on the Ben Johnson joke many times before. Damian guessed it was Mason's attempt to fit in and knew Ben had no issue with the fact he shared the same name as a Canadian sprint cheat from the 80s.

'You see, the difference is, I didn't do drugs,' Ben said. 'Bet you have, though.'

'I thought everyone had,' Mason said.

'You thought wrong then.'

'Ben, I didn't know you did athletics?' Noah said, and Mason snorted out his beer laughing.

'It's a bit before your time. I'll explain later,' Mason said.

A debate on drugs ensued, with Mason championing their recreational use. Sarah leaned over to Damian and said in his ear, 'Are you sure it's sensible to place so much responsibility in his hands?'

Damian was unsure what she meant and whispered back, 'What do you mean?'

'Mason, I mean. You're placing a lot of trust in someone you don't know well. What if he gets it wrong?'

'Don't worry. He won't. He's a fucking genius with that laptop of his.' Damian leaned in to whisper and kissed her on the neck. 'You smell good tonight,' he whispered.

She placed her hand on the back of his neck, stroking his hair. It sent pleasurable shivers down his spine. Next, she clasped his chin and pulled his face around to align with hers. He thought he saw pain in her eyes before she placed a soft kiss on his mouth. Maybe these heists are stressing her out, he thought.

'Don't worry, Sarah, we won't be doing many more,' he said. 'Just a little problem to sort and normal service will be resumed sooner than you imagine.'

'Why, what problem?' she asked.

He forced a smile. 'Nothing I can't handle.' He stood up and beckoned Ben to join him, picked up the bottle of bourbon and walked with Ben past the bar, through the sports lounge and out the back entrance. For the first time Damian was conscious of the stares from Anderson's friends, who were standing around the pool table as usual. He silently chided himself for his blindness to the uncomfortable situation he'd placed Ben in so many times before.

'Anything wrong?' asked Noah, shuffling back around the curved seating to Sarah. He looked across at Mason, who seemed preoccupied with a tablet – another one of his many gadgets, she guessed.

Noah leaned in close and whispered to her, glancing back across the bar from time to time. 'I like your perfume,' he said. He moved closer and she could hear him breathing in the opulent aroma. The perfume was an expensive limited edition, and she was pleased it was noticed.

She leaned forward to pick up her drink, detaching herself

from Noah in the process. She sensed him studying her as she sipped from the bottle.

'Madam,' he said in a mock-British accent, 'I think you may be drunk.'

'Whatever gives you that idea?' Sarah countered in a slurred voice.

'Er, I think I may be too.' He lifted his beer bottle to his mouth, pretending to miss. The joke backfired – the bottles were fresh and full. Some splashed down the front of his shirt and onto his lap. 'Shit!' he said, which made her laugh loudly.

Mason looked over momentarily.

'We can't take you anywhere, can we?' She grabbed a paper napkin from the table and dabbed his chest. She heard his breathing quicken as she pressed the napkin lower down his shirt.

Noah glanced nervously towards Mason. He was absorbed in his tablet, oblivious to the game she was playing with Noah across the table.

'What type of stiff takes a tablet on a night out?' Noah whispered.

'Look, I missed a bit.' She dabbed further down and felt him tremble. She pitied his nervous inexperience, but his helplessness unleashed a sense of power in her, acting as an aphrodisiac. Her hand moved increasingly lower until it reached the damp patch of spilt beer on his crotch. The infraction made him shudder even more. She enjoyed teasing him, caught between the tenderness of their friendship and a desire to be wanted. Sarah had always been an overt flirt and knew Noah fancied her. But she had never been unfaithful to any man she'd been with.

Damian's recent behaviour made her question that loyalty. She considered what it would be like with the dashing young driver, but quickly dismissed the thought. Noah was needy and lost without Damian's leadership. She knew Noah was a rescue job, much like herself, but ultimately more reliant on the rescuer. Noah was weak-willed.

After years living with her weak mother, she enjoyed the certainty of being with a strong man. She also enjoyed the lifestyle that came with it. She had kept Damian's house clean and tidy and offered herself completely to him, without question. She thought back to a few months ago when Damian's behaviour started to change. What had started as fun sexual experimentation become cruel, enslaving her into a darker world of rough sex videos and more extreme demands. It seemed the more power Damian built in his business world, the more controlling he became in their private life.

The last few weeks had been the worst. Since that man had called around and tried to bribe Damian, his violence had grown. She had seen his temper and stammered cursing flare up from the kitchen door. Was he punishing her for having seen that? She had no leverage and resigned herself to increasing abuse.

Leaving Damian would be difficult. And being with Noah would be the death of them both. As the thought flashed across her mind, she checked herself, realising she needed to back off from the intimacy she was encouraging in the youngster. Noah's hand was edging up her inner thigh. Although her leg was hidden under the table, she was scared Damian would return and see what was happening.

'There, there, Mr Chauffeur, all cleaned up after your little accident,' she said, giving Noah one final big dab with the serviette and removing his hand from her thigh. Jumping up from the table, Sarah flashed a smile. 'Excuse me, I'm gonna use the john.'

'Are you kidding me?' Noah exclaimed, drawing Mason's attention.

Sarah walked towards the bathroom. Regretting her last comments, she looked back to see Noah's gaze burning holes into her. She should probably be more careful around him. There was a lot at stake.

Maybe Damian was too trusting when it came to Noah. She was unsure how reliable the kid was. It was clear he'd betray his boss for sex, given the chance. Would he do the same for money, she wondered. Damian also seemed to be placing a lot of faith in Mason's technical abilities to burglarize. She hoped Damian's trust in them both was not misplaced.

By the time she re-entered the bar, Damian and Ben had also returned.

Damian was slumped in his seat. The bottle of bourbon in front of him was half empty, and he seemed to have downed a bottle of beer too. *That was quick.* He had the half-closed eyes of a drunk trying to make sense of his surroundings. Ben looked grim, making her wonder what they had been discussing outside.

The dark cloud seemed to extend out across the group, the party atmosphere flattening out like the surrounding swampland. Damian, Ben, and Noah wore expressions of distant reflection. Only Mason seemed happy, swiping away on his tablet.

But the drinking continued. It always did with her boyfriend.

She sidled in next to Damian and joined in the group's silence. The background rock music – something by Bruce Springsteen – provided cover for the awkwardness. She would try to cheer him.

'I know, I'll take you shopping,' she said. 'I'll get you those Gucci shoes we saw' – she ran her fingers up and down his lapel – 'and what about a lovely new Boss jacket?'

'This jacket not good enough, then?'

'No, that's not what I meant, I …' She had seen him drunk many times before, but his reaction came as a surprise.

'Come on, tell me. What the fuck's wrong with my jacket, I'm sure we'd all like to know?' Damian's raised voice attracted glances from others near the bar.

Sarah felt hijacked. Everything had been so relaxed and, even by Damian's unpredictable standards, the outburst was ridiculous.

'That's not what I meant.'

'That's not what I meant?' he mimicked. 'Well, what the fuck did you mean?'

She rose from her seat, announcing, 'He knows I like that jacket. He knows it! I was there when he bought it.'

She looked around the table through teary eyes. Noah was fiddling with the label on his beer bottle. Ben was staring at

Damian and shaking his head. Mason's jaw had dropped. He looked aghast.

The truth is out about you, heh, Damian?

This was a side of Damian that she imagined was new to Mason, who stood up. *He's going to walk out, she thought. That'll teach you, Damian.* Except Mason did not walk out.

'Boss, boss, look at this ...' Mason indicated his tablet. 'I think I've got it – our next job.' Holding the screen in a more convenient position, Mason looked earnestly at Damian.

For one moment Damian looked confused. His eyes followed Mason's, staring at the screen. Then his features transformed, his face lighting up into a broad grin. Slapping Mason on the back with pantomime theatrics, Damian's smile now extended towards the whole team.

'I told you this man was good!' he said, ushering Mason away from the table, his demeanour as businesslike as over half a bottle of bourbon would allow.

Ben stood up a moment later. 'Don't be hard on him, Sarah,' he said. 'There's a lot going down, that's all.' He gave her shoulder a pat and walked over to join Damian and Mason.

Sarah watched them talking in a space nearer the bar and could hold back no longer. Her tears flowed and she was aware of Noah closing in warily to comfort her, his earlier hurt seemingly dissipating into the bar's musty atmosphere. He was rubbing her arm blind side of their inebriated leader.

Noah offered her a napkin and she snorted a laugh through her tears, remembering its earlier use. He half laughed too, although he looked as forlorn as she felt. She knew the truth of her situation and there was nothing she could do about it. *Soon, though, soon ...*

A few minutes later Damian returned with Ben and a smug-looking Mason, a fresh bottle of champagne in hand. The next job had been agreed.

She saw the jealous look flicker across Noah's face and felt his resentment that the new member of their team had stolen the limelight. Noah welcomed back the thief with what seemed an insincere back slap. Glasses were raised and Damian flipped back to being all charm and wit.

She felt resentment bubbling like the mousse rising in the champagne flutes they all held aloft.

EIGHT

Noah staggered through the shared hallway and into the small condo rented out to him by Damian. He felt ill and regretted joining in with the champagne and shots.

Damian expected them all to drink, which no one seemed to mind, not when the alcohol was free. The whole night was paid for by Damian. He had a tab at the Rebel Yell and an account with the cab company, which meant their rides home were also covered.

Damian even allowed Noah to stay in the condo rent-free.

Yes: Damian – *the perfect boss.*

At least he did not have to chauffeur Damian and Sarah back to their home on such nights. Damian called them his party nights.

Noah slung his jacket over the back of a chair and slid the balcony door open. It was another sultry night and he sat down and rolled a joint. He lit up and took in a long drag, looking along the line of balconies on his floor. Even through the dividers, he could tell no one else was out at such a late hour. The cute girl he liked in the next condo had left months ago. She used to talk to him across the partition and had even invited him over for dinner. Work had stopped him going, and then suddenly she was gone. He had no idea which day she had moved out, or why. She had not bothered to let him have a forwarding address.

Noah took another drag, thinking about the missed opportunity.

Another girl had moved in soon after. She was about his age and looked like a model. He remembered the first time he saw her and the way she said, 'Oh, *hello,*' across the hall in a surprised voice.

She smiled at him, showing her perfect teeth. He smiled back, just as the boyfriend walked out of the lift, glaring at him like a lunatic. 'This is Dan,' she said. Dan was a lot older and jacked on steroids. As big as Ben, but bald and ugly. Noah did not understand what the girl saw in him. Dan, the googly-eyed, iron-pumping asshole. *Life is so unfair.*

Settled down with his joint, Noah thought about Sarah. He felt a wave of loneliness and pain. He felt the contradiction between his desire for Sarah and his anger at her earlier slap-down. He did not deserve that, and she did not deserve what Damian had said tonight either. The disdain towards his boss was growing like a cancer. One day he would stand up to Damian and tell him what he thought about the way Sarah was treated.

He wanted to be his own cool alter ego. The mean and decisive Noah of his dreams. His mind wandered in a cannabis haze. *Shit, this stuff is good.* He liked to fantasise – it was his escape.

Assured and in control, he was a martial arts expert, holding Damian in a death grip as the woman he desired looked on in awe.

'You leave her alone,' he purred.

Damian looked worried for a moment and then grinned. 'I saw you touching her. Do you think I'd ever give her over to you?' He twisted back, smashing Noah's head against the bar floor.

Noah started. He knew he had been tripping, except he remembered the fantasy. Who was he kidding? Even in a dream, his self-loathing was unlocked and laid bare. He was a failure in his father's eyes, beholden to a gangster in Chicago and another one here, risking jail time to make enough money to go home and repay his debts. Worse than anything else, he felt desperately alone. He had no real friends in life and had to chauffer the woman he desired.

He craved to be a part of something better and to belong again, like he had in Chicago. He regretted going against his father. He had given up everything a man his age could wish for. Spending time at the track practising and then going down to *da Lake* to meet up with friends and girls. They would cruise Lake

Shore Drive and take his father's dinghy out, drinking beer from a cool box. He missed looking at the stunning Chicago skyline from the lake, shimmering in the late afternoon sun.

He stubbed out the joint and went inside.

In the bathroom he splashed cold water on his face and stared at his reflection in the brightly lit mirror. His eyes looked tired, and he made faces at himself. It made him laugh and his reflection laughed with him. He pulled a tousled piece of hair down and peeked out from under it, cocking his head to one side, pouting. He nodded. *Not bad, sexy man.*

Everything would right itself. The gang would not be permanent. It was just a temporary means to an end. One day he would have saved enough money to square his debts and try again for NASCAR. Maybe with Sarah by his side and his father cheering from the pit lane.

It was not fair that Damian treated his girlfriend as a possession, like a pedigree dog to be paraded around and shouted at. He would treat her far better, he was convinced.

He drifted towards sleep and entered a delicious fantasy. She was forbidden fruit, and they were kissing. He believed she felt the same way about him.

NINE

The meteor strikes a fortnight earlier had triggered a genesis

The alien matter carried by the meteor fragments had set to work immediately. Absorbing all localised life, a fusion of converted material was spreading across the dankness of the building's back wall, permeating the more porous, crumbling sections of the brickwork and reaching the outside world.

Gently pulsating, the stain of fused matter had become visible on the outside of the construction, spreading like a virus across the wall and into the soil towards the waterway.

Warped creatures devoured each other mercilessly, fragments of their previous hunting instincts still prevalent, but equipped with new physical attributes. A spider's unnaturally large pedipalps extended out to hold a mouse in place. The spider's fangs crushed down on the mouse's head, injecting its deadly mutated serum into the helpless rodent.

The mouse's mandible cracked with the pressure of the arachnid's bite, taking the furry creature to the absolute brink of where life gives way to darkness. On the edge of death, however, the essence of the rodent mingled with the greater mass. The mouse ceased to exist as such. Its biochemistry was now in synergy with its growing host, as mouse DNA fused with that of the collective.

The exoskeleton of a beetle surfaced from the collective soup. The alien's voracious appetite to assimilate new organisms meant that Earth-formed life had gained ascendency. The original alien life contained within the meteor was now the minority partner in a new order of combined matter.

Relentlessly reaching out to absorb more organic lifeforms, the material contained a small and growing cross section of animals familiar to humans. Yet the process of absorption meant that traits of living beings diffused into the pulsing mass were slowly becoming unrecognisable.

The alien's path was set on an unconscious mission to devour and absorb anything biological. Altering the pattern of genomes that had coded all life on Earth since the first single-cell entities, the matter was building new strands of DNA, creating genes not previously found on Earth, and slowly spreading to touch every living thing within its reach.

TEN

Ben killed the motor and allowed the boat to drift down the channel until a tangle of cattails halted its progress. He removed his ear defenders, allowing all his senses to take in the atmosphere. Since losing his wife the previous year, he lived for nights like this. The stillness of the air married to the unearthly hush enhanced his senses, supercharging the adrenaline of anticipation.

With the moon in a new phase, there was no celestial torch to show the way. Everything outside the spotlight's shallow arc was invisible to him, but not to them. The water appeared as an inky black sheet, darker than hell, he imagined, extending its reach to infinity. The strange absence of any sounds added to the eeriness. Despite his long association with the swamps, Ben felt an icy chill run down his spine. He had never known it this still, which served to enhance the aphrodisiac of fear that accompanied such encounters.

They would be there, somewhere – watching him. They were always close-by because he fed them regularly.

They liked to wait among the vegetation on the opposite bank, where the dominant one had built her mound. She was the one he called Thunder and was around nine feet long. Although larger males sometimes visited, she ruled this stretch of water.

He first saw her four years earlier, when out fishing during a storm. The boat drifted too close to her mound, and she had slammed her full weight into the haul, unbalancing him as he stood watching his rods on the other side. The crash of gator against boat coincided with a load clap of thunder.

He was fortunate not to have fallen into the water. Since then, he'd been careful not to go near a mother gator's nest containing hatchlings.

Thunder's favourite trick was to swim under the boat, rising the other side to tear flesh attached to lines he dangled out for her – typically scraps of meat and offal given to him by someone he knew at the abattoir. Beef, pork, horse and even llama. His friends in the swamp welcomed any type of flesh, and tonight they would be given a treat that had only appeared on the menu once before, three months earlier.

He remembered the first one like it was yesterday. The man had tried to blackmail them – a weaselly man called Randal Button. Not a bright Button though, he had joked with Damian. Button had been naive to believe Ben was meeting to hand over money. It had been strangely easy to strangle the thief, bring the body to the warehouse, and dump the corpse in the waterway – away from prying eyes. Gators could consume a human body within minutes, digesting flesh and bones in strong acidic gastrointestinal tracts. They left no evidence.

Ben remembered watching with morbid fascination as Thunder thrashed to release the body from the weights keeping it submerged, twisting and chomping bits of the body in a gruesomely efficient feeding frenzy.

He had felt a little sorry for Button, who made the wrong choices, giving them no option other than to end his life. Ben looked down at the uncovered body on the boat floor, confident no one would be around at this late hour.

The dead man was known as Rico. Ben had no idea if Rico was his real name. Unlike the unfortunate Mr Button, Rico had known what he was doing, and had posed a bigger threat to their business. He'd intentionally moved in on their turf to gain traction with Damian's network of thieves. He intimidated contacts and threatened them if they did not work for him. The night the gang celebrated their successful second heist at the Rebel Yell, Damian had received a disturbing text message.

The message was from their best and most lucrative burglar, known as Gold to his peer group. The text said it was no longer in Gold's interest to continue working for Damian. It also advised Damian to 'watch his back'.

The message confirmed what Damian had been hearing over previous weeks. Ben's intelligence suggested that Rico's gang was into drugs and prostitution. Fencing stolen goods seemed like an opportunistic land grab; not taking Damian and Ben seriously.

Ben casually kicked Rico's body with a feeling of satisfaction. Rico had made a huge mistake underestimating them. He heaved the weighted body overboard, watching it slip below the surface as if sucked into a black hole.

Now all he had to do was punt himself to a few yards away and wait. He did so and settled back to watch, contemplating the situation.

Men like Rico would have difficulty replicating Damian's and his business model. Rico would not know there was still a lot of old money in the state – the legacy of former times of enslavement and forced labour. Slavery had afforded the privileged the opportunity to live in opulence. Ben knew that high-value jewellery and other rare objects were rarely locked away in bank vaults. Most items languished in less secure home safes. Easy to access by persons with the right know-how.

He admired Damian's gift for fencing stolen goods. He had buyers waiting in LA, Vegas, Chicago and Boston. Damian's preference was for jewellery so it had become their speciality, but they could also fence furniture, paintings, collectibles, memorabilia, and all manner of other heirlooms.

Ben had a network of tradespeople who operated legitimate businesses and had access to rich Floridian houses. They would secretly take photos of paintings, reproduction classics and anything they suspected to be valuable. This allowed Damian to case a property without entering it and then research the items.

Damian also scoured the internet for pictures of socialites attending balls, events and parties wearing family heirlooms. Identifying valuable jewellery and matching it to people was easy.

The modern generation loved having their pictures or pouted self-ies splashed all over social media. Finding out where they lived was an easy process. Some fools would even pose in their own houses, right in front of valuable objects. That always made Damian laugh the most.

Sometimes associates found the exact location and make of safes secreted within homes. Victims never seemed to link robberies back to handiwork carried out by their contacts. Not one of his associates had ever been questioned by police in connection with a robbery because they would wait a year from receiving intel to having a thief act on it.

Taking such information in exchange for cash on completion of successful jobs was a long-term process requiring much patience. Damian often told him that leaving over twelve months meant other people would have been in the houses and previous visitors forgotten. Damian also said the police were not resourced to trawl back over months to cross-reference tradespeople to other robberies. Ben admired his friend, who was astute for a young man.

And as far as he was concerned, there was nothing wrong in liberating such ill-gotten gains from wealthy fools. Ben was doubtful Rico could establish such a robust process of identifying key targets, right down to where safes were hidden in houses.

Ben also believed the night in the Rebel Yell to be a seminal moment. They had decided to limit the number of heists, and Damian agreed to end his association with the racist Anderson. Ben explained to his friend that Anderson was resurrecting the Brevard County KKK. Damian said he had found out about the Klan that very night. They agreed that after Rico was eliminated, Damian would help him remove Anderson. Killing Anderson would take time and the murder would have to be carefully constructed, but he would be patient. He looked forward to feeding Anderson to Thunder.

First Thunder would feast on Rico. Isolating Rico from his gang had not been easy. The gangster travelled with a bodyguard and packed a weapon of his own. Ben caught him alone though, leaving the apartment of an expensive whore. She was one of those uptown escorts who guaranteed discretion from Mrs Rico. That discretion played right into Ben's hands. Rico's weekly solo visit proved a fatal error – it established a pattern that Ben could exploit.

He had ambushed Rico exiting alone – no bodyguard in a poorly lit private parking lot, no CCTV, and no witnesses.

Ben jumped Rico, broke his neck and crammed him into the trunk of his Ford Fusion. The big gangster man put up a disappointingly poor struggle. There was no blood and no trace of a man who did his best not to be seen there in the first place.

He drove the body straight to the warehouse for the late-night feed – the most dangerous and thrilling time to be around the ancient monsters.

As a teenager Ben had worked at an alligator farm near his home. He witnessed an experienced worker lose his lower leg to an alligator at feeding time in front of a crowd of tourists. Ben thought the worker had disrespected the reptiles by playing to the gallery. The gator knew it was being taunted and had its revenge. Fair enough.

Damian knew all about his love of the animals and Ben would point out gators on their many airboat trips. Seeking them out was a ritual between the two of them. Damian would tell him if he missed one and once asked how Ben was so good at spotting alligators. He replied, 'A hungry gator will always be where you least expect it.' It was a stolen line he enjoyed using to spook people. He hoped Thunder was hungry tonight.

Crocodilians could devour massive meals very quickly by diverting blood to their digestive systems and away from their lungs. He prided himself in knowing everything there was to know about alligators, snakes and other reptiles. Benjamin had flunked school but would have gained an A-star if there had been a subject entitled 'Reptiles of the World'.

His favourite of all was the Komodo Dragon, yet he had only ever seen one in Brevard Zoo. Ben had never ventured outside the USA, but that was going to change. With the money saved from his work, he was going to visit south-eastern Indonesia to see the Komodos. He was then going to venture to the Northern Territories of Queensland to see salties. He was going to pay for or volunteer to spend time on a farm with a crocodile wrangler. He'd go out with the wrangler and learn how to snare and move the crocs. His ambition was to catch a twenty-foot monster.

The urge to travel had taken hold. In a year's time, when both his boys had finished college, he would go. Losing the love of his life as her cancer returned the previous year had been the catalyst for his travel plans. Damian had helped him and the boys through the grieving process, but he'd not got around to telling his friend yet.

Ben brought himself out of his reverie and checked his watch. Ten minutes had elapsed without incident. Another five long minutes of silence unwound before the airboat's spotlight picked out reflections of gator eyes. The creature waited a few moments before diving down to tear into the body beneath, its death roll breaking the surface. Two others quickly joined it in a feeding frenzy of twisted scales and armoured tails.

He watched with morbid fascination in the hope that Thunder would arrive, and was not disappointed. He recognised her battle scars as she surfaced over the feast and dived into the depths to stake her claim on the pickings. The others scattered, leaving his favourite gator the remaining spoils.

It was over. The waters calmed and Ben caught his breath.

Damn. In his excitement he nearly forgot. *Damian will be wondering if I'm alright.*

Ben took the small burner phone from his pocket and texted the words 'pets fed.' There was only one bar of signal, so he stood up on tiptoes, waving the cellular in the air. Looking back at the screen, he was satisfied the message was delivered.

He crushed the cheap burner in his hand, threw it into the water and started the motor. He expertly U-turned the boat in a tight curve and drove it up the concrete ramp into the shed. Once stationary, he pulled on the joystick, turning the boat on the spot through a hundred and eighty degrees so its nose faced the exit ready for its next use. He cut the power and took in the silence again.

With a final glance into the blackness, he slammed the shutter down and locked it into position. His nose twitched. Was it his imagination or had the building taken on a foetid aroma since his last visit? Something was deeply unpleasant, and he checked his boots to make sure he had not stepped in anything.

His soles looked clean under the shed's artificial light. Satisfied, he flicked the lights off, walked out of the front entrance and locked the shutter from the outside. He climbed into his Ford Fusion and stared at the warehouse. He could not get the aroma from his nostrils and, for the second time that night, Ben felt an icy chill run down his spine.

ELEVEN

Sarah felt more concern for Damian than she believed he had a right to. It was the morning of the next heist, and she found him waiting in the kitchen, impatient for Noah to arrive. He stared out towards the pool looking like a lost soul.

In the days and nights following the Rebel Yell celebration she had felt trepidation about Damian, but he had left her alone. As well as a welcome respite from him, it had given her time to think. She knew Damian had a business trip to Boston planned for the following week and she was mentally counting down the final days with her abuser.

She wondered if Damian also felt their relationship had run its course because he was spending more time than usual with Ben, often stopping out for dinner and sleeping in his old bed in Ben's basement. He'd asked her if she minded, and she'd faked disappointment. But not too much disappointment to make Damian return home.

Ben's two boys regarded Damian like an uncle. He had taught the boys to play soccer or, as Damian called it, football. It had been hard on them, losing their mom. Damian was a natural with children and it saddened her that she no longer wanted to carry his offspring.

He had stayed in their own home the previous night, staying up late, and not touching her when he'd eventually come to bed. He'd been on edge all evening yet had made dinner and been kind to her – more like the old Damian. *Less cocky.*

'Let me look at you,' she said, pushing down his polo shirt collar riding up at the back. She surveyed him carefully.

'You'll do.'

Damian smiled back weakly, and she knew something was still wrong. The lead-up to the other two raids had not felt this tense – there was something else. Silence intervened and while she made herself a coffee, he occupied himself scrolling through his cell phone.

'Hurry up, Noah,' he said out loud and added, 'he was meant to be here by six.'

She looked at the oven clock. It said ten to six. Noah was not late.

Finally, she plucked up the courage to ask. 'What's bothering you? Something you want to share with me?'

Damian put his phone away and smiled at her. She felt a tinge of sadness for the loss of their past – and better – life together.

'Sorry I've been so distant recently,' he said. 'The last few weeks have been very difficult, but I promise you it's all sorted now. Last night, actually.'

'You want to talk about it?'

Damian hesitated slightly before saying, 'Seriously, don't worry. Ben had to sort a problem with our supply chain. You know how it is.'

'Well, not really.' She didn't know what the problem had been.

Damian laughed. 'Ha, it was nothing really. Just business, that's all.' He lifted her long night T-shirt and squeezed her behind playfully.

She was unconvinced. 'You definitely want to go through with today? I can tell something's been bothering you.'

'Yes, definitely. Today's taken a lot of planning, so I'm not pulling out.'

'I just wish you wouldn't. You know what I think. It's dangerous – anything could happen.'

'Really, honestly, don't worry. The problem had nothing to do with today. It'll all be fine.' He cupped her face, kissing her gently, staring into her eyes. 'You know, I've been thinking on

61

what you said about Mason. Guess what he did last week?'

She had no idea and shrugged.

'The fucker asked for a bigger cut. It really pissed me off.'

'That's not a good sign,' she said.

Damian looked back with a resigned expression. 'I know …
Now the problem affecting my supply chain is sorted, I'll make
this heist the last one, and ditch Mason.'

'And go back to selling stuff?'

'Exactly.'

'You know, I want things to go back to how they used to be,'
she said. 'I want us—'

The faint noise of a car pulling up outside silenced her.
Damian gave her a big hug. He had not been this nice – no, this
normal – with her for a few months.

'I do love you,' she found herself saying.

'I love you too. Sorry I've been shitty lately. Chill out this
morning and drive over to the warehouse after lunch. We should
be back by then. Maybe we can talk about this tonight. Just you
and me.'

'OK.' She could hardly get the word out as a wave of
emotion hit her unexpectedly.

She followed Damian out of the kitchen to the hall and
held the door ajar as he walked out to a black Audi A8, its engine
idling on the roadside. The Audi stayed with Noah for his driving
duties. It was certainly better than her little old Toyota, parked out
on the drive.

Ben climbed out of the front passenger seat to get in the back,
where he was joined by Damian.

Please don't go. Please don't do the job.

Damian paused before closing the door and blew her a kiss.
Ben laughed, but not in a bad way. She liked Ben. He was a
stand-up guy and looked out for them.

Noah looked over from his driving position and she hid
further behind the door to protect her modesty. She watched the
Audi set off and felt hot tears of confusion stinging her eyes.
They tumbled down her cheeks, confirming she still had feelings

for her partner. She'd wash them away in the shower and fight the inner turmoil that threatened to derail her escape plan.

TWELVE

The journey took over half an hour longer than the seventy-five minutes a tourist would take, because Noah avoided Interstate 95 north to Highway 528. He cut across on Highway 192 through Osceola County instead, before heading north to Orlando on urban streets from Kissimmee. Noah was confident he'd bypassed potential LPRs mapped out by Mason, and the route avoided being recorded at toll booths. He had screwed a new set of false plates onto the NV, but it remained safer to avoid Interstate patrols.

Noah understood their third heist had been scoped out by Mason. Their target was a bureau situated in the popular tourist area of Orlando. Noah hoped it would pay out as well as the last job, yet it niggled him Mason was at the centre of the planning. There was something about Mason he disliked.

As it happened, the journey was uneventful. Damian ran through everything one more time. He explained mornings were best to hit the bureau. Mason's research suggested fresh dollars were delivered first thing and they wanted to strike before the dollars were dissipated in swaps for foreign currencies and diminished against card transactions. It surprised Noah how many transactions were still carried out in cash using foreign currencies.

Noah knew Damian preferred dollars, and laundered cash through offshore accounts to hide his wealth in Floridian property via overseas bank loans. Damian liked to confide in him and, during one of their nights out, Damian revealed he used an accountant who 'cooked the books', which Noah thought was a cute English expression. There was no way Damian would confide in Mason like that. The thought gave him a sense of satisfaction on the drive off Highway 192, up through Orange County and into central Orlando.

He parked the NV on a quiet back road, two blocks from the target, leaving the engine idling. Despite the early hour, the sun was gaining heat as it climbed on a journey towards its daily apex. Shadows cast by adjacent buildings were shortening across the heat-shimmered road. Noah knocked the aircon up and, for a while, its blast was the only noise to accompany tapping from Mason's laptop at the back of the van.

Mason seemed to sense the attention and said, 'Wi-Fi dongle, dynamic IP, connecting to the internet via a VPN.'

'VPN. Yes, I remember you explaining that last time,' Ben said.

'Don't worry, it just means our location source is untraceable. I'm reconnecting to their security system. I know the way in because I hacked it last week.'

When the tip-tapping of Mason's laptop keypad fell silent, Damian asked, 'Is it done?'

'Yes, their security's down. Alarms, cameras, all offline. They'll just think it's an IT fail. Now to cut off their path to fix it …'

Ben was in the back with Mason and opened the door.

'Don't cross here. Cross up by that fire hydrant. They have cameras pointing out from that gym,' Damian said.

Noah watched as Mason, wearing AT&T overalls and holding a toolbox, pulled down the peak of his baseball cap, jumped out of the van and walked up the road, level with the fire hydrant. Mason checked both ways and crossed to the exchange box. He opened the box, knelt in front of it and, less than two minutes later, returned to the van.

'Done,' Mason said as the door banged shut behind him.

That was the trigger.

Noah revved up and slammed the van into gear. *Now it's my turn.*

He drove fast but smoothly around the corner and pulled up adjacent to the currency exchange.

Rather them than me, Noah thought as Damian and Ben exited the van wearing heavy-looking ski masks, despite the harsh morning sun. Noah saw their guns already in hand as they entered the exchange.

In the back of the van Mason was still on his laptop, making sure connections to the security link remained down. He had seen Mason do the same on the last two jobs and felt safe, knowing the computer-driven alarm system would be inoperative. Mason told him, 'If I can't get in, that means they can't send out comms either.'

While Mason tapped away, muttering to himself, Noah checked his rear-view mirrors. It was his job to sweep the road for anything threatening or unusual. A Ford F-Series opposite caught his attention. While it did not have the feel of a police car, the tinted rear windows made him nervous. A man in bright shorts and a Toronto Maple Leafs top walked past carrying a large breakfast bag from Keke's. The man crossed over to the Ford, got in, and drove off. Of course, he should have realised, the Ford had Canadian plates. *Snowbirds.* Like thousands of other Canadians, they had driven south to winter in Florida. The symbiotic relationship was an annual invasion of elderly Canadians, often golfers, from which the local economy benefitted.

Noah's wandering mind was brought back to sharp relief as a very loud alarm went off. 'What the—' came a cry from the back of the van as Damian and Ben sprinted out of the bureau. Doors slammed shut and he hit the accelerator.

'What the hell happened?' he screamed above the noise of the revving engine.

'You tell me,' Damian shouted, looking over his seat to the back of the van. 'I thought you said the alarms were offline.'

'They are,' Mason said, 'they must have a backup.'

Damian exploded. 'A backup system? A bit fucking late to be telling me now.'

'I-I know. I don't understand.'

Noah felt vindicated. He knew Mason was a smug prick who should not have been trusted. 'I knew we shouldn't have trusted him,' he said.

'Alarms can sound on their own circuits, you know, without computer contact with the outside world. The system I hacked was fully integrated. It's not my fault they've two systems. How was I to know?'

'Maybe because it's your job to know, man. It's your job,' said Ben.

Noah agreed. 'Yer, it's his fucking job ...'

'I know it's my job. I know! I'm sorry, right?'

'Jesus, I don't believe this,' said Damian.

More recriminations followed as the van sped on, threading its way back down and past Kissimmee. He concentrated, keeping his driving precise. He did not want to get pulled over for missing a Stop sign.

He took the 192 back east and, by the time he had driven under I-95 and turned north on the South Wickham Road, the group had calmed down. They were back on familiar territory. South Wickham morphed into the North Wickham Road, heading to the intersection with Lake Washington Road. It was a much-travelled route for Noah, and a left turn down the Lake Washington Road heading west would take them towards Damian's canal-fronted home.

'Do we stick to the plan, or should we take the van to yours?' Noah asked.

'Stick to the plan,' Damian answered, 'I don't want the van at mine.'

Noah did as instructed, ignoring the turn to Damian's, instead following the asphalt further north. The road continued for a couple more miles until it bent ninety degrees to the west and back inland, past Brevard Zoo and under I-95.

Damian tapped Noah on the shoulder and waved a holdall. 'Every cloud, mate. We still managed to get some money,' he said. 'Had to shoot the bitch though.'

This was news to Noah. He had not heard any shots from the van. Neither had Mason because, after a moment's silence, he asked Damian in a shaky voice, 'You shot someone – is he dead?'

'*She*,' Damian replied, 'Yes, probably. I'm not sure.'

Noah did not know what to say and stared ahead at the road. They passed Duke's Diner. The nose of a patrol car was jutting out from a clearing next to Viera Wetlands. Strange, on a backroad, he thought. He glanced sideways at Damian who pulled a face, confirming he had seen it too.

They reached the end of North Wickham Road and passed River Lakes Conservation Trailhead's parking lot. They were now on the uneven track that led back to base.

Noah kept a keen eye on his rear-view mirror as he continued. He slowed considerably, not wanting to create a dusty cloud on the trail that might hang in the air. The NV jolted its way over the uneven surface till the warehouse came into view.

Noah thought about the police car, suspecting it to be Florida Highway Patrol off Interstate 95 to have a snooze. Lazy blue force, he thought.

They had not been followed.

THIRTEEN

The Burmese python waited patiently under the shade of a semi-submerged bush, eyes unblinking currants of death. An amoral apex predator measuring just over fifteen feet long and weighing in at 150 lbs.

The snake should not have been there. Introduced by humans, this non-native killer was an unwanted success story, one of an invasive population now numbering in the tens of thousands, wiping out south Florida wildlife and posing a threat to domestic animals, even pets. Global warming was allowing the python population to take hold around Kissimmee to the west and they were now slowly infiltrating the St John's River system.

Having not eaten for nearly a month, the fully gown adult female was hungry. She was on the hunt for the more substantial local species, such as white ibis or limpkin. The serpent's menu also extended to smaller alligators. But that competitive indigenous reptile was not the snake's present focus of attention. Tongue flickering, tasting the air, the python felt tremors of movement as a large rat scuttled along the side of an adjacent wall, stopping to sniff at something.

The rodent presented a mere snack to the fifteen-foot python, but hunger meant the treat would not be overlooked. Using the waterline as cover, the snake advanced stealthily towards its target. Apart from its body twitching erratically, the rat was not moving. The snake paused, its senses heightened by the hunt, tongue and delicate nasal receptors taking in unfamiliar aromas.

The aroma was confusing. Rotting animals, suggesting larger carrion worth investigating, but there was something potentially dangerous. The snake was torn between an instinct to flee and the need to eat. Hunger won.

The Burmese python struck the quivering rat from behind, biting down on the rodent. The force of the strike killed the rat and, sensing this, the snake's mouth dislocated a fraction to take in the food, but the rat would not move – it was attached to something.

At close quarters, the snake's poor eyesight focused on the mass in front of it. Other semblances of creatures could be seen. The snake, unable to comprehend what was happening, tried to disgorge the three-quarters-swallowed vermin. But it couldn't. The rat was stuck inside its mouth and the helpless reptile was starting to fuse below its neck to the fabric of the living wall confronting it.

In desperation, the snake's lower body flailed. In abject panic the powerful animal managed to rip away a section of the wall, though the segment remained attached to the snake. Pain seared through the hapless creature as its head pushed through into the swampy fabric of the wall, becoming visible from inside the building.

The putrid wall contained so many micro-organisms that it had crumbled and dispelled brickwork, cement, and concrete. Non-organic matter disintegrated and collapsed, helping to accelerate the fusion of other lifeforms. Large sections of the back wall were fully organic.

The python became another element of the wall, writhing and surfing in and out of view as its tortured assimilation continued.

FOURTEEN

'Get this van out of sight,' Damian said to Noah as Ben hauled up the building's front shutter. Noah nodded and reversed the van in tail to nose with the Audi A8. Ben hauled the shutter back down.

Damian hit the light switches and stopped as a stench met his nose. 'Jeez, what the fuck is that?' he asked.

He shot Ben a glance and asked in a low voice the others could not hear, 'What did you do with Rico?'

The insinuation was understood, and Ben nodded towards the airboat. 'Out back, like last time.'

Noah joined them. 'Are you talking about that smell? What is it?'

Damian felt uneasy. 'I don't know, but we can't keep the shutters open. Not with that in here,' he said, looking at the van.

Noah nodded. 'I'll soon have it resprayed and the plates changed.'

'We can't even move it to get the A8 out. Not till dark. Fucking patrol car.' Damian saw the despondent reaction on Noah's face and added, 'It's not your fault, Noah. You did good, despite the shitstorm.'

They looked over to Mason, who kept his head down, rummaging through the bag of cash on the table.

A shaft of light, penetrating a gap in the roof at the building's far corner, caught Damian's attention. He watched the flickering beam as he considered what to do about Mason. A large hand on his shoulder interrupted his thoughts. 'You noticed that too,' Ben said, following Damian's gaze.

'Hmm, the roof needs fixing. That smell must be where the rain's got in.'

'It's not rained for days,' Ben muttered.

'Well, it needs sorting because it's making me feel sick,' Damian said.

Noah stared towards the far corner. 'Something doesn't feel right.'

Damian laughed and tried to lighten the mood. They had not been stopped and his confidence was increasing. 'Don't let things get to you. It's been a shit day, but we made it. Mason, you might as well take the bag and get it counted.'

'I think we need to, erm, you know, discuss what happened first, don't we?' Mason said, his voice shaking.

'I think we do,' Noah said with an accusatory stare back at Mason.

'There will be plenty of time for all that,' Damian said. 'I need to get my head around it first. Then we can talk.'

Ben looked from Noah to Mason. 'The boss needs time. Do the count first.'

Mason shrugged, opened the office door and peered hesitantly into the darkness. Damian watched Mason's hand scrabble across the wall to locate the light switch. He flicked the button and fluorescent lights stuttered into life.

The door to the side office closed and Damian shook his head. *The idiot can't even turn on a light.* This was the last heist, for sure. He had promised Sarah, and today confirmed she had been right: it was a mistake to place so much trust in Mason's ability.

He joined Ben and Noah at the table.

'Noah, you go make some drinks, heh?' Damian said. 'There's a good bloke.'

Noah showed no enthusiasm but stood up to do what was asked.

Half an hour later Mason stepped out of the side room and placed the bag on the table.

'Well?' asked Damian.

'Eight thousand. Give or take.'

'They were opening the safe, man,' Ben lamented. 'Another minute and I would have had all the green.'

'Bollocks,' Damian said. 'That fucking alarm going off. Not great.' He glared back at Mason who averted his eyes.

A vehicle could be heard pulling up outside and the gang froze, looking at each other. 'Sarah,' said Damian, looking at his watch. 'I completely forgot. I should have told her not to come.' He peered through a small gap in the blacked-out, barred-up window. The visitor was not Sarah, it was David Anderson.

'That's all I need,' Damian muttered. 'Hide that bag.'

Ben reopened the shutter.

Anderson seemed in a rush and spoke quickly. 'I appreciate we said the exchange would be at the weekend, but the event's been pulled forward. I tried calling, but I've been going straight to voicemail. Decided to try my luck here.' Anderson glanced strangely at Ben and said, 'And I could really do with that thing you've got me.'

'Ben knows all about the cross,' Damian said, deadpan, 'but you're in luck. I have it here.'

The silver Anglo Saxon cross stolen to order for Anderson from a museum in Georgia was tucked in the trunk of the A8. Damian had taken receipt of it two days prior but not yet arranged the exchange with Anderson.

'Sorry, my phone's been switched off. Meetings. You know how it is. You got the cash?'

Anderson nodded. 'I also got the liquor we agreed. Thought I'd save you the trouble of sending your man around this time,' he said, looking towards Noah.

'I'll go get the cross while you bring the boxes in. I'm in a rush, so just dump them here.' Damian waved in the direction of the front wall by the shutter. 'Then we can deal with the cash.'

Anderson popped the trunk of his car and started lifting out the boxes of liquor. 'I also managed to get that twelve-year Bowmore malt again. You know, that bonus I promised.' Anderson's muffled voice echoed from the trunk.

Ben wandered over to help speed things up. Anderson hesitated a beat and let him lift a box. Damian nodded to Noah, who jogged over to help.

As the boxes stacked up, Anderson mentioned casually, 'I see something big's going down near here.'

Damian frowned. '"Something big". What do you mean?'

'You know, the police and all. You must have seen them.'

'No.' Damian knew his reply was too sharp. Ben and Noah stopped moving boxes and were looking at Anderson.

'Heh, this hasn't got anything to do with you boys, has it?' Anderson joked, but his voice sounded less assured. He kicked some gravel, feigning indifference.

'Us?' Damian laughed and shook his head. 'Just interested, that's all. Nothing ever happens around here. Where are they?' he asked, recomposing himself.

'Everywhere. Lots of cherry tops around the old farms and out near Duke's Diner.'

Although Damian tried to feign disinterest, the location given by Anderson was only two miles away. He heard a vehicle approaching and his hand subconsciously hovered over his Glock. To his relief Sarah's car appeared around the dusty bend. She jumped out looking panicked and called out, 'Damian, thank God you're back safely. The police are up at Duke's and there's talk of a shooting in Orlando on the radio.'

Damian felt his blood rising. The stupid bitch. Anderson's car was right there with him standing by it. *What is she thinking?*

'Shooting, you say?' asked Anderson.

Anderson was old Floridian. Stolen collectibles were one thing, but he knew Anderson's list of friends included senior ranking officers in Brevard County Sheriff's Department. Damian had met a bunch of cops in the Rebel Yell who were tight with Anderson. It was possible some were old-time WASPs involved in the new KKK.

Anderson was now a big problem.

Damian considered his next actions. The currency exchange teller was probably dead. Anderson was bound to hear the news and make the connection to what Sarah had just said. Could Anderson be counted on to keep quiet, even bribed to do so? Damian doubted it very much. It was status more than money that Anderson craved.

I can't trust Anderson to walk out of here. He knows something's wrong.

Anderson turned towards his car. 'Let me just get you those last boxes and I'll be on my way.'

Damian signalled Ben, who had edged around to block Anderson's route.

'Now hold on there a minute,' Anderson said. A huge forearm clamped around his neck. Ben's other arm blocked Anderson's right hand as it moved for a concealed weapon. Anderson thrashed wildly – even so, the weapon was expertly liberated from his grasp and pocketed by Ben.

Ben pushed Anderson away from his car and rolled up his shirtsleeves, grinning. Anderson looked at the huge man blocking his path and turned hopefully towards Damian.

Damian decided to let events play out and shrugged.

Ben jabbed out at Anderson several times with restrained force, drawing some blood from cuts to Anderson's lip and under one eye. As Anderson became punch drunk, the mismatch continued, with Ben aiming a few body blows.

Damian was fascinated by the sight of Ben exacting revenge for years of innuendo and racial slights. Ben was far brighter than Anderson realised. Ben understood local history and, no doubt, every crude racist reference Anderson had ever made. Damian regretted his own failure in that respect and now revelled in his friend's actions. This was to be welcome payback.

A hammer blow to the stomach doubled Anderson over. Ben grabbed Anderson's hair, jerked back his head, and stared disdainfully into his eyes. Blood trickled from a facial cut and Anderson stared back, whimpering, knowing he was facing death. 'Where're your Klan friends now?' Ben said, drawing back a clenched right fist.

Sarah, watching wide-eyed, shouted, 'Enough. Ben, please!'

Ben hesitated and, instead of delivering the coup de grace, let go of Anderson's hair, pushing him to fall backwards into a crumpled heap like a rag doll. Anderson's head hit the gravelly track with a sickening thud.

Ben looked towards Damian for direction. He gestured towards the warehouse and watched Ben and Noah drag Anderson into the dank building. They sat Anderson on an old chair at the back corner of the warehouse, binding the hostage tightly with packaging tape. Ben, grinning all the while, rammed an old rag into Anderson's mouth. They left Anderson and followed Damian back to the table.

FIFTEEN

Brevard County's Sheriff Marty Wiles pulled into the parking lot. A female had been shot and seriously injured in a botched heist over in Orlando. CCTV footage from near the currency exchange had identified the robbers' van and that information had been broadcast statewide.

The fallout had interrupted the sheriff's weekly fishing trip, yet he was not unhappy. He was not the sort of constitutional sheriff who limited activity to sitting behind a plush desk in Titusville. Wiles was at the scene quickly and wasted no time confronting the unfortunate deputy who had let the criminals slip through his fingers.

Surveying Deputy Rodrigo Gonzalez, Wiles asked, 'So, let me get this straight. You saw the vehicle pass you just after noon? And you are positive it was the van. The van?' Wiles cursed his luck it had been a rookie deputy on patrol. He spoke to the young officer like he might a naughty puppy pissing on his carpet. 'The Lord knows what you were doing parked up there in the first place.'

Gonzalez looked sheepish. 'I had to answer a call of nature, sir, but I got the license plate, look,' he said, waving his notepad.

'I can see that. So, can you tell me why you didn't pursue?'

'I did.'

'What, *immediately?*'

'Well, I, erm, I figured it best to check it was the one on the BOLO.'

'I see. You didn't set off in pursuit straight away. There was a delay.'

Deputy Gonzalez looked down. 'That's right, sir. I radioed in to check first. I thought I was mistaken – that it couldn't be the same van.'

'Except it was the same van. Why not just run the check on the move?'

'I don't know, sir.'

'You don't know?'

'No, sir.'

The sheriff allowed the admission to hang a while, like a verbal noose tightening around his rookie's neck. Satisfied his point was made, Sheriff Wiles signalled other officers, who came over. They had set up a temporary field base in the parking lot of Duke's Diner. Several patrol cars were parked up. Brevard County Sheriff's Office deputies, and State Highway Patrol officers mingled, many carrying takeouts of Duke's coffee and their famed donuts.

A map was spread over the hood of a patrol car and Wiles waited for attention. 'Right, we're looking for a white Nissan NV. I want you to divide up the remaining ground.. Check all, I repeat, all buildings. Even the derelict ones. Check the woods in case they have a cosy little camp thing going on. Push right out to St Johns. State will keep the blocks on surrounding highways while we put the squeeze on here. If the van's still around, we'll find it. Remember, these people are armed and dangerous. Orlando PD believe there's likely to be three or more. If you find them, call for backup. I don't want any heroes out there today. Especially not dead ones. You got that?'

Officers crowded around to be given their search areas.

Wiles wanted the bust. He knew his men did too. It would be a coup for the Brevard County Sheriff's Office. The longer the situation went on, the more likely the suspects would escape the net, if they hadn't already. If he was lucky, they could get a result soon, before state troopers crashed the party.

It was extremely good fortune that Gonzalez had been parked there and had seen the van in such a remote location. Sure, Gonzalez had messed up, but there was a good chance the van was still in the area. He believed the gang did not have time to get clear before the major routes had been blocked off. Checkpoints were searching all vehicles leaving the area, and he would order searches of vehicles entering the sealed-off zone too.

He also had detectives trying to link the van to its owner. So far, they had drawn a blank – the plates had been matched back to another van. That van was accounted for and could not have been involved. The van had to be local to be seen this far off main routes. Someone would know whose it was.

As his local deputies dispersed, he walked through the double doors of Duke's. He needed a coffee and donut. He may have missed out on his fishing, but this was potentially a more prestigious catch for the recently elected sheriff.

SIXTEEN

Anderson's eyes flickered open, adjusting to the gloom. A choking stench invaded his nostrils. Old-looking fluorescent lights barely illuminated his corner of the warehouse. He recognised his car and the one driven by Damian's blonde piece parked up immediately to his right. He could also see a white Nissan van and a black saloon parked tightly together, deliberately hidden from outside view, he imagined.

He was secured to a chair and sensed he'd been out cold for some time. There were slivers of faint daylight from holes in the roof, meaning it was now late afternoon or early evening. His hands were bound tight behind his back, and he could no longer feel them. There was no feeling in his legs either. He could not move. A cloth stuffed into his mouth made breathing difficult, so he had to breathe deeply through his nose, sucking in more of the rancid air.

The smell. He wanted to vomit but knew it would choke him.

Low muffled voices reached his ears from the other side of the van. He felt his mind swimming and tried to concentrate on the voices. He recognised the British-accented twang of his captor and the excitable tones of his Illinois gofer.

Cold penetrated deep into his bones and he shivered. It added to his fear and desperation.

Gent. You bastard. How could you do this to a friend?

Anger welled up and he struggled to free himself, but something was wrong. His brain did not seem to be connecting to his hands or arms. His legs felt fixed to the floor, and he could not feel his back.

My God! Have they broken my spine?

Although he struggled hard to move his body, the chair remained static. Trying to focus, he blinked several times. His blurred vision played tricks on him, making the floor appear to move.

The floor was moving.

His eyes, adjusting to the dimness, took in the horror around him. He was sitting over a seething swampy mass. Semblances of creatures he recognised appeared and then merged back into a tangled mat. Insects, bugs, and other things.

He craned his neck to get a view around the side of his body. His trousers had disintegrated. Instead of legs, he could only see a continuation of the contorted matting that extended around the wooden chair he was tied to.

His breathing quickened as he looked down at his legs to see that his boots were not there. Or his feet. His legs looked like twisted stumps of rotting garbage wrapped in frayed packaging tape. Twigs. Moss. Grass. What looked like the back end of a rat oscillated where his left knee should be.

The visual realisation of his situation was a precursor to extreme pain, agony kicking in like a wave of fire, burning his body at the extremities. Panicking, he tried to shout, to alert the gang the other side of the van to his predicament. The cloth filling his mouth made vocalising impossible as searing pain reached levels his brain was unable to cope with. As his head contorted in abject terror, his mouth foamed.

Unable to breathe, Anderson felt himself suffocating. Hysterical, he gagged, choking on his own bile, realising that the savagery of his death was saving him from a more painfully protracted demise.

At the front side of the storage unit, Damian sat with his gang around the table. Mason was using an old scanner radio to listen to police chatter and discovered their van had been caught on surveillance close to the crime scene.

That was not a problem, except Mason also heard local cops had cut a lucky break, seeing the van pass only a couple of miles from their base. It confirmed Damian's fears and was the terrible slice of misfortune that prompted the police activity Sarah had seen.

Mason explained the whole area was sealed off by police conducting building-to-building searches. Early reports hadn't seemed too bad, centred more on new housing off I-95, but during the last hour, chatter revealed the net closing in. They recognised more of the locations Mason gave out as rural properties, one a nearby campsite. It was increasingly likely the police would search down their small dust track.

He came to a decision. 'We have to leave.'

'What, right now?' Sarah asked.

Damian nodded. 'Yes, now. If they find this place, we can't be here. Sarah, you drive home. You're not involved. If you get stopped, come up with something good.' She nodded as Damian continued. 'If they turn up here we're fucked. Anderson's car, our van—'

'What will happen to us?' Mason asked, his voice shaking again.

'The chair, that's what will happen. If they find us,' Damian replied.

'But *you* shot her,' Mason said, looking accusingly at him.

'OK, stay here and tell them that, and see how that works out for you. The rest of us are leaving. If we're lucky, the police don't find this building or guess who we are.'

Ben looked grim. 'The scanner makes me think they'll find this place.'

'Or they could just follow their noses,' said Noah, pulling a face.

'Safest to assume they will look here. But, if they don't, we may be able to come back.'

Ben looked at Damian with concern. 'I am truly sorry, my friend. After everything we've been through together, I do not think there'll be any coming back here. We'll have to start again. All of us.'

Damian felt resigned and nodded slowly, and then remembered Ben's boys. 'What about Adwin and Chaka? We can't just leave them.'

'I will figure a way. It will be OK.'

'*We'll* figure a way.' Damian said, feeling wretched about the future his friend now faced. Knowing they had been waiting around too long, he stood up. 'Sarah, you get going. Everyone else, get your stuff together and we leave by boat now. Our guest too.'

Noah also stood up. 'I'll go get him.'

'No, leave him to me,' Ben said, disappearing around the side of the van.

Moments later a cry reverberated around the warehouse.

'Ben?' Damian shouted. Gun in hand he charged around to the other side of the vehicles. The others followed more cautiously. Ben was bent over the seated Anderson. The light was shadowy in the warehouse's far corner, but something was wrong. Ben was hyperventilating and turned to him with an expression of panic on his face. 'Please, please, help me,' he shouted.

Ben's hands held on to what Damian assumed was Anderson's shoulders. Except it was not Anderson. His facial features were recognisable as Anderson, but his lower body was shrouded in a blanket of gunge. The debris around Anderson seemed to be pulsating, obscuring most of his chair and joining the space between what had been four wooden legs to the floor. The material extended outwards from the chair, rising to join the back wall.

He stared at the bigger picture emerging from the gloom. The back wall was saturated with the same frothing morass that enveloped Anderson. It hung from the ceiling in the corner and there were things moving in the shadows. The turgid aroma was worse that side of the warehouse and made Damian feel nauseous.

Strands were lapping up one of Ben's legs.

'Please, Damian, please!' Ben looked helplessly back at him. 'I can't move. I can't move.'

For a moment Damian could not move either. Fear had

frozen him to the spot. 'I-I …' he said meekly, unable to comprehend what he was seeing.

'In the name of God, *please* help me. Help me!' Ben pulled hard against the forces holding his hands in place. His right hand seemed to be pulling away, with slimy strands stretching back to what had been Anderson, like melted cheese from a pizza slice.

Damian recovered himself and edged forward to help, but felt a hand hold him back. It was Sarah. She looked as terrified as he felt. 'Don't touch him, Damian. We don't know what it is.'

'I have to do something,' he said, stricken. 'I owe this man everything.'

'I really wouldn't,' said Noah, with a wide-eyed expression. Damian followed his gaze to the wall.

A snake-like creature was emerging from the foam. It coiled itself around Ben, who screamed. The coiled monster pulled the big man tightly against the living wall. Python-like patterns punctuated its considerable length, yet the snake's head was less well defined. It was a mossy tangle with two currant eyes. The coils pulled hard against Ben's torso, constricting his exhalations, and both of his arms were swallowed up within the seething matter.

Damian stood by helplessly as the boundaries blurred between where his friend ended and the wall began. Anderson's warped shape had been pulled into the wall with Ben. Anderson's face moved onto the wall. It seemed to be fusing with Ben's upper body.

Gasping, Ben managed to speak. 'Kill me, brother. Shoot me. Please. Please. In the name of God, shoot me.'

Damian shook his head, mouthing a soundless 'No'. He felt tears welling up in his eyes. 'I can't do it,' he said. He looked around the group, helpless, imploring, hoping for a miracle. His faithful ally was dying in an agonised twisted torture, pleading for help Damian knew was unthinkable.

'Please, friend. For what you did for Kayla, thank you.' Ben grimaced before continuing. His voice slurred and he was losing the ability to speak. 'Shoot me, brother. If you … love me, … you'll do it.'

Damian squeezed the trigger, and five rapid shots were discharged into Ben's body. He choked back tears as he saw the life leave his best friend's eyes. 'Sorry, my brother. I'm so, so sorry.'

He felt Sarah put a protective arm around his waist. She was crying too. Noah and Mason closed ranks and they collectively took a couple of steps backwards, staring at what had been Ben.

Without warning, the figure lurched forward, straining against the fronds wrapping themselves around him. Despite five bullets hitting its torso, the body exhaled a rasping unearthly howl. The primeval shriek filled the warehouse, the sound echoing, driving fear into Damian. As he watched, the snake-like coils pulled the remains of Ben back into the morass.

'He's still alive,' Sarah cried out.

'I don't think that was Ben,' Mason said. 'We need to get out of here.'

'He is alive,' Damian countered. 'Look'.

Ben was looking at them peacefully. His mouth was moving like he was singing an old gospel hymn. Was Ben grinning at them? Maybe he was making his peace with God, Damian thought, taking a step forward, mesmerised. He hoped against all hope that his loyal friend was going to a better place.

'Watch out!' He heard Noah's shout too late as a tentacle shot out and attached itself to his forearm. Crying out in pain, Damian struggled to release himself, finding his arm held firm.

Noah uttered a profanity and rushed forward to grab Damian's unattached arm. Other tendrils flailed out, one skimming Noah's shirtsleeve.

The closeness of the attack seemed to galvanise Noah to find extra strength. Damian felt the grip on his arm tighten as Noah yanked with all his might. Sneakers planted into the squishy mass, Damian drove his legs hard in a tug of war action, in time with Noah's pull. The combined effect succeeded, his arm detaching itself from the tendril with a sickening Velcro-like ripping sound.

He let out a yell of agony as a chunk of his forearm was torn away, his skin still visible against the kaleidoscopic earthen colours of the pulsating tendril that carried it off.

The counterforce of detachment made the pair stagger backwards. They both fell and Damian looked quickly at his hands. Thankfully, they had both fallen onto dry concrete, beyond the living carpet advancing across the warehouse.

Another tendril flared outwards, touching his sneaker. The tentacle crawled up his sock and for a moment Damian feared it would attach itself to his leg. With no living matter to fuse to, the writhing arm snaked away, and they scrambled to their feet, distancing themselves from the menace.

Damian's arm was burning, and he gagged at the sight of his own flesh being absorbed into the wall before their eyes. A rotting aroma emanated from the gash to exacerbate his terror and he retched; all the time unable to take his eyes off the continuing fusion of human forms on the wall.

They needed to get out. He backed away from the terror, eyes alert to the danger of another strike. The others were doing the same.

His last view of Ben was the stuff of nightmares. Ben's face was fusing with Anderson's. A sense of irony seeing their features merging flickered into Damian's thoughts before he turned his back on the wall to join the others.

SEVENTEEN

Ten Minutes Earlier

Sergeant Paulo Conti walked down the dusty track with three deputies in tow. They were arguing about recent public comments on the Brevard County Sheriff's Office Facebook page. 'Why do we even bother responding to those conspiracy theory posts?' Millar was saying. 'We should just take them off. Better still, lock up the bozos on Code 373.'

'Incitement?' Conti liked a good debate but was flagging in the wilting heat and wanted to get home. 'Crazy idea. The First Amendment wins every time,' he said. He didn't miss Miller pulling a face towards Warner and Grimes as if to say 'Watch it, the sergeant's on one.'

He was on one. The new sheriff was a dumbass getting personally involved, pinning hopes on the Nissan NV being holed up in a local building or residence. Conti guessed the criminals would have turned south down Lake Winder Road to slip the net of checkpoints on the main routes to I-95 at Stadium Parkway, Viera Boulevard and North Wickham Road. They would be miles away by now. He'd drawn the short straw when Wiles gave him a big chunk of the extensive River Lakes Conservation Area to search. The vast area of marsh plants and scrub ran from Lake Winder down the St Johns river to Lake Washington.

They had parked up at a windshield repair building off a track past Lake Winder Road, then moved their car north to the conservation area's trailhead parking lot and searched the surrounding campsites for another two hours.

A departmental drone would have made their job much easier, but none of his search party were licensed to fly one. The Brevard County Sheriff's Office Aviation Unit was no help either. Three of their seven helicopters were involved in the hunt, all without success. He had no idea why they needed to duplicate an aerial search of open countryside from the ground.

The sultry conditions and the need to be wary of wildlife added to the gruelling nature of their foot search. At least their search area contained few buildings and most of those were campsites too small to hide a van. Even so, he would have preferred the tedious house-to-house hunts around the many artificial lakeside estates that stretched north and east beyond the Space Coast Stadium.

By the time they reached the building at the end of the narrow track, the sun was petering out in the west. His legs ached and his sweaty shirt stuck to his body. He thought it ironic that they had gone on foot at his insistence. It was his idea to park and walk up to buildings, so as not to alert any potential fugitives of their arrival. It was a decision he regretted because the track was further than it looked on his map. They needed to check this last building quickly and get back to the parking lot before dark.

He glanced at his watch – the Florida Gators would kick off soon and he had some money riding on the result. The thought of watching the state showdown against the UCF Knights with a cold beer in hand was a mouth-watering prospect.

He placed a finger over his lips, signalling his fellow officers to be quiet. The sticky air felt unnaturally calm. There was something odd about the scene. It was the deathly hush – there were no animals sounds. This time of evening they should have been greeted by dusk-calling cicada and frogs. The atmosphere felt eerily silent to him – almost supernatural.

Up ahead stood the last unchecked building on his map, silhouetted against the glow of dusk. Light leaked through chinks in the blacked-out window and he heard faint sounds of voices from within, carried along on the stillness. The building was obviously occupied, but there was no Nissan, or any other vehicle, parked out front. Conti felt uneasy. Despite his impatience to get home and watch the game, he decided to approach this one cautiously.

He sent two deputies around the back while he and Miller crept up to the front. It was impossible to see much through the small chink in the blacked-out window, apart from an unoccupied set of garden furniture and the unmistakable shape of an airboat beyond it. He could also make out the front edge of a white van and a large black sedan beyond it. The sedan looked like an Audi, but he could not see the van's logo. He wanted to check across to the right, but the gap in security masking was too small. Even so, he had a feeling the nearer vehicle was the all-important white NV, mostly hidden behind the shutter. There were car tracks of various types on the road surface. They looked recent.

'There's a white van in there. I can't make it out well, but it could be the one.'

'Should we bang on the shutter?' asked Miller.

'No, we have instructions. We stay put and call for backup,' Conti replied. 'We need to pull back to a safe distance. Go round the back and ask the boys to fall back. Keep it quiet. No radioing.' He retreated to the side of the track, under the cover of the wooded scrub. He would radio in at a safe distance.

A few seconds after Miller disappeared around the side of the building, deep cries for help came from inside. Things quietened for a short time and then five shots rang out in quick succession.

Conti ran around the corner and caught up with Miller, who had his back against the wall, most likely stopped in his tracks by the sounds from within. Conti gesticulated for Miller to follow him.

Miller did so, retreating quickly to the adjacent foliage. The shots had come from inside the building, and there was no sign of the other two deputies.

Conti was about to radio base when they heard a terrible howling sound that made his skin crawl.

'What the hell was that?' Miller asked.

'I don't know. Sounded like an animal of some kind,' Conti replied and lifted his radio. 'Conti to base, over.'

'10-2, over.'

'We have a code 33. Repeat 33. Request immediate assistance, over.'

'10-4. Please state your location, over.'

'I'm not sure, control. We're at the end of a small track. It runs along the north side of our search quadrant up to Winder, over.'

'Hold on. Yes, I think I can see it. Does it meet water at the end? Over.'

'Yes, that's where we are now. The building's at the end of a track. What's your 10-52? Over.'

'Five minutes.' The female voice of the colleague he knew well softened. 'Stay safe, Paulo, over.'

'Roger that, over.'

As Conti considered his options, Deputy Warner sprinted around the corner, sliding to a halt next to him. Warner looked desperate and blurted out, 'It's Grimes, he needs help.'

'What, has he been hit?' Conti asked.

'No. he's stuck.'

'Warner. For God's sakes, calm down! What do you mean "he's stuck"?'

'I don't know. He was leaning on the wall and now he's stuck. We heard the shots and that noise from inside. It sounded like a God-damned wolf. I know it sounds crazy, but the wall's kinda got hold of him.'

'Inferno di fuoco,' Conti uttered as he looked at his confused deputy. 'This is a nightmare.'

The remaining gang members were hurrying their escape. Damian grabbed a medical kit from the office and wrapped a bandage around his arm.

He knew the best chance they had to avoid police was to flee by water. The cops were looking for a van, not a boat.

His immediate priority, however, was to get out of the building and far away from whatever it was that had attacked him.

Ben had been right about having to start a new life again from nothing. He was not sure if it was the pain of that knowledge or his arm that hurt the most. Everything he'd built had been destroyed in one lousy day. Even in his panic he pitied himself for having to flee a second time in his life. His one consolation was the thought that he had enough money hidden away to start again elsewhere. He just needed to retrieve it.

First, they needed to get their swamp boat out of the building and onto the water. To do that they needed to open the back shutter. The metal itself still looked untouched, but the fabric of the surrounding wall was a writhing mass.

'What now?' Sarah asked. All three were looking at him for instruction.

He looked back at the shutter and knew going near it was a risk. It would be easier to leave by the front, but the airboat was blocked in and could only exit from the building's back shutter.

'OK, I'll get the shutter open,' he said. 'Sarah. Here's the key.' Damian nodded towards the boat. 'Can you start that thing?'

'Yes, no problem,' she said and jumped onto the craft.

'You guys get on too. Just stay off that stuff.' Noah and Mason shot each other a glance as they eyed the carpet of debris encroaching over the right side of the floor by the shutter.

As Damian gingerly stepped past a patch of matted gunge, he was relieved to find clear concrete at their planned exit. He unlocked the shutter and hauled it up. As he did so, the boat's motor roared into life. The boat could traverse the ramp down to the water without any of them needing to have feet on the ground.

Ignoring pain shooting up his arm, he clambered onto the front of the boat as it moved out of the shed. As the boat edged forward Noah and Mason climbed on board too.

'Police! Freeze, now!' The warning had sounded from his left, and he reeled around to see three cops pointing guns in their direction. Loud screaming started from the other side of the boat. Turning a hundred and eighty degrees, he saw another officer.

Instead of pointing a gun, the cop was melting into the other side of the wall from where Ben had been killed.

One of the cops to his left let off two warning shots over the boat. 'I said freeze!' the cop shouted over the din of the boat's propeller.

The lead officer said something to the other two and all three backed up quickly, but strangely, did not open fire. Damian realised the stricken officer on the right side of the boat was in their firing line – too close for fellow officers to risk taking shots. Instead of feeling panicked, Damian felt incredibly lucid. He knew he had a tactical advantage.

He looked quickly at the officer to his right. The man had his back to the wall, but his arms were stuck to the wall either side of his torso. His hands were fused into the wall so there was no chance of him producing a gun. They needed to stay clear of the building, but in the line of fire between the other officers and their colleague. Damian pulled out his Glock and held it above his head, so that the officers could see he was armed.

'Keep the boat still for a moment and don't hit the ramp until I give the signal,' he shouted back to Sarah. He heard the propeller slow as Sarah held the boat at the ramp's apex.

I need to survive. The thought reverberated inside his mind. He felt the mantra taking hold and realised he would do whatever it took to escape. He turned back towards the three officers. 'You want to help your man? No one shoots and no one will get hurt. You understand?'

The trapped officer continued screaming, begging for help. The smaller, dark-haired officer seemed to be in charge and took half a step forward with his arms raised. He wore three stripes on his sleeve. *Sergeant.*

'OK, I just need to get to my man there. Just let me help him and I promise you we won't shoot.'

Damian calculated that, in the dim twilight, the sergeant could not see the squeamish detail the other side of the boat. He sensed the man's heart racing and believed the cop meant what he said. He felt the survival instincts in his mind working furiously, weighing up the options.

A plan had formed which he now executed, the words he needed to say coming easily. It felt as if someone else was saying them, such was the assuredness they carried. 'Listen carefully. This is what's going to happen. Your man is caught in our security trap. The trap is going to kill him. Only I have the keys.' Damian waved the keys to the warehouse and continued. 'We are taking our boat out onto the water. If you shoot you lose these keys, and your friend dies. Once the boat is out there, I will throw the keys and you can help your friend. But first, all three of you need to throw your guns into the water and step away.'

The three cops looked at each other, unsure. Their fellow officer's screams rang out with renewed vigour. It was a choking, gurgling sound that told Damian the man did not have much time left.

Good timing, officer.

Despite the screams, the sergeant looked like he was not going to comply. One of the officers behind said something and the sergeant hesitated, shaking his head. He looked resigned and threw his weapon out into the water. The two officers behind did the same.

Damian's outrageous play was working. The din of the boat and hysterical cries of the trapped officer made rational thought and negotiation difficult. Capitalising on the situation, he sensed fear in the face of his cold demands. All three officers slowly stepped back. Damian lowered his weapon and, with his other hand, held the keys aloft to affirm his good intentions.

It was like an out-of-body experience. Damian heard his robotically smooth voice make the next demand needed to secure his safety. 'That's good. Right, now lie down on your fronts, where you are. Hands behind your heads.'

The officers followed the instruction and Damian gave the signal for Sarah to get going. 'Gently down the ramp. If you hit the water hard, we'll sink,' he instructed. The airboat shuddered as it started moving slowly down the ramp and to the edge of the water.

You need to do this to survive.

He tossed the keys over the side onto the ramp, freeing up his left hand to cup under the handle of his semi-automatic to aim at the grounded officers. He discharged the remaining twelve rounds into the three officers. Each pull loaded the next round into the Glock 19's firing chamber, allowing Damian to fire more than once per second. Yet the scene played out in slow motion for him as if every move of the three targets was being mapped independently in the split screen of his mind's eye. The officers tried standing to run for safety, but they stood no chance. Damian felt his aim tracking efficiently, hunting them down one by one, in the manner of a deadly assassin. He figured that each officer had taken at least two bullets. He knew he had hit the third officer in the head and watched the man slump to the ground.

The boat was now waterborne, and he turned on its spotlight and pointed it back towards the grounded officers. The light shone over the back of the warehouse and he absorbed the scene, knowing it would be the last time he saw the building. Swinging the light down a fraction, he picked out the grounded cops. One was twitching, but the other two showed no sign of movement. He turned to smile his satisfaction at Sarah, Mason and Noah. They weren't they smiling back as he expected. Instead, they stared at him, looking dumbfounded.

Then he understood. They were weak and did not realise that he had bought them all the valuable time needed to execute the next stage of his escape plan.

I will survive this.

'Get us away from here,' he said to Sarah as the boat negotiated the small tributary and entered Lake Winder.

EIGHTEEN

As the boat's spotlight vanished from sight, Sergeant Conti struggled to free himself from under Warner's weight. Warner was dead – a bullet to the cranium that had exited through an eye socket.

Conti pushed the body to one side to concentrate on himself. He felt the wounds in his shoulder and below in his stomach and realised he was haemorrhaging blood. He crawled over to Miller and felt for a pulse but couldn't find one. Miller had managed to get up first and had made it a few yards before being hit.

The desolate scene was shrouded in near darkness, yet he could still make out Grimes's shape against the back wall. Managing to stand, he staggered to where he saw the keys land. He needed to free Grimes from the trap and scrabbled about to find them. There they were, partly covered by some grasses. He picked them up and took a few steps towards Grimes. A large shape had pushed out from the wall. It was enough to make the sergeant hang back.

Through the darkness he could see the wall was moving. Instead of the metallic snare he had imagined, the whole facade was writhing with life.

He scanned the shifting morass and realised it extended down one side of the ramp to within inches of where he stood. He staggered back and felt a wave of nausea sweep through him.

Grimes was still moving but had fallen silent. A strange head appeared on a stalk protruding from the wall. It pushed itself towards Grimes and paused next to him. The structure of the head was human-like. It hinted at dark skin, maybe mixed race, although the blend was patchy. It seemed to sense him watching and its eyes opened, staring back. The eyes seemed to look straight through his soul. They were like black beads, looking at him as if they could pierce his thoughts and feed off his fear.

There was no trap. He had been tricked by an act of witchcraft or sorcery. Grimes had been trapped by a conjured evil-eyed demon whose head swayed, nose pointing up, although there was no nose that he could see. The fiend's head tilted as if taking in the still night air. A pungent aroma played in the background, accompanying the horror story, reinforcing his terror. He dropped the keys, clutched at a small silver cross through his shirt and said out loud, 'Father, this prayer is said for Peter Grimes and I pray it works, in the name of the Father, the Son and the Holy Spirit. Malocchio, leave this man.'

The head turned back to the trapped deputy, aligning itself with Grimes's face as it opened its mouth. The saliva-strewn aperture slowly widened to envelop his head. The mouth resembled that of a reptile, dislocating itself to take in its prey, yet the face remained human-like. This was greater than a Malocchio spirit and Conti realised that his prayers were useless against the monster. He stood transfixed by the unholy visage, which appeared to him as a fusion of demons combining to consume his colleague. The extended jaw of the creature slipped over the doomed deputy's face and his fair hair until nothing of his head remained visible. The mouth now expanded further and slid effortlessly over Grimes's shoulders and down his uniformed torso.

Grimes's arms were no longer discernible as human. The snake-like monster sucked those in with the torso and finally, legs, feet, and even the matted ground beneath them disappeared into the monstrosity as if it were feeding on itself.

The end of days. Conti believed he was witnessing the heralding of the Beast's arrival on Earth. He sank to his knees and prayed for God to have mercy on his soul in the face of the Devil.

Staring at the ground he became vaguely aware of the foliage being illuminated by shifting red and blue lights. The path to Hell was opening before him.

The slam of car doors jolted him back to reality and he realised reinforcements had arrived to the front of the building, their flashing lights a lurid kaleidoscope against the pulsating matting creeping out of shadow towards where he knelt. The new lighting revealed more detail. The ground in front of him was a seething mass of life. Patterns were shifting and Conti saw shapes of small animals among the frothy substance. The snake creature across the ramp from him remained in shadow.

Several state officers ran to his aid. 'Behold, the Gateway to Hell,' he said, pointing at the scene. He felt hands on his shoulder and concerned voices asking if he was OK. He looked from face to face, but he did not recognise the officers. 'We sit in the Last Judgement. This is the End,' he said, looking to where Grimes had been moments earlier.

One of the men cried out, 'My God, what is that thing?'

So, the officer could see the deformity too. *It was real.* He was not losing his mind. The serpent was morphing back into the portal to Hades. Two of the officers fired weapons into the shifting shape.

'It's too late,' he shouted as loud as his remaining strength allowed. 'It has already taken one of us.'

The officers continued taking shots at the beast until it had been absorbed back into the building's living fabric. One of the officers was standing on the rippling matting. 'Get off that thing, now!' Conti cried out in panic. 'You don't understand.' The man looked down and stepped back several paces quickly. *God has spared this one.*

Conti looked at the bodies of Miller and Warner and hoped they were in a better place – not where Grimes had been taken.

Unlike Grimes, he had been saved. Maybe he had been chosen to fight *Il demonio.*

Then Conti remembered he had been shot. The bullet wounds were taking their toll. He heard voices telling him to 'stay with us' as his vision faded to nothing.

NINETEEN

Lieutenant Izard from Florida State Police's Orlando office arrived as Conti was being strapped to a trolley and wheeled to an ambulance. The gang believed to be responsible for the shooting in Orlando had crossed county lines, so he would be running the investigation team. The Brevard County Sheriff's Office had argued over jurisdiction but were cooperating.

Izard was relieved to see Conti still breathing. He did not know the local deputy sergeant, but that did not lessen the impact of seeing a fellow officer down. Three more deputies were reported dead or missing. The seriousness of his investigation had escalated beyond what he imagined possible a few hours earlier.

His primary task was to question those arriving on the scene first; he considered it likely they had stumbled on the fugitives from the Orlando shooting. Evidence proved there had been a shoot-out, but officers could not gain entry to see the plates on the white Nissan NV inside the warehouse. Its plates were hidden from view behind an Audi and the Audi's plate was not visible either, blocked by a stack of boxes.

That was when things really got strange. Izard asked why they had not entered the building and the officer spoke of 'stuff oozing out of the back' and they had seen 'a creature' disappearing into the wall. There were other creatures in the substance, and no one was prepared to go any nearer.

Even stranger, the officer reported that the sergeant taken away in the ambulance had been ranting about the end of the world and demons.

Izard listened with incredulity, doubting the validity of his officer's report. 'Show me,' he said. He was escorted carefully down the side of the building. He could see two bodies a couple of yards apart from each other next to a ramp. All other officers had pulled back. One of them looked at Izard and said, 'I really wouldn't go any nearer, sir.'

'Don't be so stupid, man,' he said and pushed past the cordon of officers watching the scene. He sensed their fear and turned back towards the officer. 'What is it? Why are you back here?' he asked.

None of the officers replied, but one was pointing.

'Give me that flashlight,' Izard said and shone the beam on the bodies. The first body was half covered in some kind of sludge. One arm of the second body was also hidden by the stuff. 'What the hell?' he heard himself say.

'It wasn't like that before you arrived, sir,' the officer who'd greeted him said. 'It's creeping out along the back.'

'Did no one think to move them away from that stuff?' Izard said to the group. They all remained silent, which added to his feeling of helplessness and anger. 'I know it's a crime scene, but someone should have moved them.'

They stood watching the slow crawl of the substance for a few moments more. He needed to do something but was unsure what. Izard did not like what he was hearing or seeing. The cops had radioed in for backup saying the fugitives must have been trapped inside the building. Had the gang been consumed by the substance? Had they created whatever it was? Regardless of the answers, safety was the first objective.

'Set up a cordon down that track. No one goes near until I've had time to think. We're not taking any chances with this stuff,' Izard instructed.

TWENTY

Damian unhooked a pair of ear defenders and put them on. The loud roar of the propeller was painful, and his ears felt more sensitive than usual. He killed the spotlight and took over the steering from Sarah. He knew the waterways well, even in the dark. The moon's beams reflected off Lake Winder, giving it the appearance of shiny silver glass. He headed south to where the lake narrowed, continuing as the St Johns River. The river was a mere trickle here and he followed its path south, upstream, towards Lake Washington. Everything outside the silver sheen was pitch black, marking out his route – *just keep on the shiny stuff.*

Obstacles loomed out of the darkness, odd shapes distorted by the watery shadows they cast. The occasional reflection of eyes from the banks reminded him of the presence of alligators, but he knew they avoided boats. As Ben had loved to tell him, travelling the swampy waterways at night was not for the faint-hearted. Poor Ben. The image of his friend being taken by the snake-shaped monster burned in his mind.

He had made this journey with Ben many times, carrying goods between the warehouse and his canal-fronted home off Lake Washington. He half expected search beams from police helicopters to appear from the air, or to encounter police patrol boats. Neither happened and the river was traffic-free. If they could make it off Lake Washington without being spotted, they should be OK.

After thirty long minutes they arrived at a weir. The weir kept the water level upstream high – Lake Washington was the primary water source for Melbourne. Damian accelerated to gain the impetus the airboat needed to ascend the weir. The fact that the water flow meant south was upstream used to confuse him, but now he was used to the paradox. The journey would become easier from here; the river widened and the boat entered Lake Washington.

The river entered at the north-west point of Washington and he headed for the opposite side of the lake and hugged the bank heading south, looking out for Bullgators Adventures to his left. He recognised its jetty, though the building was in darkness, closed for the night. Another two hundred yards or so past Bullgators he slowed, looking for the outlet that allowed access to his canal-fronted property on Pina Vista Drive.

He felt lucid, despite the continued pain in his left arm spreading out down his side. His physical pain was juxtaposed against a clarity of thought he had never previously possessed. He thought about their situation and believed it must be the van, not them, that police had been searching for. The van was on false plates. They had worn masks in the raid. Even the warehouse was not owned in his name. Very few people knew about the warehouse and one of those, Anderson, was now dead. The Audi A8 worried him though. It was registered in his name and would be a link to where they now headed.

A photo-like still of the warehouse was framed in his memory. It was what he had seen looking back from the boat at the dead officers with the warehouse behind them. He mentally zoomed in on the image of the Audi through the open back shutters. Boxes were piled high behind it, blocking the view of the A8's rear. He knew police would be unable to step inside to look closer.

I'm safe for now. The thought had entered his head with the confidence of a new intelligence working within his consciousness. It felt like a moment from the Stephen King books he read as a youth – his own detached voice talking to him from within his mind.

The voice was planning his escape. All he had to do was gather up all his cash and get out. It should not take long.

Damian thought about his shooting of the obstructive cashier in Orlando. It was the reason the hunt for the van had gone statewide so quickly. Why had he been so hot-headed? Something inside his brain told him that man was his *old* self. He felt calmer now and more in control. Even so, she was the one who had pushed the alarm. *She only had herself to blame.*

As the new self-awareness took hold, he felt it fighting for dominance with James and Damian. The imprints of his former lives and their memories seemed distant and out of kilter with how he was now processing thoughts. He knew his thinking had something to do with the warehouse and the infection taking hold of his body, but not how.

His emotional behaviour was being underpinned by cold instinct and, above the physical pain he felt, he was enjoying the new feeling of power. Sheer cold logic and incisive thinking were helping him form a plan.

Damian pondered the possibilities. It was doubtful the police knew who they were, but he was going to put that theory to the test. Until they had discovered the warehouse there had been little chance of police connecting him to the robbery. Sarah's car had not been stopped and checked on the way in and neither had Anderson's. They might see Anderson's and Sarah's cars in the warehouse and visit the Rebel Yell. But Anderson would not be there. Had Anderson told others where he was going and who he was visiting? That was unlikely because his intention was to collect a stolen cross. There was no other human element to connect Anderson to the warehouse. He also wondered how long it would take the police to gain access to the warehouse with the snake monster writhing in the wall.

With the warehouse discovered, the clock had started ticking. How long would it take for his ownership of the building to be unpicked? Without knowing his identity, the police would not yet have his home under surveillance. A lot hinged on the efficiency of the police. Logic told him to assume the police would be efficient. It all came down to how much of a head start he had.

The first part of his plan was to moor up at his house and switch to another vehicle. From there he would drive to the discreet marina he used to hire boats, only this time he'd have to buy one of them, no questions asked. He had used the boat hire service to smuggle stolen items and cash to the offshore haven of Bermuda. He hoped to access his offshore bank accounts before they were frozen, but first he would retrieve the cash hidden in the safe at home. There was enough to buy a boat and survive for some considerable time. There would be no return journey and he knew Bermuda had extradition treaties with the United States of America. He would not be able to stay on the island for long and would worry about where he travelled on to later.

The notion of killing Mason and Noah entered his thinking. His companions were weak and would hinder his survival. He'd need to work out a plan to kill them and dispose of their bodies, though not yet. For the time being he might need them, even as bait or a distraction for the police. He would travel with Sarah to provide cover, like a normal couple on a romantic break.

As he turned the boat down the narrow channel that served as boat access to Lake Washington between Laguna Vista Drive and Pina Vista Drive, he knocked the power down to its lowest level and the boat edged its way down the canal. Noah and Mason had taken up positions away from him to the front of the craft. The thought they were terrified of infection was an amusing one. Did he have the power in his hands to infect them with the disease he now carried? He was not sure. He was no longer sure it was a disease. Could it be a blessing?

Noah was looking at him.

'I'm fine,' he said, 'but I could do with some medicine to ease the pain.'

Lifting a piece of tarpaulin, Damian uncovered a battered tin box. He released a catch on either side and opened the lid. From it he produced a bottle of bourbon, unscrewed the cap and drank. 'This should help.' He smiled. The others exchanged nervous glances.

He gulped down the fluid and immediately felt a wave of relief sweep over him – the alcohol quickly eased the pain but helped focus his mind on the present. He used some directly on his arm, lifting the bandage to let the liquid wash over his wound, hopefully keeping infection at bay. He had seen them do it in films.

Damian felt alive, his body tingling, its senses heightened. He believed the alcohol had lifted his spirits. Except there was something else too. He dismissed the thought and concentrated on his escape plan. They were only yards from his house's jetty, and he was confident that they would elude capture.

TWENTY-ONE

The Brevard County Aviation Unit's prized Huey hovered above the warehouse, its spotlight illuminating the back of the building. The swampy area across the back of the tributary meant it was easier to use helicopters to relay quick pictures of the scene to Izard. Two five-hundred-horsepower Water Thunder airboats were on route from the Marine Unit's fleet. The airboats would be able to get ground-level eyes on the back of the warehouse, now sealed off to foot access.

It had taken Izard a few minutes after his arrival to report that the fugitives had potentially escaped. He kicked himself for relying on the assumption that the gang had shot the deputies from within the warehouse. Images from the chopper showed the two dead deputies had disappeared, consumed by the creeping carpet. Staying clear of the deceased deputies had been the right call.

The images also showed a gap where an airboat may have been. He believed it likely that the gang had escaped on water, rather than been trapped inside the warehouse. The shooting of three, maybe four, officers supported the escape theory.

He talked to Sheriff Wiles, who agreed to sanction more Aviation Unit helicopters taking to the air and various inshore boats to search the long stretches of the St Johns River, lakes and their tributaries. The sheriff informed him that housing developments and their canals punctuated the waterways. The county had seventy-two miles of coastline and two intracoastal waterways. Despite the resources he was able to offer, the sheriff believed the gang could be almost anywhere by now, though it was likely that they would make land again, rather than stay out on waterways at night.

After reporting the fugitives' escape and issuing search instructions, Lieutenant Izard turned his attention to the matter of the 'missing' deputy, Grimes, and the two dead deputies. He needed a drone to fly inside the warehouse and obtain the vehicle license plates, hoping they would reveal the identities of gang members.

Izard was also desperate to see the warehouse interior to understand more about what they were dealing with and the danger it posed. Some of his men were talking about aliens and monsters. He needed to quell speculation and report facts. The explanation had to be simple, so he called the Florida Fish and Wildlife Conservation Commission. After much delay and insistence, Izard was patched through to a weary-sounding woman who had taken his name and asked how she could help.

His description of the incident was met with scepticism. She laughed at the notion of contagious spores covering concrete. Yes, there were non-native species of large snakes living in the swamp area, but the vast majority were in the Everglades, further south. She told him Burmese pythons reached sizes of twenty feet long, but she'd never heard a single report of them eating humans. Did the lieutenant not realise that pit bull dogs killed more humans in Florida than brown bears, alligators, wolves and snakes combined? Their owners were the problem. And yes, the lieutenant may have expressed surprise, but there were wolves in the Everglades. The rare red wolves were being reintroduced to Florida and liked eating snakes and their eggs, so she hoped they would help keep a check on the growth of the python population. Elsewhere in the United States the red wolves were mating with coyotes, producing coy-wolves, which could spell the end of the species. That was the problem with forcing nature into unnatural habitats, she had warned. Anyway, she would have someone come over to take a look for signs of the reported reptile in the morning. She wished him a curt goodnight.

Frustrated by the call, Izard checked for progress on ownership of the warehouse. Detectives had not yet established a link from the warehouse to a person. The building's ownership was in the name of Titusville-based 'Brevard Swamp Tours', but it was a bogus business with no phone numbers or website. Its registered address was a rented postbox at a post office in Bermuda. Detectives were working on the renter of the box, though eligibility dictated that they must be a Bermudan Citizen. Izard was advised the person renting the box was most likely doing so as a proxy and would not be one of the gang members they now hunted. It was clear that whoever ran the operation was hiding behind a few layers of secrecy.

The ground hunt was proving equally frustrating. Seventy officers were involved. The sheriff's office was throwing a bunch of their resources at the problem, including four choppers and eight patrol boats. Izard believed the fugitives had to live in Brevard, Osceola or Orange, within easy reach of Lake Winder. Would they head back to accommodation of some description? Or would they assume their identities were known? Would they stay together or split up? These were all questions he discussed with his team.

Izard guessed the gang would assume their identities had been discovered, meaning he would have to widen the search in case they tried to leave the state.

A surveillance van arrived, acting as a temporary command centre. He was eager to look at images relayed from the Brevard Aviation Unit's powerful high zoom and infrared cameras and crowded around one of the van's screens with fellow officers.

As the camera zoomed in, they could see the material contained lots of small movements within it. Strangest of all, it displayed a heat pattern that suggested the matted area was alive. All of it. It supported the deputies' earlier reports of something retreating into a wall, which the helicopter's tech suggested was a living entity.

At last, the Brevard County drone arrived and was quickly deployed. A local deputy gave Izard a tablet to watch images beamed back from the drone's camera.

'We need to check no one is hiding in there and then get license plate numbers,' Izard explained as the drone flew out of their sight to the back of the shed. The open shutter was now obscured by what looked like creepers hanging down. The sinewy cover was preventing any obvious point of entry.

'Why don't we force open the front shutters instead?' the deputy suggested as he kept the drone hovering several yards away from the back entrance.

'We already considered that option,' Izard said. 'The problem is, I can't risk anyone touching the building. Not after what happened to your man. We have no idea what's behind the shutter. I know it's tight, but we need to get eyes inside. Please give it your best shot.'

The deputy nodded. 'I'll try to squeeze it through that larger gap to the right,' he said. A group had gathered around Izard's tablet, transfixed by the drone's images. It edged into the gap and made it through.

'Nice. Now do a one-eighty,' Izard directed.

The drone was hovering over a garden furniture set and turned around. The image displayed was still of the table.

'Can't we widen the field?' Izard asked.

The deputy moved a small joystick on his remote and the image on his tablet moved up over some boxes to show the shuttered opening from inside. The dim warehouse lights fizzed and one popped. The drone was now operating in darkness.

'I have something to help with that,' the deputy said as a circle of light appeared, 'but the spotlight does reduce battery time.'

'OK, move off to the right and see what we can see.'

The spotlight picked out some of the back wall. It appeared much the same as from outside.

'Let's look down and see those license plates.' The spotlight looked down at the roof of the Audi and then over its bonnet. The van's plate was mounted high enough up on the right side of its back door to see. Izard squinted at his screen as the camera homed in on the detail to help. 'Yes, that's the one from Orlando. At least we know that with certainty. Now swivel round and get the plates from the cars.'

'The van is blocking me from getting low enough to see the front, but if the car's registered in Florida, there won't be a plate anyway. I need to get to the other side.' The drone reversed towards the back of the building. The image showed the trunk of the Audi and the teeming floor behind it.

'I need to take it lower to get an angle,' the deputy explained as the drone's feed slowly moved down to a lower aspect of the car, its spotlight reflecting off the A8's back window.

Something waved across the screen. The image fizzed and went blank.

'No, no, no,' said the deputy. He pushed buttons and moved levers, but the image on his remote-control display, and on the tablet Izard held, remained blank. The deputy looked at him and shook his head in the manner of a surgeon losing a patient mid-operation.

'Sorry,' Izard heard himself saying, and handed back the tablet.

He once again needed thinking time. The substance in the warehouse could kill and had knocked out a drone. He recalled his conversation with the Wildlife Conservation representative. She had not taken him seriously, and he surmised the problem must be new to the area. He needed a professor of biology, tropical diseases, or an expert on parasitical behaviours. He would start with the universities.

His phone rang. He did not recognise the cell number but decided to answer it.

'Lieutenant Izard?'

'Yes, who is this?'

'Dr Nathan Goodhew at NASA. I understand you have a problem?'

TWENTY-TWO

Barely an hour after launching the airboat, Damian killed the motor and allowed the craft to drift the final yards to his home's small jetty. A long stretch of well-kept lawn led up to his house and its metal-grilled swimming pool. The annual hunt for new real estate meant his house encroached into a large wilderness. The meshed fencing kept those in the house safe from snakes, gators and crocs on the outside.

His property was one of many thousands over Florida, Sarah had told him, that chewed into natural habitats. Ben had said much the same and explained that, since the 1970s until the property crash in 2008, legislators had given up protected wilderness to property developers. The landgrab of natural habitat had since recommenced, Ben had lamented, when they discussed who to vote for the previous November.

With the boat's motor silent, the sound of crickets stridulating a cheerful chorus of chirruping became noticeable. Damian liked the sound, and it was a welcome contrast to the still silence they had experienced at the warehouse. A strange thought occurred to him. Nature *was functioning normally on this stretch of water and he was safe here.*

The unfenced side of the house led up to an adjoining double garage. Damian discarded his now empty bottle of bourbon. He had drunk a full litre and still felt sober, which was odd, but he did not care. He was starting to feel euphoric.

All four stared up towards the property, looking for signs of a police presence. Damian knew there was no one there. His senses told him so.

'What do you think?' asked a furtive Mason.

'Let's go see, shall we?' Damian grinned. 'All of us.'

There would be no easy separation for the others – he needed to keep them close. He could not allow them to separate and fall into the hands of the police for a while yet.

Striding confidently up the path, Damian was followed timidly by the others. A slight breeze was blowing towards the water from the direction of the house, giving Damian the advantage. There was no one around. No humans. Other non-threatening aromas reached his nose, but he dismissed them.

I can distinguish between humans and animals. There was that feeling again – of invincibility.

The home's side door led into the double garage, which meant their entry was not visible from the front. Lights flickered on, revealing Damian's Ford Mustang. His prized possession gleamed under the lights and he recalled how Noah had taught him to race it around Bradenton Motorsports Park near the west coast. It was the feeling of speed and taking man and machine to the limit of their capabilities around the sharp corners of the track that excited him the most. With sadness he realised he'd have to leave the Mustang and, as a tender farewell, stroked its sleek bodywork. The others exchanged glances. Damian nodded beyond the Mustang to the less conspicuous Volvo station wagon, a car they used to collect and deliver items. 'We'll be taking that one,' he said, 'but first I have to get the keys.'

Damian beckoned them through a door leading into the large single-storey house and on into the open-plan kitchen, scene of previous social gatherings.

'What I need is along the hall. Sarah, you come with me,' he said. 'Noah, grab some food to keep us going. We keep bags in that drawer.'

Sarah followed him down the corridor to the main bedroom.

Damian went to the wardrobe and opened a door. He pulled out some shoes, rolled back a piece of carpet and removed two loose planks, setting them to one side. He punched numbers into a safe, smiling to himself. Mason would admonish him if he

111

realised his safe had been built into a wardrobe, like everyone else's. It mattered no longer. The safe would be empty in a few moments.

He pulled out wads of notes and stuffed them into a large holdall. The safe was deep and it contained dozens of bundled notes, mostly hundred-dollar bills. It also contained a bag of jewels. He finished emptying the safe and stood up.

'Well, you devil,' he heard Sarah say. 'All the times I've slept in here, I never knew you had a little stash going on.'

He looked at her and smiled. 'I like to have a few secrets. Let's call it our getaway fund.'

'How much is in there,' she asked.

Damian considered a moment before deciding to tell her. 'Half a million in cash and probably the same again in gemstones.'

'How?' she asked, looking incredulous, which amused him.

'The stones are held back from robberies. The cash is from property transactions. Ben and I have quite a portfolio now. It's the easiest way to launder cash from sales.'

Sarah was looking at him and he realised his mistake. Ben. 'Fucking hell, Ben,' he said and felt the strength leave his legs. He sat down on the side of the bed.

After a moment he looked up and saw she was staring at him wistfully.

'What is it?' he said.

'Ben,' she replied, 'I know he meant a lot to you.'

He looked back at her. She was right. Ben meant the world to him. Within days of Damian's arrival from the UK, it had been Ben who rescued him from a street gang in Miami and taken him back to his house. Damian had been holed up in a hotel and had stupidly tried to join a local gang. Back then, that was all that he knew. They had beaten him and threatened to kill him, demanding he brought them money. Then Ben appeared from the side door of what turned out to be his uncle's restaurant. The kids all knew Ben and ran off.

What was meant to be one night to recover at Ben's house had turned into a week. Then he found out Ben's wife, Kayla, had

112

cancer. They were struggling to afford the remaining treatment. Ben had saved him from having his money taken by the street gang, so he decided to give Ben all the money he had brought with him from London, to help with Kayla's treatment. Months later, Damian realised it was not a lot of money – not compared to the cost of cancer care in the United States. Yet the big man had cried when Damian handed ten thousand dollars over in a little paper bag.

From that moment, Ben and Damian had become inseparable. He had only seen Ben cry once since, and that was the previous year, when the cancer returned to take Kayla.

The biannual scans had become annual ones and, just as the hope that Kayla had beaten cancer seemed a reality, the cruel monster had chosen to return to her body and take her life. It still angered Damian that Kayla's cancer reappeared a decade after being told she was cured, and that no amount of money had been able to save her.

Kayla had not only left Ben, but two sons no longer had their mom. Adwin and Chaka relied fully on Ben, and Damian realised he would somehow need to reach out to them to look after them financially. As he sat there it occurred to him that the boys did not know their dad was dead. The thought overwhelmed him, and tears flowed.

'Hang in there,' Sarah was saying. He felt a consoling hand on his shoulder.

Eventually the feeling subsided. They needed to move. He wiped his face with the back of his hand and looked at Sarah. She did truly care. He could see it in her eyes and felt a pang of shame and regret.

'You know, Damian, you could have treated me better. I mean, it's been great. I really mean that. But just recently, you know …'

He looked back at her with sadness. 'Yes, yes, I know. It could have been better. I mean, I could have treated you better. I wish I had, my princess.' He stroked her cheek.

His admission seemed to surprise her, and he saw a wave of emotion flash over her soft features, heightening his sense of regret. He knew they were both struggling to hold it together after the manic circumstances of the day – the shooting, the thing in the warehouse killing Ben, his arm and the pain he was in. It felt as if the new calculated way of thinking had deserted him. Sarah was crying and he felt his eyes welling up again as he allowed himself to yield to his emotions.

'Thinking about it, I've been a bit of a git, haven't I?' He laughed out the comment between the tears now streaming down his face. Sarah returned the teary laughter and they held each other in manic, tear-fuelled hysteria.

'Yes, you have, haven't you? You've been a complete asshole. You know that, right?'

'Yes, I know. And I'm so, so sorry,' he replied, wiping a tear from her face, and suddenly they were kissing with the passion he had enjoyed in their early times together.

'We've had some good times in this house.' He spoke softly.

He felt her body shaking with the release of deep-seated emotion. Her kissing became greedy, her hands behind his neck, locking him into her embrace. Fear of infection seemed to have left her, and he felt something stirring inside him too. To his surprise she was unfastening his belt and he hitched up her skirt, pulled her panties to one side and was feeling her.

'I want to feel you inside me. The real you,' she said.

He unzipped his trousers and pulled them down just enough to hoist her up and pin her against the wall. She gasped in surprise. He had never done this to her before, yet he was able to lift her easily – holding her softly but firmly as he entered her.

'This is the real me,' he said. 'The new me.'

He felt himself deep inside her. She shuddered and winced slightly, then he saw pleasure taking hold as he pushed himself deeper still.

'So, this is the new you?' she asked, gasping.

He did not answer. Holding her tight, kissing her neck as she offered herself to him completely. He felt the explosion within her body as she climaxed. He felt himself climax too, his body shuddering as he did so.

For a while he held her there, both panting, savouring the feeling.

'Oh my God. That kind of hurt. But in a nice way,' she said.

He lowered her down and they quickly sorted themselves out, adjusting their attire while looking at each other the whole time, transfixed, laughing guiltily like naughty teenagers after being caught kissing by their parents.

'I can't believe we've just done that,' she said.

'Me neither,' he replied, pausing by the door. He looked at her intently. 'You know, you and I are not that different, Sarah.'

'How so?' she asked.

'We're both survivors.'

'Yes, I suppose we are.' A wistful look returned to her face as if she were recounting her life experiences, before snapping back to reality. 'We'd better get going. They will wonder what we've been doing.'

He followed her out of the room. He knew that Mason and Noah feared him, but not Sarah. She was made of stronger stuff, and he admired her for it.

Mason could tell Noah's impatience was growing.

They had filled two bags with snacks from the cupboard and fridge. They had also found some small water bottles and cans of soda. That had not taken long, and the extended wait was causing unease, neither knowing quite what to do next. Mason worried the police would be arriving any moment, but also wondered if their arrival might be for the best.

As he unscrambled the day's events, he tried to imagine if he could come out of the situation being viewed by police as a minor accomplice. Shooting cops was not cool though. Any association with the killer would not go down well. Reality took hold because he knew they'd all be named as accessories to the murders. They needed to leave the house quickly. Damian and Sarah had been gone over twenty minutes.

'What's taking them so long?' asked Noah. 'Do you think something's happened?'

'No, I went to check five minutes ago. I could hear them laughing so they must be OK.'

Noah frowned. 'I didn't see you do that.'

'No, you were in the john.'

'You heard them laughing?'

'Yer, sounded like they were having a party. Messed up, right?' Mason said. He could feel his agitation increasing by the minute.

'Laughing – wow. We really do need to leave, like now,' Noah said.

Mason was prepared to make the move to leave without Damian and Sarah. He figured it would be better to be apart from the cop killer. He had not pulled the trigger at the heist. He had not shot those three cops. That was down to Damian. 'Shall we get out of here now?' he asked.

'No, that's not what I meant,' Noah said. 'I was just wondering if Sarah's OK. Are you sure they're still in the house? Maybe *they've* left us?'

'I don't think so. I can still hear their voices.' Mason pondered their next move. 'Let's get out of here now. Without them. Noah, you can hot-wire cars, can't you?'

Noah nodded. He did not want to leave Sarah, but he was spooked by the long wait. 'I'm not sure … what if he comes back?'

'What if who comes back?' It was Damian. He was leaning against the door frame, smiling, with Sarah behind him. Mason was unsure how much Damian had heard.

Damian held a bulky black holdall.

Had they been spending all this time packing, like they were going on holiday? Mason wondered. Damian went to several boxes on shelves at the back of the garage. He pulled a large bottle of bourbon from one, wrapped a paper bag around it and put it in the holdall, zipping the bag back up.

Damian produced a key from his pocket, which he pointed towards the Volvo. The indicator lights flashed on the station wagon in time with the clunking sound of its central locking popping open. He opened the tail and placed the holdall carefully inside, then moved to the driver's door. 'OK, let's get going.'

No one moved.

'Come on, get in.'

Noah looked doubtful. 'You know you can't drive.'

'Yes, I can,' Damian returned.

'No, I mean you're banned, you know, drunk driving.'

Damian laughed manically, unsettling Mason further.

'Do you really think my driving ban's an issue now? "I'm arresting you for murder, armed robbery and, oh yes, driving while disqualified".' Damian scoffed. 'Here, have the fucking keys. I don't care, you drive.'

He tossed the keys to Noah who caught them one-handed. Noah headed around to the driver's side and they got into the car. The automatic garage door slid open and Noah put the car into drive.

As the car exited the house's long driveway onto Pina Vista Drive, Mason knew they had burned vital minutes. Noah was instructed, once again, to avoid I-95 and head west on Highway 192 to pick up the 441 south towards Lake Okeechobee. It proved to be a hundred-kilometre drive, taking them nearly two hours with a quick roadside comfort break included. Mason realised that Damian was not giving up his whole escape plan. He tried listening as Damian made a cryptic call from a burner phone, giving an instruction to 'Get her ready for an early start' and 'Yes, I'll have the cash.' Damian did not explain his call and Mason imagined they would only get the escape plan in instalments.

At the end of the 441, Damian instructed Noah to drive east through Cypress Quarters and head south-east on the 710. Damian said he had a stop-off in mind, within striking distance of the following morning's destination.

Noah drove on another twenty miles until they reached Indiantown. 'Slow down. It's somewhere down here on the left,' Damian said, leaning forward.

'There, it's the motel on the left, after Dunkin' and that pizza place ... here.' Damian pointed unnecessarily; Noah had already slowed to make the left into the motel's parking lot. A neon sign informed them that the motel had vacancies. Damian pointed Noah to the lot's far side, out of the glare of its main lights. 'Yes, anywhere here will be fine.'

To Mason's relief, Noah turned off the engine and they could get out. It was just past 10.00 p.m., yet it felt like midnight. So much had happened that evening and everyone looked exhausted. He was keen to stretch his legs to shake out some cramp in his left foot. Damian had jumped out of the station wagon and lifted the tailgate to retrieve his holdall, coming back around to where Mason was stretching out.

'Do me a favour and check us in, Mason. Go get us a room. Try to get us a family room, if they have one. We won't be crashing here for long, so just make sure it's the one room. We'll be setting off early to meet my contact.' Damian was rubbing his side and looked in some discomfort.

Mason took the cash Damian handed him and headed around the front to reception. The motel was one of those family-run independent mom 'n' pop motels he had stayed at numerous times on family trips as a kid. The reception looked dilapidated and Mason hoped Damian would not be angry if the family room proved to be similarly run-down. They did not do family rooms, however, so he settled on two adjoining rooms on the upper level.

Again, he hoped Damian would not mind.

TWENTY-THREE

Dr Nathan Goodhew arrived with an assistant a few minutes after Izard had taken his call. The two were ushered to the van from which Izard conducted operations.

'That was quick. Dr Goodhew, I presume?' Izard said, extending a hand.

Goodhew's handshake was firm. A lanyard was half-hidden under the doctor's unzipped jacket. 'May I take a look at that?' Izard said, gesturing towards it. 'Just a formality.'

The doctor held it up for him to see. The laminated card confirmed the identity of 'Dr Nathan Goodhew, Chief Scientist, NASA'.

'Thanks, Doctor,' Izard said, impressed.

'Nathan, just call me Nathan. Yes, we were already on our way when I called you. In any case, we're practically neighbours. I'm situated over in Kennedy. Same county.'

'Hmmm, well, I'm from out of town, but this site has now become my problem.' Izard nodded to the cordoned-off warehouse.

'I love the uplighting,' Goodhew said. 'Reminds me of a sightseeing trip to the Valley of the Kings.'

Izard looked at the dilapidated spotlit building and laughed. He had no idea if Goodhew's icebreaker was meant to be sincere or ironic.

Do you mind if I take a look?' Goodhew indicated the taped-off area and received a nod of approval.

'Just be careful,' said Izard. 'There's some kind of organic matting around the back. I know this is going to sound crazy, but the stuff swallowed two, maybe three deputies.'

'So I'm given to understand,' Goodhew said.

Izard watched the doctor and his companion approach the edge of the infestation. They stared intently at the shifting matter that extended down the boat ramp. Goodhew's brow furrowed and he exchanged a few words with his colleague. The assistant took some large gloves from a bag and put them on. He bent down, using an implement to scoop up samples into a receptacle, which he then carefully bagged.

'Are you sure that's safe?' Izard shouted and, to compound his point, something snaked out and they backed away.

Goodhew looked grave. 'I fear this won't be your problem for much longer, if that's any consolation, Lieutenant.'

'Why not?'

'I'll explain more in a bit. First, we have to remove your men from the area. I want an exclusion zone of at least a hundred yards.'

It was not a directive Izard could accept. He had made little progress at the scene and the fugitives were still at large, meaning he was feeling heat from superiors. 'You've got to be kidding me. This is a crime scene. An officer has gone missing, and two others are dead. There's vital evidence inside that building we need to get at. I have a 360 on its way, so we can get a peek inside.'

'You'll have to hold back on the excavator,' Goodhew said, 'until I run some tests.'

The doctor's tone was matter-of-fact and Izard felt irritated. 'Doctor Goodhew. Nathan, sorry, no. My people have to get in there. We will just have to work around each other. You do your job and let me do mine. If you don't mind …' He wanted to side-step the doctor, but Doctor Goodhew did not move as Izard hoped.

The doctor was rubbing his chin, looking quizzically at Izard before speaking. 'OK, Lieutenant, let me explain. This stuff, as you call it, could be highly contagious and until we know what we're dealing with, I insist you keep your men away from the site. It could contain viruses or be toxic. It could even be parasitic, if your reports are accurate.' Goodhew turned to his assistant. 'I never thought I'd say this, but will you instigate Protocol 84.'

'Eighty-four?' the assistant repeated, hesitating. 'Now?'

'Yes, Greg. Now. And also mention that it might be connected to the meteor shower we tracked. I think we've found where the meteorites impacted.'

Izard was puzzled. 'What's Protocol 84?' he asked.

'Protocol 84 was set up by President Truman in 1947, named after Hangar 84, Roswell. The protocol is initiated by a call to the White House. We're just about to make that call. I'd prefer you not to mention anything to your men. Best tell them there might be some volatile chemicals on site. I need government agencies on the ground here to help me coordinate. In the meantime, I could do with your help, until we get the military in.'

Izard felt his irritation levels rise further. 'Roswell. I mean, really, Doctor?'

The doctor gave him a disappointed look, as if addressing a failed student. 'No, I am not referring to little green men with buggy eyes, if that's what you're implying, but we do know there are things out there other than us.'

Izard imagined being NASA's Chief Scientist put Goodhew on a much higher pay grade and meant the man was very important. But Izard could not recall anything in his training that suggested a situation where NASA personnel could outrank him in a civil police matter. 'I don't want to sound disrespectful, but you don't have any kind of jurisdiction here. This is my crime scene. I need to see behind that shutter.'

Goodhew smiled at the comment as his assistant, Greg, walked purposefully back to their car. Placing a fatherly arm on Izard's shoulder the doctor said, 'On the contrary, I do. I'm acting under special government powers. And as of this moment, so are you. We will clear that up shortly, but time is of the essence. Right now, I have some questions. I need to know exactly what happened here. Tell me as best you can, but I need to know fast.'

There was something about the doctor's air of authority that made Izard believe him. He was too controlled to be faking.

121

Izard took a deep breath and tried to explain. But it all came out a jumble. What had started as a shooting in Orlando had escalated when the getaway vehicle was reported in this general area. Local deputies discovered the gang holed up here. Shots were fired. He had arrived expecting a shoot-out, or at least some kind of stand-off leading to arrests. That was not how things had played out.

On arrival he discovered two dead deputies and a sergeant in a critical condition. He believed the gang had escaped, unless they had been trapped inside the warehouse. Three state officers reported seeing a strange snake-like head appearing from the wall that swallowed the missing deputy. The state troopers were his own men and were experienced, reliable witnesses. Yes, it was dark, but he believed them. The officers had obviously seen something. They were in shock and at the sheriff's office now, waiting to be debriefed. Did he want to interview them?

The doctor looked thoughtful. Again, he was rubbing his chin. 'That's a good summary, Lieutenant Izard. Very useful.'

One of Izard's detectives approached. 'Sir, we have boats out on St Johns, Washington and north on Poinsett, but still nothing.'

Izard was frustrated. It seemed they were no nearer finding the fugitives. Without access to the building, he was pinning his hopes on a quick answer as to who owned the building. Dr Good-hew had stepped to one side to make a call. He was pacing around a few yards away, keeping his voice down. Izard knew it was something important and waited for the doctor to finish.

'Sorry, Nathan, will you tell me how we resolve accessing the building? Izard asked.

'If you don't mind, that can wait. This is far more important.' Goodhew held out his cell phone. Izard hesitated and took it. He listened intently to the voice at the other end and glanced up at Goodhew in surprise before answering a series of instructions. 'Yes, sir, I understand, sir. Yes, I will certainly do that. OK, we will keep the area locked down until your boys arrive. Yes, you can count on me, sir. Thank you. Yes, I'll hand you back, sir.'

Izard returned the phone to Goodhew who wandered off a few yards again for privacy. Izard took out his own phone and tapped a name into Google search.

'Who was that, Lieutenant?' asked one of his detectives.

'You're not going to believe me,' Izard replied, staring at his phone's screen.

'Well, try me.'

Izard's cheeks blew out. 'That was one of the president's Joint Chiefs of Staff.' Izard noted the sceptical look on his detective's face. 'Yes, I know. Sounds far-fetched right? But look here.'

Izard held out his phone and the detective held it steady to view the screen. They both read the profile. 'Seb Lewis, Joint Chief of Space Operations.'

The detective whistled. 'Space Operations? Really, we have one of those?'

Izard had no idea about the finer details of Protocol 84, but it evidently worked. The Joint Chief of Staff had asked him to enforce a tight exclusion zone around the site. The army were on the way and the scene would be handed over to the military. In the meantime, Izard was 'officially requisitioned' to work on behalf of the President of the United States of America. He was not to pass on any information Dr Goodhew shared with him.

'My wife is never going to believe this,' Izard said to everybody and nobody. 'I'm working for the president.'

TWENTY-FOUR

Sarah, Noah and Mason stood by the motel bed, watching Damian as he unwrapped the bandage on his arm. Sarah was shocked to see bumpy green-grey swelling around the flesh tear, although the wound itself seemed to have closed up, as if it had healed itself.

Sarah exchanged awkward glances with the others, guessing no one wanted to say what they feared. It was clear Damian was infected with whatever it was that attacked him in the warehouse. His mood had changed too, the kindness she had seen at his house four hours earlier seemingly gone.

She looked at him, wondering if he really was morphing into the snake thing they'd seen at the warehouse and if he might attack them. She also thought about their moment of passion earlier. The potential repercussions filled her with dread.

Damian was lying back on the room's double bed and, not for the first time that day, seemed to sense her fear. 'I'm alright,' he said. 'I'll be fine. Really.'

Except she could see that the pain had returned and despite his efforts to hide it, he grimaced and touched his side.

'I'm fine,' he repeated.

'Maybe you should get that seen to,' she said.

'I don't think that's a good idea, do you?' Noah replied, listening from the open door of the adjoining room.

Damian was finishing the bottle of bourbon from his holdall, gulping it down like water. 'I need some more of this,' he said, wincing with pain. He dropped the empty bottle to the floor.

'What will be open at this late hour?' Sarah said.

'Hold on, I'll check.' Mason typed something into his phone.

Damian frowned. 'Have you had that on you all day? What happened with the no-phone rule on jobs?' he said.

'Don't worry, this one's a burner and I only take it on jobs as a backup, in case I need to tether it to my laptop, or use it outside the van.'

Sarah looked at Damian, who seemed satisfied with the answer. She wondered how many risks Mason had taken on jobs. The police could track phones and would surely be filtering cellular activity to arrive at suspect devices.

'There's a Circle K at the gas station. Have to rush though – they stop selling alcohol at midnight. You want me to go?' Mason asked.

Damian nodded and held out some cash, which Mason took.

'I won't be long. It's only a bit further on, towards Burger King.' Mason left the room – a bit too quickly, Sarah thought. She wondered if they'd see him again.

An uncomfortable silence ensued as Damian slumped back across the bed. His breathing was laboured. Sarah watched him, unsure what to do next, replaying the day's events. She had not been involved in the robbery, yet her proximity to the gang put her in danger, both from the police and from whatever was infecting Damian. Her mind felt fogged by anxiety. Despite her earlier reconciliation with Damian, she started thinking how to get away from him and the others. She'd missed the chance to go to the store and make her escape and kicked herself for not spotting the opportunity. She guessed Mason was making his move at that very moment – he'd been gone a while.

She looked over at Noah. The poor kid looked petrified. He had seated himself on a desk chair across the other side of the room, keeping a wary eye on Damian. What was going through Noah's mind? Maybe she should try to make her escape with him? He could hot-wire a car and put some distance between themselves and Damian.

Then she looked at Damian. Back at his house there had been a reconnection. There was still something good between them, worth holding on to. Damian's eyes were now closed, and she mouthed silently over to Noah, 'Is he sleeping?'

Noah looked at Damian and cautiously replied in kind, shrugging. 'Don't know.'

Believing Damian to be asleep she moved around the room to talk in a hushed voice to Noah. 'That thing eating Ben, it's like a nightmare. Please tell me it didn't really happen.'

'It did. It nearly got me too.' He touched the top of his arm.

'Damian told me about Ben today. Did you know that Ben saved Damian from being killed when he first arrived from England?'

'Yes, didn't you know that? I've known about it for ages. Ben also told me that his wife—'

'Kayla?'

'Yes, Kayla. She got cancer but they had no insurance. Damian gave him all the money he had and then worked with Ben to help pay back a loan from Ben's uncle in Miami. His uncle owns a few restaurants down there. Damian and Ben worked on ways to make money until Ben had paid back every last penny. Tens of thousands worth of cancer treatment.'

Sarah and Noah looked at Damian, who was moaning incoherently on the bed.

'Why did Damian do that?' asked Sarah.

'Ben saved Damian. A gang were going to kill him. Ben's family took him in and looked after him like one of their own. Damian was only nineteen when they first met. Ben said Damian was scared and desperate. Can you imagine? In many ways, Ben and Damian were like brothers.'

'Incredible,' said Sarah, shaking her head. 'I had no idea. Why would Ben tell you that and not me?'

'We spent a lot of time together. I drove them round, don't forget.'

There was a gentle knock on the door. It was Mason. To her surprise he had returned and was holding a large paper-wrapped bottle. 'I don't like it out there in the dark,' he said. 'I can't shake that thing out my head. What if it tries to follow us? What if he turns into it?' The three looked at Damian, who looked like he was

126

in the middle of a bad dream.

'No, I don't think so,' said Sarah. 'He looks the same as he did when we first got on the boat. That was a long time ago now.'

'I don't know,' said Noah, 'that thing we saw appeared out of a wall. Maybe it's inside him. You know, like in *Alien*.'

'Noah, please don't. That sort of shit's not gonna help,' Sarah said.

'But he could be right. You saw that snake thing too. What if there's one in him?' Mason said.

Damian started and sat up like a bolt. His hands went to his chest. His breathing suddenly became erratic as he gasped, 'I can feel something inside me. Help me. Get this thing out of me. It's bursting out.'

Damian lurched forward, throwing his arms wide open, screaming. Sarah took a step back before realising that there was no bodily explosion or blood. Mason had dropped the bottle. Luckily, it did not smash.

'Give me the bottle, you fucking moron. There is no alien,' Damian said.

'You're an asshole.' Noah laughed. 'I think I've just shit myself.'

Sarah laughed nervously as Mason picked up the bottle and laid it on the end of the bed, which appeared to have become a quarantine zone.

'Don't do that again, do you hear?' Mason said, visibly shaken.

'I think someone really did shit himself,' Noah said, looking derisively at Mason.

'Noah!' said Sarah. 'Leave him.'

'Yer, you're the one who said he'd shit himself,' Mason said.

'God, chill, man, I was joking.'

'Now, now, children,' Damian said, grunting a laugh as he picked up the bottle and unscrewed the cap. It was another one-litre bottle of bourbon. He gulped down a few measures and poured some on his arm, from which vapour fizzed like dried ice.

Sarah glanced at Mason who looked aghast, like he was witnessing a pet dog ripping up and eating the neighbour's cat.

Damian closed his eyes and looked like he was sleeping again, but she was not sure. She decided to move to the bed in the adjoining room and try to get some sleep too. It would be a long night.

TWENTY-FIVE

It was after half past four in the morning and Damian slowly raised himself from the bed. He was still holding the bottle of bourbon, which had not left his grip since he dozed off at midnight. He lurched towards the door. 'I think I need some air,' he said. 'Maybe I'll go meet my alien friends outside.'

Sarah had slept little and was sitting on the bed in the adjoining room, talking to Noah about some of his trips out with Damian. It was clear she knew very little about Damian's business dealings.

The adjoining motel door allowed her to watch Damian walk around the bed. He stopped briefly and smiled in at her. He had picked up his black holdall and she heard the door open and close as he left the room. She had no idea where he was going, but it gave them the freedom to talk openly for the first time since escaping the warehouse.

She woke Mason, who was slouched in a chair in her room. She could tell he was now terrified of Damian. 'Don't worry, he's gone,' she said.

TWENTY-SIX

The cooler night air blew softly against Damian's face. The light breeze refreshed him, relieving pain like a cold swab on a burn. Taking another few swigs from the bottle, he felt happy to leave the confinement of the motel room behind. His arm and torso tingled, but the suffering had subsided. Feeling better than he had done since their arrival at the motel, he staggered on, but with no real direction. He needed to clear his head. His thoughts during the escape had been clouded with strange feelings and imaginations.

He wondered how it was possible to feel lousy on the airboat, then OK at his house, only to worsen during the journey to the motel. He could still recall some of his nightmarish dreams from earlier. In his delirium, he had been sinking below the surface of a swamp, with something hunting him. The predator's face was that of a large snake but, when it had come to eat him, the face had morphed into his stepdad's. The snake was consuming him, biting down on his head. He was being swallowed whole and could see another world of animals squirming around next to him, turning on him and biting too.

Damian steadied himself, leaning against a wall for support.

A female voice called out from close by. 'You OK, Chico? Maybe you should stop now.' The source of the voice walked over and nodded towards the bottle in Damian's hand.

The distraction was a welcome one. It had snapped him away from the lurid daydream he was re-entering. Taking in his surroundings, Damian realised he had walked down the street outside the motel. In one direction he could see the motel and noticed the Dunkin' logo beyond was no longer lit up. In the direction he was walking, Burger King and McDonald's signs were still lit bright against the darkness.

'Maybe I should stop,' Damian replied, 'unless you want some too?' He lowered his bottle and tried to focus on the Hispanic figure in front of him, but his sight was strangely tunnelled. He could smell her well enough. The aroma of cheap perfume mixed with sweat pervaded his nostrils, as did the smell between her legs. He could tell she was in season but did not question how he knew.

'How much?' he asked. He sensed something else about her. Not fear. She did not fear him – it was desperation, like she needed something. She was eyeing his Rolex and smiling. 'A nice man like you, a hundred and fifty bucks round the back or, if you want a room, two hundred.'

She needs money.

Damian nodded. He followed the hooker and waited as she unlocked a ground floor motel door and beckoned him in. The woman turned on a light and looked at him. She looked at the rip in his shirt and hesitated.

'Heh, you been in a fight?'

'No, all good. Just a little accident, that's all.'

'OK. But I don't want no funny business, you understand?'

'Don't worry. I'm not like that.'

'Money first. Nothing personal, just business.'

The pheromones he was picking up were sending him into a frenzy. He knew he had to have her, like his life depended on it. He had to fight back the instinct to rip her clothes off as he dug into a pocket and pulled out a wad of notes. He did not know quite how much was in his hand as he thrust it into hers. Satisfied, she disappeared into the bathroom. 'Just a minute, Chico,' she said, smiling back gleefully. He guessed she had been provided with a bumper payday and did not care.

He heard the grinding of poor plumbing as a tap was turned on. The sound of water splashing into the sink seemed like it was right next to him. His heart was pounding, heightening his senses to provide an aphrodisiac that made his loins throb in readiness. He placed the bourbon bottle and holdall by the bed and sat expectantly, head turned towards the bathroom door – knowing his prey would enter the room any moment. The door handle turned. He felt every revolving click in the mechanism. He had never been with a hooker before, the idea used to revolt him, yet now he allowed the blurry outline to push him back and take control.

She straddled him, lifting her skirt so it rode around her waist. Damian unzipped himself. Pulling a condom packet from her shirt pocket, she expertly tore it open with her teeth, took it out and pulled it down over his penis.

She looked surprised. 'Heh, you not as drunk as I thought. Very hard, yes?' she said.

She must have already taken her knickers off in the bathroom because he was easily able to enter her, thrusting in time with her movements. After a couple of minutes, he stopped.

'You finished there?' she asked.

He looked up at her face; she was close enough for him to see her Latin-American features. Still inside her he could feel her heartbeat, her sexual heat, and taste her loins just by breathing her in. The heady aromas were intoxicating. His mind swam in a heady storm of deadly desire. Underneath it all he felt confusion and self-loathing.

'No, I'm OK,' he said and continued.

He grabbed her hips and the intensity of his thrusts increased. The girl looked nervous, the previous faked pleasure he disliked having disappeared. With each new jolt the cheap-looking bed rocked and squeaked. She removed her flattened palms from his chest and, shifting to a more upright position, clenched her hands into fists, grimacing. He sensed her discomfort and did not care.

Entering a rhythmical trance, Damian felt his swollen penis reaching out inside the hooker. He closed his blurry eyes and was transported to his home in North London.

He no longer held the power. A force was striking down on his head – the pain of old nightmares resurfacing to join the new terror within him.

'Please don't, please ...' He heard his mother's sobs as the drunken blows from his alcoholic stepfather rained down on him. At that moment he was James Wardell, his terrified eleven-year-old self, taking another severe beating.

'You good-for-nothing lazy little shit,' his stepfather was saying, 'after all the things I do for you.'

The father figure James craved had morphed into a vindictive bully.

This was the man who, as part of 2 Para, had taken on the Argentinians at Goose Green and survived. Eighteen of his comrades had not been as fortunate, a point repeated to James in one of his stepdad's many 'You should count yourself lucky' speeches.

The process of bullying was insidious. It started with breaking the tight bond with his mum. James loved to cuddle up to his mum on the sofa, watching TV, and had never left the house without a kiss goodbye from her. Now he had to 'man up', 'stop being a pussy', and kisses from his mother were banned.

'Forgive him, James, your dad has PTSD. He saw a lot of bad things in the army,' she said. His mum was stroking his hair – the tyrant was at work. James had no insight into the psychological darkness of PTSD but certainly knew its consequences at the hands of his mum's new husband.

Then the cruel monster was home after a bad day at work, and his mum shrieked as another blow from his stepdad landed on him.

The pitch of the shrieking intensified and stopped.

Damian was back in the motel room.

He was still inside her and found himself stroking the girl's long raven hair, hanging down seductively, tickling his face. The prostitute was quite still, breathing softly, letting him touch her tenderly.

He missed his mum and intentionally visualised her. There she was, flickering into his mind's vision.

His mum stood watching helplessly as his stepdad spoke. Damian could see himself standing at her shoulder, watching the scene play out. He was detached and looking in at his younger self. He felt tiny fragments of understanding clicking into place to complete the jigsaw puzzle he'd kept boxed up, tucked out of sight for over a decade.

'You need to let the boy grow up. You're doing him no favours by mollycoddling him. He'll turn into a wuss and get bullied.'

A big hand swept down and caught him on the side of his head, making his ears ring.

Another beating. This time, using a pillow to lessen the chances of telltale bruising. The regime was systematic – James's preparation for life. He saw the look on his stepdad's face.

He enjoyed hurting me.

The scene faded to another. James and his mum were looking through some old school photo albums. There were photos of him at summer football camp, proudly wearing his Charlton football shirt. Then there was one with his father on the beach in Cornwall. His father looked so handsome and young. It was the last holiday they had together before his dad died on the building site. The door of the lounge opened and there was his stepdad home early from work, watching them, eyes narrowed with suspicion. James was asked to leave the room and he heard them arguing. He never saw the photo box again.

You were jealous of what we had.

Damian saw his stepdad's fear clearly now. He understood fear and visualised the irrational disease taking hold of his stepdad, that the enemy on the photo might one day return from the dead to his old habitat and reclaim the family death had taken. The notion was as absurd as it was impossible.

James, in the meantime, was the Argentinian being stalked around the household. The enemy within, to be locked up, punished and forced into submission.

Damian felt himself sinking deeper into his recollections as memories untouched since childhood resurfaced. He knew he was in a deep trance and decided to stay in the unconscious state – to finally face up to his boyhood nemesis.

His stepdad entered the next stage of his campaign against James. He was using repetition of mantras to reinforce the household's new code of conduct, codes that James was failing to keep. He forgot to put his dirty washing in the laundry basket. He was negligent in his task of loading and unloading the dishwasher. His worst crime was spending too long in the bathroom and using up the hot water.

'Once you sign up you have a responsibility. You are failing in your duties, soldier,' said his stepdad's beery voice, his rank breath hot against James's face.

Living at home was a war. From buffing up his school shoes to 'parade standard', to homework 'passing muster'. Daily communication was steeped in military jargon. He was a cadet who was never going to 'pass out'.

His stepdad's desire to see failure in James was relentless, becoming a self-fulfilling prophecy. James avoided coming back to a home that had become his own version of Goose Green. Except James's avoidance of home had consequences. Delaying getting home meant hanging around the shops and park, leading him into the company of a local gang. All this came during the intensely self-reflective period of puberty. The awkwardness of physical change exacerbated the daily mental challenges he faced.

Damian looked on, watching the boy waiting on the corner for his new mates to arrive.

Through a systematic process of verbal abuse, the innocence of youth was dissipating, trust and acceptance giving way to confused, angry cynicism. Damian watched two years fast-forward, the carefree eleven-year-old mutating into an angst-ridden teenager. Within three years that teenager was walking around the neighbouring estate carrying a knife.

I knew it! You did this to me. My life choices are your fault.

Damian could see their old family doctor talking to his mum while James looked silently on. 'Your son's affliction is at the lower end of the Tourette Syndrome spectrum,' the doctor was saying, which was no consolation. He now had an 'affliction' to compound his feelings of uselessness. He stuttered when nervous, particularly when using the letters 'd' and 'f'.

He felt himself blush and throw his head to one side in time with the 'd-d-d' accompanying stammer. He dreaded teachers asking him to read passages out loud in class. He saw himself stuttering through a scene of Othello, as Iago played mind games on his unfortunate self. A razor-edged feeling of shame sliced through him as other children sniggered. After school, some gathered around him in the playground.

'You f-f-f-uck off. Fucking leave me alone!' James shouted. He hit the ringleader hard and felt the satisfaction as blood burst from his tormentor's nose. The boy was screaming. The screaming was getting louder.

No, it was not the boy at school. Damian was back in the motel room as the girl on top of him thrashed around wildly, screaming. How had he been so detached as to forget her? he wondered.

He held her there, watching her face twist in agony.

TWENTY-SEVEN

Sarah felt guilty for plotting with Mason and Noah. They sat on the double bed eating snacks, watching an old B-movie. It was Mason who'd insisted on switching on the wall-mounted television. She found it extraordinary that, despite everything, Mason had wanted to watch an old sci-fi channel.

The movie itself could not have been more unsuitable. Entitled *The Brain from Planet Arous*, it was about a criminal alien brain that took over a human. She could not watch the screen. The irony seemed lost on Mason, even though he was totally absorbed in the movie from the start. At least it seemed to calm him, she thought.

The discussion had been a difficult one, not just because the dramatic music and barking dog in the movie were off-putting, but because they were openly discussing taking the Volvo and leaving without Damian.

Noah and Mason argued what she already knew to be true. They had not shot the teller, Damian had. He had also shot three police officers. It was his fault they were in this mess. Noah even blamed Damian for whatever it was that killed Ben and Anderson in the warehouse, suggesting Damian had been stealing toxic chemicals from a lab in Palm Bay to sell on.

'What if he'd been storing some at the back? Maybe that thing was a chemical mutation.'

Sarah did not believe she had witnessed a chemical mutation. She also thought it unlikely Damian was stealing chemicals, but Noah said it had to be true because Damian had once commented about the security protocols at FAR Chemicals when they drove past.

On the television, the lead character, Steve, had developed strange shiny metallic eyes and had shot the sheriff.

'Do we have to watch this?' she said.

Mason turned to her. 'I don't take these old films seriously, you know. But that does not mean aliens aren't here. What we saw proves they already are,' he said, 'and they plan to kill us all. We were lucky.'

Noah shot Sarah a look, making fun of Mason, except part of her wondered if it could be true. None of them could explain what they'd seen. It brought her mind back to Damian's arm and what happened between them. She could not shake the sickening thought that she might be infected too.

More time passed and she began to doubt that Damian would be returning. He had the holdall so he did not need them any more. The other two believed he'd just gone out for some fast food and would be back soon. They didn't know the bag Damian took with him contained enough cash and gems to start a new life somewhere else. She wished she'd emptied Damian's bank accounts and disappeared before all this happened. She believed capture was inevitable and considered handing herself in. Noah and Mason preferred to go on the run. She figured that was because they faced more jail time.

On the television the man with shiny metal eyes was in an official-looking room with military personnel sitting around a table. He was looking out of the window at a nuclear explosion. He was laughing manically as the room caved in around them.

'No, sorry, no more. I really can't watch this.' She jumped up to look for the remote control.

'OK, let's get out of here,' Noah said. 'I have the keys, and I can see the Volvo from here.' He was looking out the window with his back to them, like the man with spooky shiny eyes in the movie. She wanted to get out of the room and away from Damian. Common sense told her it would support the narrative that they were unwilling accomplices to his crimes.

Mason sighed and stood up. He had the remote and switched off the television.

As the room fell into silence, they could hear loud shouts.

'Is that Damian?' Noah said.

The three stood still listening.

'That's definitely Damian's voice,' Sarah said. 'It sounds like it's coming from the room below.'

The shouts stopped and were followed by a female screaming. It sounded like she was screaming for her life.

'Damn, what do we do?' Sarah said.

Noah looked at her bleakly and she could see he was frightened.

'He's got someone down there. We can't let him kill her,' she said.

Damian looked up at the girl. He could tell she was terrified, yet he had done nothing wrong. He knew her screams could attract unwanted attention.

'Shut the fuck up and get off me,' he shouted.

He thought he heard her say, 'I can't,' but her voice was cracked. One of her hands was reaching out, grabbing at something. It was the bottle of bourbon on the bedside table. She held the neck like a club and swung it at his head. He managed to catch her hand before the bottle impacted and held it there, hovering inches from its intended target. Half a litre of undrunk bourbon glugged out over his face, neck and chest, soaking his shirt.

He felt a distant pain that brought him back to reality. It felt like an explosion both within his loins and in his head. He felt triumphant. Invincible. He had escaped his stepdad. He had escaped London. He would escape this mess.

The prostitute, meanwhile, was silent.

He sensed movement from outside the motel room. Fists pounded on the door. It was Sarah shouting, 'Damian, let us in. Stop what you're doing. Stop.' He heard desperation in her voice.

Withdrawing from the woman, he looked down at his penis and immediately felt sick. For a moment, protrusions writhed from its shaft. They looked furred up. Infected. The condom had disintegrated, rubber shreds hanging off small barbs. It was covered in blood that now spurted out from the woman and was soaking the bed sheet in a widening pool.

As he stared down in horror, he saw things return to normal. Or near normal. As his stiffness relaxed the strange barbs retracted and he could see no sign of them, other than small greenish markings where they had appeared.

He looked at the limp body of the female. She lay face down, motionless on the bed. There was no sign of her breathing. He had killed her. His 'thing' had killed her. He was changing into another being. A creature.

'What the f-f-fuck am I?'

On the other side of the motel room door, Sarah stopped hammering and was left struggling with indecision. Noah had followed her, but not Mason. The screaming had ended abruptly. Too abruptly.

The silence stretched between them like a challenge. They stared at each other, both waiting for the other to react. She took in deep breaths to calm herself and looked at the door, half expecting Damian to burst out. The anxiety of the silence was terrifying.

'OK, stand back,' Noah said at last.

Sarah was surprised. 'Are you sure?'

'No,' he replied and then shouldered the door, like the cops do in films. Instead of the door bursting open, Noah bounced straight back. Despite herself, Sarah laughed. The indignity galvanised Noah, who resorted to kicking the door several times.

'How can – doors be – so solid – in this – shithole?' His words punctuated each kick.

'Try higher, just under the lock.'

He did, but the door held firm.

He looked at her, shaking his head in disbelief at the absurdity of the situation. 'I don't believe this. Why am I trying to get in there?' He took a step backwards to get a run-up, and the door opened from the inside.

Damian stared impassively back at them. 'You guys want to come in?'

TWENTY-EIGHT

Dr Nathan Goodhew checked his phone. He was rounding up his team of NASA scientists based at various facilities around the United States of America. The space receiving laboratory at the Kennedy Space Center was readied quickly, having been built with such contingencies in mind. After all, Kennedy was located at the site of seventy-eight Shuttle landings on its single 15,000-foot concrete runway, north-west across the Banana Creek.

Speculation as to what missions might carry back from space had not just been confined to the movie industry but, as a rocket scientist, Goodhew knew what they faced was not his field of expertise. He had been appointed NASA's Chief Scientist in early 2023. Launching satellites was big business globally and his skills were in great demand. He knew he needed the biologists over at Houston to join him and their space receiving analysts at Kennedy.

Despite his engineering skills, being NASA's Chief Scientist had meant gaining an understanding of the wider scientific operation. Part of that education informed him the possibility of space exploration bringing back new diseases had been taken seriously by NASA as far back as the 1960s. An interagency committee on interplanetary quarantine had formulated a national policy for handling spacecraft and material returned from other planets, in advance of the lunar landing. The first space receiving lab built at the Johnson Space Center in Houston was followed by a smaller, covert version at Kennedy to support Shuttle and other missions. Goodhew was in charge of all the labs – even the ones that housed biologists rather than physicists and propulsion engineers. He never imagined he'd have to actually work so closely with the space receiving labs.

Remaining at the Lake Winder impact site, he organised the extraction of samples from the unidentified biological carpet. This was to be done using two Mars mission excavators brought over from the Space Center.

Live footage of the samples being extracted was to be relayed to the White House. Seb Lewis, the Joint Chief of Staff for Space Operations was an ex-colleague and had taken his earlier call seriously. The president and Joint Chiefs of Staff gathered around a large table to view the footage.

Goodhew nodded to several technicians standing at a table resembling the lighting rig controls at a rock concert. They pushed some buttons and two Mars mission excavators trundled down the side of the building towards the infected area. Their names were proudly displayed along their metallic flanks. One said 'Bob', the other 'Sally'. Their extendable arms carefully scooped up and quarantined scraps from the matted floor and placed them into canisters set out along the perimeter.

Goodhew watched on a monitor from a safe distance. The scene resembled an old motion picture: poor connectivity and dim lighting adding to the juddery 1950s B-movie feel.

Sometimes, when the wheels of the probes touched the shifting material, it reacted. Fronds shot out attacking the small excavators. The attacks seemed random and ineffective until Bob became caught up in the quagmire. Stalk-like strands hooked around one of Bob's metal arms and, like tyres spinning in snow, its wheels dug deeper into the gunge. The strands acted as a tightening lasso, pulling Bob onto its side making it impossible for the excavator to escape the seething mass.

Bob disappeared from view as the collective enveloped it. Was the material defending itself or acting as the aggressor? Was the activity committed consciously or was it some kind of reflex action? Goodhew was uncertain which.

After losing her mechanical partner, Sally was kept to the periphery of the material. Her remote-controlled arms managed to slice more small samples and deposit them into canisters without attracting serious attacks.

Sally picked up the canisters one by one, driving up a ramp and placing them on racking inside the decontamination unit, and a heavily armed convoy escorted the samples back to clean rooms at Kennedy.

TWENTY-NINE

General George Schmidt sat back on the leather seat on-board Air Force One with a glass of bourbon in hand. He was an hour into the five-hour flight and his annoyance had still not abated.

Schmidt accepted a generous top-up from the steward, while contemplating how his day could have taken such an unexpected turn. One minute he was leaving his Pentagon Office to go home, the next he was called to the White House to attend a crazy live video stream. Soon after, the president had ordered him to board Air Force One to be her 'man on the ground' at the Kennedy Space Center.

He believed Protocol 84 was complete hogwash, and the new president was wasting everyone's time by sending him down to Kennedy.

That's what you get when you vote in a woman to do a man's job

After her recent election win, the president had kept him on as Chairman of the Joint Chiefs of Staff, so he had resisted the temptation to make his feelings clear before departure. He wanted to keep the prestigious post, although her entourage of advisors was already proving to be a pain in the ass.

Her policy advisor and her communications advisor looked no older than college kids and were the two who'd suggested the general be sent down to Florida to 'control the situation'. The kids believed what they wanted to see, and Schmidt was confident the footage was not what it seemed. Even the president had asked if it was 'a joke they play on all new Presidents' – yet she still took the idea of an alien threat seriously. The general knew there had to be another explanation. Seeing the excavator disappear had an eerie finality about it, but the grainy live feed was inconclusive, and they were relying too much on the word of the NASA guy – Goodhew.

Annoyingly, the Joint Chief of Space Operations, Seb Lewis, had vouched for Goodhew, his NASA crony. NASA had gained too much influence during the new global space race. The general preferred the days when it was Uncle Sam against the good old USSR. You knew where you were with the Soviets. Now every man and his dog were blasting off into space. Fast forward to 2025 and the United States of America was competing against the United Arab Emirates on Mars missions. Now that was a sick joke!

The general was mystified why the president had acted on the strength of NASA paranoia. Seb was nothing more than a glorified pilot. Sure, the guy was a decorated astronaut, but try asking him to fight Special Ops in Iraq or Afghanistan, and then see how brave he was.

What had Seb said to the president about Doctor Goodhew? – 'I can vouch for the doctor, he's solid.'

Solid? Cheers, Seb, you're the reason I'm flying to Mosquitoland.

The general drank his remaining whiskey but the alcohol was not helping. The whole situation was unnecessary, and the list of wrongs spun around his head. The live feed was unreliable, as was assuming the material could be alien, Madam President ordering him onto Air Force One, her staff of pimple-faced kids, having Space Ops as part of the Joint Chiefs of Staff, and Goodhew invoking an obscure protocol. More than anything, sending him, Chairman of the Joint Chiefs, down to Florida on a wild goose chase – it was all totally ridiculous.

He would deal with Goodhew on his arrival.

THIRTY

An hour after leaving the impact site, Goodhew was overseeing canisters of samples being offloaded from the mobile decontamination unit and into the space receiving laboratory at Kennedy Space Center.

Several reinforced glass tanks lined the main lab. Doors led off the main room to sub-rooms where other experiments were being set up. Goodhew also ordered areas in KSC's corrosion technology laboratory to be given over to the large team being assembled.

It was fortunate that one of his first tasks as Chief Scientist had been to oversee the OSIRIS-Rex team to ensure the safe touchdown of the sample return capsule in Utah in September 2023. The capsule contained samples taken on the Bennu asteroid. Samples had been taken to Johnson's state-of-the-art curation facility, built specifically to handle material from Bennu. The relations he forged with the experts at NASA's Astromaterials Research and Exploration Science division, known as ARES, would be important to him now.

Kennedy's ARES technicians were already in place, initialising the experiments set out by Goodhew and from biochemists seconded to explore the answers. The ARES team from Johnson would be arriving in the morning – he was going to need all the expertise he could muster.

Goodhew sat at his laptop in a side office, looking over the list of experiments lined up. For the time being the alien substance remained an unknown quantity.

It didn't help that General Schmidt had sent him a directive forbidding non-governmental help. For the time being, he would have to rely on NASA scientists to decode what he believed to be alien material. It meant missing out on brainpower from further afield, and he believed the general was more concerned with saving face than saving the planet.

The impact site was the doctor's primary concern. He would recommend a project to stop water flowing past the site. He hoped to contain the biological threat, though he realised the horse might have bolted where that idea was concerned – it was possible the alien substance had already been spread by water. Maps of the surrounding waterways told him that any floating material would already have spread beyond the point of containment. Like the substance he'd seen moving along the warehouse ramp, the potential horror they faced had been creeping up on him.

A new email prompt popped on his screen, signalling a message from General Schmidt. The general was due to arrive around dawn and was emailing from the air.

The email was a list of questions the general wanted answers for. The list contained nothing already covered in his own list of intended experiments. It was the final sentence of the email that Goodhew found worrying.

'I expect immediate answers on arrival.'

His heart sank further. How did the general think science worked? They would run experiments as quickly as possible, but each one would have a process requiring time to yield robust results. The demand was nonsense.

Goodhew considered his response for a moment before typing.

Subject: RE: My Arrival at KSC

Can confirm experiments already in progress.

It is now a priority to carry out the following:

o Containment of alien material at impact site is vital until we learn more about its infectiousness

o Suggest the stemming of water flow feeding the channel passing the impact site

148

o Recommend damming off and redirecting adjacent river and ringfencing the site. Ringfence materials recommendations to follow initial experiments

A quick answer is requested in relation to water-flow project.

Thanks,

Dr Nathan Goodhew

Chief Scientist, NASA

The doctor paused and reread his email before making two amendments. 'A quick answer' was deleted and replaced with 'An immediate answer'. Under cc. Goodhew typed in the email of the Head of Space Operations 'sebastian.lewis@nasa.gov' and hit send. If the general failed to respond to the request, he knew Seb would.

Satisfied, Goodhew called Lieutenant Izard. There was a long wait before Izard answered. Goodhew could tell the lieutenant was driving and asked, 'Lieutenant, are you not at the impact site?'

'The what?'

'Where you met me ... Dr Goodhew from NASA.'

'Yes, I know who you are, Doctor. I'm no longer there. I'm parking up at the sheriff's office in Melbourne.'

'Sheriff's office? I thought you were overseeing things at the site.'

'Not now. The army turned up to control the crime scene and the FBI is taking over the manhunt. I was told to situate myself here and help the FBI. Didn't you know?'

'No, I didn't. Where did your orders come from?'

'From my commander in Orlando.'

'Where did your commander get their orders from?'

'He got his orders from the FBI, I guess. My department is still out there though, with county cops, looking for the fugitives.'

Goodhew thanked Izard and placed his cellular on the desk. A dark thought had crept up on him during the call. Everyone attending the impact site should have been brought into the clean rooms at Kennedy for examination and potential decontamination. He admonished himself for not considering that earlier. Allowing Izard and others who had been very close to the impact site to continue as normal was a mistake. There had also been a serious breakdown in communications he needed to bridge. How could he contain a situation when so many other people were now involved, and he had no idea who was controlling what?

Everyone who had attended the site before the cordon was set up needed to be rounded up and brought to KSC, as did anyone they'd been in contact with. It was night, so he prayed that list would be limited. Should he be calling in the World Health Organisation? There were so many things the doctor felt he should be doing but hadn't yet. His mind was in a spin.

He needed to share the load and would start by appointing a clean-up project leader from his team at NASA. They could start with bringing in Lieutenant Izard and work out from there. Izard's star status had been short-lived, relinquishing control of the exclusion operation only a few hours after being handed responsibility. Goodhew knew it was the right move and understood the need to use the military to keep the area secure.

He believed things might quickly spiral out of control and needed Izard's military replacement to talk to his clean-up leader. There was no time to lose.

THIRTY-ONE

Sarah was lost for words because Damian seemed extremely calm. 'Mason not with you?' he said. She could see bloodstains down his shirt and trousers.

'No, I think he's cleared off,' Noah said.

'Has he now?' Damian said, raising an eyebrow.

'Yes, I knew we couldn't trust him,' Noah replied.

Sarah tried to recompose herself. A few minutes earlier they'd been listening to screams coming from the room Damian was now blocking. 'What's just happened in there? We heard screaming.'

To her surprise Damian stood back from the door, inviting them in. 'Be my guest,' he said.

Sarah edged cautiously into the room, followed by Noah, who was eyeing Damian. The sight that met them confirmed her worst fears. A woman lay on the bed, her head to one side. Her features were contorted, revealing the agony of her final death throes. The bed was soaked in blood. Not just a little – the white sheets had turned crimson. A pillow had been placed over the woman's middle parts, blocking the view to what appeared to be the epicentre blood flow.

'God, Damian. What did you do, stab her?'

Damian pondered; his answer seemed detached. 'Yes, you might say that, but not quite how you'd imagine.'

His aloofness was unnerving. It felt like she was talking to someone else. 'Why, Damian? What made you do this? I don't understand.'

He turned from the bed to look at her. 'I didn't know what I was doing, Sarah. It was a complete accident.' He looked from her back to the bed, his manner changing, imploring. 'Something's happened to me. Something bad. That thing in the warehouse. It's infected me.' He lifted the side of his shirt to reveal a myriad earthen hues underneath. 'Parts of me aren't human any more.'

To her surprise, Damian broke down in tears, shaking. He looked overwhelmed, struggling to find the right words. 'I'm changing into … a thing. A freak. Look what I've become, Sarah. Look at me! I've turned into a monster.'

Sarah looked back at him, shaking her head. 'No, Damian, you were always a monster.'

The words had been uttered without an edge of anger as she looked at the man she once loved. He was shaking, his face looking ravaged and sallow. His eyes were the only part of Damian that seemed unaffected by his recent physical metamorphosis, and they looked out at her pleadingly. 'You have no idea what I've been through,' he said.

'We do, Damian, we saw what happened in the warehouse.'

'No, not that. You have no idea. He used to beat me, stub cigarettes out on me, for fuck's sake. He hurt me, Sarah. Really hurt me.'

'Who did those things to you? Who hurt you?'

Damian raised a shaking hand, outstretched, towards his girlfriend. 'I do love you, Sarah. You know that, don't you?'

'Then let me help you, Damian,' she faltered. 'We can find help for you. I'm sure we can. There must be a doctor or something.' She looked towards Noah for his affirmation to help, but he was shaking his head at her, looking incredulous.

'This is all very nice, but we need to get out of here. That screaming. The police will be here any minute,' Noah said.

Sarah took a small step towards Damian.

'No! Sarah, don't touch him! He'll infect you too.'

Damian turned to Noah; his voice sounded distant. 'Noah. My trusty friend. The boy I took under my wing. The boy I saved by paying off his debts.'

Noah looked puzzled.

'What do you mean?' he asked.

'Yes, you didn't know about that, did you? I squared things in Chicago. I paid your debts. I bought your freedom.'

'I had no idea, Damian. I hoped they'd given up looking for me. I—'

'People like that never stop looking, Noah. Never.'

The three stood in exhausted silence. Noah chewed down on his bottom lip, like he was trying to comprehend Damian's revelation.

Damian spoke first. 'So, Noah, the boy who thinks he's a man. What's your grand plan, heh? Tell me.' He lurched forward and grabbed Sarah's wrist. She wriggled, but his grip was extraordinarily strong. She grimaced in pain and submitted. 'Planning to drive off into the sunset with this one, are you?'

Sarah saw a flush of colour rise on Noah's cheeks. It seemed to confirm Damian's suspicions. 'Don't think I haven't noticed the way you look at her. Don't think I haven't noticed the way you act around her, and don't think I haven't noticed the way she looks at you. Yes, you, Sarah, you! I've tolerated it for far too long. You've both made a fool of me.' Damian's grip tightened further, forcing Sarah to her knees. 'Maybe it's better if neither of us have her.' His gaze was locked on Noah.

'It doesn't have to be like this,' Noah said. 'Don't get me wrong. I'm grateful for your help, but this, it's fucked up, man. Stop.'

'I gave you both everything. Everything! At great personal risk where you're concerned.' Damian sneered at Noah. 'For what? Answer me … So you could run off together?'

Damian pulled Sarah's hair back so that she had to look up at his face. At closer quarters she saw a greenish tinge of veins running down his neck and a strange, matted texture down the left side of his face. There were tiny, barely visible perforations on the side of his nose. He lowered his face, his mouth barely an inch away from her lips as he whispered, 'It's been one hell of a journey, Sarah Mitchell. I'm afraid it ends here.' His free hand went to her throat and squeezed.

153

Sarah stared up at him helplessly, trying to catch her breath. She pulled on the hands holding her throat, but they were immovable. Her sight blurred as dizziness took hold. She felt strength leaving her and loosened her grip from the hands choking her. Life was draining away and there was nothing she could do to stop it.

A muffled crack of gunfire sounded somewhere in her consciousness, a pause, followed by two more in quick succession. Sarah felt like she was hearing sounds underwater as something vaguely thudded to the floor next to her. She became aware the tension on her throat had gone, air finding its way back to her lungs as she gasped short, panicked breaths.

Someone was grabbing her hand, helping her stand up. She felt her chest pounding, recovering enough to respond. As her vision cleared, Noah's face came into focus, looking into her eyes with concern. He led her to the motel room door then stopped. She leaned on the door frame as he ran back inside, opened the wardrobe and searched inside it.

'Where is it?' Noah said. He edged past Damian's legs to look under the far side of the bed. He pulled out Damian's black holdall, tiptoed gingerly around the body and laid the bag on the bed's unbloodied near corner. He unzipped it and looked inside. 'Ha! I knew it.' Noah put the gun in the bag and zipped it up again, casting a nervous glance towards Damian.

She tried to keep up as he ran to the car. Noah looked back as if expecting to see Damian, then he unlocked the car and opened the passenger door for her. He ran to the other side, slung the holdall onto the back seat and sat down in the driver's seat, shaking visibly, fumbling with the key.

The engine stuttered but did not engage.

'Please start!' he said as again he looked across the parking lot. His behaviour put her on edge. She had heard three shots but had no idea how many hit their target. 'I thought you killed him?' she said.

'I did,' he replied.

'Then calm down. This isn't one of Mason's movies.' She

154

looked across the lot. There was no Damian lurching his way across – no grizzly half-human maniac hammering on the car window.

'Was that Damian's Glock?'

'Yes. I saw him reload it on the way here and hide it by his bed.'

'Thanks,' she said. 'I mean it.'

Noah turned the key again. There was a moment's silence before the engine sprang to life. He reversed quickly, throwing up gravel and dust. The car thudded into something and he slammed on the brakes. 'What was that?' he shrieked.

'You've reversed into something,' she said.

There was no other sound, so he released the brake and reversed further. Something was dragging on the underside of the car, flapping against the axle noisily.

Looking in the side mirror Sarah saw what he'd reversed over a small pile of empty cardboard boxes left to one side of the garbage. He laughed manically, engaging drive. 'Boxes, only boxes. Would you believe it?' Noah grinned at his passenger, but she was looking beyond him.

Noah must have seen the fear in her eyes because he put his foot to the floor. Wheels spun, tyres threw grit into the air as the station wagon accelerated.

Damian slammed against the side of the car, splintering glass over Noah. His hand swiped at Noah's face as the Volvo gained traction on the loose surface. The car quickly reached the parking lot exit, and Sarah looked up at the rear-view mirror expecting to see Damian on the ground, but he had disappeared.

Surely not. He couldn't have managed to hold on to the car, could he?

Noah must have been thinking the same because he also looked at the shattered window to his left. A bloodied hand was clinging on to the window's framework, a shard of glass sticking through the punctured skin. Noah screamed, and she screamed too.

The lacerated hand tensed as the other hand grabbed the

door frame. Sinuous arms pulled hard, hauling Damian's body weight up until his face appeared at the window. The face was the manifestation of pure anger, his eyes drilling into Noah's, their faces only inches apart.

Damian looked like retribution in waiting, letting out a howl of absolute rage. Somehow Damian released one of his hands and clawed at Noah's face, scratching him.

Sarah screamed again, clambering across Noah as the Volvo picked up speed on the highway. She removed a shoe from her foot and smashed its heel into Damian's fingers. 'You – fuck – off.' The emphasis of each word coincided with the strike of the heel, which made for an effective weapon because Damian was gone.

She heard the thud and looked back. Damian's body rolled on the road. He must have clung on to the car for close to a hundred yards. How was that possible? *What had Damian become?*

It was ten minutes before she could allow herself to believe they had shaken the demon – that Damian was not going to reappear around the bend or in the side mirror. Noah turned off the main road and onto backroads leading inland.

As Noah drove on into the night, she knew the police would be close.

They needed a new plan.

THIRTY-TWO

Aboard Air Force One General Schmidt only napped briefly and was tired, although his anger had subsided. The journey was allowing him time to think. He considered the substance engulfing things in Florida could be a foreign manufactured bio-chemical threat. He needed to take charge and ensure it was kept in check. And then he could discover its secrets and harness it for the United States military.

He did not want civvies controlling the scene's security cordon. The situation required speed, which meant enlisting the nearest military base for help. For expediency, he contacted the brigadier general in charge of the 45th Space Wing headquartered at Patrick Space Force Base across the Banana River from the Kennedy Space Center. Despite being woken up in the dead of night, the man had been battle ready. His team was at Schmidt's disposal and, within thirty minutes, a 45 SW colonel was in position at the impact site. The police had been told to stand down at Lake Winder, although the colonel would leave them to brief the FBI on their arrival in Melbourne.

As an army man, Schmidt considered the irony of deploying the 45th Space Wing, assigned to Space Operations Command, to control the area Goodhew was describing on emails as 'the impact site'. He was truly living in a new age where the United States Air Force had a prized Space Wing. The wing also controlled the Cape Canaveral Space Force Station and knew how to protect large areas of sensitive land.

The general discussed the situation with the colonel and was surprised to learn that 45 SW had trained for containment contingencies involving unknown biohazards. They agreed the operation was to be conducted on a need-to-know basis. Only those he trusted would know the full story and that did not mean the president's entourage in DC.

The Space Wing colonel had called back to report the media had already descended on the impact site. The genie was out of the bottle, it seemed, with speculation on social media including words like 'aliens', 'UFO crash' and 'Roswell'. Reporters were being kept outside a wide exclusion zone which the colonel had already extended to air space. Media helicopters buzzed around the area until the colonel imposed a ten-mile no-fly zone for non-military aircraft. The general quickly warmed to the Air Force man. He was efficient.

The president's communications advisor was soon on the line. The White House press office was being bombarded with enquiries about the situation and she wanted to know what the deal was with a no-fly zone. The general had bigger fish to fry and told her there had been no attempt to justify the unusual measure. The advisor seemed relieved, agreeing that a temporary news blackout was for the best. 'Any excuses would only fuel media speculation until we know what we are dealing with,' she said.

The general's staff on Air Force One showed him lurid stories of aliens eating police officers appearing on social media. In a world of mobile technology, some officers must have leaked what they heard from fellow officers to family and friends. Like the substance itself, it was spreading out from the site. In a matter of hours, rumours had circulated worldwide.

A deluge of emails arrived from the president's obsequious communications advisor. The general disliked the entitled Harvard graduate; she was too visible for his liking whenever he visited the West Wing. He'd had to fight for his opportunities in life – literally fight in some cases.

He skimmed the advisor's latest long email to get to the punchline. There it was, at the end of her missive. In her opinion, the difficulty of rebutting the truth about the impact site meant they were to maintain a news blackout. There would be no fake holding positions, because they always came back to bite. She preferred not to add fuel to an 'already blazing inferno of social media speculation'. *Isn't that what we already agreed on the phone?*

General Schmidt looked at his watch. The journey was dragging on, but it allowed him valuable thinking time. He reconsidered the live feed from earlier that night. There had to be an explanation other than Goodhew's theory that the threat was alien. The doctor was held in high regard at NASA and in Washington.

The Chief of Staff for Space Operations, Seb Lewis, had informed him Goodhew was in charge of putting military satellites into orbit. Yet, with all that expertise, the doctor instigated what the general believed was a defunct protocol. At best, he considered Protocol 84 too obscure to carry any policy weight. Why would such an intelligent man do that? Schmidt opened his laptop and looked up Goodhew's profile on the NASA site.

There he was, Doctor Nathan Goodhew, NASA's Chief Scientist, smiling shyly at the lens in his publicity shot. He had been the scientific lead on several space missions. He was also involved in the hallowed Mars space missions. The successful Perseverance Rover space mission launched in July 2020 had paved the way for further missions to the red planet. The general was well aware that the United States aimed to beat China and the UAE to Mars to claim its newly discovered mining riches. He also controlled the latest lunar landings in competition with Russia and China's new base on the dark side of the moon. It seemed Goodhew was a rock. Dependable. And yet he believed in little green men from outer space.

What if it was true? What if the material was alien? *No, surely not.* The general tried to dismiss the notion, but the possibilities started to intrigue him.

Among the conspiracy theories surrounding Covid, the most popular was the Chinese created the virus in a lab and then held back on the vaccine they invented. The United States had developed its own vaccine and it had taken most of 2021 to vaccinate the population. The general agreed with much of the thinking and the siege mentality prevalent in the States was a narrative he had sympathy with. Anything that gave the United States an advantage was welcome. What if something extraordinary had literally fallen on their laps from the sky?

Stretching to close the lid of his laptop, he saw an email ping in from the president's office, subject, 'EO Number 14,595'.

The email outlined an executive order to commence an engineering project at the impact site. The aim – 'to stem the spread of the infestation'. The flow of water to the channel passing the warehouse was to be dammed and redirected. The order also gave the green light for the construction of a barrier around the disaster area. The president was calling the defence her 'ring of steel'. The word 'alien' was not mentioned anywhere, he noticed.

The email contained three separate PDFs expanding on the factual nature of the EO. They were entitled 'FEMA and Military Logistics', 'Background Context' and the third one was headed 'Communications'.

The FEMA PDF explained that US army engineers had been called up and were being flown in. The Administrator of the Federal Emergency Management Agency was a cc. on the email. Instead of reporting to the US Department of Homeland Security, he would have a direct link to the president. The general knew reporting directly to the president's office was expected during periods of disaster response.

It seemed FEMA had been busy. Steel structures had been sourced from a huge engineering project in Georgia and were already being prepared for transportation south, pending confirmation from Dr Goodhew that the unknown material would not penetrate a steel barrier.

At the same time, drilling rigs were being requisitioned from oil companies working in the Gulf of Mexico. The email outlined Doctor Goodhew's suggestion to take deep samples from the ground to verify the extent of any spread.

The general clicked on the PDF marked 'Background Context'.

The short document outlined the premise that the risk of holding back and doing nothing was greater than spending federal money and later realising such measures had been an overreaction. The American economy could not withstand another lockdown or another one and a quarter million pandemic deaths in the face of an unknown public health threat.

The background document also cited Dr Nathan Goodhew as the source of the intelligence on the threat and went into detail about what he'd reported. Wow, the president certainly knew how to cover her back, he thought. The president had positioned Goodhew as the patsy, should she have to justify the federal expenditure at a later date. The general wondered how Goodhew would react when he read the email and determined he would be careful not to set himself up to be thrown under a bus later.

A soft glow of sunlight appeared over the ocean on the horizon. The first faint light of dawn was always a sight to behold, which was why he preferred the port side of an aircraft when flying south as night turned into day. The captain of Air Force One announced their position and the expected weather in Florida. The general had left temperatures similar to the interior of a refrigerator in Washington, but it was going to be touching on ninety-two in Florida, unseasonably hot for the first day of March. *Global warming.* They would be starting their descent into Kennedy shortly.

Schmidt clicked on the PDF marked 'Communications'. The White House document confirmed that a media feeding frenzy was underway. The news outlets had realised something substantial was happening down in Florida, big enough for the news-hungry celebrity presenters to feed off. The PDF was signed by the communications advisor, repeating much of what he'd read on her emails. She advised access to the disaster epicentre was to be strictly limited. No more than a dozen key personnel could

161

be permitted within two hundred yards of the warehouse. The general smiled. He was one step ahead, having put similar measures in place with the help of his Space Force colonel.

A huge invasion of army engineers, scientists, and soldiers was on its way to Brevard County, Florida, and he was the man overseeing the whole operation. The situation suddenly felt much bigger than the July 2024 ops he'd directed in Africa against the Chinese-backed insurgents. Maybe the trip would be far more interesting than he'd first imagined.

He settled back to watch the strengthening glow in the east.

THIRTY-THREE

FBI Executive Assistant Director Walker received the call to curtail his scheduled week at the Charlotte field office on Microsoft Way slightly before 3.00 a.m. He packed, checked out of his hotel, and made the journey – walking into the Melbourne Sheriff's Office on 1515 Sarno Road just before dawn.

His brief was sketchy, and he'd used the ninety-minute flight time to talk to both Orlando Police Department's Lieutenant Izard and Brevard County's Sheriff Wiles to acquaint himself with the situation on the ground. On touching down at Orlando Melbourne International Airport, a car had greeted him at the steps of the FBI-owned Gulfstream V and driven him the mere thousand yards north to the sheriff's office in Melbourne.

After talking about the local geography with Sheriff Wiles, Walker accepted the offer to set up operations at the sheriff's Melbourne office. It was a question of convenience. The FBI's Tampa, Jacksonville and Miami field offices were too far away from the epicentre of the situation. While the Tampa office served Brevard, its satellite office in Melbourne was too small for the scale of operation under way and its resident agents would join him at the sheriff's office.

The physical geography of Florida presented other problems. Walker was going to need all the resources at his disposal to track down any potential fugitives, including the Brevard County Sheriff's Office, the Fish and Wildlife Commission, the Orlando PD and the Melbourne PD. Heads from each force had been notified to join him.

The Chairman of the Joint Chief of Staff, General Schmidt, was on his way to coordinate military interventions. The situation was unprecedented, and Walker was unsure what to expect.

Sheriff Wiles had come down from the county seat of Titusville and was already there to greet and show him around. Desks had been cleared in the main office and Wiles introduced him to his new team. He explained that three of their fellow deputies had been killed and that a sergeant had been seriously injured in the earlier shootings – he was still in a coma. Accounts suggested Sergeant Conti held the key to what really happened at the crime scene. It was unfortunate he was unable to talk. 'I need to know as soon as he comes round,' Walker told the sheriff.

The commander of the Melbourne Police Department, located around the corner from the Sheriff's Melbourne office, joined them. At first the commander seemed more interested in a petty squabble over the jurisdiction of the manhunt. He expressed concern that the sheriff's deputies had set up roadblocks the previous day within his city limits. He also questioned the presence of Lieutenant Izard from Orlando PD operating out of his jurisdiction. The minor irritation did not concern Walker; federal agencies always trumped state, county and city. All local law enforcement was gathered to help the FBI. Whatever had gone on before no longer mattered. His team would show them how to conduct a manhunt.

Satisfied he'd enough of a picture to create a search strategy, Walker quickly converted the office into an incident room, with intelligence streaming in. The only piece of the jigsaw missing was the science behind what had happened at the gang's warehouse. The building could not be accessed. General Schmidt had explained on their earlier jet-to-jet conversation the Chief Scientist of NASA was involved and had barred access to the warehouse.

It was safer to assume the gang had escaped the building. The absence of an airboat at the scene made the escape scenario all the more likely.

Walker understood he was the first outside of the White House and Dr Goodhew's team to know the whole story. The capture of escaped fugitives exposed to a deadly unidentified substance added a new dimension to the manhunt. Dealing with deadly substances was more the territory of CIA spooks, so he would have to lean on Dr Goodhew for advice. He would talk to Goodhew as soon as possible.

The challenge of capturing the gang without exposing more people to the risk of contact was paramount. It meant making it clear to his own staff and local police that there was a threat of contagion. Walker pondered the problem and realised he'd have to issue instructions without revealing that the fugitives could be infected with a Chinese or Russian biological weapon, which seemed to be General Schmidt's belief. He certainly was not going to repeat the line being taken by NASA – that the contagion might be alien. Walker knew he'd be laughed out of the office by his team.

He would put out instructions saying just enough to make officers wary of close contact with the gang, and not enough to raise suspicions or cause panic.

With so many local officers enlisted on the hunt, experience told Walker details would leak out. People and media outlets illegally monitored police radio airways. Despite warnings, some officers would be careless using social media. They already had. It would be impossible to contain rumours, and stories of captured 'snake aliens' had already appeared on Facebook, Twitter and TikTok.

Walker aimed to dilute rumours to something less problematic than a spreading contagion that could devour people. If officers wanted to believe there was a flu epidemic or a new Covid variant, that was preferable to the reported truth for the time being. The government's comms team was engaged in creating rumours of a serious chemical leak.

Walker's team in Washington were at work trying to learn the identities of the gang. Without forensics from the warehouse or car plates, the starting point had been unravelling ownership of the building. Izard was investigating that line of enquiry, but not yet established a link to anyone. The warehouse was held in the name of a defunct Titusville-based business called Brevard Swamp Tours.

Brevard Swamp Tours had been registered at a non-existent address. Walker was handed a sheet by one of his special agents, detailing the findings.

'Talk me through it,' Walker said.

'Sir, the County Recorder's Office shows the property was built by Mormons last century. They sold it to Industria Estates, based in Miami, back in 1974. Industria Estates looks legit. They buy up bits of strategically situated property on the cheap in places they believe will be developed – new airport extensions, new shopping malls or coastal resorts. Some win and some lose, but they make serious money selling on land to developers when they win.'

'Was this one a win?' Walker asked.

'No, the opposite, sir. If they speculated on some kind of new waterway, water treatment plant, residential properties or holiday resort being built, it never happened. What we do know is that they sold the property at a loss to Brevard Swamp Tours in a cash transaction in 2018.'

'What happened to Swamp Tours? You said they are defunct.'

'The company wound up voluntarily, with no debts. Their assets were sold for a nominal fee to a Bermuda-based trust fund, which has owned the warehouse ever since. And the trust has bought other properties too, although for much bigger sums.'

'Sounds like a front to launder money – buying properties through trusts. Who's behind the trust?'

'The trust was set up in Bermuda to keep ownership hidden. We don't know yet, sir, but one coincidence stands out,' the agent said.

Walker smiled at his agent. 'Go on.'

'Records show the voluntary liquidation of Brevard Swamp Tours was handled by the same accountant whose name is on the transfer tax declaration on behalf of the offshore trust buying the warehouse. We've traced internet activity from the accountant to an offshore bank in Bermuda. It's very likely that the bank holds the account of the Bermudan registered trust.'

'So, this accountant is the one who set up the trust and its bank account?'

'Yes, metadata shows the accountant has emailed the bank on a few occasions, although the content of those mails was encrypted. He also made a visit to the island on the date both the trust and bank accounts were set up. And on later dates too.'

'We have flight records confirming that?'

'No, he travels by chartering a boat. Quite a long journey – three or four days, I think. He must pay for the boat by cash as his accounts show no financial records for the journeys. But there are records of his arrival with border control in Bermuda and those records state the method of entry into the country. Always by the same boat, owned by Key Charters. The boat is moored at Key Charters' marina down the coast in Jupiter.'

'Interesting that he chose not to fly. Easier to take cash in on a boat than through airport security checks. Money laundering seems likely. Odds on it's connected to the gang who fled the warehouse. So, where is this accountant? Find him and he'll lead us to the gang.'

The agent returned Walker's smile. 'The accountant is local. Very local. His office is walkable from here. This is him and his wife, taken from her Facebook account. And we have an address for his house. Less than an hour away down on Vero Beach. I have a real estate photo of his beachfront home. Look.' The agent offered over a printout picture of the huge gated property.

'And they say crime doesn't pay. Let's get there.'

'I took the liberty. We have agents on the way now, sir. We know from telemetrics that his car is there, so we assume he is in. We just need your permission.'

Walker was impressed by the local agent. 'That's excellent work. Excellent. I want a surveillance team watching

Key Charters straight away. The fugitives need a route out so it's likely they will reach out to known contacts to escape. Alert the Coast Guard too. Have them detain any boat owned by Key Charters. The gang will want to access their accounts in Bermuda, so notify our people to be on standby there. As for the accountant, bring him in and we'll find out how deeply he's involved, and who he's working for.'

THIRTY-FOUR

Noah's winding route took them south-west out of Palm Beach and into Hendry County. Sarah emphasised the need for caution, and he promised to keep them away from populated centres.

Trying to avoid main roads, he'd driven down dirt tracks, hit dead ends and had to double back a few times. He'd never explored the depths of Florida before and found the small roads daunting. They cut through vast swathes of ranches laid out like a patchwork quilt, and then into a Wildlife Management Area.

The staccato route stretched out his perception of time. He had been driving for what seemed like hours, except the dash clock insisted it had only been two.

Noah kept glancing at Sarah and each time she was just staring ahead into space. He thought she looked sad. In contrast to how she looked, he was experiencing an adrenaline-fuelled release. Like his best laps on the track, he had been pushing to the limit. Thoughts shot through his head like the messages on advertising hoardings whizzing past at the circuit.

Why should he feel guilty about leaving Damian on the road? The man was a monster who would be captured and locked up. Noah hoped Damian was dead. With his mentor out of the way, the dream of being with Sarah would come true.

Thoughts of a new life circled his mind. Damian's revelation that Noah no longer had enemies in Chicago meant he could start a new life with the money in the holdall. All these thoughts connected back to one thing – his desire for the woman sitting to his right.

He glanced at her again. Exhaustion had taken over and she was sleeping restlessly. He slowed the car and watched her pupils move under closed eyelids. Little sighs permeated her slumber. She looked sexy and he fantasised about waking up next to her, stroking her body.

He would look after her. She needed him.

As if reading his mind, she stirred, her eyes flickering open, squinting against the first rays of dawn. She yawned, brushing strands of hair away from her face.

God damn, she looked so cute.

'Morning, Sarah. Got some sleep in there?' he said.

She looked at him a while, taking in their surroundings. She touched the area under her left ear and on her windpipe. It looked sore.

Wilderness and water seemed to surround them, and Noah felt proud to have picked his way through so many unmarked tracks.

'How long have I been out?' she asked.

'Not long,' he replied.

'Where are we?'

'We ducked under I-75, just north of the Cypress National Preserve,' he said, 'heading south.'

'Heading south, where?'

'Shark Point.'

'Shark Point? You are kidding?'

'No, not kidding,' said Noah. 'I saw it on a travel show. It's the most remote spot you can get. We'll be safe there.'

'Yes, I know, I used to work in tourism. Good plan, except that they only have a couple of platforms and those get booked up months in advance.'

'Platforms?'

'Literally platforms at sea to camp out on. Plus, I'm not sure you can get down there without hitting major roads. They'll be watched.'

'Oh.'

Noah had been running the GPS on silent as a rough guide, following his own route to keep them in remote areas. Now he was lost but was not going to admit that to Sarah. He pressed a button and traced the forward direction. Sarah was right; it looked like he'd have to risk main roads and head back east again to get to Shark Point, though he suspected there would be more tracks, like the one they were on, not shown on the display.

'Damn,' he mouthed under his breath.

'That GPS,' she said, 'it's not on live Wi-Fi is it?'

'Wi-Fi? No.'

'You sure?'

'Of course I'm sure. It runs off a disk. This car doesn't have Wi-Fi.'

'Good, though I don't know if car Wi-Fi is trackable anyway. I just think we should play safe.' Sarah said. 'The west coast is good. But we can hide out without booking or heading as far down as Shark Point. I mean, that place is in the middle of the ocean. You need a boat transfer. And we'd need all the camping equipment. You thought about that?'

Noah fell silent, his bubble of euphoria burst. He felt resentful, hating the way she treated him like a child.

'OK then, since you're the expert, you choose somewhere.'

Sarah fell silent and he watched her ponder a while.

'Is your phone still off, Noah?' she asked eventually.

'Yes. Why?'

'Just checking. You know you can't turn it on. The police will be looking for our signals. In fact, best we dump them.'

He looked at her warily. All his contacts were on his phone. 'I'm not dumping my cellular,' he said, voicing his thoughts.

'You are, and I'm getting rid of mine too. You sure you've not turned it on? Not even for a minute?' she asked again.

'Yes, yes. I promise. I did like you said. I haven't touched it.'

'Where is it then?' she asked.

He pursed his lips and shook his head to hold back on the anger he felt welling up. 'Wow, man, what the hell's wrong with you? I told you, didn't I? I haven't touched my cell. It's right here, in my pocket. Switched off.' He fished it out and tossed it petulantly across the car. It bounced off the door and landed on her lap. 'Check if you don't believe me.'

Sarah fell silent once more and he hoped she felt bad about the way she was treating him. She turned to him and said in a softer tone, 'OK, Noah, I just needed to be sure. The police will be all over us by now. They must be. What with, well, everything.'

Noah deliberately fixed his gaze on the road. He was not going to be nice to her while she spoke to him like he was an idiot. His knuckles showed white as he gripped tightly, transferring his mood to the steering wheel.

They hit another dead end with water ahead and on both sides.

'Fuck!' he shouted. He slammed the car in reverse and spun it around as only a racing driver could. It was a cool move and, despite himself, he glanced sideways for approval. Sarah gave no reaction to boost his frayed ego. Once again, awkward silence took over.

Finally, Sarah let out a big sigh and spoke. 'I've been thinking about this. They'll have found Damian's body. They'll know what car we're in and most likely who we are. They'll have our details, cells, bank cards. Everything.'

He could tell she was looking at him for a response, so he continued staring at the road ahead, unable to work out what she was thinking.

'You've done well,' she said at last. 'Continue to keep the car off highways and we'll follow your plan.'

'My plan?' He adjusted his grip on the steering wheel and glanced at her.

'Yes, though instead of Shark Point, we'll head a bit further north. There are campsites with small lodges we can stay in,' she said, glancing at the bag on the back seat. 'We can pay cash, hide the car and buy some time. I might even know a site that's deserted, if it's not been bought up by anyone. We'll head there.'

Noah felt the dark cloud lifting. 'Yes, let's do that,' he said.

'I've also been wondering about Damian's plan. I think he was intending to get us to a boat this morning. I think he was planning to take us offshore. Maybe the Bahamas? Or Bermuda? Maybe we should do the same,' she said.

'I'm not sure. I used to go to the Bahamas on holiday with my parents. It's not a big place. Everyone knows everyone. And money won't go far there. It's not cheap.'

Sarah gave him a surprised look. 'Good point,' she said.

'We'll stand out on either of those islands,' he confirmed and thought about what Sarah had just said. *Of course.* Why had he not realised earlier? 'I know where Damian was going to take us this morning,' he said. 'I've driven him there.'

Sarah looked stunned. 'Where?' she asked.

'I've driven to and collected him from a marina in Jupiter a couple of times, but I've forgotten its name,' he said.

'OK, maybe we avoid the whole Caribbean thing. Too close to home and they have extradition. From the west we can get across the Gulf of Mexico and up to Texas or Louisiana.'

Now he was surprised. 'Really? You can get there by boat?'

'Yes, for sure.' Sarah laughed. 'The Gulf of Mexico touches a few of the Southern States. We could sail all the way into New Orleans if you wanted.'

'Cool.' He spun the idea around in his head. 'Let's do that. We can fit in there. Start again.'

'Exactly. We have the money to buy new IDs, disappear and start again.'

'Start again ...' Noah repeated.

The sun had fully risen behind them, to the east. The dawn of a fresh day took on new significance. He was free from any obligations and felt a renewed confidence. He had no debt in Chicago, he had his ex-boss's money, and he had his girl. New hope filled his heart.

The words 'start again' buzzed around his head like a cool aphrodisiac. He realised that he was driving with an erection.

THIRTY-FIVE

In the sheriff's office interview room, the accountant shifted under the gaze of Walker. 'They've told me who you are and I'm not answering any questions until my lawyer arrives,' he said.

'That won't be happening,' Walker said with a deliberately nonchalant air.

'I know my constitutional rights.'

Walker eyed up the accountant. He knew from his file sheet that the guy was fifty-two, except he looked over sixty – sallow-skinned, overweight and sweating profusely. Too much money and poor lifestyle choices, Walker thought. He took an instant dislike to the self-indulgent crook.

'Sixth Amendment's guarantee of counsel is not applicable in your case,' Walker informed him.

'And why not?' asked the man, who was looking greyer by the minute.

Walker slid over a document. The accountant looked at it but seemed confused. 'What is this?' he said.

'This document sets out to enable police assistance to meet an ongoing emergency. In your case its practical application is a rogation of your Sixth Amendment Rights. It's signed by the president.'

'Rogation? What do you mean?'

'Curtailment, I suppose. It withholds those rights.'

'It can't do that. Can it?' The accountant was sounding less sure of himself and Walker smiled back.

'Yes, it can. The National Emergencies Act of 1976 allows the president emergency powers.'

'What emergency?'

'I'm not at liberty to say because this is a matter of national security and that trumps your rights to a lawyer. Now, let's get down to business.'

The accountant stared blankly at the document. It was a printed copy of a scan, with the new president's name at the bottom, under the signature, in clear letters.

'Is this real?' the accountant asked, his voice faltering.

'Yes, it's real. I'm not in the business of faking documents. That's what you do. Let's make this quick. For everyone's sake, including your own. I only have a few questions.' Walker slid a photo of a battered old warehouse across the table. 'Firstly, tell us about this building. Who uses it?'

The accountant blinked, looked at the image and laughed. 'I get involved in many property purchases. You don't expect me to know them all by sight?'

'A purchase, you say? I didn't mention anything about a purchase. Think harder,' Walker said, leaning in, 'time is pressing.'

'Well, transactions then,' the accountant said, looking at the photo. 'No, I don't recall this one.'

'It's a building paid for in cash, through a trust you set up.'

The accountant looked up but said nothing.

'This is your signature on the trust documents – a big mistake when that trust is involved in money laundering. We linked the trust to offshore bank accounts in Bermuda, and these are the dates and amounts of cash deposited into those bank accounts.'

Again, Walker slid paperwork over the desk.

'These are the HM Immigration, Customs and Health Clearance documents you signed on entry at St George's Harbour, Bermuda. Each one marries up with the time periods cash was deposited. Always arriving on the same boat out of Jupiter. This one.'

Walker slid over a picture printed from Key Charters' website. It showed a very large pleasure craft, the one he knew the accountant had taken to Bermuda on nine separate occasions.

The accountant eyed the accumulation of copied documents, but left them on the desk, untouched.

'What can I say? I like Bermuda. I go there often. I never visit banks though.'

'No, you deposit the cash by proxy, using a resident, Adam Brooks,' Walker said, playing his trump card, sliding across a surveillance image of Mr Brooks standing in front of a teller desk in one of the banks.

The accountant looked up at Walker incredulously.

'You want to know how we did this, don't you?'

Walker was not going to satisfy the slime ball opposite with an explanation. Finding the intermediary had actually been fairly easy. Not many people would visit three different banks the trust held accounts with on the same day the accountant happened to visit the island. His agents had filtered down to just one common face on the banks' security cameras and used a little facial recognition software to identify that person. It was the speed his agents conducted the work that Walker found the most impressive.

'I have no connection with this man,' the accountant said, recovering his composure.

Walker laughed and looked across at the agent standing by the door, who shook his head.

'Enough, now. You studied accountancy and finance at university with this man, Brooks. We will soon uncover any communications between the two of you.' Walker pushed the photo a little closer to the accountant. 'We will have him in custody on the island soon.'

The accountant tried to hide behind the veneer of professional decency. He maintained that there had been nothing illegal in setting up offshore trusts. He had been acting under instructions from his client to purchase the warehouse as tax efficiently as possible.

Walker knew there was no time to wait for his fellow agents to entice Brooks to corroborate the evidence. Nor was he going to have a philosophical debate on the niceties of smuggling large sums of untaxed cash out of the United States of America into Bermudan accounts to pay off loans taken from the same banks to buy property back on the mainland. He needed a name, fast, which meant speeding up his usual questioning techniques. He would have to resort to threats and bargaining. For expedience Walker decided to offer a deal, something he generally preferred not to do.

He stood up and walked to the one-way mirrored window. He faced the window with his back turned to the accountant, an old ploy he liked using to make the detainee wonder who might be standing the other side of the glass, and what power they might yield. After a few seconds Walker turned around, his expression deliberately monotone and almost weary.

'We are not interested in you and your petty frauds,' he began, 'but understand this. The maximum penalty for a violation of 18 USC section 1956 is imprisonment for twenty years and a fine of $500,000. Or twice the value of the properties involved in money laundering transactions, whichever is greater. And believe me when I tell you, unless you cooperate, we will make sure you get the full twenty. And that lovely wife of yours, I don't think she'd thank you if we seized your assets and made her and your son homeless?'

Walker slid over a Facebook picture of the accountant and his much younger silicon-enhanced wife, allowing time for the information to sink in. 'Her social does suggest she likes the finer things in life. Your second wife, I believe. And two children to support from your first marriage. That can't come cheap.'

The accountant stared down at the Facebook picture. His pasty face drained of all remaining colour.

Walker sat down again, fixing his gaze on the crook sitting opposite. 'Or you could give up a name and get away with five years. I could see to it that you get released in little over two and with a nominal fine. With the right help. Now, what would you prefer? Twenty years and lose everything, or two years and come back to that lovely beach-front house of yours?'

Walker left the thought hanging in the air.

177

'This is what happens next. I am going to give you ten seconds to give up a name. After that ten seconds I am going to leave the room. If I leave the room without a name, my agents will spend the next few days unpicking your life. Every client. Every trust set up to launder money and demand justification for every single dollar you ever earned. Because there will be other frauds, reaching out like an infection. There always are with people like you. After that, the full force of the state's prosecution will rain down upon your head. From the moment I leave this room, you'll be on your own.'

Walker stood up and slid his chair under the desk to emphasise the finality of his threat.

'One, two, three, four, five ...'

Walker turned and headed for the door.

'Six, s—'

'Alright, alright.'

Walker stopped, still facing away from the accountant to the door.

'Damian Gent. The name you're looking for is Damian Gent.'

The accountant gave Walker Damian Gent's Pina Vista Drive address without looking it up. It was a legitimate property purchase, so was not listed on the Bermudan-based trust's properties currently being visited by the FBI.

Agents were quickly deployed to Pina Vista Drive.

Other agents got to work gathering information about Mr Damian Gent.

In a matter of minutes, Walker was back at his temporary desk, receiving more intel.

Damian Gent had associates. An employee called Noah Scott. Another called Benjamin Johnson. Both were on his payroll.

He had a girlfriend, identified as Sarah Mitchell.

Walker was not a man to take chances. He sent agents out to all addresses and considered the possibility of unknown gang

178

members.

Agents set about examining cellular records from the warehouse area. Walker hoped calls from the area would identify accomplices. While the net closed in on the gang, the FBI's primary focus was Damian Gent. The gang leader would most likely determine any escape plan. Where might he go? Who might provide a haven? These were questions Walker asked his team to explore.

The top-line intelligence on Damian was that he had no criminal convictions, other than a driving ban for DUI. The ban explained the employment of Noah Scott as a permanent driver. Walker considered the amount of revenue required to maintain such an expensive luxury.

Damian Gent was not a common name. There was only one Damian Gent on the birth and deaths records in the whole of Florida, and that Damian Gent had died at the age of three. Walker believed Damian Gent's name was a false identity and that he'd found the man leading the gang responsible for a shooting in Orlando less than twenty-four hours earlier, a man with a crooked accountant stashing cash in Bermudan bank accounts. Those assets would soon be seized following a process the FBI needed to go through with Bermudan authorities.

Mr Gent would not want to give up that cash and Walker figured that Damian's next move would be to escape the United States of America to recover the money to fund a new life.

Would Damian be heading to the boat charter company used by the accountant? That was considered the most likely scenario. As well as agents, a decontamination unit was deployed south towards the Key Charters boatyard.

Damian owned three cars. Their license plates were placed on the hotlist for Floridian ALPR systems. If the cars passed highway patrols or cameras, they would be pinged.

General George Schmidt was updated on progress through a secure line from Air Force One as he came into land on the Shuttle landing strip. The general's instructions to Walker were that all gang members and those who'd come into contact with them were to be taken for screening at NASA's research unit within Cape Canaveral's Kennedy Space Center.

In less than thirty minutes from the initial identification of the accountant, Damian Gent and his associates had become the USA's most wanted.

THIRTY-SIX

It was an hour before dawn, and it took Martin County Deputy Frank Harris less than three minutes to leave his desk and arrive at the scene. His nightshift at Martin County Sheriff's Indiantown Substation was several hundred yards up the other side of Highway 710 from the body of a male found outside the Mobil gas station, on the side of the road. A truck had pulled over, shielding the body from traffic. The night worker at the gas station had come outside to ask the truck driver why he was blocking the forecourt's entrance. They were standing back from the body, talking excitedly.

The body presented a strange sight, with coloured growths down one side of its neck and arms.

Other deputies soon followed and made the possible connection to BOLOs to find and apprehend the gang connected to a shooting in Orlando. Instructions to be on the lookout for a gang and to exercise caution had not changed, though mention of a Nissan NV had been dropped. The gang's current vehicle was unknown.

Additional instructions were unlike any BOLO Harris had heard before. There was to be no direct physical contact with suspects. The instructions detailed a 'risk to life' from close proximity to gang members. The coloration on the body led him to guess at some kind of virus. Florida had seen the third-highest number of COVID-19 cases in the United States, so he took the instructions seriously, regretting feeling the body for a pulse on arrival.

Worse was to follow. They were called to the nearby motel by its manager. He showed them to a room with a female corpse on a blood-soaked bed, saying the room's door had been left wide open. The manager also reported the possibility of gunshots being fired but was unsure because he'd been listening to music through headphones at the time. The motel manager had left it a while before he looked outside, which was when he discovered the body in the room.

The deputy was angry with the manager for not reporting the gunshots immediately, thereby allowing time for suspects to disappear from under the noses of the nearby Indiantown Sheriff's Office. 'You realise you can see the sheriff's office from here? Next time you think you hear shots, call straight away, sir. The shooter will be miles away now.'

Harris called his findings in and was told not to allow medics to examine the bodies. They must have just missed the murderer by less than ten minutes, he thought, and asked to look at video surveillance from the parking lot to identify suspect cars. He also felt a headache coming on and hoped he had not caught whatever the dead guy with a green face had.

By the time FBI and military police arrived to talk to Harris, visibility of the motel's blue neon sign had faded against the morning sky.

Local paramedics milled around, unsure what to do, given their instructions not to touch the body. There were no signs of life and they agreed the subject was dead. A female FBI agent politely thanked them and asked them to leave.

Military medical officers arrived in camouflaged trucks, forming part of what they called a 'contagion isolation unit'. One truck carried the international sign of the red cross on the side, and personnel donning green protective suits alighted from the back. They erected sheeting around the body which extended out as a tunnel to the back of the truck. It reminded the deputy of a scene from the movie *ET.*

Even more extraordinary was the video surveillance from the parking lot. He ushered an agent into the motel's back office to watch it.

Walker listened to the report from his agent at the scene of the shooting in Indiantown. He privately congratulated himself on having the foresight to send an isolation unit in the direction of the Key Charters marina in Jupiter. The motel was only ten clicks north-west of Jupiter. Their analysis was surely correct; the gang was intending to access a boat and escape US waters.

But something had gone wrong and a body, now confirmed from photographs to be that of Damian Gent, was lying on the side of a road. Another body, identified as a local prostitute, had also been discovered, though her connection with the gang had not been established.

The other fugitives had disappeared, but not to the Key Charters marina. An incoming call from an unidentified phone had been received on the boatyard's landline the previous evening. The call had been traced back to a cellular mast in Brevard with audio from a male instructing 'Get her ready for an early start.' FBI surveillance revealed that a boat had been made ready – the same boat they knew the accountant had used for his Bermudan trips – yet it was still moored up. Damian Gent and his gang had been a no-show.

Forensics studied the area around Damian's body. A line of blood marks and disturbed grit lines on the roadside suggested the body had been dragged along the surface for a hundred yards.

Walker's special agent was thorough, describing the scene to him in detail. He waited as she paused the call to climb into protective clothing to shoot live video for him. She called back and he watched the footage as she moved through a flap in the tent erected around Damian. The image showed another plastic flap. The image on Walker's phone whited out as the plastic sheeting brushed the camera lens.

Finally, video of Damian came into focus. His white shirt was dirty and punctuated by holes and blood. There was surprisingly little blood from the gunshot wounds, despite the proximity of his heart.

'Move up and show me the face,' Walker said.

The camera slowly moved up the body, past a rough green-tinged neckline, and settled on Damian's face. His eyes were closed, his face motionless. The left side of the face was accented by scaly greenish-brown skin. There was a gash to the top right of his forehead and, again, little blood.

'Move in closer. Let me see,' Walker insisted.

The image was unsettling. There were obvious signs of infection.

Would all people, if infected by the virus, look like Damian, with almost lizard-like skin, a swollen neck and blackened lips? Walker wondered.

THIRTY-SEVEN

Damian felt cold to the core. He straddled the zone between reality and hallucination, and was strangely conscious of that fact. It felt like he was watching some distant footage of his life as his younger self, James, yet he held the remote control of the video. A nagging thread in his mind told him to press the 'off' button, but it was a place he needed to go. Something deep inside told him the catharsis was necessary.

His body ached from another beating at the hands of his stepdad. His release was to walk and curse. He was feral and out of control, throwing a brick through a parked-up van, shouting, 'Fuck-it! *F-f-fucking arseholes!'* He was showing off to his new mates and they were running together, laughing with him.

The shame of swearing at the most inopportune moments – on a busy street, in a shop, or even the school corridor – was acute, although visits to that educational establishment became rare events as a new life in the gang gave him a sense of belonging. His new friends played along with his stutter and seemed to accept it as part of his make-up.

An epiphany burst into his consciousness as he finally understood how his swearing was framed by Tourette's. Frustrated by the unfairness of life, he relived bad moments in his head shortly after they happened, making swearing the release valve for his exasperation. Damian had never realised that before. It all made sense now as he watched the young version of himself standing defiantly before his stepdad as the man opened another letter from school. The letter was concrete evidence confirming the tyrant's dim view of him. Terrible school reports and an upset mother led to even angrier stuttered exchanges between him and his imposter dad.

His stepdad's enjoyment of his affliction compounded the cruelty, casting a shadow of misery that its creator relished, leading to more bad behaviour. That was the irony. He hated how his stepdad revelled in his discomfort. Whenever the tic revealed itself, a suppressed down-mouthed smile would wash over Michael. James wanted to punch that look off his stepdad's supercilious face. And he imagined other retributions.

Choosing to avoid home, he lived on fast food paid for by money earned running errands for his new mentor, Big Mac. Mac was indeed big and had a Scottish surname. Oddly, he preferred KFC to McDonald's. Mac's gang, the West Drive MOB, which stood for Money Over Bitches, dealt drugs on their small patch.

His release from home torture was that no one in the West Drive MOB seemed to care about his stutter, because he did the deliveries into crack dens the others avoided. He also collected a couple of long-standing debts. Fellow soldiers took note and an aura sprang up around him of someone not to be messed with.

Other gangs considered West Drive small-time, yet their gang grew, taking on more action. James became main within the MOB and Big Mac even gave him runners for support on drug deals.

On the streets he was fearless.

At home, he watched his stepdad growing older and weaker, while he metamorphosed into something physically stronger – a young man.

One glorious day, at the age of sixteen, he grabbed the old man by the throat and warned Michael never to touch him again. His stepdad's beatings stopped.

At the age of eighteen, James became Mac's lieutenant. The gang was embroiled in a turf war with the neighbouring Albanian gang, Original Albanian Gangsters. OAG was now running the estate. They carried guns and used them.

Mac got hold of a couple of zip guns and things took a turn for the worse. Word got out to the Albanians via a drill hip-hop track laid down and spread over social media by MOB's MC. Describing their beef with OAG, MOB's threatening rap was a challenge to OAG and got an immediate response.

Mac survived a drive-by but ended up in Whittingham Hospital. The bullet had shattered his left collarbone. The seriousness of the confrontation had escalated, and Damian watched in as he decided to exact revenge. He wanted to reach into his dream and stop his young self, but the path of history was set and Damian knew how the following scene would play out – the same way it always did.

The attack took place on a dark, drizzly December night in Haringey, North London. James had done his research to find the home of the Albanians' elder. James and one of his runners, Junior, waited for nearly an hour, hiding in a bus shelter on the estate, with eyes across to the housing association address they'd been given. The wet and cold helped conceal them on the empty street. No one was out in the weather and they were on the verge of jacking it in to go home when a hooded figure appeared from the house.

They followed the hoody a while and caught up as he cut through a deserted children's play area. James pulled him around by the shoulder to face them, to find the man was a kid, far too young to be the gang leader they expected, although he did look a lot like their intended target's profile pic.

The kid was tall, but only looked about fourteen. He looked them up and down, clearly unimpressed. 'Who the fuck are you two?' he said.

'West Drive MOB, init,' Junior said.

'West Drive? You're that plastic gang. What you doing in my ends?' The boy was grinning as he patted a pocketed gun. The hint of an Eastern European accent accompanying the street patois gave the kid menace, confirming to James the kid was part of OAG.

He exchanged nervous glances with Junior, knowing MOB was not on the same level as the Albanians. Junior had started backing off down the street, which was when something inside

James snapped. He took a step forward, hand hovering over his own jacket pocket.

The OAG member pulled out his gun. It looked like a serious piece compared to James's home-made zip and he regretted his audacity. The Albanian pointed the gun at James in an outstretched hand, rotated ninety degrees in the time-honoured fashion.

Junior was holding up his hands, wide-eyed. 'Oh, my days,' he said.

Deep into the hallucination, Damian felt his heart racing but was too invested to pull out. The scene felt real, and his out-of-body self wondered if he really was back in North London.

'You ain't listening, tourists,' the Albanian kid was saying. The trigger clicked, but no bullet fired.

James and Junior glanced at each other, speechless. The Albanian looked panicked. He hadn't released the safety catch on the gun and they were on to him, pinning him to the ground. Defiance returned to the boy with a confidence that belied the downturn in his fortunes. James was considering his next actions when the Albanian spoke up. 'What the fuck? Get off me. You know whose this is, yer?' The kid nodded at the gun that had fallen to the pavement. 'It's me bruv's, and he'll find you. You can run to your 'rents, but we'll find your yards.'

Anger again exploded inside James. The street was his new home and West Drive MOB his family. He had earned respect on the street, but this upstart was trying to take it away. If he let the gangster go, Albanians would be round his yard in no time to kill him. Leaving the zip in his jacket pocket, he pulled out his blade and stabbed the gang leader's younger brother. He plunged the knife into the boy's gut and held it there for a while before pulling it out, bloodied.

He had been threatened and given no choice. It was not his fault.

Blood quickly spread over the pavement. It was seeping out of the abdomen wound quickly. Junior looked at James incredulously. It was clear neither had seen so much blood.

They both turned and ran.

Walker looked at the lifeless face on his screen. The facial expression seemed tense, as if Damian's dying thoughts had not been good ones.

Odd. Walker thought he could see some REM.

'Will you zoom in a bit furth—'

Damian Gent's eyes flickered open.

Despite his experience and training, sitting miles away in the comfort of the Melbourne Sheriff's Office, Walker nearly dropped his phone.

'Jesus!'

Damian Gent was alive and staring back at him through the lens, smiling.

THIRTY-EIGHT

The general and his aides' arrival was a tour de force, sweeping into the complex without the niceties normally associated with a governmental visit. Dr Goodhew had been informed of their arrival and was waiting as the entourage entered his main lab.

'Dr Goodhew?' the general asked.

Goodhew put out his hand. 'Yes, sir, a pleasure to meet you.'

'OK, Doctor, let's dispense with the formalities. What do we know?' The general's Midwest drawl was cutting.

Goodhew decided to view the general's abrupt approach as a positive, indicating the seriousness of the threat was understood. Goodhew was happy to get straight into discussing the science. 'We're struggling to understand the exact nature of the threat,' he said.

'Struggling?' The general made a sweeping motion with his hand. 'With all this at your disposal?'

Goodhew was taken aback by the affront but managed to collect himself. 'As you know, we extracted samples from the site. While you've been up in the air, we've been conducting numerous experiments.'

'Yes, as we discussed, so please get to the point. Are we looking at another Covid here? A new virus?'

The conversation was not going as expected. Doctor Goodhew paused, gathering himself for what he was about to say next. 'No. Far from it, I'm afraid. As I first suspected, the subject matter is alien. The materials feeding into the alien mass at the site are of this world. Living creatures, plants, animals, and humans. Anything with a living cellular structure is being absorbed into the mass. I think you saw earlier footage from the site?'

'Yes, I saw it. Go on.'

'What our tests show is that after absorption into the base matter, anything introduced slowly degenerates until it becomes unrecognisable.'

'Unrecognisable? How so?'

'I think it's easier to show you than explain. We have some time-lapse footage.'

The doctor nodded towards a large monitor above their heads which held a static image cued up for the general. The picture showed a substance that looked like greenish-brown pond sludge.

'The quantity of the alien substance on the screen is on a much smaller, controlled scale than what you may recall viewing last night. This was filmed two hours ago, in one of the tanks in an adjacent clean room,' Goodhew said.

'I hope you're not squeamish,' Goodhew's young lab assistant added.

The general shot her an irritated glance and said, 'Do I look like the squeamish sort to you?'

The assistant tried to recover from her nervous blunder. 'What I mean is this is not what you'd describe as pleasant.'

She tapped on a keyboard as everyone in the lab paused, focusing on the image appearing on the overhead screen. A cursor pressed the play arrow and a digital time-date stamp in the top right corner of the screen began ticking. The times on screen moved forward one minute at a time, each minute taking only a couple of seconds of real time. After twelve seconds the on-screen clock had moved on six minutes but nothing much had happened.

Twelve seconds began to feel like a long time under the glare of the general, who Goodhew noticed was frowning, looking impatient. 'It's worth the wait,' Goodhew said.

At nine minutes a mouse appeared on the screen, having been introduced to the tank. Stills suggested the rodent was sniffing at the mound of gunge. The frames moved jerkily forward four minutes and the mouse remained in place, seemingly

191

unable to move. The rodent began struggling on the time-lapse, glued in place by its nose.

A few frames later and its whole mouth was covered. The mouse looked dead.

'We believe it suffocated or was killed by an infection,' Goodhew said.

The strange mass enveloped the mouse's feet and lower body.

About forty-five seconds into the time-lapse, the rodent was barely recognisable. Strange bulbous eyes were protruding from what had previously been its head.

The assistant hit a button on the keypad and the image froze.

Goodhew turned to Schmidt, whose frown had deepened. 'Let me explain. What you are seeing there is the result of an earlier part of this particular experiment. Prior to the mouse, we had introduced a large insect – a cricket – to the tank. It seems that certain physical characteristics of the cricket are being assimilated by what was the mouse, and vice versa. The mouse seems to have taken on physical aspects of the insect.'

'You're saying they are being mixed together?'

'Exactly that, yes. In terms of structure, we believe their orders are losing individual characteristics and starting to share DNA.'

The general said nothing.

The footage restarted. Within another twenty seconds the mouse was barely recognisable as such. The video stopped.

'That's all you need to see really, sir,' said Goodhew. 'We have other experiments running simultaneously, all delivering the same results.'

The general looked at Goodhew. 'Tell me what this means, son.'

'What it means?' The doctor exhaled, not knowing how the general would react to the news he was about to deliver. 'In the short term, this thing is going to keep spreading. Absorbing everything in its path.'

'And in the longer term?'

'In the longer term, General, this is the end of life on Earth as we know it. Unless we find a way of stopping it, we are looking at the new dominant species on Earth. One that assimilates every other living entity.'

The doctor felt the effect of his words as they brought the lab to a temporary halt. He realised he was postulating the threat of Armageddon, an apocalypse not previously imagined or prepared for. Meteorite impacts, volcanic eruptions, the melting of the polar icecaps, nuclear war, deadly viruses, even attacks by other species, had all been discussed within government, NASA and the US military. But not this. A creature devouring everything in its path, assimilating biological matter into a mutated new mass was a new prospect, both terrifying and real.

The general looked reflective and said, 'How long have we got, Doc?'

Goodhew realised the impact of his earlier statement and put on a brave face.

'There is some good news coming out of our data, sir. It's a bit early to be too precise, and we need to run more experiments across a wider range of biological cells. The absorption rate is calculated at only a few metres a day at present. But that comes with a caveat. The absorption rate might accelerate as its mass increases. We don't know yet.'

'Can we contain it?'

'Hopefully, General. What I mean is the recommendation I made last night was the right call. Erecting a ring of steel around the impact site should contain it. At least buy some time until we figure out what to do next.'

'Can't it go under the steel? Through the planet even?'

'We're not seeing evidence of that. It's not been able to absorb pure rock. In other words, as long as rock is not permeated with living cellular structures, it acts as a barrier. So does metal. This matter can only absorb biological structures.'

'What about water? I believe this thing made it to a waterway behind the impact zone. If that's the case, won't it be statewide by now? And God help us all when it makes it to the ocean.'

Goodhew watched the military man shaking his head, no doubt strategizing, playing out a doomsday scenario in his mind. 'Doctor, are we already past the point of no return?'

Goodhew returned Schmidt's steely gaze. He had played out that scenario too. Not just in his mind, but on computer simulations containing hundreds of variables. If the initial tests were wrong and the alien matter could transmit itself through rock and metal, the simulations all pointed to one conclusion: the destruction of all life on Earth.

'Transmission of the substance through liquid has yet to be confirmed, sir,' said Goodhew. 'We are continuing with those tests and I hope to have clearer findings back shortly.'

A soldier stepped forward and talked in hushed tones to the general. The general turned to the doctor. 'There are reports of a shooting across state and it looks like we've captured one of the fugitives. If the reports are accurate we need to isolate the other felons, now we know what they might be spreading.'

The news offered them a crumb of comfort, although Goodhew had no idea if the fugitives were contagious or not. Early experiments on potential gas-carried transmission of the substance had not identified it as having the ability to fragment into airborne particles like a regular virus. Goodhew suspected the only way a contaminated human could infect another would be through physical contact. It would be interesting to look at an infected host to understand if his theory was correct. 'General, we are already talking to the FBI, and my clear-up team has isolation trucks waiting in the field.' At least in this respect he believed he was ahead of the general.

The soldier turned to address Goodhew. 'Doctor, I can tell you the captured felon is being prepared for transfer back here in one of your vehicles as we speak.'

'Good,' the General said and turned to his soldier. 'We need the others locked down too. Anyone who has so much as looked at these felons must be rounded up and put in the doctor's trucks too.'

'Understood and already in progress, sir. We are liaising with an Agent Walker and his team.'

Goodhew listened intently and addressed the soldier. 'Please stress the importance of following contagion protocols.'

'That's a given, sir.'

'Good,' the general said again. 'Keep me updated.'

The soldier left. Goodhew realised the contagion genie might be out of the bottle and feared the worst. He hoped the gang had not already spread the alien substance to a wider population.

THIRTY-NINE

Noah pulled the Volvo to the roadside. He looked tired and Sarah could tell he was losing heart.

Trying to drive a direct route had taken them down tracks not shown on the outdated GPS. They had made three U-turns in the last ten minutes. Their planned destination meant heading west. She was convinced they needed to avoid busier routes, so did not want to loop back east and around the southern tip of Florida to pick up obvious coastal roads.

'Look, a building,' Noah said.

As they got nearer, a sign above the entrance told her the building belonged to 'Jake's Swamp Safaris'.

Next to the brick building was a dilapidated shed like the one they had fled from by Lake Winder. The building's doors were open, and a ramp led to the waterway.

Through the door they could see a couple of boats. Outside, in a compound, were older airboats and inflatables in various states of disrepair, one with a 'For Sale' sign stuck to it.

'That's bad,' said Sarah. 'It means we're close to main roads. These tourist places are always near towns, hotels, resorts.'

'Yes, but if I can get in, I can steal a boat. We can ditch the Volvo and go by water.'

He drove them a little closer and they parked up, continuing on foot the rest of the way. They hid to survey the property. The place did not seem to be too busy. Several vehicles were parked out back, but they could only see one person in the office. She was sitting at a desk, working on a laptop.

Noah nodded towards a couple of airboats moored up close by. 'Too dangerous,' Sarah said. 'Even if you could start one of those things, she'd hear it.'

Noah nodded.

They'd have to start the engine several hundred yards away, she thought. Or, maybe, there was a better way.

'That boat's for sale. I can't see the price. Can you?' she asked.

Noah squinted in the bright sunshine before answering. 'The sign says "Call for a Price".'

'OK, so how much do you think it will cost?'

'I don't know, ten thousand. Maybe more. Maybe less. I only know cars.'

'Can you see security cameras?'

'Yes. One. No, two. There and there. Might be more round the back.'

'OK, let's try this. We pull the vehicle up into that blind spot. We take in some cash and we buy a boat. One of us drives the car and the other one the boat. We meet back up the road at the last dead end. We hide the car and use the boat to travel on. I think we can get to where I plan to take us on water from here.'

Noah did not seem convinced. 'I'm not sure.'

'What's the alternative?' she said.

He fell silent for a while, contemplating. 'Who's going to drive the Volvo and who's going to drive the boat?'

'I've piloted boats before, in my old job. I used to move quite big boats around the marina.'

'I'd prefer to do that,' Noah said, with an edge to his voice that betrayed his paranoia.

'I'm not going to leave you, if that's what you mean,' she said, half laughing. 'I mean, what good would it do me if you were caught? They'd soon find me. Now just relax. Let's do this thing together, honey.'

Noah flushed with embarrassment. 'Sorry, I know. I know you wouldn't. It's just …'

'I know. Don't worry. It's not been easy.'

Her words seemed to work to ease his fears, and she was soon walking into the office, Noah holding ten thousand dollars of cash wrapped in a plastic bag.

The receptionist turned out to be co-owner. She insisted the boat was worth nearer twenty thousand. Sarah cringed as Noah spun out an unlikely story about needing the boat for a fiftieth birthday gift for his dad and there not being more cash.

'This is all we've got,' he said, indicating the bag. 'It's for a birthday trip next week and I'd hate to let him down.' Sarah thought his Illinois accent out of place in the local context of his lies.

The lady paused a beat and offered a compromise.

'If that's your limit then there is maybe something I can do. Follow me.'

She led them through the side door into the adjoining shed. As well as airboats, there was a fibreglass-hulled boat with a logo reading 'Boston Whaler. Outrage 22' on the side.

'Now, this one is due to go on sale at twelve thousand dollars. But since you're paying cash, I can let you have it at ten.'

Sarah looked at Noah. She knew he was not sure if they were being done over either. Maybe the lady was genuine.

'May we have a moment, please?' Sarah said.

They moved to one side of the office, but the discussion did not take long. They needed the boat.

'Yes, we'd like to take it,' Sarah confirmed.

The Volvo's rear protruded stubbornly from the gurgling water. Bubbles of escaping air rose to the surface, but it was clear the sedan was not going to disappear completely.

Despite them pushing it with a good run-up, the slope into the water had not been steep enough. The vehicle hadn't gathered enough speed to move through the tangled mud and weeds of the shallow bank.

'Now what?' Sarah asked.

'We'll just have to leave it. I think we should get going quickly.' Noah pointed at a large alligator on the opposite bank.

He was sweating under the blaze of the Floridian winter sun. His feet were wet and muddy. He had been driving most of the night and must feel frazzled, she thought.

'I doubt anyone's going to find it here – it's a bit of a dead end. Come on then, let's go,' she said.

Noah looked relieved. He helped her into the fibreglass boat with exaggerated gallantry, all the while checking the alligator had not moved from its mound opposite.

He pulled the engine's cord and the 200hp Johnson outboard rattled into life first time. The cooling momentum of the boat helped her think. They'd managed to get a couple of Jake's Safari lunch packs and a fuel canister thrown in as part of the ten-thousand-dollar-cash deal. False details had been given to the owner, but Sarah doubted Jake's would want to raise any issues following their cash transaction. The cash sale would be an easy IRS tax dodge for the owners. Sarah knew how these things worked.

She guessed they'd been ripped off but didn't care. It had been Damian's money and very soon she'd be free.

Except Noah was a problem. He glugged greedily on a precious ice-cool bottle of water from the lunch pack. He was likely to get them both caught. That story about the fiftieth birthday gift had been feeble. Somehow she had to figure out how to get away from the entitled boy from Chicago – with the money and the gems.

FORTY

Damian woke feeling groggy, and guessed he'd been sedated. People in green protective suits, surgical masks and plastic visors blurred into vision. He tried to turn to look around but found he couldn't. He'd been strapped to something that resembled a dentist's chair. He felt restraints across his chin and forehead, holding his head tightly to the headrest.

After struggling for a while, he gave up, feeling weak. The straps pressing against his throbbing temples were inducing anger. He shouted out for help through his haze, but the green suits seemed oblivious to his plight as they scurried out of the room. Although he could not see behind him, he knew he was alone. He sensed it.

A camera mounted on the wall above drew his attention. It pointed down at him, watching. He had been positioned facing an observation window. The chair was elevated enough for him to look forwards, towards the glass. The room beyond was in darkness, so he could just make out his reflection.

He was looking at a changed person. Pushing his chin down against the strapping to get a better angle, he blinked. The reflection blinked. His skin looked strange, but it was unmistakably his own reflection staring back.

Memories flooded back into his consciousness.

He'd been attacked in the warehouse by that thing. It had gripped his arm. Despite being ripped away, he realised the substance had invaded him. He remembered a sickness taking hold, spreading through his body. Yet the malady had given him strength, allowing clarity of thought, and made him feel powerful.

He remembered the prostitute, and the strange thing that had happened to his penis – had it become an alien part of him? The thought made his stomach churn. Wanting to see the rest of his body, he struggled with his arm restraints, hoping the motel image was a bad dream. He had been dressed in orange overalls, like those worn in a penitentiary, and could not get his hands down to check.

He needed to see his body, to know what he'd become.

Lights flickered into life, revealing a room the other side of the glass. It was another sterile, stark, metal-walled room. He heard a click. A door opened at the far side of the second room and two figures walked in.

One was military, a big man wearing a jacket with medals and stripes and a crisp shirt with perfect tie. Immaculate. The stark lighting of the lab illuminated the man's silver hair, buzz cut close to a balding scalp. The hair glistened nearly as brightly as the metal buttons on his tunic. Damian imagined military man was nearing the finale of a distinguished career and instinctively felt an antipathy towards him. There was something in the cold nature of the stare. He knew the man was like a silver-fox predator – a killer.

The second man was less impressive. He looked to be a similar age or slightly younger than the first. His hair was also grey – the murky grey he imagined that women wouldn't find as attractive. He had a small beard and moustache over pallid skin. Unhealthy. Damian assumed he did not get out much. He wore a white lab coat that bulged out slightly at the stomach. A uniform for indoor work. The second man seemed non-threatening, if not a little tense.

The two sat down the other side of the screen. The lab-coat man leaned forward and pressed a button. A speaker above crackled into life. It was the man in military uniform who spoke first.

'Good afternoon, Mr Gent. I am General George Schmidt. This here is Doctor Nathan Goodhew. We're here to ask you a few questions, you understand?'

201

The words came out of a mind fog. Whatever drugs they had given him were making listening difficult. He had already forgotten their names.

'I said, do you understand?' the military man said again.

'Yes, I understand,' said Damian, eyeing his straps. 'But is this necessary?'

'Aha, the accent I was told about. British. You know, one of the technicians had you down as Australian. To be honest, you Brits and Aussies sound the same to me.'

'The straps,' Damian said, again looking at the harnesses keeping him at bay.

'And yes, those are necessary. At least until we know what we are dealing with.'

'Dealing with?'

'Yes. It may have escaped your attention, but you're not a well man. You picked up some kind of infection at that shed of yours.'

The lab coat interjected. 'We need to ask you about that. The warehouse. What happened in there?'

Medal man glanced at the doctor with a look of annoyance. 'Yes, later. First we need to find out who you were with and where they are now. Your friends. Are they infected too?'

'Infected.' He laughed. 'No, no, they're not infected. I'm the only one it attacked. Apart from Ben, that is.'

Medal man referred to some papers in front of him, shuffling through several sheets.

'Ben. Ben. Ben, aha. It says here Benjamin Johnson was a member of your staff. Where is Benjamin now?'

Damian felt the sadness return. 'Dead,' he whispered.

'Sorry, I did not catch that. Will you kindly speak up for the microphone?' medals said.

Damian looked defiantly at the man, his voice now more forceful. 'Dead, I said. Killed by that stuff. It covered him. Ate him alive. When I tried to help, it attacked me.'

'Attacked?' asked lab coat. 'What do you mean by attacked?'

202

'It grabbed my arm. I was pulled away and it took some of me with it.'

'Tell us what happened then.'

'And then I started to feel bad. To change. Into what you see now.'

'Do you still feel change going on?' the lab coat asked with a look of concern.

'I don't think so,' Damian replied. 'I hope not. You've seen what I've become. That not enough for you?'

For a moment he was James again. He felt the same sense of shame he'd had stuttering in front of classmates. He was unable to hide his sadness.

The lab coat looked back compassionately. 'We get that. It must be terribly confusing for you. I'm having tests run now to confirm the infection has stabilised,' he said.

At that moment Damian heard clicks, like a door latch catching. He looked towards the door of his room and was surprised when the one at the back of the room beyond opened instead. He must have heard it through the glass screen, he thought. He felt his earlier wooziness lifting and watched a new arrival sit down next to the other two.

The new man was younger, well-groomed, in a charcoal grey suit and matching tie. He turned to the other two and said, 'Hello, General, hello, Doctor.' The general leaned forward and touched a button on a mike protruding from the counter. The wall speakers above Damian buzzed as the mike was silenced. And yet, he could clearly make out the voices opposite, even through the glass.

'Don't worry, we've not got far,' the doctor was saying, 'But he told us that the subject Benjamin Johnson is dead. Killed at the impact site.'

'Yes, that tallies with our intel,' grey suit said. 'Video surveillance from the motel shows Damian Gent arriving with his driver, Noah Scott and his girlfriend, Sarah Mitchell. There is another gang member with them who we also see later, walking out of the parking lot, but the image is so poor we haven't been able to get a match on facial recognition. There was no sign of

Benjamin Johnson, so Gent may be telling the truth.'

The general spoke with urgency, telling grey suit that they needed to get the unidentified man's name. Damian watched him intently through the glass. It was clear to him that tracking down his gang was the priority, and that Sarah, Noah and Mason were still at large.

'OK. We need to press on,' said the general, and turned on the mike. The speakers crackled loudly and a new voice came through.

'Apologies for being late. My name is Assistant Director Walker.'

'Walker here heads up national security at the bureau,' the general informed him.

Impressive, thought Damian, despite himself. They really were wheeling in the big hitters.

Walker looked concerned. 'Please excuse the strapping, Mr Gent. A temporary measure, we hope. Would you like some water? Are you thirsty?'

Damian was momentarily confused. His first thought was to ask for whisky, but the idea now made him queasy. 'Yes, some water please,' he said instead.

The doctor looked up into a camera and said, 'OK, that can be arranged.'

Walker continued. 'Let me start by saying that we are concerned for the safety of your friends. We really appreciate your cooperation to help us find them. You were talking about Benjamin, just before I came in.'

The interlude had helped Damian recover his senses. 'Why should I help you? How will that help me?' he said.

The general smashed his fist against the counter. 'God damn—'

Walker held out a warning hand in the direction of the general but maintained eye contact with Damian. Walker said calmly, 'We realise this must all be very frightening for you.' He nodded towards the doctor. 'Please understand, we are going to help you. And we also want to help your friends. What you and your buddies need now is science, and we have the science. We have seen what this thing has done to you. Help us and there's every chance we can figure out how to reverse it. Would you like that?'

Damian looked into Walker's eyes. He seemed to be telling the truth about the science, like he believed in the possibility. And yet they seemed promises born of ignorance. Damian knew how deep the transformation had gone and could not imagine the process being reversible. This FBI man was too smooth, saying all the right things. Trying to push his buttons to get what they wanted.

'What if I don't cooperate?' Damian asked. 'I mean, it can't get any worse for me. Look at me.'

The general answered. 'Believe me, sonny, it can get a whole lot worse for you. When my men are finished on you, the state you are in will seem like a picnic. Now, do you want to put that to the test or let the good doctor here help you?'

Damian weighed up his options. He was captive. He felt barely human. He had no idea if the infection had spread to his gang and owed them nothing – they had tried to kill him.

Also, he sensed something in the general. It was a dark desire to hurt him. He did not know how he knew, other than feeling a threat in the general's demeanour and voice. There was something else beyond his conscious understanding that told him the general was set in attack mode. He took the risk seriously.

Damian felt his mind clear once more and his thinking lucid. He had to do what was best at that moment to survive, and that was to give the general what the man wanted. Or nearly everything. He would not tell them the part where he shot law enforcement officers and kidnapped Anderson.

'OK, I'll tell you what you want,' he said.

FORTY-ONE

The first thing Walker did as he exited the lab was call in the name of Mason Reeves, given over by Damian Gent. He hoped the name was not a spoof and would show up on the bureau's files.

He drove the short distance back to the Brevard County Sheriff's Office to brief his team. As an FBI Executive Assistant Director, Walker was more used to running National Security Branch operations from a desk in Washington and making courtesy visits to main field offices. He was looking forward to spending some time back in the field working a case.

Accessing the building at the public reception desk, Walker made his way to an open-plan but small incident room, given over to the FBI by Sheriff Wiles. A wall of sticky tension hit him on entry, excitement and overcrowding created its own energy in the small space.

The room was crammed with over a dozen of the FBI's finest. Some perched on the edge of desks, while others stood. The list of special agents gathered was impressive. Even so, the scene was one of managed disorder.

Walker knew he could dispense with the preambles. He took off his jacket and slung it over a nearby table. He informed the team that Benjamin Johnson was assumed dead within the confines of the impact site. The fact Benjamin had not arrived at the motel with the rest of the gang reinforced the belief he'd been killed. An agent at the back joked it was lucky they didn't have to chase Ben Johnson. Some older members of the team laughed at the reference. Walker did not mind the banter, but knew time was precious.

'So, let's sum up what else we know,' Walker said.

Individuals from the team spoke out, summarising the current status. Assuming Benjamin Johnson was dead, another three fugitives had avoided capture so far. The belief was they'd split up.

A rap sheet for Mason Reeves was handed to him, which Walker glanced at.

Walker updated his team on some of the details of his earlier interview with Damian Gent, but he adapted the part where Damian described his friend Ben being absorbed into the warehouse fabric, appearing later as a snake eating a local deputy. Holding back on detail would help avoid histrionics and he was not sure he believed Damian's story.

Aliens, UFOs and snake men – none of it was real. There would be a reasonable explanation for what had happened. There always was. In real life the division of the FBI dealing with X-Files was simply relooking at unsolved cases, not hunting aliens.

Among assembled bureau staff, only Walker knew the full picture, and chose to outline that there was a strange material, as yet unidentified, which had enveloped the area, covering Benjamin and four local deputies. The lost NASA excavator and the lost police drone had confirmed the warehouse contained a substance capable of consuming objects and probably people. He was careful not to mention the word 'alien'.

Walker explained that the crime scene was still cordoned off by the military and considered too dangerous to send in forensics. The news prompted lively discussion in the room. What was the substance? How had it got there? Could it be a foreign attack? The debate was exactly what Walker was afraid of, knowing it would detract from the manhunt.

'Let's leave the speculation to the scientists,' he interrupted above the din. 'They will let us know soon enough. In the meantime, we remain focused on the capture of the remaining fugitives. Let's start with Mason Reeves.'

Mason's rap sheet outlined a conviction for online fraud, which carried a jail sentence. Scrutiny of his finances suggested he was earning money illegally. Three bank accounts had all been receiving irregular cash deposits. The entries were all under $10,000 and not frequent enough to raise Suspicious Activity Reports from banks. Without a SAR, Mason Reeves had never been investigated by the Financial Crimes Enforcement Center.

When combined, the cash sums were significant, especially for a man with no documented employment and who paid no tax. Despite his money, Mason was listed as having 'no fixed residency'. Correspondence from the court at the time of his arrest had been sent to an address in Florida City, down in Miami-Dade County. The property was owned by Mason's father and agents had already been despatched to the address.

The intel supported an account of a man fitting his description hitchhiking south, picked up by a truck outside Indiantown around the time of the shooting.

While Walker was satisfied with the answers he was receiving about Mason, Noah and Sarah were proving elusive. Despite hundreds of FBI, army and police being involved in the search, they had disappeared off the grid. They were either lucky or holed up somewhere, trying to ride the storm.

Walker looked up at a large map of Florida and surrounding waters pinned to the incident board. The gang's base north-west of Melbourne, designated as the impact site, was circled in red. The motel at Indiantown and the marina at Jupiter down the coast were also circled. An agent circled Florida City, home of Mason Reeves's father.

It had been several hours since Noah and Sarah had fled the motel and General Schmidt had questioned him why no capture had been made. Walker was not a man to panic, having overseen countless manhunts. They nearly always played out with a capture. This would be no different.

This time is different, he reflected. Much different. There was a possibility the fugitives were infected. If they carried the contagion he'd witnessed first-hand at the NASA lab, it would already be too late.

'OK, let's go over this again. What are we missing? Based on what we know, what're their plans?' he said.

A female agent he knew from Washington stepped forward. 'I have an update on Mason Reeves,' she said.

'Go ahead, Agent Zhang.'

'We know Noah Scott and Sarah Mitchell left the motel at precisely twelve minutes past five this morning. We have established that Mason Reeves split off from the other two shortly before, hitchhiking south towards Miami. We interviewed the truck driver who is now in transit to KSC where we can question him some more.'

Another agent shouted out from his computer terminal. 'No need, we have Reeves.'

'Captured?' Walker asked.

'Not yet. We have surveillance showing him getting on a train heading southbound at Government Central, Miami. We are also tracking a cellular number active at the station. The same phone was active in Indiantown last night, Lake Winder yesterday afternoon, and in Orlando yesterday morning. It has to be his.'

'He's using the same cellular at multi-sites? Not too smart,' Walker mused.

'No, we're all over him now. He's now off the train and on a metrobus at Dadeland South Metrorail Station. That route terminates at Busways West Palm Drive, a short walk from his father's house in Florida City.'

'What's his ETA at Busways?'

'It's an hour thirteen bus trip. Gives us time to get ahead and stop the bus.'

'No, just follow the bus and watch he doesn't get off. He could be armed, and I don't want a confined shoot-out. Better let him get to his destination and away from people. We can take him down away at the station.'

'On it now,' the agent said, picking up his cellular.

'Any updates on the other two?' Walker said, looking around the room.

Agent Zhang spoke up. 'We know they took Damian Gent's Volvo from the motel. The car has not been pinged by LPRs. They've either dumped it or hidden it somewhere. We've got the state on lockdown. Roads, airstrips, ports and marinas. There's nowhere left to go.'

'So, let's look at their remaining options,' Walker said. 'There's a lot of swamp and wilderness out there. We already have helicopters in the air and boats on the water. If that's where they are, we'll find them. But, in case I need to remind you, they may be carrying an infection. I learned earlier that this infection can be transmitted to animals.'

'Like bird flu?' an agent asked.

'I'm not sure. I understand that contamination spreads via direct physical contact. Early tests suggest it is not airborne, thank Christ.'

'So how do we handle arrests, sir?'

'Yes, I was coming to that. There must be no direct skin-on-skin contact. If they do not surrender and voluntarily enter containment vehicles, our instructions are clear – shoot to kill. We have a duty to protect citizens and ourselves. All operations must work in parallel with decontamination units.'

A murmur went up as agents digested the information.

'What about people they come into contact with?' an agent at the back of the room asked.

The implications of the question were mind-blowing, and Walker hoped they would have the resources to cope.

'Yes, good point. They will need to be isolated and taken to KSC. That means anyone he sits next to or may have touched. Time is critical, with containment being the primary goal. I just hope we're not too late.' Walker grabbed his jacket and made a move towards the door. 'Capture and handling protocols are being emailed over to us any moment. Please read them carefully and, Agent Zhang, kindly circulate to our field operatives. I'm heading back to Kennedy. I have a few more questions I need to ask. Let me know when we have Reeves.'

He stopped at the door and turned back. 'And will someone please see about getting the aircon fixed.'

FORTY-TWO

Fifty-five minutes later Walker was back in the lab. Doctor Goodhew and the general were standing in front of several screens, looking at the camera feeds from experiments. The doctor was explaining something to Schmidt and smiled towards Walker as he crossed the room.

'This will be useful for you to know,' the doctor said. 'I was just telling the general that what we don't understand is how the alien mass is managing to stay alive by blending what we know is incompatible DNA. In layman's terms, I could try mixing your DNA with a flower, but it would never work. The DNA structures all contain the same elements, but they are sequenced completely differently. So we shouldn't see plants growing out of your face, for example. But the alien structure possesses something that facilitates multiple and diverse structures to bond and merge. It's physically impossible, yet we can see it happening before our eyes.'

'Can you isolate that *something,* Doc?' the general asked.

'That's what we're trying to do. To understand exactly what it is that facilitates DNA fusion.'

'I mean, can we apply it to marrying up animals of our choice?' the general asked.

The doctor frowned at this question. 'That's akin to Nazi experiments,' he said with a note of disdain.

The general did not reply.

'I think the overriding objective, General, should be to get this substance off the planet.'

It was clear to Walker that the general's line of questioning concerned Goodhew. He was picking up on an uneasy tension between the two men.

'I'm talking hypothetically, of course,' the general said, his tone lighter. 'I understand your concern, but you can see there might be applications beneficial to humanity.'

By 'humanity', Walker guessed the general meant 'the US Military'. The doctor collected himself and continued his technical explanations.

'We are trying to understand the DNA fusion process, but it's working at a subatomic level. We know that a mixture of atoms forms an ordered structure called a molecule. And molecules make up living cells. In organic cells, atoms have a recognisable structure. But in the alien DNA, molecules are being shared, spread out, even fused.'

'Sharing atoms? You're not suggesting nuclear fusion?'

Goodhew turned to another man in a white lab coat who had been hovering behind the general. 'This is Professor Nyman. He'll be able to explain. He's been conducting experiments using electron microscopy.'

The professor stepped forward. 'I have been examining the cellular structures within the DNA. I'd expect structures to remain independent of each other, but there is a window where we can see atomic arrangements moving across from one cell to another.'

'Wow, I feel like I've gatecrashed a science lecture,' Walker said, finding himself struggling to follow.

Once again, the general was silent.

'You mentioned independent structures. What do you mean by that?' Walker asked.

'I mean where we introduce a new animal to the alien substance – during the initial stages we can see what should be independent sub-cellular atomic patterns moving from the animal into the immediate alien structure.'

'And then?'

'And then the atomic patterns fragment beyond the point where they are recognisable as DNA molecules.'

'But how?'

'That's the thing, sir. We don't know how. According to conventional science, it's not possible.'

The general looked thoughtful as Nyman shuffled over to colleagues gathered around a nearby computer screen.

'We do have some good news, General,' Goodhew said. 'Very good news, in fact. Experiments suggest the alien matter cannot be transmitted through water. The matter will attract any waterborne organic matter, but the mass is not fragmenting to be carried off by H_2O. We're now testing other liquids.'

'Not carried off by H_2O, you say? Meaning we didn't need to drain the surrounding waterway?' the general said.

'Sir, that was necessary. For all we know, water flow may carry off fragments of this material to other areas.'

'I'm confused. Water can carry the threat then?'

'Well, sort of. Let's put this another way. The alien matter does not separate out of its own accord. When water comes into contact with it, the main mass is not releasing a sub-mass. Rather the main mass absorbs any biological matter present in the water. Which is surprising, really, as splintering the threat in liquid would surely expedite its promulgation. That's a weapon the alien does not seem to have.'

The general had held up his hand towards Goodhew.

'I think I get your drift, sonny, but it seems to me you swallowed a whole dictionary on that one.'

'Please excuse me. My wife picks me up on that too,' the doctor replied. Walker could see that Doctor Goodhew was trying to break the tension and laughed with him. He had been analysing the conversation. The general's body language was aggressive and Goodhew's defensive. He could see antipathy between the men. It made him feel uneasy too; after all, the planet's survival depended on their joint leadership.

'Sorry, I have to run through this again,' Walker said. 'For the safety of my agents I would like to understand what we are facing. Are you saying that this bonding process takes place only within organic matter? There is the potential for water to carry fragments of the alien matter, like a river carries a leaf along in its current. The stuff could already be everywhere by now.'

'It could, but we don't know for sure. The alien matter bonds biological material together very strongly. So well, in fact, that we have not seen material fragmenting and breaking free unless subjected to extreme force. That is why we have not detected any new areas of infestation. If we're lucky, draining the channels and erecting the ring of steel around the impact site will isolate the material, stopping its spread.'

'It might,' the general agreed, 'unless the three remaining fugitives are infected too. Which reminds me …' The general turned his attention to Walker. 'What are you doing here? Why aren't you out there finding them?'

'Be assured, my team is on it, sir.'

'Well, shouldn't you be out there with them?'

'My duty extends to their safety,' Walker said. He was not going to let the general bully him. 'I requested capture protocols. Have they been emailed out yet?'

'You best ask the doctor.'

'Yes, I checked. They'll be with your team by now,' said Goodhew.

'That's good.' Walker smiled. 'I need to understand what we're dealing with here. I came back because I have a few more questions for Mr Gent that might help us capture his associates.'

'Mr Gent is not to be disturbed at present,' the general cut in. 'If there are any remaining questions you neglected to ask earlier then address them through me. I will ask our guest later.'

Walker opened his mouth to respond and decided against it. He held as much seniority as the general, yet also knew the general's influence within government. He'd taken a close look at the general's background. The man was hard line when it came to the defence of US interests abroad. His recent actions, forcing the Chinese to back off in a conflict over the Democratic Republic of Congo's newly discovered dysprosium deposits, had made him a hero. The general was not a man to mess with. Walker knew his approach required diplomacy.

'Sir, my intention is to understand the threat. The nature of the threat informs tactics on the ground. Our teams need to know what they're dealing with. They are directly in the firing line, as it were.'

'Yes, indeed they are, Assistant Director. Goodhew here will feed you that intel. In the meantime, I suggest you get out there and join your team.'

'Of course, sir.' Walker nodded in the direction of Doctor Goodhew and turned to leave.

As he reached the main lab door the general called over. 'And Walker, I don't want to see your face in here until we have these fugitives captured, you understand?'

For the second time Walker opened his mouth to say something before deciding to keep his own counsel. *Discretion is the better part of valour,* he recalled, exiting the lab.

Moments later Walker was sitting in his vehicle. He paused before turning the key, reflecting on what the general had just said. The Executive Assistant Director of the FBI's National Security Branch did not take kindly to being spoken to in such a way. He would humour General Schmidt, for now.

FORTY-THREE

Mason looked at the old man sitting on his porch swigging beer. His father must have noticed the lights because he looked up from his bottle. Blue and red flashing lights reflected against the nearby trees and bushes.

He could hold off no longer and stepped out from the darkness. 'Pa.'

'Mason, is that you?'

'Pa, I had to come back – I saw them following me. I forced the driver to let me off at your street.'

'What do you mean?' his father asked.

'I just wanted to see you one last time – to put things right.'

Mason looked around as the flashing lights entered the driveway.

Officers leaped out, silhouetted against the dazzling red and blue backlighting, most pointing guns at him.

'Freeze, or we shoot,' came a call from one.

'Don't shoot. I have no weapon. I'm just here to see my Pa, then I'll come.'

'Hands in the air now.'

Mason ignored the request. He took a step towards his father.

'Pa, I needed to see you.'

The shadowy figures had moved forward, all wearing dark vests with 'FBI' emblazoned across the front.

'Mason, my boy, what have you done?'

The lead FBI agent was much closer now and did not have to shout. 'Mason, put your hands above your head where we can see them and kneel down slowly,' she instructed.

Her words seemed distant in the exhausted desperation he felt. The experience at the warehouse had stalked him on his journey from Indiantown, haunting his thoughts. He wanted to tell his father and warn him about the monster he had seen. He needed to explain what had happened and ask for forgiveness.

'I was there. But I'm not a killer,' he said, taking another small step towards his father.

'I said freeze. Right now. Not one more step.'

'I don't understand what happened, Pa. I'm sorry.'

Another small step.

'Kneel down now, Reeves. This really is your final warning. Don't make me do this.'

Mason stopped edging forward.

His father struggled up from his chair to address the FBI agent standing to the side of his son. 'Please don't shoot him. Can't you see he's unarmed? What's he meant to have done? Son, tell me what's happening?'

Mason's voice was barely audible as he replied, 'I've not hurt anyone, Pa. I don't understand what's happened. It's too crazy to explain.' He took a hesitant step forward. 'I'm so scared.'

'I'm warning you …'

'Son, no. Stop there.'

Mason turned to the officer. 'You can cuff me. I'm not armed. Just let me talk to my Pa, that's all.'

The agent kept her distance from Mason and answered, 'We can't do that – you may be contaminated. We need you to kneel down there, sir.'

'What do you mean, contaminated?' his father asked.

'I'm OK, Pa, it didn't get me. It was after the heist. I was in the van the whole time. They killed someone.'

'Son, you're making no sense. If you're innocent, they'll listen. Just stay calm. Please, Mason. Listen to them. Listen to me.'

'You don't understand, Pa. Afterwards. That thing. It killed them. There was nothing any of us could do. A monster, Pa. I swear to you, I saw it with my own eyes. A monster coming out of the wall. It killed them.'

A tear tumbled down his father's cheek. 'Mason, let them arrest you. We can sort this.'

'You're not listening, Pa. I saw a creature. It ate one of us. You've got to believe me. I saw it with my own eyes.' Mason started sobbing uncontrollably, staring into the distance at his imagined snake monster.

'Son, son. Hold on right there … you're not talking sense. Let me help you.'

His father moved towards him, arms outstretched for a hug, until an agent held him back.

'Can't you see he's traumatised?' Mason's father struggled against the agent holding him back. 'Let go of me.'

Mason stared out from his imaginations and held out a hand to his father, whimpering, 'It's useless, Pa, it's going to kill us all anyway. It's coming for us.' He walked towards his father.

Flashes from a firearm lit up the darkness as three neatly consecutive cracks of gunshot reverberated in the stillness. Mason fell to the ground, looking towards the old man standing up on the stairs of his porch.

'I'm sorry, Pa.' His final words were barely a whisper.

As his vision blurred, he could see his father trying to approach. Another FBI agent intervened, so that there were two holding the old man back. He felt blood choking up inside his mouth and tried to hold out one hand to reach his father, to bridge the gap.

Mason felt his emotions distilled to several yards of separation, but over a decade of hurt. Anger and resentment were forgotten in his lonely desperation, wishing he'd been less rebellious. But time had run out on them both, the distance between them splintering into eternity.

The old man wept as his son's shadowed face ceased moving. He knew Mason was dead, and stared transfixed by his son's skin coloured intermittently by the lurid reds and blues from the FBI vehicles. The red blood trickling from Mason's mouth appeared black and yellow in the colour subtraction from the flashing lights. Men in green hazmat suits positioned themselves around the fallen figure, carrying sheeting that blocked his son from sight.

The old man wondered what terror had tortured his son's mind during the final moments of life.

FORTY-FOUR

Walker turned his car's aircon to full blast and opened the vents to aim cold air at his face. The drive back from Kennedy slowly calmed him down, the aircon's frosty blast tempering his boiling blood.

Refreshed, he stepped back into the incident room and was once again hit by a wall of stale foetid air.

'Did anyone call for an aircon engineer?' he shouted above the buzz.

Zhang wandered over. 'Good meeting?' she said with a strong hint of irony.

'You noticed.' Walker smiled. 'Not the best. I'll tell you later.'

'They promise to sort an extra aircon unit,' she said, nodding in the direction of two of the sheriff's deputies at the back of the office.

'They promise? What about actually getting it done? It's stifling in here.'

'Go easy on them, sir. They've just lost fellow officers and their sergeant is still critical. We all know how that feels.'

Zhang was right – many agents had suffered the loss of close colleagues, himself included. How had he allowed the general to get under his skin? He would have to guard against that in future and stay focused on the manhunt.

'Don't worry, sir, we do have some good news,' Zhang said, walking over to the incident board. He saw a thick red marker-pen cross through the photo of Mason Reeves. 'Aha, we have him.' *One down and two to go,* he thought.

Zhang updated him on news of the shooting in Florida City. He looked at the photo of Mason Reeves. It was an old police ID photograph, from when Mason was in custody. *What a waste.* Mason's background notes told the story of an intelligent man from a good background – an IT genius who had graduated top of his class. And all for what?

Now Mason Reeves was bagged up in a decontamination truck on its way to KSC. The fugitive no longer posed a threat and, as far as Walker was concerned, gave the general one less thing to bust his balls about. There was no room for sentiment in the FBI.

Better still, reports suggested Mason Reeves' outward appearance gave no indication of an infection, something he hoped the NASA lab would confirm.

Damian Gent's photo was above Mason's and the other gang members on the board. The positioning reflected the gang's hierarchy. It was fortunate Damian was captured, because there was precious little information to produce a robust profile. The picture of Damian Gent had been removed from his house. It showed him in a local bar, holding a bottle of bourbon. Damian was smiling enigmatically – a snapshot to happier times, Walker imagined.

Pieces of string fanned out from a pin holding Damian's photo to the board. One string stretched out to the right of the board to a picture of a female lying on blood-soaked sheets, an empty bottle of bourbon next to it.

The bar in the photo of Damian presented another mystery. The bar owner, David Anderson, had been reported missing. While his movements and the timing of Anderson's disappearance meant he couldn't have been at the Orlando crime scene, Walker had to consider the possibility of his involvement. It was possible that he was a silent partner in the gang.

The potential connection was strengthened by interviews with staff at the Rebel Yell bar, who reported Damian as a regular there. Stories suggested Damian liked his drink. A search of his house revealed both fine wine and Scotch whisky collections worth thousands of dollars.

Drone footage from the warehouse showed a car matching the description of Anderson's. While the drone had been unable to gain the license plate before disappearing, the evidence meant Anderson's portrait was pinned to the board as a possible gang member.

Walker, however, was unconvinced. Background intel showed Anderson as being well connected, owning a bar and several holiday rentals along the coast. There was legitimate money in his bank accounts. Lots of it. The idea of Anderson being part of a small gang pulling off heists seemed at odds with his wealth and social standing. A bit of digging revealed Anderson was involved in a far-right racist group. Walker could find no trace of Damian having fascist affiliations. The fact that Damian's business partner was Black made the notion of Damian being involved in far-right political activity even more unlikely, Walker thought.

Had Anderson tried to escape with the gang on the airboat, or had he been killed at the impact site along with Benjamin Johnson? It would explain his disappearance and seemed a possible scenario. Anderson and Damian made unlikely bedfellows and Walker reminded agents that Anderson was not seen at the motel.

Damian had made no mention of David Anderson during his earlier interview. Why would he omit to mention Anderson? Sergeant Conti's recovery held the key to answering that mystery and the need to interview Damian again was now more urgent.

Walker's attention turned to the photos of Noah Scott and Sarah Mitchell. These two were most likely together. Damian Gent's east-coast escape route was blocked off. No air traffic had left the area and the Coast Guard had put a squeeze on all sea traffic.

Agents were working on the possibility that they were receiving help and being hidden somewhere. Failing that scenario, there seemed to be only one viable escape route, which was into the vast Floridian wilderness.

Walker focused on the picture of Sarah Mitchell. She had lived on the edge of Fort Lauderdale in a trailer park with her mother. Was she receiving help from family and friends to smuggle her out of the state?

Interviews, social media, phone, text and email records did not lead Walker to believe that scenario. Agents had already interviewed her mother, who was a druggie and estranged from Sarah for about fifteen years. Field agents went as far as to suggest her mother would give Sarah up for a few dollars, if only she knew where her daughter was.

The disconnect happened during the time Sarah Mitchell was at university. It struck Walker that this was a significant event in her life. Sarah had managed to put herself through university without outside financial support. He concluded that university had been a new chapter, elevating her above trailer-park life. Walker doubted Sarah would seek help from the mother she'd shunned. His lead profiler agreed with him, writing in her analysis: 'Sarah Mitchell has broken free of the trailer-park bonds she despised. She will not want to admit failure or face ridicule by turning back.'

There was no need to pour much energy into that line of enquiry, but they were keeping an eye on the park.

Agents were also looking at her university life, visiting and interviewing people on her social media friends list. So far nothing suggested she was being shielded by ex-students or university staff.

Walker turned his attention to Noah Scott, whose handsome boyish features stared down from the board. What was a potential NASCAR pro from a good family doing working for Damian Gent in Florida? All incoming communications to his known Chicago associates and family were being monitored and, so far, had drawn a blank. Agents in Illinois had interviewed his mother and father, reporting there was a rift between the father and son. The father had been frustrated by Noah turning down a test driver position for a NASCAR team and they had become estranged.

Noah Scott's profile was of someone who lacked patience and who would take shortcuts. This could play into their hands.

Looking at the two profiles, Walker's team had concluded that Sarah Mitchell would be the natural leader. She was determined, strong-willed, and knew Florida well from working in tourism.

All her booking history had been pulled from her previous tourism employer. Any interaction with accommodation in the region was being examined. Walker's profiler believed that Sarah would be confident enough to go it alone and seek refuge somewhere remote but familiar. Somewhere she knew would not attract attention.

Social media and her private Gmail account proved she still had friends at a few tourist destinations. But there were no recent conversations to indicate an escape route. Hotels, campsites and marinas were all being monitored. Undercover agents had been sent as tourists to sites favoured by Sarah, or sites with staff still in contact with her. The agents would bed in and watch out for the fugitives' arrival.

In the meantime, ten helicopters and over thirty boats were scouring the waterways of Florida.

Walker believed capture was only a matter of time.

FORTY-FIVE

Damian woke to the realisation he was being watched like an exhibit through gallery glass. The observer's facial features were hidden under the visor of a green hazmat suit. Damian recognised the gait and stature of the figure and had no idea how long the general had been there.

A pattern of six bleeps was audible to Damian as the clean room's door clicked open and the general entered from the observation area.

Damian watched the general until he disappeared behind his field of vision. The general reappeared at his other side, coming into view like a vulture circling its prey. Damian's newly honed survival instincts screamed danger and he tugged on the bindings holding him down.

'It's just me and you now, boy. Me and you alone, you understand?'

Damian stared back. Through the light reflections of the general's visor, he could still see ice-blue eyes fixed on his. 'Yes, I've been looking forward to our date night. I see you got rid of the medals and put on that sexy outfit I sent.'

The general laughed loudly and glanced down at his protective suit. 'I do like gallows humour,' he said, moving out of sight.

Damian thought the green hazmat made the general look more sinister and preferred his stalker in its natural guise.

A chair scraped over the floor, and the general came back into vision, straddling it, arms folded, leaning forward against the chair back to face Damian. The general removed his visor, tossing it onto a stainless-steel bench. An arrogant smirk was etched on his face, reinforcing Damian's feelings of danger. He sensed the general revelling in his power as the big man leaned in menacingly.

'In case you're wondering, I don't need a visor. Seems your DNA stabilised. You've got some weird stuff going on in there though. Want to know what, or do you already know?'

Damian craved answers and found it difficult to feign indifference.

The general obviously savoured the moment. 'Son, you look as nervous as a whore in church.'

'Just get on with it,' Damian said.

'Looking at your criminal activities, I'd be inclined to call you a snake. Yet, according to our tests, you really are. Can you believe that? Part reptile. Even some insect stuff thrown in there. Seems you really are a bastard.' The general laughed loudly.

The insults felt rehearsed to Damian; however, they made sense. It confirmed his own suspicions. Since acquiring the infection he'd felt his senses heightened, except for his eyesight, which seemed worse, if anything.

'You don't look surprised?'

Damian shook his head as far as he was able under restraints and asked, 'It's stopped now though – so this is it for me?'

'Well, yes and no.'

'What's going to happen to me?'

'Now, my boy, that is the right question.' General Schmidt surveyed his subject in mock pity. 'The choices are: you go to trial and the judge puts you in prison, forever. The biggest freak in the God-damned freak tank. Or …' The smirk had returned. 'Or you can repay Uncle Sam for his kind hospitality over the last few years. You know, being an illegal alien. Robbing our citizens. Murdering them. It's a debt that needs repaying. You'll be pleased to hear we start collecting now.'

'Collecting?'

The general looked up at the camera and nodded.

'Collecting what?' Damian asked again.

'You are going to be my new prototype. The first of many. Seeing as you love change so much, let's see what else we can do for you.' The smile was gone.

'What debt? What are you collecting?' Damian realised he'd broken his feigned indifference. He'd not wanted to give the cold predator a sign of weakness and sensed his time was running out.

'Whatever I tell you, it won't make any difference.' The general left the words hanging and Damian felt more threatened than he'd ever done in his life. He felt evil pulsing from the general and knew he was staring death in the face. Its harbinger hesitated at the door.

'Before I leave you, let me console you with this. What we learn from you and the others will go down in folklore. Though you are history, you are also the future. Just you remember that, Mr Gent, as you die.'

Damian struggled wildly to break his bonds.

'Now don't get yourself all worked up, you hear. There are a few friends I want you to meet.' The general waved towards the observation window.

The lab door opened and several people in hazmat suits entered. A couple of stainless-steel trolleys were wheeled in, carrying glass tanks and what looked like surgical equipment. Damian could see one tank contained an assortment of amphibians and another fish. Damian smelt the vile odour that had permeated his warehouse and realised one of the tanks must contain the stuff that had torn his arm and invaded his body. Realisation dawned on him as he understood what the general meant. They were going to reintroduce the infection. Experiment on him.

General Schmidt turned his back to address one of the scientists. 'OK, just as we discussed,' he said. 'And turn that thing off.' He nodded up at the wall-mounted camera.

Damian continued to struggle frantically, pulling at the straps binding him to the trolley. There was no give. He was helpless. He looked at the general. 'Stop this now, General. You know this is wrong. I have my human rights.'

General Schmidt remained impassive. 'Human, you say?'

'Yes. I'm still a human being.'

'What sort of human being are you, though, to have killed other humans?'

'What sort of human being are you, torturing people?'

The comment seemed to amuse the general.

'Torture isn't new to me, son. We do all sorts of things we don't like in the theatre of war. And we're fighting a war for resources now against the Chinese. We need all the advantages we can take, and you might just be one of them.'

With that the general nodded towards a scientist. Damian recognised the unspoken instruction to begin whatever experiments the general planned. He felt a needle prick his arm and his senses dull as the room blurred into darkness.

Damian Gent woke. Cold permeated his torso and he felt the danger of being pursued. He was running as fast as he could through the North London drizzle. The Albanian was probably dead, and the kid's elder brother would be coming for him soon. Heart racing, he reached the front door and fumbled for his key. His instincts were locked in flight mode and his hands shook under the adrenaline rush.

His stepdad looked up fleetingly from his phone as he ran past the living room. 'I see Al Capone's back,' Michael muttered as James ran up to his bedroom.

Damian felt the out-of-body sensation he'd experienced the previous night. He was looking in at his younger self again, except his emotions were not distant memories. The need to escape felt real. He watched James pull his bed from the wall and lift the carpet, revealing a loose floorboard. He lifted the wood, hoping the TV in the living room below would mask any sounds.

Glancing cautiously towards his bedroom door, James removed an envelope containing nearly £6,000 in cash. He had about five thousand in his current account and would empty that out in the morning. The cash in the envelope was not his though. It had been collected from running drugs on the estate. James knew

Big Mac would miss the money.

He needed to breeze off – anywhere out of the Smoke to buy time to plan his next move. He threw some garms and a few essentials into a Nike sports holdall.

He opened his top drawer, grabbing the passport only used once, on a week's holiday to Majorca with Big Mac the previous year. He pushed it into his front pocket.

He pulled on a fresh T-shirt and a clean sweatshirt. The one he'd taken off had blood on the front. He'd have to get rid of it in a bin somewhere. Heart still racing, he ran into the bathroom to relieve himself and grab some of his toiletries, which he placed in a washbag and into his holdall.

He bounded down the stairs and past the living room door. His stepdad was watching an football match. He'd wanted one last glimpse of his mum, but it was Weight Watchers night. She'd be back soon, but he dared not risk the wait. Not being able to see his mum made him feel wretched.

Hesitating at the door, he considered stabbing his stepdad. He was the cuckoo who'd stolen into their cosy lives. No, his mum would get home and see the body and the police would definitely be on to him then.

Closing the house door behind him, he was back on the streets. The rain lashed down into his face as he buried his bloodied hoodie at the bottom of someone's skip. He ran two blocks to get on the Northern Line, known by his friends as 'Stab Alley'. He looked at the Tube map by the ticket machine and traced the route to Victoria. He'd need to change at Warren Street. From Victoria, he would catch a train on to Gatwick, find a B&B, and buy a flight out of the UK. He'd fly to Australia, Canada or the USA – anywhere English-speaking, as long as it was far away. He bought tickets to Gatwick.

The Tube carriage he chose was nearly empty. He felt steam rising off his body and his heart rate lowering. Other confused feelings invaded the scene. The metal of the carriage became unnatural and frightened him. He wanted to be outside in the open. He pictured greenery and water and felt something menacing stalking him from the depths.

He knew that Original Albanian Gangsters might soon be on his trail. He feared them a lot more than the police and hoped Junior would not squeal. Maybe the Albanians would not realise that his gang was behind the killing. OAG competed with much bigger fish in the drugs pond of North London. Maybe there was an advantage to being thought of as inconsequential.

At least the Tube carriage was warm, and he felt the chill of a dark London winter's night leaving his body. James felt the sun on his face and the carriage faded away.

He was in a swamp. A hot sun beat down on his face, heightening his senses as the enemy surrounded him. After all these years, the Albanians had caught up with him. They were holding him down and pain tore through his body as a machete blade pierced his arm.

The agony lacerated his consciousness, but he needed to live. Suspending his pain receptors, he ripped free of what was holding him down. The aggressors still surrounded him, yet he felt renewed strength flowing through his limbs.

The combination of pain and strength fed energy into his psyche. The power was underpinned by a burning rage at lingering memories of injustices. The anger ramped up to fever pitch, bursting from him like an explosion.

He attacked.

Seizing his prey, he twisted its neck until it snapped. Other attackers were quickly on him. He repelled the first attacker easily and then unleased his wrath on another. He held on to this one, feeling the sweet taste of blood on his palate as he bit down on raw flesh.

His jaws ripped through a neck and he swallowed a whole chunk, feeling the blood of his quarry spray over his face. His eyes were closed to protect them at the moment of incision, a reflex action at the strike. Not only could he feel his own potency, but he also understood he was in control of its power.

He was the alpha predator now and sensed the other attackers dispersing.

Damian tilted his head to be met with blinding light and realised it was not sunlight. A strong lamp was shining directly into his face and moving shadows appeared around it, screaming and fleeing. He pulled at something holding his legs in place and felt it give way.

At the moment of wriggling free, he felt a pinprick in his arm and, like the time before, his energy drained. As sunlight faded away the commotion dissipated, darkness enveloping him like a shroud.

FORTY-SIX

The general and his team stood outside the lab, looking in at the scene through the observation window. Damian lay unconscious on the floor; two men in military uniforms added heavy-duty strapping to his surgical chair, eyeing the motionless subject warily. Blood covered a wide area around the chair and was being cleaned from the floor. It was also concentrated around Damian's mouth and gown.

Other technicians and medics cleaned around an overturned trolley, removing broken glass and surgical instruments that had been scattered over the tiles. One technician was trying to capture frogs hopping around the lab floor. The general watched his inept attempt to capture the animals and, while it made a comical juxtaposition to the grizzly scene, he was not laughing.

Damian had killed the Chief of Naval Research Science and Technology and it was left to other officers to explain what had happened, the highest ranking of whom looked at the general and said, 'In the light of this, we need to suspend plans to experiment on the others.'

The general held up a hand for silence as two corpses were wheeled from the lab past their group. A blood-splattered arm hung down from the cover hiding one of the bodies. Three of Goodhew's own NASA scientists had arrived and instructed the bodies be taken to a separate clean room for monitoring. General Schmidt waited for Goodhew's team to leave the observation area before speaking. 'I see no reason to halt the experiments. As soon as new restraints are in place, strap him in and continue.'

The senior officer stood firm. 'We can't continue on safety grounds, sir.'

The general took a deep breath. 'I have not brought in the best brains at the Army Research Laboratory and the Office of Naval Research to give up at the first setback.'

'With respect, sir, I am advising to suspend activity until we understand more.'

'That is exactly why we have to continue, so that we can understand what has just happened. That man has strength beyond any other human. Just as we'd hoped. Imagine the potential if we can harness that power.'

'That's entirely my point, sir, we don't know if we can harness it. We've just lost two senior officers in there.'

'What's your rank, son?'

'I was a company commander before my transfer to ARL, sir.'

'OK, I have to make a call to Washington. Once I return, we resume the experiments – that's a direct order. Check those bindings. Safety is now your responsibility, commander.'

The general turned to walk out of the lab just as Dr Goodhew walked in. He guessed Goodhew had been woken and told about what had happened. Goodhew was followed by more of his own scientists and the expression on his face was one of fury. He blocked off the general's exit.

'Where are you going? We need to talk,' Goodhew said.

'I have matters to attend to, so it will have to wait.'

'This won't wait,' said Goodhew. 'I need to know why your soldiers are cordoning off parts of this building and what the hell's just gone on here. Who are all these people?'

'These are scientists from ARL and the ONR. They're with me. I'll leave my commander to fill you in on the details. However, let me make one thing clear. You're no longer in charge here. You are here to help and observe. Now, if you will excuse me, the president comes before you.'

The general brushed past Goodhew.

The commander looked awkwardly at Goodhew as Schmidt punched in the six-digit security code, pushed his finger against the pad and exited the observation room.

'Do you really know what you're dealing with here?' Goodhew said. 'Letting that man play God with stuff none of us understands?'

'I assure you that we are following your own safety protocols,' the man who Goodhew understood to be a military scientific officer responded, but did not sound too convinced.

'None of my protocols set out to introduce the substance to human guinea pigs. It's obvious what's going on here. Are there others?'

'That's classified,' said the commander.

'Classified? Is that why parts of Kennedy are now out of bounds?'

The military scientist looked uncomfortable.

'So, what is the general's grand plan then? You heard it yourself, I am here to observe and help. Tell me exactly what you did to this poor man?'

They both looked through the observation window at Damian, who was being strapped back into the chair and cleaned up. Even before Goodhew finished the sentence, a frog hopped from under the chair Damian was strapped to.

'Ha, frogs!' Goodhew exclaimed and at the same time noticed a tank containing marine fish. Details of the experiments were self-evident. 'It seems the frog's already out the bag, so you might as well let the cat out.'

The commander looked resigned. 'We took some of the original alien sample from the impact site and introduced an amphibian species and fish. Before the frog and fish were totally assimilated into that sample, we reintroduced the sample to the subject.'

'You mean you deliberately introduced an alien sample with a prevailing DNA code, hoping the subject would take on some of those characteristics?'

'That's pretty much the size of it, Doctor,' the commander said.

Goodhew learned that the sample had been introduced to Damian as he slept. The process had been extremely simple. A small amount of the active frog-and-fish-boosted sludge has been placed on his arm, where it has quickly taken hold and absorbed itself into his body.

Damian was supposed to remain unconscious for several hours, having been given a high dose of anaesthetic. But within an hour he had woken up, ripping free from his restraints, and killed two officers in a frenzied attack. He'd bitten a large chunk of flesh from one of them and swallowed it.

Luckily, one of the braver scientists had managed to anaesthetise him again, deploying a dose large enough to knock out a rhino. Damian had somehow survived the overdose. Leather strapping had been replaced by metal bonds and observation of the subject revealed the assimilation process continuing as the new sample was processed by his body.

Goodhew was thankful for the commander's honesty. The medical officer had probably been more candid than the general would have liked. He also revealed that several other potential subjects were now located on site, awaiting experimentation.

'Where has the general obtained his other guinea pigs?' Goodhew asked.

'G-Bay.'

The doctor recognised the military abbreviation for the Guantanamo Bay detention camp. The commander confirmed they were using Islamic State terrorists and Chinese militia captured during recent conflicts, and the general intended to press on with experiments.

Leaving the military scientists, Goodhew rejoined his team back at the main lab. Various tests were beginning to yield an understanding of the potency of the threat, but how and why it had initially stopped spreading in Damian remained a mystery. The doctor knew that without an inhibitor to halt the process, the reintroduction of alien matter was a death sentence.

Goodhew's scientific lead, Professor Nyman, approached. 'Doctor, I need you to come and see this,' he said, walking them towards a monitor showing live feeds from the impact site. The images were split on the screen. They showed the warehouse surrounded by the alien matter, extending towards a tall steel barrier at one side of the area. Construction work was in progress to encircle the area in steel.

Nyman pressed a few keys and the screen switched to another image of the alien matter. The blanket of matter was patchier here, as if seeping up through the ground. 'This is from outside the first steel we sank. It looks like it's already broken out.'

'We've only just started sinking the steel,' Goodhew said. 'This is a disaster.'

FORTY-SEVEN

Despite the warm night, the contrast with high daytime temperatures meant Sarah felt chilly. As darkness closed in, they moored up somewhere in the middle of the vast subtropical wilderness, away from all human habitation. Noah wrapped her in an old blanket recovered from the Volvo's trunk prior to ditching the car. Try as she might, the sanctuary of sleep eluded her.

She watched Noah through half-closed eyes. He seemed restless and she knew the noises in the water terrified him. He was a boy from Chicago, out of his natural urban environment, scanning the blackened waterscape for movement, imagining every splash and shadow to be an alligator or a snake.

Another sound was now attracting her senses. It was a long-distance hum. The hum became a thrumming until, at last, she made out the distinctive chuff, chuff, chuff of helicopter rotary blades.

Sarah rose, bolt upright, listening to the whirring echoing in the blackness, and then a beam swept from side to side in the distance. After a couple of minutes, she was certain the beam was zigzagging its way inexorably towards them.

'Shit,' she said, 'we need to move, and we need to move now.'

'I know,' said Noah. 'It's going to be over us in a few minutes.'

Noah turned the key, pressed start and the boat's engine came to life. It seemed extraordinarily loud in the stillness of the swamp. The sound bounced around nearby foliage, seemingly amplified beyond any reasonable proportions.

While the engine's noise would be a giveaway to other boats, the grubby map they'd found in the boat told them there were no roads nearby to hear their progress. They dared not turn the boat's spotlight on because it would be a giveaway from the air, even from a distance. Noah would have to navigate in darkness.

He took the boat in the direction they'd planned, and Sarah looked back at the light. She was sure it was gaining on them. 'You might have to push it a bit, Noah,' she advised, eyeing the approaching searchlight. 'That thing will probably have infrared. It will pick up our body heat, and the boat's engine too.'

'How do you know that?' Noah asked, as if amazed.

'Huh? I thought everyone knew that. Damian said it as well when we escaped the other night, remember?'

'No.'

'I knew anyway. I love watching Hunted on CBS.' She smiled. 'Always wondered if I could be good enough to win the quarter mil. I guess we're about to find out.'

Hunted? ' Noah said. 'No, not heard of it.'

Sarah looked from the search beam to Noah. He seemed oblivious to the threat, like a small child playing adult games – ironic, she thought, for someone in a gang involved in killings.

She was innocent. She had not been involved. Her only crime was the misfortune of being Damian Gent's girlfriend – something she believed would be problematic if she was captured. She preferred not to test that out.

The motel room death had unsettled her. She imagined even if she could prove her innocence, she would receive no help. The others would happily implicate her to take some of the heat off themselves. She knew how the law worked, having witnessed first-hand in the trailer park how injustices could prevail. She had seen real criminals escape while their patsies went down for long stretches.

There were too many deaths to brush off with the 'wrong place, wrong time' excuse. She should have driven away as soon as she'd learned about the Orlando murder. Instead, she'd waited around, and others had died. Benjamin, Anderson, police officers and then the strange motel death. The law had no time for people like her – trailer-park trash. She would be cast aside by the system and either thrown into jail or be given a lethal injection. She needed to keep running.

The chopper was now over their waterway. No longer zigzagging across wider expanses of swamp, it was travelling in a straight line towards them. The helicopter's whirring was noticeably louder, even above the noise of the boat's old engine.

'For Pete's sake,' Sarah said, 'you need to speed up.' It would be a matter of minutes before it caught them. Looking over his shoulder at the helicopter closing in, Noah seemed to grasp her urgency, pushing the throttle lever up a couple of notches. She felt the boat's nose rise out of the water, but even so, the helicopter still seemed to be closing the gap.

'It's closing, hurry,' she yelled, and held on to a rail as Noah pushed the boat to its max, maintaining the gap. She realised it was a dangerous tactic as the boat hit something hard and lurched to the left. Noah rallied the steering, avoiding a series of overhanging cypress trees near the bank. Both ducked, not wanting to be decapitated.

Positioning the boat more centrally in the shimmering channel he sped up to full throttle. The boat hit more bumps and she was uncertain whether their luck would hold out for much longer. They were sure to hit a log, a tree-root system, or run aground, she thought.

Sarah tried to read the flapping map but struggled to focus in the dark and with the bumpy passage. Noah nudged her and pointed ahead. They could just make out what looked to be a fork in the channels.

'Go right, go right,' she screamed, and Noah obeyed. She was sure this was a major fork she had seen on the map earlier. She knew the right-hand fork headed towards the coast, where she planned to travel in the morning.

They both looked back nervously.

The helicopter's search beams were already approaching where the waterway split. She saw a red and green navigation light and the shape of the helicopter itself now, silhouetted black against the midnight-blue sky. The helicopter remained above the fork for some time. It seemed to be sweeping the banks, its beam lighting up an old building they'd missed in the darkness.

The beam swept to the left as the helicopter followed the channel heading south. Sarah signalled to Noah to slow and he did, the engine noise decreasing as the boat's nose dipped.

She laughed. Noah looked puzzled for a moment before his face cracked into laughter too. She imagined the last ten minutes had been far more exhilarating than any NASCAR race and looked at him grinning manically, conceding to herself that he'd done well. His sharp reactions had kept them from crashing, and he had navigated the waterway quite brilliantly in the dark.

But the circumstances only accelerated her escape plan. Rather than wait until light, they would reach the intended campsite under the cover of darkness. She was certain the location would allow some respite and the opportunity to initiate the final phase of her escape.

Then she would have to find a way to ditch Noah.

FORTY-EIGHT

Goodhew stood next to Professor Nyman, transfixed by the image on the screen. There was no mistaking the now familiar sight of the alien sludge, slightly pulsing, expanding in size. It was spreading beyond the newly built section of the containment zone.

'You were right, this is a disaster,' Nyman said at last. 'There's nothing to contain it.'

Goodhew was baffled. 'How has it broken out? The data says it can't penetrate rock and metals.'

'We still don't think it can,' Nyman said. 'There was no time for protracted geological or biometric surveys before sinking the steel. Just imagine if there was just one tiny fault in the rock line under the steel, filled with biological matter. Even a fractional fault in the line would allow it to break out. We have to assume that's what happened. Maybe we just didn't drill deep enough into the rock.'

'Or maybe it had already spread that far out but was unseen, under the surface all the time. We have no way of knowing.'

Other sections of the barrier looked to be containing the spread, which gave Goodhew hope. He agreed with Nyman that the diagnosis presented mixed news, both good and bad. Goodhew asked for some data on spread rates to allow for a wider containment zone to be erected. He wanted geological surveys that would allow them to calculate a safe margin for error for the depth required to sink in new barriers. It was agreed they would sink the metal fifty per cent deeper than the surveyors' depth tolerance.

They would also triple-layer the barrier and bolster it with more concrete. They agreed to pour millions of tons of the stuff into a steel and concrete BLT to block fissures that might be filled with biological matter. There could be no way for the alien DNA to find gaps and creep under the safety shield. In the longer term they would then re-layer with even thicker steel.

Goodhew asked Nyman to hang around as General Schmidt entered the lab for an update. Goodhew nervously relayed the bad news, imagining it would be met by a barrage of insults.

'I agree, this is bad,' the general said. 'This is going to take a lot of steel. Have we got that much steel? Can it be made in time?'

The thought had already occurred to Goodhew. 'My clean-up team is already estimating its escalation rate and the projected size of contagion area over various time points. We are also surveying the drill depth and volume of steel and concrete required. All manufacturing facilities are already primed to go and just need your clearance.'

'Good, so you have this under control.' To Goodhew's surprise, the general seemed satisfied. 'Just tell me if anything changes.' The general seemed to address the last remark to Nyman, who glanced at Goodhew before nodding.

'OK, you have it. I will leave you two gentlemen to it.' The general left the room. Despite the avoidance of the general's wrath, Goodhew could not help but feel uneasy. The general's 'Everything is under control' assessment was at odds with the truth, which was far more complicated. No one knew for sure whether the present containment methodology would work. It had failed once, and the alien DNA could circumvent the tiniest of faults.

Goodhew expressed his doubts to Nyman. 'What we're dealing with here is new to science, and I have no idea what he is feeding Washington. We can put up all the steel barriers in the world, but the key to our survival must be in understanding the alien's DNA structure and absorption process. For the long-term safety of the planet, that's where we need to concentrate our efforts.'

Nyman looked down to the ground and Goodhew thought he looked stressed. Maybe Nyman was struggling with the general's interventions, adding to the pressure of the long hours overseeing intricate experiments. 'Look, don't worry, Professor. Leave me to deal with him. And maybe you need some rest, after we see where the biochemists are up to with this conundrum.'

The doctor and the professor walked over to a large bank of monitors in an adjoining lab. Each showed live feeds from experiments in progress. Both were handed data sheets, which they scanned. The sheets outlined various experiments aimed at understanding the material's ability to transmit itself through and via other matter. A new set of experiments attempting to decode the alien substance had also commenced.

'I can't help feeling that Damian is at the heart of the solution,' said Goodhew.

'Damian?'

'The subject Schmidt was experimenting on.'

'Subject Gent?'

'Yes,' said Goodhew, 'although I find the "subject" label dehumanising.'

Nyman seemed distracted, chewing his bottom lip and avoiding eye contact. Goodhew hoped the professor could cope with the responsibility he was being put under.

'Professor, has it ever struck you as odd that Damian was infected and yet the mutation halted before his capture. How was he stabilised?'

'Yes, that's been our priority since we realised his DNA had stabilised,' Nyman said. 'I took several samples before last night's procedure and also just before further access was denied, so we can continue our work.'

'Hold on, what do you mean "access was denied"?'

'The general has blocked access to the subject.'

'He's done what? I know he reintroduced the alien DNA and we all know what happened after that. I saw the aftermath. When did he restrict access?'

'Almost immediately after that, after our technicians cleaned up that area. I assumed you knew.'

Goodhew digested the information. 'No, I had no idea. What sort of game is Schmidt playing?'

'I thought he'd have told you before me.' Nyman's voice faltered.

The doctor felt anger welling up. 'This mission is tough enough without being denied access to our key source of samples.' He lowered his voice. 'The reintroduction of alien matter was reckless in the extreme. If we lose Damian, we lose the best clue we have as to how we stop this thing.'

'Yes, I know,' said Nyman. 'Though it will be interesting to see the results of the full mutation.'

A lab technician with 'Monica Devlin' on her name badge approached them. 'Doctor. Professor. Sorry, I caught that last bit. We already know what a full mutation looks like.'

'How so?' asked Nyman.

'Of course! We have another subject, don't we?' said Goodhew. 'The corpse from the motel room. The prostitute we assume had intercourse with subject Gent. Deceased, but still biological matter. She still looked human last time I looked.'

'Not any more,' Devlin said, a resigned expression on her face.

'Then please lead the way,' Nyman said.

'We cannot enter the room, Professor. That is now sealed off. Your protocols, Doctor. We do have this though,' said Devlin, pointing towards a nearby monitor.

Doctor Goodhew and Professor Nyman stared at the screen. The female body on the metal trolley looked like a seething mass of compost. Though her shape was still human, areas of her body's surface pulsated slowly with what the doctor assumed were the last vestiges of the original creatures whose DNA had been shared with Damian's.

'We have been monitoring the mutation process and taking samples at various stages,' Devlin said.

'Wow – this is what happens if you have sex with an infected person,' Nyman said.

'She was still recognisable as a human the last time I saw her,' Goodhew said, repeating his earlier comment and shaking his head. 'Why did no one show me this earlier?'

The question went unanswered as the horror of the screen's image reverberated around the lab. Goodhew decided to gather the team.

He put up the feed from the sealed-off isolation room on one of the main lab's overhead displays. Over twenty pairs of eyes followed his gaze as Goodhew started his address by looking up at the image.

'That substance, that sludge you see on there,' he said, 'was once a human being. A homo sapiens like you and me. If we do not find an antidote then one day this thing will cover the planet. There will be no humans, no trees, no animals – no life! Just a sea of that stuff.'

The lab fell silent as the articulated reality of what humanity faced sank in.

'The good news is that there is a way to halt the mutation process.' He left the words hanging. 'We have a man in this building who was infected. Yet, by the time he arrived here, the infection's spread had ceased. It's up to us now to find out what stopped the infection. Unfortunately, the mutation has since been deliberately reactivated.'

Goodhew was thankful his team was not part of the previous night's dark experiment, although he knew everyone had heard versions of what had happened. 'Professor Nyman tells me we do have several stable blood and flesh samples to work with, taken before last night's, how shall we say it … events. Let us concentrate our attention on those samples. Let's see what they show us.'

The lab got back to work, and Goodhew expanded the team already working on Damian's stable blood samples. He hoped that, by broadening that team, someone might discover something they had been missing. He had some of the best biochemists in the United States of America looking at the problem. Goodhew surmised that as the mutation process had stopped naturally, the solution would be a simple one – environmental, perhaps. He called Walker.

One ring and the cellular was answered. A voice said, 'Good morning, how may I help you, Doctor?'

Efficient, Goodhew thought. 'I'm not sure. I just wanted to ask you about where you found Damian. Damian Gent. Where was it exactly? I am clutching at straws here, but was there anything unusual about the place? Anything around it of significance? Chemicals? Agricultural? Anything at all that struck you as different? I'm trying to understand what caused the infection to stabilise in Gent.'

'Good to hear his infection has stabilised.' There was a pause at the other end of the line before the answer. 'No, nothing I can think of, Doc, but I can send you comprehensive pictures of the road where we found him. And the motel room where we discovered the corpse. I already have your email address.'

'OK, that's much appreciated.'

'No trouble. The crime scene is in a place called Indiantown. Go Google it, though I can't think of anything unusual there aside from the number of fast-food joints.'

The conversation ended and, in a matter of minutes, Goodhew, Nyman and Devlin were standing in front of a computer screen. They trawled through Google Earth views of Indiantown, aerial views and photos from where Damian was found seemingly dead on the roadside.

He clicked on Walker's shots of the motel room. The pictures were horrific. The body of the prostitute lay on the blood-soaked bed. The final shots were of the full room, taken from further back. Nyman considered the photo. 'Again, there are no materials on view that I would consider strange. Unless something is really odd with say the water supply or any foliage or natural materials outside that worked to stop the process. There's nothing unusual in this room.'

'Water supply?' said Goodhew. 'I like your train of thought.'

'Is there anything transmitted by water that can act as an agent to halt the mutation? Fluoride for example?' said Devlin.

'I'm not sure if every county in Florida allows fluoride,' said Goodhew. 'I read something about it. I know they don't over in Clearwater – they voted against it. That struck me as apt at the time, them wanting clear water in Clearwater. I am not sure about the east-side counties.'

'Anyway, I don't see how a monatomic anion can affect DNA,' Nyman said.

'I agree, I believe we're looking for an endogenous substance,' Devlin said. 'Or process.'

'Maybe, but my worry is that we're trying to find processes that originate from within cells at a subatomic level we simply cannot see,' Goodhew said. 'While the DNA fusion seems internally fuelled, I still think what halted the process with Damian may have an exogenous catalyst. Something from outside his body acting like a pathogen that caused the endogenous change, halting the DNA fusions and saving his life. For a while at least.'

'Yes, that sounds logical,' Nyman agreed. 'Not bad for a rocket man. I'll up the testing of different compounds to see if any halt the process. The general is pushing hard for that answer.'

Nyman walked off and Goodhew stopped to look at the screen showing Damian's room. There was something nagging him about Nyman. His last comment played on the doctor's mind. 'The general is pushing hard for an answer'. There was obviously a direct line of communication between the general and Nyman. Something in Nyman's body language had been offbeat too. Goodhew began to feel uneasy about the professor.

The computer display showed Damian's bio-readings had changed, his temperature dropping as his heart rate went down to only twenty-nine BPM. He'd go and look in on Damian, despite the general's order that the subject was off-limits.

The doctor checked the lab monitor showing Damian's clean room and found the camera feed had been already turned off. The general's secrecy had given him a lucky break.

'Subject Gent' might still contain clues to curtailing the *mutation process,* despite the reactivation. Goodhew also wanted to do the right thing to help prevent Damian suffering a painful death.

He left the main lab and entered the central corridor linking distinct sections of the facility. A soldier stood at the end of one and another guard barred his access to the observation room outside Damian's room. 'Sorry, sir, I have instructions not to let anyone pass.'

'Instructions?'

'Yes, from the general.'

'Was my name mentioned in those instructions?'

'Er, who are you, sir?'

'I'm the man the president put in charge here. Dr Nathan Goodhew. It says right here, on my badge.'

The soldier craned forward to look at the badge. 'Yes, I have heard of you, sir.'

'Good, now step aside before things get serious for you.'

The soldier looked uncertain but let him through. Goodhew was thankful. 'NASA Chief Scientist' carried some weight.

FORTY-NINE

He made it onto the Gatwick Express at Victoria without incident. Tiredness infiltrated his bones, making them feel heavy, a background ache that his psyche knew was the prelude to playing out his escape from London. And it signified something else, just out of reach from his consciousness.

With every passing moment he felt slightly safer. A search on his smartphone secured lodgings in a cheap guesthouse in Horley, not far from the airport. Once inside the dingy room, he recharged his mobile and Googled travel options to the USA. One site advised travellers not to forget ESTA. This was a blow. The site explained 'ESTA, set up in the wake of 9/11, is a temporary permit that allows up to ninety days travel within the States.' Ninety days was easily enough time to disappear, he thought.

Another site advised he needed to have an onward address and a valid reason to get through immigration. Although he had no 'previous' with UK police, James imagined a red flag existing on a computer somewhere to block his travel plans. He filled in the online form and paid. The transaction was an unfortunate necessity, providing police with a way to trace him. To his relief, in less than ten minutes, the response came back. 'ESTA Approved'. He'd ask the guesthouse to print off the form in the morning.

Next, he Googled 'How to become an illegal alien in the USA', followed by, 'How much money can I take into the USA'. He needed to make sure nothing went wrong.

With a full plan in place, James began his search for late flight deals to the USA. It was exciting – an adventure. And more importantly, it was an escape from his tormentor. A picture of the general fused with that of his father. Who was his tormentor? He tried to grasp the answer, but it lay in that area of the brain he knew would only allow access if he stopped trying too hard.

He'd buy the cheapest ticket to the USA from Gatwick departing tomorrow – a return ticket so as not to raise suspicion at immigration. He'd empty his bank account at a branch in Horley. It was risky, but necessary. He planned to exchange most of his cash for dollars. Mostly big bills, so the bundle would not look like an unreasonable amount on security scanners.

He boarded the American Airlines jet heading to Charlotte Douglas International Airport without a hitch, sitting in a window seat, watching the sunlight bounce off fluffy snow-like clouds. He felt himself looking down at the boy wrapped snugly in a flight blanket, drinking his first-ever whisky from the trolley, and to his amazement it was free. He asked for another, a double, yet the expected alcoholic heat did not follow. He tried to feel the connection with James Wardell, watching the boy departing his home-life nightmare, only to enter another one. He moved to pick up his cup of whisky, but metal restraints on the seat's armrest stopped him.

An image of the general materialised and he began to feel cold to the core, pain bringing him back to the place he subconsciously knew was the present. He wanted to dive back into the adventure of his flight, but slowly the surroundings of the bright laboratory came into view.

Damian stared up at the harsh ceiling lights. He was delirious and felt more changes affecting his body. He remembered the general's expression, relishing his misery and seeing the tanks full of frogs and fish. Realisation of his plight quickly followed, and he knew he was an experiment the general had ordered. He could feel his veins swell as breathing became difficult.

He also knew his time was running short. Staring up at the camera, he mumbled, 'Help me. Please. Help. I'm dying.' The internalised sound of his voice was strange, like a hoarse rasp. His vocal cords felt swollen, his skin dry and in need of water.

A door opened and steps approached. He was picking up noises from outside the room. The steps stopped the other side of the door to his room. They were light steps, not the general's.

A six-digit code sequence sounded. It had changed from the last time he heard the sounds. Damian replayed the sequence in his head.

The door opened and Doctor Goodhew entered, carrying a large canister. He looked apologetically at Damian. 'What have they done to you?' he said. 'I'm so, so sorry. This is not right.'

'Help me.' Damian felt his human self slipping away.

'This will help,' Goodhew said, unscrewing the metal canister and holding it up to Damian's lips. 'Just drink.'

Damian opened his mouth and felt cold water pouring in. He spat it out. 'Just pour it over me,' he said, 'I'm drying out.' The doctor paused before doing what he was asked. The liquid soaked Damian's head and torso.

'That feel better?'

'Yes, better. You know what I could really do with though?'

'No, what?' the doctor said.

'A bottle or two of whisky. Or bourbon. Or vodka. Anything alcoholic. I don't mind.'

'I don't think now's the time to be drinking if you're drying up. Alcohol dehydrates.'

'You're not getting it, are you, Doctor?'

'Getting what?'

'You know, for an intelligent man, you're slow on the uptake.'

The doctor looked perplexed. 'I'm sorry, I don't know what you mean.'

'I've worked it out, Doc. Worked out what made me feel better.'

'You have …?'

'I've pretty much just told you. No? What did I just ask for?'

The doctor stared at Damian for a moment, his eyes widening. 'Hang on in there, I'll be back soon,' the doctor said, running from the lab.

251

FIFTY

Less than ten minutes later Doctor Goodhew was back. He carried in a large plastic container, like the ones people buy screen wash in.

The doctor beamed. 'A hundred per cent proof, this. Pure ethanol. This should do the trick.'

Goodhew unscrewed the top and tipped some into Damian's mouth. He swallowed hard, feeling fire cut into his throat. Despite gagging, he kept swallowing the fiery liquid, spitting some back up from time to time. 'More,' he said, 'and again.'

Damian drank a quarter of the container with no apparent side effects. 'Now pour the rest over me. Concentrate on the worst areas,' he said.

The doctor unzipped the top of Damian's orange overalls and poured some over the exposed skin. He paid particular attention to where the latest alien substance had grafted to Damian's shoulder, craning forward a little, concentrating.

'What is it?' Damian rasped.

'Nothing.'

'We both know that's a lie, don't we?'

Goodhew avoided eye contact as he splurged the remaining liquid over Damian's torso and placed the empty vessel to one side.

Damian tried again. 'Tell me what it is, Doc. I want to look.'

'I'm not sure that's a good idea at this stage. I need you to focus on your recovery.'

'What are you trying to say? Do I look even worse than I did before?'

Goodhew said nothing.

'Let me see. I have to know. Go turn the light off in the other room, so I can see myself in the window.'

Instead, the doctor picked up the empty metallic water canister he'd brought in earlier. 'This is the best I can do.'

'Let me see.'

'It's not ideal. It's going to distort your features and make it look worse than it is. Are you sure you want to?'

Damian nodded and the doctor held the shiny canister in front of his face, moving it slowly from right to left like a barber showing off his work. Damian had to catch his breath as he saw the reflection. His face was only just recognisable as human. A reptilian visage presented itself, bloating out and then thinning as the canister moved across his eye line. A fairground hall of mirrors freak show, he thought.

The doctor put the canister to one side again and looked sympathetically at him as a moment passed. 'You're right. I have looked better,' Damian said at last.

'Well, as a scientist I would say you look amazing. Unique. Did you notice the gills? You might be amphibious. Can you believe that? A new species.'

'Gills? I don't want to be a fish or a frog. I want to be human. Do you not get it? Human. Not some experiment in a lab.'

'I know, sorry. Please excuse my insensitivity. I don't have anything to say that will help. You are a new evolutionary form. Incredible – the first of your kind.'

'The first, and last. Destined to die alone. A freak.'

'Hmm, this is difficult for me.'

'For you?'

'What I mean is that I understand it if you want more like you. You wouldn't want to be the only one. And when I said evolutionary, maybe that's the wrong word.'

'Wrong?'

'Well, this is not an evolution. Not as Darwin set out. This is an invasive entity, one threatening our planet. How are you feeling?'

Damian laughed, despite everything. 'Fine. You're really cheering me up. You just have the knack, I guess.'

'Do I?'

'Not really, but you know, the pain's going. I feel pretty normal.' Damian realised the incongruity of his comment and added, 'As normal as a talking frog can feel. I mean, I'm not actually the first talking frog on the planet, am I? I think Kermit beat me.'

In the manner of a local GP, Goodhew smiled reassuringly. 'Yes, very good. Let's hope the ethanol has halted the transformation and killed off the DNA cocktail they gave you earlier.' He beamed.

'Am I meant to be happy? I look like a refugee from Fraggle Rock.'

The doctor laughed. 'You've retained your human sense of humour, I see.'

'Yes, the future looks bright. I just need a princess to kiss me now. Do you know any?'

'You just never know. Although you did try to eat the last woman who touched you. That will have been the snake DNA from the impact site, I believe.'

'I thought I might have dreamt it. I remember now. How is she?'

'She's dead.'

Damian contemplated the news. 'She was trying to hurt me. She deserved it.'

Goodhew looked surprised. 'Deserved it? She had no choice in the matter.'

'You scientists, heh? Always defending the indefensible. What was she doing? Just following ze orders?' Damian said, in a mock German accent.

'Yes, you're right. There's no justification for this – for what the general is doing.'

'What is the general doing, exactly?'

'I can see you are an intelligent man, Damian. You can imagine.'

'Thanks for the "man" call-out. Appreciated. I've seen enough films to imagine that the lunatic is trying to create a new line of species.'

'Not just a line. I believe he is trying to create an elite force. Amphibious soldiers in this case. With increased strength and powers.'

'It's a joke, right? I still have my own will. My own mind. I'm not following his orders and I never will. He's deluded, and, when I get out of here, I'm going to put him out of his misery.'

'I have no idea how he expects unwilling volunteers to follow orders either. But once I report the significance of ethanol to the lab, I'm afraid it will give him the tools to halt any mutations at a point of his choosing. But I won't let it come to that. I will petition Washington. I intend to stop this nonsense.'

While Goodhew was earnest, Damian doubted a few scientists could reverse a political and military imperative. 'Let's pretend you are able to stop what he's doing to me. Tell me you can make things better. Change me back.'

'I'm so sorry, but we can't. I wish we could. The process is irreversible.'

'Irreversible,' Damian repeated.

'Yes, I don't think the new DNA can be separated out again, or the situation reversed. You are a new species. A hybrid.'

'You said as much earlier. But you said something else too. Are there more like me?'

'I hope not. At least I don't think so. But there will be, if the general gets his way.'

'Maybe I should wait then, while he creates some new friends for me to play with. A new mate maybe?'

'Interesting idea, but I don't see it working like that exactly. Not for you. You have too many other contaminants from the impact site for us to replicate an exact match.'

Damian smiled widely at the doctor. 'You may be one hundred per cent human, but you can't tell when I'm joking. You're as bad as he is. Deep down you want to know, don't you? You want to see if the general can do it.'

Silence fell between the two. Damian's hope of becoming normal again had been dashed in one word – 'irreversible'. No human would want to be near him again. He'd never find female companionship.

Sarah Mitchell, what would she think of me now?

Pangs of regret pricked his conscience. Things could have been so different. The armed robberies were a mistake, as was relying on outsiders. He'd mostly only ever had to rely on himself, since his stepdad came into his life and started abusing him and since he'd had to flee England to start a new life with next to nothing. Apart from Benjamin he had no one, and his friend was dead. The vigilante at the last heist. Why had she stood up to him? It was not her money. She was an idiot and she got what she deserved. It was not his fault; she had forced him to act, to protect himself. Why did bad luck always seem to fall on him?

And the infection from the warehouse. Why him? And now he was being used as a laboratory rat. He had become the general's pet. The general was abusing him, like his stepdad used to. Hurting him. All his abusers would pay a heavy price and he would particularly enjoy some time alone with the general.

Sick thoughts about what he would do to the general crossed his mind. Behind his fancy uniform, the man was an animal and deserved to be put out of his misery very slowly. He imagined the moment and it made him feel slightly better.

Damian's dark thoughts extended to his own physicality. Even if society would allow him to live freely, he would be labelled a freak to be hunted by the media and shunned by others. He knew that his physical make-up had changed irreparably. The doctor had been clear on that point.

Damian broke the silence. 'So, I'm going to have to live in SeaWorld for the rest of my life?'

'Well, yes, an aquarium might be necessary,' the doctor said.

'You are really something, aren't you? I was joking again.'

'Oh, yes, another joke. I see. But your skin is drying out quickly. I think you might need to live in a watery environment.

I'll have to run some checks, of course. I'll take some more bloods in a moment.'

'This is surreal. You are being serious. Between you and the general, I've become a snake-frog pet or something.'

'Or something,' Goodhew repeated, except he was reading distractedly from a nearby data terminal. Damian saw the doctor's disassociation – his submersion into a process. This was the person who'd come to help him. It was all a joke, and a sick one, he thought. Where was the compassion? The doctor perused the screen and muttered to himself.

'Doctor, please tell me, what have I got to look forward to? Being prodded about in a tank? Being sent to die in battle? A lifetime of dating on Plenty of Fish?' Damian laughed at his own joke, his hoarse laughter morphing into sobs. He was struggling to process the stark reality of his situation.

Anger began to rise. He relived his torture at the hands of the general and lamented the facility's inability to help him. The doctor's clinical aloofness irritated him. As if reading his thoughts, the doctor left the screen.

'Maybe think of it another way.'

'What way?'

'Well, you're going to be a hero. The man who saved the world. You're the person who discovered the alien substance can be halted by ethanol. Or at least it looks that way. I just need to get back to the lab and report my findings.'

'Aha, your findings now? It was my discovery just a moment ago.'

'No, I didn't mean it like that.'

'I'm never going to be given any credit for the discovery. I'll only ever be seen as a criminal monster to be experimented on further.'

'Please listen to me,' said the doctor. 'I'm going to put a stop to this. You must trust me. I'll be back with more alcohol soon, but I hope what I've administered will stop further mutations. At the very least, it will buy you some time. And after that, I think we need to get you into a water bath.'

257

Goodhew turned to face the door, and Damian pulled hard against the metal wrist restraint. The metal fractured, making a loud snapping noise. Goodhew stopped and slowly turned. The horrified 'O' shape of the doctor's mouth was a satisfying sight to Damian. 'The thing about carrying DNA from other creatures – it has made me stronger.'

He ripped free from the shackle holding his other gnarled hand in place, then strained his neck muscles and broke the collar and head restraints, allowing him to sit upright to unbolt his chest and legs. Raising himself to his feet, he looked into the transfixed doctor's eyes. He saw confusion.

'Look, Doc, don't take this personally.'

He clasped his hands around Goodhew's neck. The doctor's eyes bulged in their sockets, a blue tinge invading his lips. Damian felt life leave the doctor and let him fall to the cold floor of the lab. There was nothing more the doctor could do for him and, in admitting so, Goodhew had become expendable.

Glancing up at the camera, Damian knew he had to act quickly. He reached down, grabbed Goodhew's hand and separated out its fingers. Holding the hand to his mouth, he bit down until a crunching sound echoed in his head. He let the hand drop and took the doctor's index finger from his mouth, checking it carefully.

At the door, Damian pressed all ten keys and listened to the variance in their tones. The panel bleeped angrily and an 'Access Denied' message flashed up. He hoped the mechanism would not lock as a result of his test. He carefully entered the six-digit code he had listened to earlier: 0,3,0,2,2,5. Damian had lost track of time, but knew the code must be that day's date. Not very secure, he thought. The fingerprint recognition pad was situated under the numbered buttons. He held the doctor's finger to the pad while it still had enough of an electrical impulse to work. The door clicked, and he pushed it open.

Damian was in the adjoining observation room. He took in air through his slightly open mouth, enhanced receptors searching for signs of life and danger. He tried to pick up faint scents of the outdoors – a possible escape route.

All he could discern was a strange lingering taste on his tongue, one that he vaguely recalled from an earlier dream about the swamp. He realised it was a smell familiar to apex predators the world over. It was the bloody taste of fear and he found the taste deliciously intoxicating. It was as much a sense as an aroma, one that marked out his new being. He was to be the hunter, not the hunted.

He swallowed the taste away and another scent played on his senses. It was a person. Close by, he thought. The other side of the door.

He keyed the same sequence in on the exit pad and pressed the doctor's severed finger onto the fingerprint reader, hoping the code was universal within the complex.

A click told him it had worked.

Quickly he pulled the door open and stepped through. A soldier stood there, looking startled, expecting the doctor to walk back through, no doubt. As the soldier raised his weapon, Damian grabbed its barrel and twisted it free. Reversing the movement, he drove the gun's metallic butt into the soldier's chin. The soldier's legs crumpled and Damian, sensing someone else close by, gently lowered him to the floor to minimise noise.

He stripped the soldier of his camouflage to swap with his conspicuous orange jumpsuit. He tried the boots to find they did not fit. His feet had swollen, looking much bigger than usual.

There was webbing between his toes.

FIFTY-ONE

Damian rounded the corner and walked towards a soldier guarding the end of the corridor. The soldier was typing on his cellular and, despite glancing up, appeared oblivious to the approaching danger. As Damian closed the gap, the guard's expression changed to puzzlement.

'Heh, who are you?' the soldier said, but within seconds of pocketing his device, Damian had snapped his neck. Sensing no one else around, Damian let the guard fall to the floor.

There was no key code entry to the next corridor, so he pushed the door open with one leg and dragged the guard through, hiding him from the main corridor.

Shiny metal doors punctuated one side of the corridor at regular intervals. Unpainted new plasterwork around the metal and remnants of debris on the floor told Damian that the reinforced door frames were newly installed. The building work stood out in a facility where everything else looked pristine.

The now familiar taste of fear seeped from behind the doors. He knew the rooms were occupied and tried one of the handles. Locked. Of course, it had to be. They would all be locked. He recalled the general's words: 'What we learn from you and the others will go down in folklore.' These were 'the others', he guessed.

Sounds from beyond the main door and towards the end of the next corridor caught his attention and he regretted wasting precious seconds. Capture was unthinkable and he needed to move fast.

He smelt the air, hoping for a clue to the direction of outside. A slight shift in ambient temperature came from a ventilation duct above his head. The cooler influx mitigating the building's internal heat seemed icy cold to Damian. Sounds from the next corridor continued to get louder and Damian looked up at the duct. The ceiling was impossibly high, yet something in his brain told him to jump. He sprang up and felt a surge of joy, knowing he had jumped higher than any human had ever jumped before, and grabbed hold of the metal ducts.

Hanging on to the metal grid with strong claw-like fingers, he swung his feet up to the ceiling to exert downward force. He pressed upwards and the screws holding the hatch in place pulled out, fracturing the plasterwork they were secured to. Damian let go and fell backwards, managing to right himself like a cat, his feet touching down softly on the corridor floor. He kicked the obvious bits of fallen masonry to the side of the corridor. The hatch was now hanging, bent open, two screws precariously gripping the ceiling at two corners on one side. He heard several pairs of boots pounding the corridor around the corner. The steps sounded like heavy military boots, and Damian knew they were on to him.

He jumped up again, beating his previous world record by a fraction, this time gripping inside the hatch entrance with both hands. He pulled his body upwards, twisting his arms and shoulders to heave himself into the narrow ventilation shaft, barely wide enough to receive his frame. Reaching down, he yanked the grate off the corridor ceiling and turned it, pulling it through the diagonal of the square opening. More bits of plaster fell to the corridor below and Damian wondered if his idea of escaping via the ventilation ducts had already come unstuck. He laid the vent cover over the square opening from the inside of the shaft, hoping it would not look too obvious from the corridor level, though he was doubtful.

The induction grill's angled slats gave him a reasonable view of the corridor. Moments later he heard the corridor's end door open, and soldiers jogged past. They seemed oblivious to his presence above their heads. Damian could not see him, but the taste of his adversary was distinct – Schmidt was in the group.

Damian decided to head in the opposite direction to the flow of icy air behind him, hoping to find an external outlet to the vented system. Scrabbling forward he reached a junction in the ventilation. The junction narrowed to the left. There was no way he would be able to pass through the gap, so he was forced to turn right. If the vent narrowed ahead, he'd be trapped. Hearing voices below, Damian shimmied along as quietly as possible.

FIFTY-TWO

General Schmidt surveyed the scene with cool disdain. Damian had managed to escape, killing Doctor Goodhew and two soldiers in the process. The general had the whole building on lockdown and figured Damian could not have got far.

Goodhew's body stared up at him, a bewildered death grin betraying the pain of his final seconds of life. Despite the grisly scene, the general felt satisfied, seeing the irony of Damian's escape. Goodhew knew far too much and was threatening to blow the whistle on his plans. Unwittingly, Damian had solved a little problem.

With Goodhew out of the way, the general knew Nyman would be able to keep a lid on the human experiments and cooperate with his military scientists. He had obtained a dossier outlining Nyman's dirty little secrets. Nyman had too much to lose and would do exactly as he was told.

The general's main concern was how many NASA scientists had already accessed the observation lab immediately following Damian's previous attempted escape. He resolved to monitor NASA workers and purge the site of any who looked to endanger his project. He had made sure he left no paper trails or e-trails. There was nothing in existence to suggest that the general's work inside Kennedy was anything other than acceptable military biochemical weapons research. There was certainly no approval from the White House to use prisoners in experimentations.

An opportunity had arisen to create a force so powerful it would be able to protect American interests across the planet. He considered it his duty to carry the torch of American dominance across the globe and progress experiments.

US foreign policy had switched from its position as leader of a NATO-centric world police force to one of unilaterally defending its own interests. That meant obtaining new raw materials for American business and disrupting foreign powers encroaching on global trade routes.

General Schmidt knew his compatriots in Early Light were on-board with the opportunity that had presented itself. His secret group of military leaders and conservatives wished to turn back the clock. They needed to ensure that unfettered neo-liberalism and the rise of globalism would not go unchecked. Chinese investments in US business were eroding American power from the inside. Facing up to America's militarised corporate enemies in the new battlefields of rich mineral deposits was just one facet of a multidimensional global game of chess – a game America was currently fighting economically and territorially.

The US's failure to face up to Putin during Russia's invasion of the Ukraine in 2022 had made him angry. But he was more worried about China now than the ostracised Russian state.

The Chinese had laid claim to new sea channels opening up in the Arctic Circle, where global warming was making access to natural resources far more accessible. America's single nuclear icebreaker was unable to compete against the large nuclear-powered fleets of its competitors. It had been a massive fail by previous US administrations – one he hoped to rectify using US elite forces, which could operate in extreme cold, sabotaging Chinese, Russian and Scandinavian activity in the polar region.

It helped that the new president had convinced a majority of Americans that the USA's problems in the world stemmed from aggressive trading blocs like the Chinese dominated RCEP, as well as the territorial encroachment of Russia. It was reassuring that presidential electioneering had finally caught up with the major threats Early Light considered had been facing their nation for years.

The new political realism had only occurred because American forces were facing new flashpoints across the globe.

The majority of new flashpoints were against the Chinese, whose trade policy involved sending military-trained settlers into regions to mine raw materials. Millions of Chinese migrant workers were dispersed to strategic strongholds, with the ability to defend Chinese interests in those areas, if required.

The hard-line rhetoric of the president's election campaign had surprised him. The supposition that the United States was not to be pushed around by China was one his group had been working towards for over a decade. He hoped to subtly sound out the new president and test her suitability as a member of Early Light – he hoped she would be the first president to be a member of the group. Her involvement would make the experiment process easier.

The general considered the strategic importance of new elite forces across the globe. The dual function of Chinese migrant workers in Africa was proving a huge problem. Their ability to support local militia to control trade was blocking out US mining companies. The USA was losing the new scramble for Africa – the fight for raw materials. The general's successful 2024 skirmish was only the first step in turning the tide, as far as US foreign policy was concerned. Now even Australia was having its head turned by Chinese money, securing their huge reserves of cobalt.

The problem needed a new, more covert, approach. When the opportunity to create a new elite force had presented itself, Early Light was quickly on-board with the concept. The first mission for such a force was already being considered by the in-Congress assembled leadership of Early Light, although any plan rested on the success of his experiments.

His preferred starting point was to protect US access to the North China Sea. China had ramped up ownership claims to the water routes in the region. Their policy relied on manufacturing new islands, creating them by dumping millions of tons of dirt into the sea and then building airstrips and new naval ports on the reclaimed land. The encroachment had to be curtailed.

The problem had been discussed many times within the privacy of the Oval Office, without any clear vision of how the Chinese could be stopped. Early Light had much clearer ideas.

They needed to implicate Japan and South Korea in attempts to sabotage Chinese activity in the South China Sea. The stealth of anonymous amphibious assaults conducted with pinpoint accuracy could spark a regional dispute that would distract the Chinese, affect RCEP trading, and allow America to take advantage in other zones, particularly Africa and the Arctic Circle.

The takeover of Hong Kong and pushing for 'reunification' with Taiwan was indicative of the Chinese squeeze on Western influence in the Far East. The Chinese goal of blocking peaceful access to free trading routes could not be tolerated. And now the means to stop them had presented itself. An incognito force that could meet new threats and challenges from China.

Each division could be genetically tailored to the task in hand, starting with an amphibious assault unit that could sneak in and destroy ports and airstrips in the South China Sea.

Once the science was perfected by experimentation on prisoners, his operational units would be willing volunteers who would have great rewards bestowed upon them for their sacrifices. Once his scientists figured out the DNA combinations for the most militarily effective mutations, they would be standardised. His volunteers would be compatible mutations, allowing them to live together in luxury as faceless heroes of the state – in secret locations of course.

He would be the one to lead their creation and take the United States of America to ultimate victory. The general believed he was destined to become a hero. His historical legacy would be global peace, with the United States rightfully reinstalled as its guardian and protector.

Military medics covering Doctor Goodhew with a sheet broke the general from his reverie. Wishy-washy do-gooding liberals like the doctor would have no place in the new order.

The same weak-minded liberals with no grand vision had allowed a Chinese multinational to make a hostile takeover of his father's factories. Weak US laissez-faire economics had led to his pop committing suicide. It was unforgivable that company law allowed the invasion of foreign powers by corporate stealth. The desire for revenge burned deep, entering his thoughts on a daily basis.

He turned his attention to a lieutenant. 'OK, the prisoner has to be somewhere. Check every inch of this building. Reinforce the perimeter, get an air picket up and set up thermal tracking weapons at the outer fence. I have a feeling that's where the toad will be heading.'

'Yes sir.' The lieutenant saluted and turned to go.

'And lieutenant, get tracker dogs in here. His stink must be highly individual.'

FIFTY-THREE

Damian listened from a vent thirty yards away and pondered what the general meant by 'thermal weapons'. It sounded like the outside fence would soon be booby-trapped. He needed to move fast.

Damian continued to crawl along the shaft, thankful it retained a manageable width. A welcome aroma of grass and vegetation met his nostrils. He could visualise the greenery and knew it had to be close.

A few yards further on he came to a vertical hatch and knew he'd reached the building's outer wall. His heart sank – it was too narrow to climb through. He'd have to reverse his way down the long shaft backwards and hope to find a safe exit point somewhere else within the building.

Lying still for a few moments, he felt his skin ache as it dried out, telling him his remaining time was limited. In his new state he needed more water. Looking through the grill he was thankful it was night-time, doubting his body could survive the blazing Floridian sun.

In my new state. Damian repeated the notion in his mind and reassessed the grill. It was secured in place from the outside, which meant pushing against it to force it off, not knowing who might hear it clatter to the ground and hoping it would land on something soft. It was a chance he'd have to take.

Placing his flat palms against the grill, he pushed. The fixings were stronger than the grill, which buckled against the pressure from his palms, but stayed in place. He tried again, pressing harder. One side of the corner fixings gave way, leaving its screw in the outer brickwork, and then another corner broke free, leaving the grill secure by only its two bottom screws. Damian was able to push the flimsy covering so that it bent until the other two corner sections snapped free of their wall fixings, leaving him holding the grill in one hand.

There was no way he could pull the vent cover inside the shaft and squeeze past it. He had to take a risk and let it fall to the ground below. Angling the metallic cover as a mirror, he could just make out that the ground below was entirely concreted, with another building about forty yards away. The opposite building was so tall, he could not see its skyline, and guessed it must be the iconic Vehicle Assembly Building.

He pushed his arms forward so that they extended outside the building as far as his elbows. It meant contorting his body where the interior shaft narrowed, squeezing his torso and restricting his breathing. He flipped the grill as far as he could, using his wrist to send it out like a frisbee to clear the concrete immediately below, not wanting it to land in his fall zone. He heard the metal clatter against concreted ground, echoing between the surrounding concrete monoliths. Nothing seemed to be going smoothly.

With no grill to hold, Damian pulled his arms back to the outside wall so that they acted like a lever to pull his weight outwards. The angle was against his joints and for a moment he felt himself wedged. Panic rose in his throat as he struggled to breathe. He imagined the general being shown his body at dawn, laughing at the sight of arms pushed out of a gap in the wall, and at the thought of the escape attempt literally crushed in its own stupidity.

Fury took hold and, instead of relaxing as he imagined he should, he decided on the do-or-die option. In a double-jointed manoeuvre from the elbow, he pressed his hands flat against the outside wall and managed to pull himself further forward. He felt pressure on the side of his skull as it compressed to fit through the aperture with his arms alongside. He endured his bones giving way under the tight squeeze, compressing to the point of cracking, yet not doing so. He was in tune with what his malleable body was capable of and felt his bones bending to accommodate escape.

One more pull and he was through.

He stopped there, his head and torso hanging out of the opening, staring down at a twenty-yard concreted drop, held only in place by pressure exerted by his legs against the walls of the interior vent's sides. Another few inches and he'd be tumbling head first to the ground. Composing himself, he pulled himself out the final few inches, which allowed gravity to take hold. He fell to the ground, hitting the concrete hard. He felt bones along his left side fracture under the impact, but he had survived the fall.

Winded and in pain, Damian leaned against the wall to recover, taking in the welcome aroma of sea air. He looked around, unprepared for the scale of the complex, which he found astonishing. Which way should he go? He'd lived in Brevard County for over a decade, but never been close to the Space Center's main hangar where rockets were assembled and housed. The complex always looked impressive from across the Indian River in Titusville but, looking up from underneath now, he had an unexpected reality check as to its size.

To his right, tall double fencing stretched out to the distance, the other side of which looked like a double motorway. The double tracks had to be the route connecting some kind of transportation system taking rockets from the Vehicle Assembly Building to launch pads further out.

To his left a raised corridor connected the building he had escaped from to the Assembly Building opposite. He edged along the wall to his left and looked out from its corner to see a string of parking lots stretched out beyond the double security fencing. The double wire fencing was too high and possibly electrified, he was not sure. He was trapped.

Taking a few deep breaths, Damian cautiously looked around the corner and down the long side of the building that had imprisoned him. A road ran down the side to security booths positioned either side of an entry gate. Pedestrian crossings led across the road from the first parking lot the other side of the fencing, telling him the gate allowed both vehicles and pedestrian access. Despite it being night-time, there were over a hundred cars in the parking lot and Damian imagined security guards would be used to pedestrians coming and going at regular intervals. He would have to risk it.

Physical changes and injuries made it impossible to stride purposefully, as he'd intended, towards the security station, and Damian hoped whoever was inside was not positioned to look out in his direction; they would see a hobbling creature in camouflage with no boots. Relieved to reach the booth with no reaction, and knowing his feet were now hidden from view, he walked past the outer window, nodding towards the security detail sitting inside. The man hardly glanced up, and he was allowed to walk on to the pedestrian gate. He heard a lock release click, no doubt triggered from within the booth, and pulled the gate open to exit the inner Space Center and enter the parking lot.

He staggered across the parking lot until he met a deserted road with a helpful road sign telling him it was Saturn Causeway. Crossing the causeway, he reached a dried-out creek, which he decided not to follow because it seemed to lead back towards the rocket highway to his left. Detecting an expanse of water ahead, he stopped before a strip of rough grass which led to a smaller road. The smell of the sea was much stronger now. He could taste it.

Flashlights were visible at a fence beyond the small road, and he remembered the general's heat-sensitive weapons. Would they be able to detect his thermal signature and shoot automatically? As he pondered, a clarity of thought took hold. Damian felt close to death, dehydrated to the extent his throat burned and his head pounded. Yet he was lucid and knew what he had to do. His body and mind were acting in unison, talking to him. He had felt that way from the moment he had freed himself from his constraints.

There was a strange four-part shed-like construction a few yards to his left. He hunkered down behind one. Consciously and deliberately, he slowly closed his body down, his heart rate dipping to a distant murmur. As he looked up through slatted concrete at the stars, the blood pumping oxygen around his body slowed and stopped as he entered a state of hibernation. The stars looked bright tonight, he thought. A snapshot of ancient cosmic

history. An internal clock told him that it would not be for long –
just long enough.

He slept.

FIFTY-FOUR

They reached the remote campsite under the cover of darkness. Sarah had chosen the site because she knew it had gone bankrupt the previous season and did not think it had been reopened.

She was relieved to see she was right; it seemed deserted.

Better still, there was no evidence of on-site security.

There had only been a few months of disuse, but already the holiday park looked in disrepair. The single tarmac track snaking through the property was crumbled with weeds and, where there had been lawns, now there was rough scrub.

She mused on the voraciousness of nature. Despite humanity concreting the planet, wherever it was left alone, nature had an incredible tolerance and ability to bounce back. Builders had once invaded this small patch of national park, but after only months of disuse, the local wildlife had moved back in. Flora was finding weaknesses in the concrete. Expanding into gaps, roots taking hold, to crumble the invasive infrastructure from within. Its decay was exponential.

Sarah pointed out one of several small dwellings set back from both the service road and main waterway. 'That one looks best,' she said.

Noah piloted the craft down a small side channel and tied it to a tree stump on solid ground. A large overhanging tree branch afforded cover, making the craft invisible from the air.

Even in poor light, the holiday rental looked dilapidated. There was not a whisper of a breeze and the waterways resembled dark mirrors, perfectly still and flat. They seemed to be absorbing both light and life. The eery quiet of the sullen scene made her uneasy, as did Noah's mood. In stark contrast to the scene, he was excitable and had begun talking about them being together.

He broke into the dwelling fairly easily, looking at her for approval like a child. They entered cautiously. As expected, it was unoccupied. Their footwear scuffed against the dirty wooden floor, untouched for months. Most furniture had been removed, but built-in cupboards remained. As did a double bed with a bare stained mattress.

It would be dawn soon, and Sarah decided to stay hidden away during daylight hours. She planned to approach a small marina not far up the coast under cover of darkness the following evening.

Her uncle Billy had operated from the marina a decade earlier. Sarah had got on well with Uncle Billy. She'd heard the stories of his exploits, trafficking illegal immigrants into the country, right under the nose of the US coastguard. Billy had been legendary within her family circle, but he had died several years back.

Following the second incident fighting off one of her mum's drunken visitors in the trailer, Sarah had pleaded with Billy to let her spend the summer with him. Her uncle understood the personal issues of his alcoholic sister well and agreed to let his niece spend that summer on the west coast, which was how Sarah ended up living on one of his boats at the marina.

While her uncle was out at sea, Sarah would do odd jobs in the marina office. Sweeping, cleaning, tending the small shop and running other errands. The couple who owned the marina were called Carol and Alan. They were kind to her and would watch over her during her uncle's absences. Although it was strange for a thirteen-year-old to be left alone, no one seemed to mind. The local community was close-knit, and she was viewed as one of their own – part of an extended family of fishermen and human traffickers.

Sarah confided in Carol that one of her mother's boyfriends had tried to rape her just before school was out. From that moment Carol had taken care of her, treating her like a daughter. It was the long summer spent helping out at the marina that had sparked her desire to work in the Floridian leisure trade.

The marina was one of many around the Gulf of Mexico where the smuggling of illegal immigrants into the USA took place. In those days it was not seen as a political imperative to stop the trickle of illegals into the States. Back then the coastguard had different fish to fry, Sarah recalled. Their priority was to stop the flood of drugs entering the country from Central America. That had been the case for three decades since the days of Reagan's war on drugs. Uncle Billy had explained the history to her many times – he had made a decent living out of human trafficking.

Sarah wondered if the activity was continuing, particularly in the current political climate. She had thought very hard about her next steps and decided to outline her intentions to Noah, stopping short of telling him she was unsure if any boats still operated human trafficking from the marina. She would explain more later, on the way up the coast after sundown – the marina was only a few miles away from where she stood.

There was no other way. She could not foresee a situation in which she could ditch Noah and keep herself from being discovered. Noah would have to come along for the ride and meet Carol and Alan.

While she'd not been in direct contact for a couple of years, Sarah knew from Carol's Facebook posts that they still owned the marina. Sarah had recently viewed posts of the marina's old shop expanding to include a café bar and had liked it with Facebook's little heart option. The digital offering was a tiny form of support and a distant connection with one of the best summers of her life.

For now, she turned her attention to gaining some rest and her spirits lifted on finding the water utilities still turned on. The tap groaned and spurted into life and, after the initial dirty discharge washed away, the flow of clean water was gratefully gulped down. The electrics were not working, which meant no hot water.

They took turns to shower. The cold of the water provided relief from the acrid atmosphere inside the small tin box with a powerless air-conditioning unit.

When they settled down either side of the bare double mattress, Noah made his first move. Such an approach had not crossed Sarah's mind. He was subtle to begin with, trying to stroke her hair and whisper pleasantries. With each rebuttal he became more insistent, until, at last, frustration got the better of him.

'Isn't this what we've been waiting for all this time?' he said.

'I think you've misread things,' she replied. 'Please, Noah, we're friends, that's all. Please don't mistake me wanting to help you for anything more.'

The remark seemed to sting. 'Wanting to help me?' he scoffed. 'I'm the one rescuing you.'

Sarah recognised his volatility and decided to placate him. 'Yes, of course, Noah. And I am grateful. You know I am. But it's been a long journey and we both need to rest.'

Noah seemed doggedly determined and held her shoulders. 'Come on, Sarah, I've waited a long time for this.'

She had initially dismissed his approach as immature bravado, thinking she knew him. She had hoped he was just another man trying it on with her. But, as Noah reached out and fondled her breasts, she saw the dark expression on his face – an expression she had seen before as a child. The beast had taken over and Sarah recognised the threat.

'Really, Noah. I mean it. Stop now. Before we both regret it.'

'We won't regret it. You know how much I love you.'

'You don't love me, Noah. You may think you do, but you don't.'

'Sarah. I do, and I know you love me too. That night at the Rebel Yell. The way you looked at me. Sarah, don't fight it.'

Noah pulled her towards him, his mouth upon hers. She pushed back again, a sinew of saliva bridging their lips.

'Noah, I'm warning you …'

He was on top of her before she could finish the sentence, straddling her waist and pinning her hands above her head. She felt him adjust his grip so that his one hand held down both of hers. With his free hand he fondled her breasts, pushing down hard inside her top. She could feel his stiff penis press against her as he hitched up her skirt. He moved his hand down, clawing at her panties, but she made it difficult by wriggling wildly.

'Oh no, Noah. Not you too,' she cried. 'You fucking bastard.' She had survived fending off her mom's drunken bums, only to be attacked by a man she believed too decent to ever consider the crime. She faced the stark reality that, holed up with Noah in a remote bunker, rape was exactly what he was attempting.

Still holding her hands above her head with his left, he fumbled to undo his zipper. She saw in his ineptitude how he'd misread the degree of difficulty in keeping her still while undressing them both.

And he misread her determination.

'You absolute fuck. You're no better than any of them, you entitled prick.'

She managed to detach one hand free of his grip and gouged his eyes with a snake-like strike.

Noah recoiled, one eye reddened from her defence. 'What the – you bitch!'

She saw fury in his eyes as he hit back hard, using a clenched-fist punch.

The hit left her dazed, and he took the opportunity to use both his hands to unzip himself fully and pull her panties to one side. He thrust forward, hurting her as he forced his way inside. As Noah continued to have his way with her, she began to recover from the punch.

She played dead for longer but watched him through narrowed eyes. He repeated his frenzied thrusts, his exhalations timed with each lurch, bizarrely reminding her of the stray dogs she saw mating on the trailer park, frightening her when she was tiny. His groin felt rough against her body's dry objection. Then his face distorted as he discharged himself in a shuddering climax.

The lycanthropy was complete. She had seen him change from a man into a wolf.

She knew this was her chance and struck out with all her might. The palm of her hand smashed into the bottom of his nose, which exploded into a crimson flow. He knew she had broken his nose and his animal roar chilled her.

His hands closed around her already sore neck, squeezing hard as blood flowed from his nose, dripping down onto her. As he shifted his weight forward to gain more purchase on his stranglehold, it created the space she needed to bring a knee up into his genitals. Noah caught his breath as it struck home with force. She tipped him off her and rolled away before jumping to her feet.

'Just you wait, bitch,' he said, rounding on her.

At that moment she was thirteen again, back in the trailer, poised for her attacker's next move.

Noah ran at her and she swayed to one side, managing to parry him. She could not shake the shock that he was no better than one of the drug-fuelled down-and-outs her mother used to invite home. Noah should have known better, she thought. She was his friend, for God's sake, which made him worse than any of them.

Sarah ran to the bag by the side of the bed and pulled out Damian's gun. Releasing the safety catch she pointed it at her assailant. Noah blinked in disbelief and stopped.

'Nah, you wouldn't,' he said at last.

'This is not a game, Noah. I mean it. I'm going now, but come anywhere near me ever again and I will fucking kill you.'

She picked up the holdall with her other hand and said, 'Now step back.'

Noah's look of confusion morphed into a lopsided grin. He looked from the gun to the bag. She could see him computing the situation, knowing the bag contained money he would also need to escape. Shaking his head, he stepped towards her.

'Sarah, I'm sorry. Just put down the gun, and we can talk.'

Lots of thoughts mingled with the physical pain of being raped. Her loathing of Noah; the memory of her mother and being attacked at her trailer park home; and strangely she thought of Damian's face and the infection spreading down its side. Whether she was still dazed from the earlier strike to her head or whether survival instincts were kicking in, it felt like she was having an out-of-body experience, looking down on herself facing the wolf in front of her.

Unwelcome childhood memories galvanised her resolve. She stood passively as Noah edged his way towards her, holding out his hand, ready to take the gun. His face morphed into one of her mom's grubby one-night stands – the filthy man whose attack had been the catalyst for her to leave home and work at the marina. The dank cabin reminded her of his sweaty odour and the powerful smell of her attacker now pervaded her thoughts. It had been an aroma seeded in her mind, one that would allow uninvited nightmares to crash into her psyche on dark nights.

Except now she was living another nightmare in real time – years later, but a new attacker. A friend. A wolf in sheep's clothing.

Noah took more steps towards her, seemingly gaining confidence, his hand reaching out towards the pistol.

'Stop right there,' she said. 'I know what you're trying to do.'

'I'm not trying to do anything, Sarah. I promise. Just put the gun down and we'll be OK.'

'We won't be OK. We will never be OK. You raped me, Noah. You fucking raped me.' Sarah felt overwhelmed and, through teary vision, saw confusion flash across Noah's visage.

He was frowning. 'Rape, rape?' he stuttered. 'It was you that led me on and broke my nose.'

'Ha, ha. Are you mad? Can you hear yourself? You're deluded.' Sarah half laughed and half sobbed at Noah's ridiculous blame reversal. She saw his inadequacies spiralling into renewed anger as he made a grab for the gun. The weapon boomed, echoing in the confined space of the room. The shot was to his stomach and Noah sank to his knees. A look of confusion once again spread over his face as blood quickly soaked into his shirt, mingling with the splatters from his broken nose.

His fingers clutched his abdomen as he looked up at Sarah. 'Why?'

Sarah did not answer as she watched him juddering on the dirty floor. Years of fear and anguish were expelled in the pull of a trigger. He had raped her and had paid the price for trying to take something that was not his to take.

She went to the sink and tried as best she could to get Noah's blood out of her clothing, but it was a hopeless task. She filled a water bottle, grabbed the holdall, and opened the door to the outside world. A faint glow on the horizon heralded the coming of dawn. Looking back at Noah on the floor, she was surprised to see he was still alive. Blood was spilling into a pool that soaked into the shabby old wooden flooring and she knew he did not have long.

'Oh Noah,' she said, 'I thought you were better than that. You see, the thing you need to know about me is, I'm a survivor.'

She closed the door and, tired though she was, decided to push on to the marina in daylight. Her small consolation was that it would be easier alone, increasing the chances of a new start in life.

Carefully navigating the boat through Ten Thousand Islands National Wildlife Refuge, she saw other marine craft and knew she could not be too far from her intended destination.

She would weave up the coast as far as she dared before making the last leg into the marina on foot.

A feeling of sickness had entered her stomach as she tried to shake the vision of Noah lying on the floor from her head. There had been no choice, had there? It had been kill or be killed, she thought. Maybe Damian was right about her. Maybe they were similar. It was strange that in separation she felt closer to her dead lover than she had felt for a long time. Like him, she was one of life's survivors.

She sang 'I'm a Survivor' by Destiny's Child. It had been a mantra she had sung to herself since childhood and gave her comfort, motivating her as she navigated the small boat around the reedy headland, in sight of the small town.

Destiny had brought her back to what had proven a haven during a wonderful summer as a teenager. She hoped it would remain a refuge – a place where she could disappear and start again.

FIFTY-FIVE

General Schmidt was furious. 'Where did you get these mutts from? They couldn't find a hooker in a whorehouse.' The two German Shepherds cowered behind their Kennedy-based K-9 operations handlers.

The general continued to shake his head as he turned to his lieutenant. 'People don't just disappear into thin air. He may be sub-human, but he's not a God-damned poltergeist. I suggest you find him, quickly, or your next tour will be in the Congo.'

The lieutenant stood his ground. 'Sir, we have eighty troops around the perimeter, covering all roads out, and thermal arms covering one hundred per cent field of view within fifty yards of the waterside eastern fence. Anything so much as twitches in that space … We have checked sewage pipes and all utility outlets. Nothing is accessible. But we have cameras down them, checking, just in case. We will find him.'

The general considered his officer's explanation for a moment. 'Sewage outlets, you say? In case he escapes like the guy in that movie, *Green Mile?*'

'I think you mean *Shawshank Redemption,* sir.'

Schmidt looked down, imagining the pipes running under his feet. 'What's this?' he said, kicking small bits of masonry on the floor.

'Building work, sir. Reinforcing doors for our G-Bay guests.'

The general looked up and surveyed the ventilation grill. The lieutenant's gaze followed his. 'No, don't worry about the ventilation system, sir. It's the first thing we checked. There are only eight hatches this size in the building and all too high to reach.'

281

'Have you been up there?'

The general stared at the four rough holes where screws should have been. The grill was positioned the other side of the opening, which was not obvious at a glance. 'We ain't dealing with a human, don'tcha know. Get the dogs up there.'

One of the handlers looked up sceptically and said, 'I'm not sure they'd like that, sir.' The general gave him a withering look and the soldier added, 'Metallic vents. Their paws won't grip.'

'Then you get up there. Lieutenant, find these two a torch. See anything up there and you have my permission to shoot it.'

Damian was not sure how much time had passed. He woke up to the pleasant aroma of saltwater. He had been in deep stasis and did not want to emerge too quickly from it.

There would only be a small window of opportunity before his body reawakened and raised his core temperature. He faced the dichotomy of exerting enough energy to make it to the perimeter fence before increasing body heat triggered thermal sensors. Half jogging, half staggering towards the fence, he felt his body waking up. He lurched the last few paces and slumped up against steel wire meshing. He had made it without activating any weapons.

Looking up at the fence, his heart sank. It looked newly installed and was much higher than he imagined. It curved away from him at the top, in a style used widely in the area to prevent alligators climbing over from water on the other side. He could scramble up it, except the barbed-wire top would surely lacerate his already brittle skin. Time was running out and he needed water. His head spun, and breathing was becoming increasingly difficult.

He detected movement to his right and sensed the presence of humans, barely a few yards away, along the perimeter. He needed to take a gamble – maybe the last one he'd ever make.

The soldier looked confused. 'Look at these readings, Corporal. I'm getting some false positives. I think there might be something out there. See, look. Again. The machine gun is tracking the movement but is not firing.'

'That's because the heat signal is below the tolerance level. It's probably a thermal, or eddy of some kind. I found that quite common in testing. We can't have the thing firing at every warm gust of air.'

Damian had listened to the exchange and appeared from the darkness. They relaxed on sight of his camouflage.

'Jeez, you gave me a scare. You should buy a lottery ticket – you realise you just walked right in front of my thermal bang-bang?' the corporal said, nodding at the weapon. The soldier had the same accent as the general, but Damian tried to push the obscure thought from his head. He needed to focus. He stepped forward another few paces and realised both soldiers were staring down at his feet. Walking around bar foot on the grass had felt so natural, he'd forgotten about his absent boots. One soldier reacted, and his hand went to draw a pistol, but Damian was too quick, his razor-sharp claw slashing the man's throat before he could reach it. The hapless soldier slumped to the ground as Damian turned towards the corporal.

The corporal already had his pistol in hand and pulled the trigger. Damian dived and rolled like a gymnast, the bullet stinging as it grazed his shoulder. Jumping out of the roll closed the five-yard gap between them and the corporal was unable to reposition his aim as Damian gripped his pistol hand and turned the corporal around, pulling his forearm tight to the soldier's throat. Pushing against the corporal's upper back from behind with his shoulder, Damian now yanked his forearm backwards with an equal and opposite force that snapped the corporal's neck, loudly; only skin and sinew kept the head from rolling away from the detached crumpled body.

Damian turned towards the fence. Two infrared-controlled weapons were pointing along the fence line in opposite directions. Damian imagined the pattern would be repeated at intervals down the whole strip of fencing.

A wave of dizziness hit him. He knew only minutes of his life remained and he had to make it into the sea – there was no choice.

With no wire cutters, Damian would have to scale the fence and brave the barbed wire on top.

The comms piece on one of the dead soldiers crackled to life. Despite the sound being fed through an earpiece, Damian could make out some of the words: 'shot heard, report back' and 'Zone Echo status'. He imagined most of the troops positioned around the perimeter would soon be descending on his location, though he hoped the general's infrared toys would buy him some time.

Damian hauled himself up the fence and balanced on the section as it curved away to its barbed-wired end.

General Schmidt had relocated himself and a small task force to Kennedy's Protective Services Communications Center. He quickly discovered, however, that Protective Services were contracted into NASA by a company in Chantilly, Virginia, and were not military as he expected. He found the atmosphere more like a call centre than a command centre and was questioning himself for not setting up an external command centre instead of relying on KSC's toy soldiers. He was on the verge of leaving the Communications Center when two pieces of news came in.

Inside the compound one of the dog handlers had managed to crawl along the vent and discovered an open grill where the vent met the outside. That piece of information became obsolete less than five minutes later when news of a shot being fired at the perimeter was radioed in.

No communications from Echo Station made the general fear the worst. Damian had escaped via the ventilation system and taken out the two soldiers at Echo Station. How he had bypassed thermal imaging of the prototype weapons system was a mystery, but the general found the news both irritating and delicious. If just one mutation was capable of such an escape, it gave him great hope for the future of his elite forces.

He ordered soldiers from the other stations to move out towards Echo, angling their approach to avoid the thermal weapons. Other units were also deployed to cut off escape beyond the perimeter fencing.

'What's over the fence?' the general asked a member of Kennedy Protective Services Office personnel beside him.

'Your Echo Station is positioned by the Turning Basin, General,' the call operator answered.

The general learned that the Turning Basin was a man-made expanse of water that allowed barges carrying large cargos access to the Space Center. The basin was fed by a barge channel that eventually led to Banana River and the sea beyond. The Kennedy Space Center sat in the middle of the Merritt Island National Wildlife Refuge, adjacent to Canaveral National Seashore. If Damian broke free of the Space Center perimeter he'd have the advantage of water and wild scrub.

'So that's it then, we've lost him,' the general said.

'Not quite, sir. He's still a way to go and your men can cut him off from near the launch observation gantry on Saturn Causeway.' The operator pointed to the location on a wall-mounted map.

'If they don't catch him there, I'm not sure I fancy his chances in the refuge,' came another operator's response.

The PSO personnel explained how the fugitive would be at the mercy of a large local gator population. Visitors to the centre were always surprised to hear there was a local population of alligators. The fugitive would be best advised to surrender, or face being eaten alive, they gleefully told the general.

Damian swayed in the breeze, his energy spent. The barbed wire felt like an insurmountable barrier, lacerating his dried-out skin. The sounds and scent of more humans were coming to meet him, adding to his fear.

A fresh blast of open ocean met his nostrils, reinvigorating him. He breathed in the beautiful salinity. Deep down he felt like he was becoming imbued with a sense of home, an essence of life that rekindled an unconscious diadromous spirit.

He clambered up on top of the barbed wire. More of the sharp spikes penetrated his hands, his arm and his chest as he pulled himself over and fell to the ground the other side.

Torchlights flickered around him as he entered stagnant brackish water, splashing to stay afloat. The water by the jetty was stagnant and polluted with engine oil, which he felt entering his bloodstream, hurting him further. He needed to reach clean open water.

The sounds of humans and the light dance of torch beams were all around him as he dived below the surface and swam for his life. After a few strokes, the water in the basin began to feel cleaner and a soothing wash of saltwater penetrated his wounds. He felt his skin rehydrating and the sense of relief helped power him on until the basin narrowed to a thin canal and he felt vulnerable again.

Keeping his head under the waterline, he made it to the end of the channel. The water opened up into a series of creeks, where freshwater pools met saltwater feeding up from the south.

Damian relaxed a little until lights reflected off the black water around him. To his left, several soldiers were wading into the marsh, weapons raised in two hands above their heads. A beam of light flickered by his head, and he was sure he'd been spotted.

Diving down into the widening creek, Damian saw bullet traces and heard their sub-aquatic echo through the water. Another trace left a bubbly line close to his face and was met by others around him as more soldiers joined the shooting spree. They were some distance away now and the firing seemed quite random.

He felt other water splashes near him, and realised alligators were diving into the water from along the bank, alarmed by the noise. He felt a sting on his left leg. It smarted momentarily before a searing pain shot up through his spine and into his cerebral cortex.

Damian floundered, hit by a bullet, flapping helplessly in the middle of the creek.

Pain gripped his leg like a vice and he tasted his own blood in the water. He knew he was losing blood quickly and began to sink further into the depths, wondering if his plight would attract the gators.

Realisation struck. Fleeing into salty water had seemed so natural and yet, here he was, head under the water, still alive – breathing!

Breathing underwater.

And bleeding to death underwater.

He kicked his legs like a frog and swam along the bottom of the creek until he felt something big brush past. An alligator. He was bleeding and helpless, but it did not attack him.

Barely alive, Damian settled a while on the creek's bed, allowing his body temperature to drop, like he had earlier. Some minutes passed and the shooting stopped. He guessed the weapons would have thermal sights and imagined the soldiers struggling to enter the alligator-infested water any further.

After a wait, he followed the creek and clambered out. Sensing the ocean beyond, he fell in and out of silted water pools and crossed a road where a stretch of beach met ocean. Diving in, Damian used his final reserves of energy to swim past the surf and on to safety. He was swimming in a surreal dream of pain and new-found life. The salinity enveloped his being like a shroud; he realised he was a new species and hinged emotionally between elation at the incredible experience and despair at the separation from his former self.

He swam on, following the shoreline south, driven on by the desire to distance himself from his laboratory ordeal. Occasionally surfacing to take in oxygen, Damian swam out to deeper water for safety. Eventually he happened upon a small underwater opening and, instinctively, swam in. It was a good mile south from where he had entered the water – far enough away to feel safe from the bullets – and he needed to rest. Swimming upwards his head broke water. He was in a small underwater cavern.

Exhaustion consumed him. For the third time that day his body shut itself down, this time fully. His heavy, tired eyes closed as Damian gave himself freely to the sensation. Unsure if he would ever wake from the new warmth that wrapped itself around him, he saw the cave as a regenerative vault guarding his body, allowing it to live on.

FIFTY-SIX

The general was back in the lab to work on the next phase of experiments with Nyman.

He had heard the reports, but still summoned a soldier to hear a face-to-face account of Damian's attempted escape. He needed to be sure.

'He made it into Pintail Creek, sir. Marshland and alligators.'

'You saw him get eaten?'

'He didn't come out, sir. We waited a long time. No one's getting out of there alive – you should see the size of those things.'

A suitable conclusion to the problem, the general thought, and dismissed the soldier.

Things were beginning to fall into place. He considered Goodhew's elimination and then Damian's swampy demise. It certainly helped lift what his mom used to call his 'holler-tail mood', until a dark thought struck him. Damian was infected. He'd been eaten alive by alligators. Would that mean they'd now be infected too?

He'd have to talk to Nyman. Things were getting out of hand, and there were still two fugitives at large. He pressed a recently saved number on his cellular. The phone call was picked up after only one ring.

'Hello, General,' said the voice

'Good morning, Agent Walker,' the general replied. 'What's the status on the fugitives?'

'Good news, General. My agents found their car about an hour ago. Mitchell and Scott have bought a boat towards the west side of the Glades, and I think I know where they are heading.'

'So, no capture yet – that's what you're saying.'

'I'm saying it's just a matter of time.'

'Well, just how much time? We're not talking Bonnie and Clyde here.' The general disliked the slick agent and all his malarky. There was a pause on the line. He guessed the agent was considering his reply.

'I believe capture is imminent, sir. I have agents in position waiting at the most likely destinations. One in particular has a strong connection with the suspect, Sarah Mitchell.'

'OK, let's hope you're right, Agent. Let me know as soon as you find them. Have a nice day, now.' The general disconnected the call and Nyman walked over holding a container. Despite having been informed of Goodhew's death, the scientist looked happy.

'I understand we lost the subject to the gators,' Nyman said.

'Yes, I believe so. Will that be a problem?'

'Not necessarily.' Nyman was looking pleased with himself.

'Don't play games with me. What's that you're holding?'

'We found it by Doctor Goodhew. It contained ethanol. We believe he administered it to Gent. I wondered why and ran a few tests. This, General, is the answer.' Nyman waved the empty container. 'This is what stops DNA absorption. Alcohol. It was right before our eyes the whole time. Gent had been drinking himself better. You just can't make it up, can you?'

The general shook his head. 'Are you sure? Alcohol will kill off that stuff?'

'Yes, I'm sure.'

'Alcohol?'

'Yes, alcohol.'

The general laughed, shaking his head. 'Of all the things. Would you believe it? And will it stop the mutation process, you know, if we do what we did with Gent?'

Nyman looked down and nodded his head slowly.

'Well, you'd better go prepare our friends for testing,' the general said, grinning. 'Starting with the amphibious assault model, like we discussed.'

The general waited for Nyman to leave the room and took out his cellular again. He waited for his call to connect. 'It's General Schmidt,' he said, 'the danger is averted. We have a solution that kills off the alien substance … Yes, it is good news. We can start with a decontamination program. We can talk about the other thing later, but you have to be very sure before approaching the president about this. If she won't come on-board then it will blow everything wide open … Thank you, Senator, and you. I'll be here overseeing things, but see you soon.'

General Schmidt considered his next moves. As soon as his prisoner experiments produced a viable amphibious killing machine, he would begin the next phase of creating his specialist force, utilising willing volunteers prepared to make great sacrifices for the stars and stripes.

Funding and resources were being put in place by his friends in Early Light. There was even a hope that the president would come on-board. They would have to tread carefully, but the general left the lab feeling elated. Chinese and Russian aggression towards the west would be stopped in such a way that the enemies would turn on each other. At long last, it would be America in the ascendancy, with his secret army central to future success.

FIFTY-SEVEN

Damian Gent woke up.

Or what remained of the man he once was woke up.

He was lying on a ledge in a small cavern. It was dark, but not pitch black. Faint light fed in from under the waterline. Saltwater gently lapped against adjacent rocks. He raised his head and it scraped against the cave's roof; the space was barely large enough to accommodate him sitting up.

The only discernible exit seemed to be in the direction of the light. Had he really made it into the cave by swimming under the waterline?

Visions of his recent escape flashed through his mind. The ventilation system; regulating his own body temperature; climbing the barbed-wire fence; the alligator; a bullet striking his leg. The pain had been excruciating.

Tentatively he felt down the back of his leg, expecting to feel a deep wound and pain. There was a hole in his combat trousers, and he could just make out the stain where he had bled out. He examined the bullet hole in his trousers and stuck his clawed finger through, feeling. He couldn't feel a wound of any sort.

Had he been hallucinating?

He felt energised. Rejuvenated. And not just his leg. His whole body felt … he was not sure what. Stronger, maybe. He just felt good.

There was a scaly texture to the skin of his hands. He turned them around in the dimness, examining them closely. His fingers were partly webbed when he opened them.

That was new.

291

He had continued mutating since leaving the lab.

I'm still changing. But how?

Goodhew had administered alcohol but it had not been enough. It had decelerated the process, but it had not completely killed off the alien substance. His body was still synthesizing the various animal DNA that had been introduced.

How far would the synthesis continue and what would the next stages be?

Damian had no idea if the blend of DNA was a symbiosis, or whether it would ultimately destroy him. If he did live, would it take away the final vestiges of humanity left in him? His own memories. Ability to talk. Talk. Could he talk now?

'Hello, anyone there?' he said out loud.

The sentence echoed apologetically in the small cave.

He was relieved to find his human vocal cords were still intact and laughed. The cave laughed back at him. His voice had a strange grating resonance that felt like he was listening to someone, or something else.

He considered his options.

He needed to get out of the cave and find alcohol, although he knew he didn't need a drink in the way he used to – he felt cured of that curse. He sensed he needed ethanol though, to kill off the last of the alien thing that had invaded his body and was still making him change, though he believed the recent metamorphosis had saved his life.

After that he would find a refuge away from harm, with time to think. Somewhere away from his past life and from the general.

General Schmidt. Damian felt he understood Schmidt to his evil core. Damian had no doubt the general would want to deploy the full force of available resources to find and destroy him. He would have to exercise extreme caution.

Some minutes later Damian emerged from the sea further down the coastline. The coastline was comfortingly familiar. He had found his way into the Indian River, a broad channel of water that separated the ocean-facing beach peninsula from the main body of land. He had no recollection of his final swim and where it had taken him, but at least the submerged cave below a rocky outcrop had afforded him respite. Damian knew the river well and realised that he was somewhere south of Melbourne, close to Sebastian.

It was daylight and any human interaction on the land would expose him to danger. Even having his head above the waterline was dangerous – he could see several yachts and pleasure craft active in the channel. After dodging bullets, he did not want to be decapitated by a speedboat. He just needed that alcohol.

Most of the bars on the mainland were across a busy road from the front. He remembered one restaurant in Sebastian over the water, on stilts. He recalled its name, Squid Lips. The irony of the eatery's name was not lost on him and he touched his mouth, wondering how his lips must look. He'd taken Sarah to the one in Melbourne for seafood. She had craved their coconut shrimp, so they'd gone back a few months ago, when she still loved him. Before he treated her badly and before the infection.

Surveying the inner coastline, he saw the distinctive turquoise of the building he sought and swam along the sea floor towards it. He surfaced by one of its large structural timber supports embedded into the ground.

Yachts were moored up along the adjacent Fins Marina jetty. The restaurant could be accessed from land along a pier on one side and by sea via the jetty on the other. There was no activity on the decking above him. Too early, he thought. It must still be morning.

Caution prevented him rushing and he surveyed the underside of the restaurant, finding a rusty iron ladder extended from a hatch. He'd give it a try. The hatch was bolted from the inside. He pushed hard, but it held firm. Like an amphibious assault, he'd have to climb up the outer metalwork and enter from the decking.

Hauling himself over the turquoise-painted wooden railings, he was hit by sharp sunlight. Damian ran across the empty decking and pulled on a glass door – it opened.

He stepped in, his eyes struggling to adjust to the gloom.

'Sorry, we're closed. Not open for another hour,' came a female voice from behind the bar. A large expanse of empty floor extended from the door to the bar. The wood was slightly tacky, and the stale smell of spilt alcohol invaded his sensitive nostrils. He was thankful to be silhouetted against the outside light, his features invisible to the person calling out.

'I just wondered if I could book a table for tonight?' he ventured.

'Oh, of course, honey. Let me find the reservations book.'

As his eyes adjusted, Damian could make out a female shape rummaging about behind the counter. He used the opportunity to advance across the space, darting through the raised service hatch to behind the bar.

The uniformed girl looked up startled as he grabbed her wrist.

'Keep calm and you'll be OK,' he rasped. 'I just need a drink, that's all.' He nodded towards the optics hanging from the mirrored back wall. That was when he saw himself, barely recognisable as human. He looked like a lizard.

He stopped. Staring. Breathing heavily. Transfixed.

The girl screamed, very loudly, wide-eyed and petrified.

Damian lashed out instinctively, the back of his free hand striking her across the side of the head in a glancing blow. She slumped to the floor as a male voice came from the back.

'Sarah, you OK in there?'

The coincidence of the name jolted him, and he looked down at her. She was only about nineteen years old. A student job, maybe? Sarah Mitchell had been a student too. He'd seen how the girl had looked at him like he was a monster and knew this would be his life now. There would be no understanding of his plight. Her look of terror had spoken to him more loudly than her scream.

Footsteps approached from the rear and Damian knew he had to go. He grabbed two full bottles of bourbon. Clutching them to his chest, he paused momentarily, committing his mirrored reflection to memory, and ran to the door.

'Heh, you, stop there.' It was a nervous shout. Damian felt the reluctance to confront him and slowed, choosing to walk across the outside decking to the rails, vaulting them effortlessly and splashing down into the water.

Shortly afterwards he was back in the cave, drinking the contents of a bottle. It tasted vile, making his throat and stomach burn, yet he glugged it down, remembering the reflected monster in the mirror and hoping it would halt any further changes.

As soon as the bottle of the alcohol was consumed, he began to feel the effects. Damian grabbed the other bottle and lowered himself into the water. The alcohol made him feel sick, but he fought the desire to bring it up again. He needed to keep it in his system and absorb it into his bloodstream. He would drink the other later to prevent further physical change. Ducking under the water, he exited through the cave's narrow entrance.

Damian believed it would only be a matter of time before the incident at Squid Lips was reported to the general. There'd been no choice. He needed the alcohol more than his anonymity and swam swiftly along the riverbed, heading south.

As minutes of swimming turned to hours, he marvelled at the aquatic world now accessible to him. He felt a desire to head back to fresh water and sensed which way to travel. He passed schools of fish, pods of dolphins and a few sharks. Nothing in his new world frightened him and other creatures seemed to keep their distance.

His thoughts switched back to the look of terror on the face of the bar girl, Sarah. He wondered where his Sarah was now, and the thought of her maybe not being alive made him sad. Something in his gut told him she was alive – she was resourceful and had Noah to protect her. The same Noah who had turned on him, shooting him at the motel.

He had sensed the desire for Sarah in Noah. Maybe Noah could give Sarah what he no longer could, and they were together now, making love. He'd have to eliminate Noah. He was a competitor.

Even though Damian knew any future with Sarah couldn't be the same as before, he craved her company. He'd changed physically in a vital area and knew sex with anyone would kill them. Why had that part of him been so badly affected? Life had once again dealt him a shitty hand, he thought.

Maybe Sarah would see the new beauty in him – a butterfly emerging from a pupa. He now had the strength to protect her from the ugliness of humanity, even though he recognised he'd let her down in the past. He'd just have to accept that any new relationship would come without sex. If she was still alive that was. Maybe the general had caught her and was experimenting on her.

Damian thought a lot about the general, more than he did about Sarah. As he swam his mind switched between the two. With regular stops to catch seafood for nourishment, Damian's three-day marathon swim took him up an inlet and deep into the Everglades.

Physically strong, but mentally ravaged, he was driven on by the instinct to survive and by notions of revenge. Damian's instinct was to find a place that was quiet and secluded, in the depths of the swamp.

At last, he found a suitable place, abandoned and where he'd be safely out of reach. It had been an instinctive migration, like a salmon returning home, giving him a chance to stop and contemplate his next move – and spawn a new monster called *Revenge*.

FIFTY-EIGHT

The FBI agent sat at the marina café bar. He sported a white Lacoste polo and navy-blue chino shorts. His colleague also looked the part, in her anchor-print T-shirt and stripey skirt. They looked like the cover shot of *Zizoo Magazine*, he thought. The perfect nautical couple. They were blending in. Inconspicuous.

The coffee and freshly squeezed orange juice tasted good, as did his maple syrup pancakes off the breakfast menu. She was skipping the food, as she often did on stakeouts, he noticed.

They'd been assigned to the marina by Executive Assistant Director Walker. Intelligence had revealed that, among her four hundred plus Facebook friends, Sarah Mitchell knew the marina's owners, Carol and Alan Smith. While there had not been any direct messaging between Mitchell and the Smiths for over two years, older posts and messages referred to a summer spent at the marina. Historical messages between Carol and Mitchell exuded warmth.

The marina had made the very top of Walker's 'twenty to watch' list. Twenty locations with two agents deployed to each, should the Mitchell woman and Noah Scott show up.

Sarah crouched behind bushes, watching the jetty-side bar area.

She could see that there were two couples and a larger group sitting at the bar. All seemed engrossed in their breakfasts and she doubted they posed a threat. A couple of the boats in the marina showed activity. One was being washed down with a hose by an elderly gentleman. On the other, four young men were playing cards and, despite the early hour, drinking beer.

Looking back towards the bar, she saw one of the couples stand up and wander back around the marina to a small dinghy. Sarah was at the wrong angle to see the serving area behind the new bar seating. She wanted to walk around to get a better view but dared not take the risk.

She'd have to try to find Carol from the back of the building.

Walking through the parking area, she hid between large bins near the back entrance. The area was a fenced off suntrap and smelt bad. A fly buzzed past her ear. She swatted at it, missing, and it buzzed persistently close, taunting her inability to break cover.

Regretting the folly of her move into the baking hot bin area, she looked around for alternative cover. The kitchen's back door clicked open, and Sarah was looking at the much older face of the woman who had offered her kindness as a child.

'Can I help you?' the woman asked sternly.

'It's me, Sarah. Sarah Mitchell,' she replied.

Carol stared at Sarah in disbelief. For a moment, Sarah wondered if the woman recognised her, and then plump arms grabbed hold of her in a heartfelt embrace.

'Oh Lordy, it really is you. Sarah Mitchell as I live and breathe.'

The warmth of the welcome took Sarah by surprise and she felt her eyes welling up.

'Carol. I need your help. I'm in trouble.'

Carol put a finger to her lips and held Sarah's arm. 'Shh, come with me. I think there's people here looking for you, doll.'

She led Sarah inside the kitchen and closed the door. Despite the impossibility of being heard outside from the kitchen, she still spoke in hushed tones.

'You're on the run, aren't you?'

'Yes, how do you know?'

'Well, the blood down your top don't look too good. Plus, we don't get many high-ends here and there's two who sailed in yesterday on a nice boat. Their clothes are brand new. Still got creases from the packaging. They say they've been touring the Gulf for the last month and paid for a week's berth in advance. No one ever does that on a tour. I didn't believe them.'

'And you say they're still here?'

'Yes, eating pancakes out front.'

'They might be police or Feds, I don't know. But you're right, I am being hunted.'

'Ha, I knew their story was a crock,' Carol said, raising her voice excitedly. Realising, she ducked her head apologetically. 'Oops, sorry. Don't worry, they won't hear us back here. I just knew there was something about them but couldn't work out what their real story was. Why are they after you, sweetheart?'

'I'll explain, but shouldn't you be looking after your customers first? They might get suspicious.'

'Don't worry. Alan's out front. Just tell me what the heck's going on.'

'Oh God, where do I start?' Sarah took a deep breath and poured out the events of the missing years. About meeting Damian and then his gang. She described the Orlando job that went wrong and then the warehouse deaths. Carol raised her eyebrows at that bit. Sarah explained how she'd fled with Noah and how he'd raped her and then, finally, that she'd shot him and that his body was just a few miles along the coast, waiting to be discovered.

When Sarah finished, she found herself crying. She had needed the release and looked at Carol. 'Are you going to turn me in?'

'Of course we're not going to turn you in, honey. Come here.' Carol offered up another hug that Sarah gratefully accepted.

'You do believe me, don't you?' Sarah asked.

'Of course I believe you, child. You did the right thing. He raped you.'

'No, about the snake monster thing, I mean.'

'Yes, I do believe you saw something, Sarah. There have been stories on the news this morning about a chemical leak out on the east coast.'

'Chemical leak?'

'Yes, but I didn't pay much attention to it. Or to the rumours on social media.'

'What rumours?'

'That they've found a UFO and that the government is hushing it up.'

'Are you being serious?'

'Totally, it's all over Facebook. Some of my friends are saying there are aliens running about Florida.'

'Show me,' said Sarah.

Carol pulled a phone out of her pocket and scrolled through a few Facebook posts. 'You know Alan can't stand Facebook. Tells me I spend too much time on it.'

Sarah smiled at Carol. It was a criticism Damian had levelled at her on many occasions. He'd always wanted to know whose posts she was reading and why she was wasting so much time reading them.

'Here you go,' Carol said at last, 'look at this.'

Carol handed the phone over to Sarah and she read posts from a forum calling itself the Truth Movement. The thread outlined so-called evidence that a large area of land to the east of Melbourne had been cordoned off by the military. It claimed that engineers had diverted water and flooded nearby land. One post claimed people had been moved out and paid to keep quiet. The conspiracy theorists showed pictures of lorries carrying steel to the area and a secretly taken photo showed a steel wall, under the heading 'How to hide a UFO'.

The responses below the post stretched on for many pages. Most of them were fantastical and Sarah skim-read a few. Some talked about Roswell-type aliens that could morph into humans, hiding among the population, planning to steal back their spaceship. Others suggested a virus that would wipe out the Earth. 'Beware a new epidemic from space' warned one post.

Sarah stopped at a separate post liked by one of Carol's friends. It was posted by @SarahJBZ2004 via TikTok. It claimed she'd been attacked by a lizard man stealing liquor from the bar she worked in. Sarah recognised the bar chain as one of her favourites. The post had dozens of comments. One said that the incident was 'turtley freaky' and seemed to set the tone for a long string of reptile-related puns.

A couple of posts asked if the attacker was from a race of alien lizards.

Other posts were more scathing. One reply said, 'lizard man???? shock as robber wears mask 2 hide id. How original. #DumbAss #fakenews #attentionseeker'. One thing stood out to Sarah. The post referenced security footage of the robber. Instead of a video clip, there was a blank space. Over it a caption said, 'No photo description available'.

'Funny that – who's removed the photo?' Sarah said.

'Removed what?' asked Carol.

'Oh, nothing.'

Handing the phone back, Sarah followed Carol through to an office.

'Here's a fresh T-shirt. Give me yours to wash and sit here out of sight. When the coast's clear, I'll get Alan. First, let me get you a soda. You looked pooped.'

'A soda? Something stronger would be better, the way I feel.'

Carol nodded. 'OK, doll.'

Sarah took a long shower upstairs and stayed in the warm office for nearly an hour. She drank several shots of tequila and wondered if the lizard man was simply a robber wearing a mask, or could they be talking about Damian? Tiredness and thoughts of Damian consumed her until she slept. When she did wake, it was from a bad dream. Noah was on her, holding her wrists. She started, opening her eyes. Alan stood over her, gently shaking her arm.

'Wake up, Sarah, wake up. It's time for you to go,' he said softly.

FIFTY-NINE

The softshell turtle nosed the reeds cautiously. It spent most of its time underwater hunting or scavenging. Paddling, the odd-looking olive-green creature paused to check for predators. Its elongated head and snorkel-like nose took in the surroundings. It sensed danger but could not determine where from. Too late, it slipped back under the water to swim away. The predator pounced. Lightening quick, a claw-like hand reaching down under the surface, grabbing the turtle's long neck.

This was his favourite prey.

He yanked the turtle above the waterline, snapping its neck in one swift movement. Standing up from his hiding place behind a clump of spiky cattails, he waded knee deep through the water to the bank. From there he forced a path through a cluster of cypress trees, entering a long-abandoned boat shed. The shed was hidden from view by overgrown vegetation, providing him with a safe haven. He sat down eagerly on a makeshift bed and prepared to feast.

His strong fingers gripped under the pancake-shaped body of the turtle, prising its carapace away to reveal the tender succulent prize below. The cartilaginous shell was discarded, and he attacked the meat in a frenzy. Sinews from the dead animal dropped to the floor as he devoured his latest kill.

He looked up, having heard a noise, bloodied morsels sticking to his face. He took in the air, but there was no danger. No animals ever approached the dilapidated shed. Not alligators, crocodiles, or snakes. He realised other creatures viewed him as the apex predator and stayed away. He grunted with satisfaction. There was nothing to interrupt the pleasure of his meal.

Eating continued apace, strong jaws crunching down on the raw flesh. Very soon only a few fragments remained, the rest having been consumed.

He lay back to relax as strong juices in his digestive tract got to work, breaking down the meal. The kill would satisfy him until the next day, maybe the day after that.

Shafts of sunlight played on his face through a gap in the roof and covering foliage. The beams reflected off a small make-up mirror balanced by his bed. The mirror was a small concession to his human vanity. The daily inspection was part of a process – coming to terms with what he now was.

At a glance, from a distance, with camouflage make-up, he imagined his face might pass as human. Close up, however, the scaly skin and perforated neckline looked more amphibian than man.

He stared back at his own reflection. The dirt-smeared image presented an aberration. He felt the twisted fusion within his body and was trying to understand what he was. He concluded he was a tortured combination of creatures he could only guess at. A mutant.

On closer inspection there were a few clues to the creatures. An irregular beard grew in patches. Green hues ran down the sides of his neck and arms, revealing themselves again on his torso through rips in a stained shirt. At points his skin looked rough, almost scaly. His neck had small breathing holes. Gills. Strangely, some hidden parts of his body looked plant-like, with jagged barbs.

There was no longer any chance of normal interaction with other people. The prospects of friendship and intimacy were gone. He understood that well. The thought that no woman would ever look at him with desire had made him sad, yet time was healing those feelings. To be loved was no longer a necessity. He had convinced himself of that fact over the last few weeks of hiding.

After much adjustment, he felt his mind levelling out between the boundary of human reason and that of animal instinct. The line between the need to procreate and knowledge of the consequences

303

blurred. In his imagination he would vent his frustrations on the undeserving, but no dream of that nature ever involved Sarah. He told himself he would never hurt her.

The flickering sun hit his face again. It felt good. Heat and humidity, oppressive to most people, were his friends. His body had adapted to the surroundings and warmth energised him.

There were some obvious advantages to his new self. He felt stronger than he'd ever done before, both physically and, increasingly, mentally. He had powers he'd only ever read about in comic books: his sense of smell; his acute hearing; his strength; and other things he was only just starting to understand. He did not yet have full control over all his abilities, but he was learning, and his confidence was rising.

Most of all, he was no longer scared. The rage he'd carried since he was a teenager was still there; however, his confusion had vanished, replaced with lucidity of thought. Rational thinking like mathematics and science had mostly vanished from his memory. He had no need for those. Instinct had become his ally and he knew things before they happened. He could sense danger and opportunity, and now all he had to do was fine tune to harness those new powers.

The Everglades had become his domain – a far cry from the chilly rain-soaked bricks and mortar of his younger days. He sought sanctuary among the very elements that had permeated his body and affected his DNA. The environment kept him secure and away from prying eyes. The Everglades provided food in abundance, and human settlements provided a few of the home comforts he once took for granted.

He'd steal at night when people were asleep. Pillows, sheets, and a few clothes.

A small radio's crackly broadcasts kept him in touch with news.

Stations reported on a huge chemical incident near Melbourne. A major natural disaster had been averted by sealing off the waterways to prevent any spread. Reports suggested that tons of phosphoric acid, primarily used for agricultural fertilisers, had been illegally stored in a Lake Winder warehouse during the 1980s and subsequently forgotten. The acid had leaked into the ecosystem and had been counteracted by army helicopters dropping gallons of neutralising agents on the scene. Damian believed the so-called 'agent' would be ethanol.

One day, Damian happened to hear a report that two heroes of an Orlando heist gone wrong were recovering well. The report talked of the bravery of a teller, who had been shot by one of the gang members while she raised the alarm. The other hero was named as Sergeant Conti, who had tracked down and confronted the gang members. Three deputies and all members of the gang had been killed in the vicious shoot-out. Conti was to receive the Brevard County Sheriff's Medal as recognition for his bravery. The gang members were described as 'illegal aliens whose identities are, as yet, unknown'.

How very convenient, Damian mused. By not naming the gang members, the main link between the heist and warehouse was severed. The government was certainly doing its best to hide the truth, and no reports he heard suggested a connection between the chemical story and the Orlando shooting.

The news also saddened him. It suggested that Sarah was dead too. He assumed that her identify would have been linked back to the gang after her escape with Noah. Damian was sure the general would have made the connection to the truth about the chemical leaks disappear.

The government's hiding of the truth did not matter to him any longer. He'd been living in the Glades for three months now. He was feral, fearless and most importantly, he was free.

He hoped Ben's children would be alright, but knew that, of course, they wouldn't be. How could they possibly be OK? One day their father left their home, never to return. How would the authorities deal with that in relation to the news blackout on what really happened? What would happen to the boys? He had no idea, but knew he'd have to face up to them one day and explain what really happened to their dad. It was his responsibility now to ensure they were looked after longer term. Telling them the truth was a task he already dreaded.

Soon, he'd need to move on, and contemplated his next steps. He would steal money to create enough of a disguise to walk around among humans again. He'd also need a new ID.

Damian Gent had been his name out there, but it was not his real name. It never had been. That would have to be changed again and he'd need a good one, fitting for an alien species unique not just on Earth, but in the universe. His mind drifted back to the Kennedy facility and to his torture.

'Irreversible.' The doctor's word echoed in his head.

He'd already dealt with the doctor, and he would deal with the general, when the man least expected it. He would track the general down away from his entitlements, his army and his weapons, and torture him.

Damian began to imagine many ways to hurt General Schmidt and make him beg for mercy. He fantasised over several versions of the general's demise, in many locations and using many types of torture. They all had one thing in common. In each one the general would be stripped of all his dignity and humanity. He would reduce Schmidt to a whimpering, petrified animal, pleading for his life.

Revenge was his first thought in the morning and his last thought before every sleep. The time was approaching to leave the swamp and exact that revenge.

SIXTY

Sarah pushed hard, as one of the midwives squeezed her hand. 'Push, Sarah,' the midwife said, 'harder.' The pain of childbirth went beyond anything she could have imagined.

She felt the child coming out, the force of the birth tearing her.

She felt the midwife tighten her grip still further, and saw her staring at the baby, a look of terror on her face. The second midwife at the end of the bed was holding the abomination up at arm's length, screaming as the baby thrashed at her, fangs showing.

Blood spurted from the midwife's hand and wrist, and she dropped the baby onto the end of the bed between Sarah's splayed legs. Not recognising Sarah as its mother, the baby's yellow lizard-like eyes focused on her. The reptilian creature raised itself onto all fours and advanced, crawling up the bed towards her, pulling back its head and revealing those fangs again, preparing to strike.

Both midwives were screaming now, fleeing the hospital room, leaving Sarah alone to face the advancing monster. She faced her own son, knowing he was about to kill her.

She woke up from the nightmare with a start, sitting bolt upright on the chair she had fallen asleep on just minutes earlier. Her night and day terrors were becoming increasingly common. They had started a month ago but were increasingly frequent as the baby inside her grew.

Looking out from her small apartment, everything seemed normal. Children played soccer on some grass across the road. They seemed happy. She could hear their shrieks and laughter drifting in through a lounge-diner window.

She stroked the bump on her tummy. Physically she felt great, yet pregnancy had brought with it a fear of not knowing what lay inside her.

Hospital scans had been avoided. Sarah was too cautious to be registered at a hospital, and also terrified that she harboured something other than a normal child. She suspected the baby was Damian's, although it could be Noah's. She wanted it to be Damian's – a baby not conceived by rape. Paradoxically, the fear of giving birth to a monster was beginning to consume her.

The nightmares exacerbated her fear. In her mind, the dreams made the likelihood of an abnormality more likely, though cold logic also told her it was a ridiculous line of reasoning.

She'd been in the country with a name change and fake ID for over seven months. No one asked questions and the money taken from Damian afforded her sanctuary and the freedom not to have to work. Up until the bad dreams, she had been enjoying the anonymity.

The journey to Mexico had been arduous. She had been feeling increasingly sick and the Gulf's sea had been rough for much of the forty hours of travel.

And they'd been boarded by the US Navy.

A coastal patrol frigate had despatched an inflatable, allowing two navy personnel to climb onto the fishing boat and search it thoroughly. Thankfully, not thoroughly enough.

Sarah had been hidden in a very small box under the engine. It was lined with infrared blocking material – a thermal heat-shield reflector that had succeeded in preventing the detection of humans being trafficked in the opposite direction during several other such raids over the years. The boat had a people-smuggling success rate of one hundred per cent and it had come at a price.

The usual passage fee started at $40,000, including a temporary safe house in Everglades City. Sarah only paid $12,000 to go in the other direction. The price had been negotiated down as a favour to Carol and Alan. Their marina was the mooring place for this and one other boat like it. Both boats were engaged in the people-smuggling trade. The business was not a mass-smuggling enterprise like the ones that always ended up in capture, but the occasional trafficking of illegal immigrants with serious money – usually wealthy criminals – when no questions were ever asked. Only one passenger per journey could squeeze into the tiny space in the event of being boarded.

While the skipper and his one-person crew had not expected to be boarded heading away from the United States of America, they had been prepared for any eventuality. Sarah was quickly and expertly hidden via the engine's inspection hatch and a false piece of engine that hid a further cover through which she had wriggled.

She remembered being told that the cramped space vented out above the deck, but some fumes had leaked into the void. The boat had stopped to be boarded, rocking horribly from side to side, increasing her nausea. She had been very ill – silently – suffering stoically to gain her freedom.

Questions were asked above her head that seemed to go on forever, the muffled exchanges drowned out by the cladding and the sound of the boat's engine ticking over.

Carol had already told Sarah not to panic if they were boarded because the smugglers' cover story was close to the truth. The boat was heading out to catch deeper-water fish like skate, grouper and shark. The cover story stacked up on a boat designed to do just that, and which it still did as part of its day-to-day use.

The story had been given by smugglers who were also fishermen, and who had grown up living among communities of fishermen. There was no cause to doubt the cover story and the US Navy vessel had left, allowing her to journey safely on to Mexico.

In the months since her exile, she had read some American press and watched US News channel reports on the satellite TV in her small apartment. She had stayed off social media. It was clear the truth about the warehouse was being covered up. Reports suggested the area around the Lake Winder warehouse was quarantined, following a major chemical leak. She saw photos of a steel barrier cordoning off the building, named as an abandoned storage facility for phosphates and nitrogen. Army helicopters were filmed dousing the contaminated area with other chemicals.

She wanted to pick up on more local Floridian news to find mention of the Orlando raid and the inevitable discovery of Noah's body. She knew her DNA was all over the abandoned holiday home and hoped Carol and Alan's proximity to the scene would not implicate them – but any contact with them was out of the question.

Sarah had dyed her hair jet black on the boat journey over and changed her whole persona. Since arriving, she was also learning Spanish.

Intuition told her that Damian was still alive. If he was, she wondered where he would be hiding and how he was coping with the infection? Had the disease stopped spreading? Worse still, had she in any way contracted it through their intimacy? She told herself *no*. She felt well, and somehow knew the child she now carried was his.

Damian Gent had proven to be a monster and she would make sure that he never got to see his baby. She would protect it from Damian, and she would keep their association secret from the rest of the world.

It was now just a question of time, waiting for the birth to dispel or confirm her fears – to see if fate would deliver her a healthy normal child.

Watch out for …

ABSORPTION II
The Revenge

Release date TBA

For updates on the sequel and to let the author know your thoughts about Damian, Sarah and the general, follow Kelly on:

@K3llyFarrington

kelly_farrington67

About the Author

The name Kelly Farrington can confuse, but he is definitely a male, and references Kelly Jones or Kelly Slater as testimony to the fact that there are other men out there called Kelly. Now we have that sorted …

Born in London, Kelly's family moved to Leeds just before his seventh birthday, where he spent most his life. At school he worked just about hard enough to gain a place studying politics at Loughborough University. Kelly maintains a keen interest in global politics.

His professional career was spent mostly in media agencies. He left because he realised it was time to do so.

In July 2020 Kelly published his first book *Life in Lockdown,* which includes his poetry, sensitively bringing the madness of 2020 to life.

Other interests include wine, art, painting, golf, travel, and he is a lifelong supporter of Charlton Athletic.

Kelly has two sons, and recently moved to Lytham, on England's north-west coast, with his partner, Pam, where they live life in the slow lane – walking along the front and socialising with good friends.

Author's Notes and Thanks

Absorption has been a labour of love that began in September 2018 with the basic notion of DNA fusion. What if a substance could facilitate the amalgamation of incompatible strands of DNA? According to known science the ability to mix DNA is impossible. Unless DNA profiles are close enough to produce hybrid animals. For example, ligers, zebroids and grolar bears all exist. And a few more hybrids besides. The whole concept is a dark science, made darker still by Nazi experimentation trying to cross humans with animals. They were unsuccessful.

So, let's assume modern thinking is right. There is no way such a fusion can occur. There are no Damian Gents out there. No man-plant-snake-rat-frog combos sat in a swamp somewhere scaring off the alligators.

There are a few other made up and 'what ifs' in the writing of this book. 'You're not kidding' I hear some of you say.

The more observant reader will have noticed the book is set in early 2025. The date was the lab's door code, remember? As I type these notes in 2023, it is difficult to guess what will happen with Covid-19. What does the pandemic mean for the setting of the book? I wrote most the first draft of Absorption during 2019. Ironic, given I had written about a contagion and potential lockdown.

When Covid-19 took hold in 2020, like many authors, I was faced with a difficult choice. Did I want to pretend nothing had happened? Write a story ignoring Covid-19? Or, should I shift the timeline ahead slightly and write from the premise that a vaccine had been successfully deployed? I decided on the latter, which was lot easier and more exciting than re-writing the whole book with characters social distancing, I thought.

For a while I shelved *Absorption* and wrote a book called *Life in Lockdown* instead. Life in Lockdown was written during the initial lockdown period, starting on 23 March 2020. While working on the book I noted that there was a belief within the UK government that a vaccine would be successfully manufactured and released in 2021. The belief was well-founded.

As you have read, there is a bit of politics in the novel. Some may find the geo-politics relating to China a bit far-fetched too, yet the basis for the plot is all true. Read *Prisoners of Geography* by Tim Marshall, a superb book that outlines how Chinese migrant workers are being militarily trained prior to deployment. Look out for what might happen in Hong Kong and Taiwan as China seeks to re-unify lost territory. Also take note of the danger Putin poses and why he sees the Ukraine as an imperative.

The USA-based secret Early Light group is my own invention. While the group is fictional, there are parallels with recent splinter groups away from America First. Would such a group include business magnets, the military, and politicians? You decide.

I enjoyed writing a plot based around gangs. The culture of London gangs was interesting to research. Reading *You Don't Know Me* by Imran Mahmood was a great help. It's a brilliantly written whodunnit that captures the inside track on gang culture. It helped me know that I was on the right line with how a boy could get hooked into gang life and how 'plastic' gangs morph into more serious ones.

Are there bio-chemical research labs at the Kennedy Space Center described in the book? Not that I am aware of. KSC does have a large Prototype Development Laboratory at its southern cluster of buildings. Its aim: to build rockets. For those interested enough to dig deeper into the layout of the Kennedy site, I located my imaginary lab in the northern cluster and I imagined a large scale perimeter fence. All KSC land including the barge canal perimeter is marked by a three-strand barbed-wire fence, but I have used some artistic license to slightly alter its footprint.

Alligators at Kennedy? Yes. True. Around 5,000 of them. Mostly in the fresh water to the west side though. The animals are seen in the Banana River and occasionally on tourist beaches along that stretch, before being removed. The KSC is located on Merritt Island National Wildlife Refuge and is also home to endangered manatees.

You've reached this part at the end of the book. I hope you were able to suspend your disbelief and enjoyed reading the book as much as I did writing it.

I would like to thank my partner, Pamela Gregory, for her patience and support throughout the process. She gave me the confidence to press on to make the vision a reality. Thanks also to a list of beta readers who waded through first-draft typos to offer great advice. Mark, Jenni and Ian, I salute you!

I also want to thank all my other friends who have offered support and encouragement throughout the process.

I'd like to acknowledge the *Society of Authors* and their north-west group, anchored by author Simon Michael, for welcoming me into the world of writers. It was a Zoom discussion within the group that helped me decide to place my plot in a post-Covid world.

Thanks to Dea Parkin at Fiction Feedback for her support and advice about the publishing process and her fellow editor Lesley Jones for a thorough copyedit.

Finally, in a book with underlying themes of displacement and unwanted predators, it is great to see my beloved Charlton Athletic survive such a blatant attempt to asset-strip by imposters. Only Addicks will get that.

HELPLINES:

The book touches on some very difficult subjects such as rape and domestic violence. If you or anyone you know suffers such abuse, please seek help. I have included the numbers of two UK groups, but there will be others, perhaps local to you:

Rape Crisis helpline: 0808 802 9999

National Domestic Abuse Helpline: 0808 2000 247

(Both numbers are 24-hour, and free to call.)

Milton Keynes UK
Ingram Content Group UK Ltd.
UKHW010657091123
432260UK00006B/216